Growing up in Surrey, Clare always dreamed of being a writer. Instead, after gaining a degree in history and an MA in Women's Studies she accidentally fell into a career in IT. After spending many years as a project manager in London, she moved to Norfolk for a quieter life and trained as a professional jeweller.

Now, finally writing full-time, she lives with her husband and the youngest two of her six children. Weekends are often spent satisfying her love of history, exploring local castles and monastic ruins with her miniature schnauzer Fred. The family also make frequent visits to the beautiful Norfolk coast where they all, including Fred, eat (a lot) of ice cream.

You can follow her on Twitter here: @ClareMarchant1

By the same author:

The Secrets of Saffron Hall
The Queen's Spy

The MAPMAKER'S DAUGHTER

CLARE MARCHANT

avon.

HarperCollins*Publishers*
1 London Bridge Street
London SE1 9GF

www.harpercollins.co.uk

HarperCollins*Publishers*
1st Floor, Watermarque Building, Ringsend Road
Dublin 4, Ireland

A Paperback Original 2022
3

First published in Great Britain by HarperCollins*Publishers* 2022

A catalogue copy of this book is available from the British Library.

ISBN: 978-0-00-845438-8

Typeset in Bembo by Palimpsest Book Production Limited, Falkirk, Stirlingshire
Printed and Bound in the UK using 100% Renewable Electricity
at CPI Group (UK) Ltd

MIX
Paper | Supporting
responsible forestry
FSC™ C007454

This book is produced from independently certified FSC™ paper
to ensure responsible forest management.

For more information visit: www.harpercollins.co.uk/green

For Des,

who steers us through calm waters.

Prologue

Amsterdam, Low Countries. 1569

Freida curled herself into a tiny ball, forehead pressed against her knees, eyes squeezed tightly shut. The coarse hessian of her loose gown grazed her face. It was musty in the cupboard, but Mama had told her it was imperative she didn't make a sound, so she held her breath and hoped she didn't sneeze. The smell of the grain that used to be kept in there, a heady pungent scent of warm summers and hot bread fresh from the oven, filled her nostrils and her mind with distant happy memories. She could also detect the sour trace of mice droppings. Vermin had been the only occupants of the store for several months, the ingredients for bread having been taken for the Spanish troops who'd invaded Amsterdam and stolen their food. Now her stomach was permanently empty, the thin tasteless soup with few vegetables and an occasional piece of fatty meat floating in it their only diet, and it barely assuaged the hunger. She knew Mama and Papa often slipped some of their food into her bowl, but it was never enough.

As if in answer to her thoughts, her insides began to rumble and – pressing her hand against her stomach – she grimaced. No noise at all, she reminded herself, as quiet as the mice she hid with. She knew her parents were on the other side of the cupboard. Mama had been holding her hand earlier but now it was so silent she couldn't even hear them breathing. Only the warmth from their bodies indicated they were still in there with her.

From outside on the street came muffled shouts and screams as soldiers ransacked other houses. Only those of the Huguenots though, who chose to worship in the Protestant church following the doctrine of John Calvin, not the Catholics. Freida had eavesdropped when people at the market spoke of the persecution of certain religions and although she didn't understand why people cared so much which church they went to, she knew from her parents' faces they didn't attend the correct one. And that was why she was hiding in this cupboard behind a press, her parents secreted beside her.

A splintering of wood and a crashing sound below them came as their door was smashed open, followed by the thunder of heavy boots climbing up the ladder to the attic before soldiers burst into the room just a few feet from where she was hiding. She squeezed herself even tighter, tears and mucus running down her face as she began to mouth the prayers her parents said every evening, hoping they'd all still be there to recite them that night.

But it was not to be. Was it her breathing or her silent incantations that alerted the intruders to their hiding place beneath the eaves? She pressed herself further into shadows as she felt the crash of the door, the wood shuddering followed by the shouts of her father as he tried to stop them taking her mother. There was a heavy thud on the floor just feet away, before high-pitched screaming and an obscene gurgling sound was followed by silence. The floor vibrated with the thud of feet disappearing back downstairs and out into the street from where more desperate shouting could be heard. For several minutes she remained where she was, her hands over her ears, wondering if her parents were going to come back for her. Or if she should go to their neighbours who'd know what to do; somehow it seemed the soldiers hadn't noticed her tiny form curled up in the corner.

After opening the door she carefully crawled out, her limbs cramped from being confined for so long. Narrowing her eyes against the bright light in the room she quickly squeezed them shut again, the scene of carnage in front of her too terrible to be true. The metallic stench of blood filled her nostrils. Slowly she opened them again. In front of her lay her parents, their guts spilled across the wooden floor, wide pools of dark red blood sinking into the boards.

'Mama? Papa?' she whispered but she could tell that they were beyond hearing her now, their sightless eyes staring up at the beams above them. Still on her hands and knees she skirted past the horrific scene, her face averted. She crept downstairs wondering if the soldiers had now gone. In her father's atelier blood dripped through the ceiling onto the floor where it lay in globules amongst the dust and dried herbs on the floor. It sank into the parchment laid on the table, blooming into red flowers and blurring the lines on the map he'd been working on. Sliding out of the door to the backyard she tiptoed along the passage between their house and next door.

3

On the other side of the wall the street was littered with bodies and limbs and, whimpering in the back of her throat and with shaking legs, she pushed open the door to the neighbours' house and slipped inside.

Chapter One

Hay-on-Wye, Wales. June 2022

Robyn opened the shop door, pushing the rubber wedge underneath to keep it there. It had rained overnight and the pavements were still damp but the sun was already drying them, thin traces of steam rising to dissipate in the warmth. An early heatwave was always useful in bringing tourists to Hay-on-Wye and all the shops, including her father's, needed the custom.

Disappearing down the long passage to the kitchen and office at rear of the shop, she filled and switched on the kettle; from upstairs she could hear her father moving about in the flat they shared, and she knew it wouldn't be long before he appeared, ready to start the day. Recently she'd started to feel that their living accommodation above the shop was shrinking, less room for them to live together amicably, and she'd taken to getting up early and escaping outside or downstairs giving them both breathing space.

He would arrive in the shop as he did every morning at

exactly nine o'clock ready to talk maps – both ancient and modern – atlases and globes with anyone who wandered in through the door. It was all a world away from her real life. Her before life. The busyness and fervour of London, her job as a journalist and the nights out, parties in chic expensive flats, the walls hung with original artwork. They'd lived the lives of bright young things and she'd thought it would never end.

But end it had, her memories of that time now starting to fade despite her desperate attempts to cling on to them. She could feel them slipping through her fingers like the sand on the beach at Les Sables-d'Olonne. Afterwards, she'd returned home to live with her father for a while in his beloved shop in Hay where she'd been brought up. Since her mother had died ten years previously, he'd been living on his own, although recently he'd started seeing Alison – a fellow bookshop owner in the town – and had found a new energy and love of life. Alison's son and daughter-in-law were now helping out in her shop, waiting in the wings until she retired and they could take it on full time.

Her sojourn was originally only supposed to be for six months while she took a sabbatical, but the time had stretched on, slipping past, and now she'd been there for years. There was a comfort to be found though, surrounded by her childhood memories of growing up playing in the corridors of darkness that led to the deep recesses and corners of the ancient dusty shop where the spirits of ancient mapmakers and explorers wandered.

These days she'd occasionally think about running a cloth over the hundreds of storage boxes, or something would be sold to one of her father's numerous dealer acquaintances, leaving a dark dust-free gap on the shelf, a fissure waiting to be replaced by more. Only the front of the shop looked vaguely presentable, where shining, polished oak racks beneath vintage ceiling lamps contained the more recent maps – all second-hand of course; there was no place for anything new here.

The muted lighting added to the tranquil ambience and it was surprising anyone came in to browse when the shop had the air of a forgotten museum vault. Hidden away for so long that nobody could even find it, a secret place lost in time. But her carefully curated displays near the window pulled shoppers in, fascinated by the array of old maps engraved before the world was fully understood. She could appreciate the fascination, because since arriving back home she'd been sucked into the world of historical cartographers and the charts they drew. Growing up she'd been bored with it all and desperate to escape what she considered a book graveyard.

The ceiling above her thumped as her father, Malcolm, made his way down the stairs and she walked back through to the shop front. As always, he was dressed as if he were on his way to a smart summer picnic in a cream linen suit and navy shirt. He may be in his mid-sixties but he refused to slide into old age, his white hair and beard kept fashionably styled and, unlike most of his friends, with no sign of a middle-aged paunch.

'You left your laptop and breakfast plate on the table.' He raised one eyebrow as he looked at her.

'Sorry, I forgot. I'll go up now and put them away.' His comments about her levels of tidiness were becoming more frequent and although she was far from messy, she knew it was another minor irritation. 'There's a cup of tea for you in the office,' she added.

'I've received an email from a fellow dealer in London. He has a customer who's a collector of French cartographers' works and he's wondering if I have anything. Fortuitously I do have a Delisle so I'm going to pack it up for him. I've organised a courier for tomorrow afternoon to collect it.' He waved his iPad at her as if she could read the email displayed on the screen.

It was the specialist buyers who really kept the shop going, not the walk-in customers buying a map for sentimental reasons or a book to try and educate a child who was doubtless completely uninterested. The internet had made a huge difference to how her father did business, attracting potential purchasers from across the world. They couldn't display the hundreds — possibly thousands — of maps they owned, but her father was known to have an extensive collection and to be an expert in the field.

'But will you be able find it in your chaotic archives?' Robyn grinned at him.

'I know you think I have no filing system, but have I ever lost anything in the six and a half years since you came home?' he pointed out.

The smile slid off Robyn's face. She didn't need reminding how long she'd been there, and although she knew her father didn't want to hurt her, his comments about the hiatus in her life were becoming less subtle, more frequent. The constant ticking of the clock, counting the days and years, was sounding louder and louder. It was inside her head all the time, tick tock, tick tock, impossible to switch off. A never-ending metronome, a constant prompt that September was not far away, and getting closer every day.

'Let me just drink my tea, then I'll man the front desk while you go and look? I'll move my stuff in the flat when we get a quiet moment.' Robyn hurried back through to the office. She'd have to pour her tea down the drain if it wasn't hot enough to scald her tonsils, so she only had a two-minute optimal drinking time. Looking up she stared at the calendar above the sink, forever open on September 2015. The image of a racing yacht, its hull high in the water as it sliced through a wave. Her father had suggested numerous times that they throw it away, but she wouldn't let him. Nearly seven years.

Taking up her position behind the counter at the front of the shop as the early-riser tourists began to wander in, she smiled at a couple thumbing through a stack of 1950s Ordnance Survey maps. Eventually they chose two they wanted to buy, explaining to Robyn why they'd decided on those particular copies: one that included the village where they'd been married forty years previously and the other that covered the Pembrokeshire coastline where they'd holidayed every year since that day. They intended to frame parts of the map to hang on their wall, a permanent reminder of the places that made them happy.

She managed to keep a smile on her face until they'd left the shop, but the moment they crossed the road and disappeared into the café opposite she let it slide off. At one point in her life appearing cheerful was simply too hard to do, but now she could slip on a polite persona like an old familiar cardigan. On it went and off it dropped, falling from her shoulders as soon as it was no longer

9

needed. Despite the permanent flame she kept burning inside, she could now feel it wavering in the draughts of time as the tick tock of the clock inside her head imperceptibly slowed down.

Chapter Two

London, England. May 1580

Freida hummed to herself as she bent over the shining copperplate reflecting a pink glow against the contours of her face. Her washed blue eyes, the colour of bright winter skies, were screwed up as she concentrated. A lock of fair hair escaped from the plain linen coif she wore and she brushed it away with the back of her hand.

What she worked on was intricate, finely tooled, but she knew she was skilled enough to do it justice. Otherwise, her mentor and distant cousin – Abraham Ortelius – wouldn't have requested that she engraved for him a map of the route across Europe that the silks and spices, the plants and fossils he sent to London travelled. It was similar to something she'd worked on when she was in Antwerp at his atelier. And now here she was in London in her own workshop and fast gaining a name for herself as a competent cartographer in her own right. A role that no other woman had ever held.

She didn't know if the skills she possessed were her heritage, the blood in her veins that her father had given her, or if it was simply that she'd grown up in Abraham's workshop helping with simple tasks as she grew whilst watching everything with her constantly alert eyes. Always on her guard though, watching and listening, ready to run and hide if she heard any noises or shouting in the street. Her cousin called her a frightened *konjin* after the rabbits who ran from their path when they walked in the countryside around their home. But she couldn't help who she was.

She'd watched intently as the hardworking women coloured the maps after the men engraved them, standing for hours at the elbow of Abraham's sister Ursula who'd arrived in Amsterdam all those years ago to rescue her, scooping her up from the family with whom she'd been staying, and taking her to Antwerp. Freida began to undertake colouring at the age of twelve, but her attention was continuously drawn to the process of engraving and often she'd slip away from her work to observe the maps growing on the plates before being printed onto parchment and passed to the colourists to complete. Some of these maps were then bound together to create Ortelius' now famous Atlas *Theatrum Orbis Terrarum*. The Theatre of the World. Everything she knew, she'd learned first from her father and then in Ortelius' atelier beside the master, but she hadn't learned to believe in herself or trust those around her apart from her close family. It had taken many years for her to accept that the danger she had run from was now far away, the fighting unlikely to extend as far as Antwerp; she could let down her guard.

A forlorn shadow swept across her face as she remembered, before she looked down to smile at the baby laid in a plaited rush basket at her feet. Eventually Antwerp hadn't proved to be as safe as she'd hoped, and once again she'd escaped, now living in London and under the protection of a Protestant English queen. She had a brave husband and a three-month-old son who was sleeping beside her, his long lashes sweeping across his flushed cheeks. His head was covered in soft wispy blond down and she pressed her palm against her heart, which hurt with the love she felt for him. Little Jacob and her husband Willem were her world now, but she couldn't quash the lump that lodged in her throat every time she thought of how fragile their lives were. She fought hard to flatten the black thoughts, the worry that had followed her since the death of her parents and yet it never completely left her.

Turning back to her work she continued, trying to get as much as possible completed whilst Jacob slept, although her eyes flicked to him constantly, checking he was safe. He lay in a shaft of light shining through the glazed window, the shutters opened wide. The rest of the small room was immaculately clean, swept each morning by Freida. Her cousin had always impressed on her the importance of having a tidy workspace, and the ash and dust produced by the fire burning in the small stone fireplace meant that a daily scrub was imperative. Freida had placed her engraving easel beside the window to gain use of the maximum light available, which often wasn't a lot in the winter.

The home she now lived in was very different to the one-room workshop and home above it that she'd been born into. Now she was a married woman living in the great city of London. Their house, backed by a courtyard, stables and an expansive garden, was fronted by three horizontal rows of oak beams, silvered and pale from the sun and rain. Between the beams narrow dark red bricks were fitted in a herringbone design, with a jetty across the top floor stretching towards the narrow twisting street. The central front door was topped by an oriel window, the tiny panes of glass stained with reds, yellows and blues. It was a house to be proud of.

She ran her hand down the dimpled grosgrain of her gown, feeling it uneven beneath her fingertips, before turning to stroke them across the cool metal plate on the stand before her. The skills she'd brought had served her well, allowing her to live in comfort as the merchant classes did.

Behind her where a thick oak door opened straight onto the street, and she was alerted to the sound of loud shouting followed by a woman screaming. Somewhere there was the crack of wood splintering under an axe or hammer, and the noise intensified.

Immediately her calm musing drained down her body to pool at her feet and her heart began to race as her breath quickened. Beads of sweat started to prickle her face and dampness collected under her arms, sticking her linen shift to her skin. She dropped the tool she was working with and snatched up Jacob's basket. He murmured in his sleep and she held the carrier close, not wanting him to wake and alert anyone to their presence. Quickly she hid him behind a collection of cupboards and presses in the corner of the room. It was where she kept the materials she needed for her work and now she was thankful they were there. Checking the wooden bars were down across both the doors into the room to ensure they were locked shut, she swiftly closed the window shutters, plunging the room into murky darkness – just small shafts of sunlight now filtering around the edges where the wood didn't fit correctly. She hoped that any soldier couldn't find leverage to prise them open.

As she crouched down in the dark, her head pressed against her knees, she shut her eyes and put her hands over her face, her lips moving as wordlessly she began to pray.

Chapter Three

June 2022

The sun was trying to crawl into the room around the edge of Robyn's curtains, although her watch said it was only five in the morning. Outside the window she could hear the abrasive screaming of seagulls calling to each other. The familiar sound triggered one of her happiest memories and for a rare moment, instead of pushing it back behind the wall she'd built in her mind, she allowed it to flood out, to consume her as she relived that day. It had begun much as this one had, waking early to sunshine and the desire not to waste a minute of it. The following day Nate would be leaving to prepare for a race and turning to face him in bed she'd seen he was already awake, his hair tousled and his sleepy face smiling at her.

'Let's escape for the day,' he'd suggested, 'and go to the seaside.'

Within the hour they'd been on their way to Brighton, singing loudly to the music on the radio in the car and laughing with the feeling of freedom. Once there, they'd wandered the lanes looking in shop windows, their fingers entwined, stealing kisses every time their eyes met. They were a married couple but it felt as if they had only just got together, the quiver of first love.

Eventually they'd taken fish and chips to sit on the pebbly beach, immediately joined by dozens of seagulls, a raucous shrieking filling the air, but nothing could spoil their day and they'd laughed as they were surrounded by the birds slowly moving closer. The sharp taste of the salt and vinegar on her tongue, the hot chips that burned her mouth, every single moment of that day was imprinted on her memory. They were often on the coast somewhere in the world as Nate started or finished a race – but nowhere was like Brighton. A day of laughter as bright as the sunlight shining off the roof of the pavilion. The skin on her face had been tight and warm from the sun as they drove home at the end of the day, the streaked sky above them on fire as the sun set.

Robyn knew she wasn't going to go back to sleep. Her day had begun. After getting out of bed, she pulled on her running leggings, top and trainers, and let herself quietly out of the flat. There was plenty of time to run to the Warren, the country park on the edge of town that led down to the river. She'd sit under their tree, the place that was special to her and Nate, where she felt closest to him. The place they'd always take a walk to visit whenever they returned to her childhood home.

It was too early for tourists to be about but already the town was waking up, delivery vans driving along the streets and a road sweeper slowly cleaning them before the new hordes arrived. She started off at a steady jog but as she reached the park she lengthened her stride, feeling the cool morning air catching in her lungs, stroking against her face. She felt alive but there was no joy in it. How could she when Nate wasn't there?

Reaching their tree, she held on to it with one hand while she bent over, waiting for her breath to slow down before crossing her legs and sitting down to lean against the trunk. She'd hoped her run would calm her, but the thoughts that had plagued her earlier were still there. They never left her.

The ground was dry and all around she could smell vegetation already warming up in the early sunshine, green and fertile. To her side, she heard a splash as a creature disappeared into the river, and a pair of ducks she'd disturbed squawked angrily. Nate always said this was his favourite place in Hay. He enjoyed the tranquillity of the trees whilst also being close to the water, to which he was inextricably drawn. He'd rarely been here at this time of year though. Now the canopy above her closed over into a green cathedral of leaves, allowing tiny shafts of ecclesiastical sunlight to filter in as if shining through the stained-glass windows of a church. They usually visited in autumn and, like the big kid Nate was, he'd jump and dance through the piles of dead leaves, kicking them in the air.

Their special tree was a lime, its leaves heart-shaped; Nate would always take one from the tree and present her with it. When they'd first found it, he looked on his phone and told her that lime trees were a symbol of fertility and so by visiting it they were guaranteed a large family. Not now. Her heart ached with the emptiness within. But at least being here gave her a place where she felt close to Nate, as she

18

had no grave to visit. Their home – the flat in London – had just been a place to sleep and often she was there on her own, but here was where they'd always been together. Until that day when her world had imploded. The day when she'd been told Nate was missing, his empty yacht discovered in the Southern Ocean. Two officials from his team had arrived at the flat to break the news. She hadn't been able to understand why they both had tears in their eyes as they explained and yet hers were dry. Because the enormity of what they were saying wasn't sinking in.

Getting to her feet she brushed the dust, skeletons of dead leaves and dried, shrivelled beechnut cases from the backs of her legs before turning to run home. As usual the tree had given her no answers, and she was beginning to realise that perhaps nothing or nobody ever could.

Robyn was helping a young family with energetic twin boys find a world atlas in the box of pre-owned children's books when the courier arrived. He'd visited the shop numerous times over the years and she gave him a quick wave and mouthed, *'He's in the office,'* pointing towards the back of the shop before she quickly rescued a book from the hands of one of the boys as he snatched it off the shelf, barely pausing as he raced past. She was relieved when the parents who were either oblivious to their sons' behaviour or considered her as a temporary nanny made their choice and paid. Ushering the children outside, they left behind a pall of dust that had been disturbed before it slowly drifted back to its original position.

The courier gave her a wave across the shop as he left and he was followed shortly after by her father arriving at the shop counter, a wide smile making his face crease up. He looked so pleased with himself she couldn't help grinning in return.

'You look happy,' she told him. 'Have you sold the Delisle before anyone has even seen it?'

'What? Oh no, I'll have to wait a couple of weeks to hear whether the buyer wants it. But when I took it out of the box to get it ready to be collected, I discovered another map beneath it.'

'Hidden underneath?' Robyn raised her eyebrows.

'No, I don't think so. I just hadn't realised it was there. I thought only the Delisle was in the box. It must've been part of the original stock when I bought the shop though, so it's been there undiscovered for forty years.'

'So what map is it? Given the fact that you're almost hopping from foot to foot and looking as if you're about to explode with excitement, I'm guessing it's something interesting. Are you thinking you can sell it for a big profit?'

'If it's as old as I'm hoping, then yes, it's potentially very valuable. It's also extremely unusual. I've never seen anything quite like it. When we shut the shop later, I'll show you.'

The moment the shop sign said 'closed' and the day's cash takings were in the safe, her father took the box sitting on the corner of the desk and carefully peeled back each layer, folding up the soft cotton wadding so they could use it to repack the item, until finally he lifted out an old frame folded in tissue.

As he removed the pale bleached paper that enclosed it, the wooden frame rough and looking as though it would fall apart at any moment, Robyn was enveloped in the scent of faded lives, old secrets, fear and the harsh salty air of the sea that drifted out. For a moment the floor rolled beneath her feet and she grabbed hold of the table in front of her. A cold draught blew gently across her face as it eddied and swirled away into the corner of the room, and she turned around expecting to see someone in the doorway. She tilted her head to one side and then the other, waiting to feel some trace of vertigo, but it felt completely normal. She must have imagined it.

'So, what is it?' she breathed. He stood up straight again.

'It's remarkable, and almost certainly old. Very old. But as I said, unlike anything I've seen before. It's possibly medieval. I suspect it's sixteenth-century because it's been printed. Such a detailed map of London, and here – look, also the south-east and East Anglia together with Holland and the Low Countries. Why would a map like this have been made? Maps in the sixteenth century were less detailed than this and it's such an unusual area. It's been coloured too, so this was top quality. Fascinating.' He bent over it again and Robyn joined him. Close up it was musty. She could still smell the trace of the sea and she wondered how long, and where, it had been hidden all these years.

Intrigued, she asked, 'Would you mind if I do some research on it, please? It's fascinating and I'd like to test out everything you've taught me. I can report back so you know I'm following all the appropriate procedures.'

'Not if you're intending it as a distraction,' he replied, frowning at her. 'Time won't stop marching on. Seven years will come around at the end of summer whether you're ready or not. You need to remember what you have to do.'

'I know, I know. This isn't me putting it off.' She sighed. His repeated reminders were starting to wear her down.

She'd managed to stop herself thinking about the act of officially declaring Nate dead over the past seven years, but now with the deadline only a couple of months away it was becoming impossible to mute the thoughts inside her head. The ones telling her that she couldn't ignore the inevitable: he'd never been found and he never would be. 'But I'm interested and it'll give me something to do in the evenings.'

Her father's face cleared and he smiled, then nodded. 'Okay, see what you can find out. And don't forget to store it in the safe when you aren't working on it; we may be insured but this is potentially hugely valuable.' Patting her shoulder he headed back through the shop to the flat, leaving Robyn with the map.

She had no idea where to start, but if she couldn't find a reference book here in her father's shop, she wouldn't find one anywhere, that was certain. Looking closer she realised she could see a pale rust-coloured stain covering almost a quarter of the map. Was that blood? She shuddered. This item had a story to tell she was certain, but the potential bloodstain made her nervous of exactly what secrets it may reveal.

Chapter Four

May 1580

The door from her workshop to the rest of the house rattled, followed by a loud knock, and Freida cowered down even further as if she could sink into the floorboards beneath her. Snatching Jacob up she held him tightly to her, fingers digging into the blankets he was swaddled in and making him murmur in his sleep. The knocking came again and this time she heard her name being called.

'Freida? Are you there my sweet?' There was a thump of a fist against the wood and her breath shuddered out in relief.

'Yes, I am here,' she called out, placing Jacob back in his basket and running across the room. She lifted the bar and opened the door a little, pulling in her visitor. She replaced the bar again. Looking up at her husband Willem, the fear bottled up in her chest poured out through the tears running down her cheeks. His brows furrowed, he tilted her face up to his, before wrapping his arms around her and pressing her face against his soft moleskin jerkin. It smelled of hot pitch and the foul-smelling river, which caught the detritus of London in its continuously flowing depths before taking it to the sea, and she knew he'd just returned from his ship hidden at the docks at Wapping-on-the-Woze.

After a few seconds he held her at arm's length.

'Where is Jacob?' His eyes darted around the dark room. She hurried over to the corner behind the press and lifted out the basket with their son still sleeping inside. Willem opened the shutters, once more flooding the room with light.

'What has upset you?' he asked. Freida explained about what she'd heard. She didn't need to tell him her fear of soldiers, those she loved being executed in their own homes. He knew her demons.

'Along the street there is a door broken,' he explained. 'I think that is what you heard. But remember it is not going to be the Spanish, not here in London. I expect it was just the city guards or bailiffs. You know you are safe here.'

Freida nodded, but her eyes didn't reflect the confirmation she'd given him. She'd spent too many years listening to the news filtering through from those who arrived in Antwerp, escaping as she had from King Philip of Spain's soldiers. And whilst the Low Countries remained a part of the Catholic Spanish Empire, her life as a Protestant Huguenot was in danger. Just as her parents' lives had been; and they hadn't been able to escape as she had. She smiled at Willem, her lower lip still trembling, arms wrapped tightly around her body she tried to control the panic careering through her. Immediately his strong protective arms enfolded her, and just as numerous previous occasions, she knew he'd recognised that her fears were threatening to overwhelm her.

'You are safe,' he reminded her. 'I am here and all is well.' But once it started she couldn't stop the memories, the sight of her parents' bodies eviscerated on the floor just yards from where she'd hidden. And their friends and neighbours hung from every available gibbet-like post. Trees, shop signs, the stinking and often rotting bodies black with clustered flies as they swayed in the wind. Her neighbour who'd managed to conceal and then save her had tried to put her hand over Freida's eyes so she couldn't see the atrocities, but there were too many to hide from. She'd seen her parents' corpses and when she closed her eyes at night, she could conjure up images of their sweet faces, her mother's clear blue eyes that creased at the edges when she smiled at Freida, their only child.

'Come, let us go through to the parlour where you can have a cup of wine,' Willem suggested, one arm tight around her waist and the other carrying Jacob as he led the way down the passage at the rear of the house and across an inner chamber to the great hall, off which lay a small room.

Her journey to London had been prompted by the renewed fighting in Antwerp, which she'd endured until she couldn't bear it any longer. Abraham had sent her to live with his sister, Liskin, buying a berth on one of the *'Sea Beggar'* ships that fought the Spanish galleons, the warships trying to deliver supplies to their troops in the German Ocean, the body of water between England and Holland.

A decade earlier whilst Freida's parents lay dead on the floor and she made her escape to Antwerp, Willem and his compatriots – other Dutch nobles – had petitioned the King of Spain's envoy in the Low Countries. They carried a list of grievances against the Catholic rule and the abominations

25

meted out to their fellow countrymen, but were met with derision. When they were referred to as beggars by one of the councillors, instead of being offended they had embraced the slur, using it as an emblem as they continued their fight.

This particular *Sea Beggar* also transported curiosities and plants, letters and foodstuffs to the scientists and botanists who were now their neighbours in this community on Lime Street. At the end of the twisting lane where it joined Fenchurch Street lived Emanuel van Meteren, a nephew to Abraham Ortelius. He was also the postmaster of the Republic of Letters for traders, and the conduit of news and scientific reports between Holland, the Low Countries and London. Their neighbours on Lime Street were mostly immigrants like themselves, Huguenot Protestants who'd escaped the persecution by the Spanish Catholics in their native homes across the German Ocean.

Walking into their hall, Freida passed Jacob to Nell, her companion and maid. Nell had accompanied Freida when she travelled from Antwerp and then followed once more when Freida was first married and moved out of Liskin's home next door to her own house.

Willem threw his jerkin onto a chest beside the door. At a small side table, he poured two cups of warming honey mead, passing one to Freida. She drank it gratefully, her heart – which was still beating erratically – beginning to slow down again.

'I hate how they can still reach out to me after all these years,' she admitted, her voice wobbling. 'Everywhere I go I am sure I can feel the Spanish breathing down my neck. They missed me when they came to our door the first time, but even now, in a different country, a Protestant country,

I can't escape the fear that follows me; they will come back for the one they missed. And for those whom I love now. Once again I will not be able to protect my family and I shall lose you both.'

'I know how frightening it is,' he reminded her. 'I am the person who holds you in the night when you call out in your sleep. But I will never allow anyone to hurt you or Jacob.'

'You say that, but you cannot be with us all the time,' Freida pointed out. 'When you are away at sea it can be weeks when we do not see you. I do not know if the *Windfly* is under attack by other ships, and then we are as vulnerable as anyone else.' She tried to smile to take the sting out of her words. She sounded harsh and it wasn't his fault; it was her history not his.

When she'd first boarded the ship that would bring her to London, she hadn't seen the captain. She and Nell had been shown to a small cabin containing two narrow bunks, a chest for her clothes and a pair of squat, three-legged stools, the seats shiny with wear. It was late autumn and the weather unpredictable; the first two days were squally and Freida's stomach churned and rolled like the waves outside whilst she alternately prayed they would sink to the bottom of the sea to put her out of the misery, or that they could outsail the bad weather and find calmer waters. Nell fared no better and they both lay groaning on their bunks.

Thankfully on the third day she awoke to find the ship barely rocking and her stomach, despite now being completely empty, feeling calmer. She realised her prayers had been answered. Not wishing to wake Nell who was still asleep, she dressed in a simple flannel kirtle over her linen smock, the only piece of clothing she could dress in without requiring assistance. With her wool cloak lined with warm coney fur gathered around her, she staggered from their cabin situated at the stern and past another small cabin beside hers, which appeared to be a room for the captain and his officers to relax in, and onto the poop deck.

Here she was delighted to see the sea laid out before her, reaching away until it faded and met the sky, now a pale blue as it chased away the night clouds still resting on the horizon. Dark grey waves rolled into peaks and deep troughs, topped with flecks of white as the now much calmer wind gently whipped the spray so it danced in the sunlight, sparkling like a thousand diamonds. The ship dipped and tilted as it rode the depths and she closed her eyes and breathed in the salty air, combined with the acrid smoky scent of frying fish.

And that was when she first saw him. A tall man in just a shirt and breeches, loose boots on his feet, which stamped across the rough boards as he appeared in front of her, bowing and holding out a pale wooden charger, bleached with the salt water it had been washed in. On it nestled two freshly cooked fish, still smouldering with their skin crisp and blackened. Beside them was a piece of rough brown bread. It wasn't the most appetising of meals, but with her stomach empty she took it gratefully.

'Thank you.' Her voice was husky after two days of barely talking and keeping her teeth gritted together to stop her bringing up the acid bile that burned her insides. To her consternation the man sat down on a barrel beside her and stretched his legs out.

'I am the captain of the *Windfly*, Willem van Hoorn,' he introduced himself, inclining his head. 'I am much pleased

I have the chance to make your acquaintance whilst the weather favours our voyage.' She knew he was teasing her about her shaky start to the journey and pulling steaming flakes of fish away from the bones with her fingers she quickly dropped them in her mouth. Looking sideways from under her eyelashes she could see he was smiling, his wide mouth revealing unusually straight teeth with eyes as steely grey as the sea around them. His deep brown hair was long, almost reaching the collar of his shirt, although his beard was clipped short. She could tell from the few lines around his eyes he was not much older than herself, but already there were threads of silver in his hair. She stopped eating for a moment.

'Pleased to make your acquaintance, Captain van Hoorn. I am Freida Ortelius and I am travelling with my companion Nell to live with my cousin in London.'

'Yes, so I believe. I am to deliver you to Lime Street with the other letters and packages I am taking to Emanuel van Meteren.'

Freida wasn't sure she liked being compared to a package, but she could see a twinkle flash in his eyes and she dipped her head, the ghost of a smile hovering at the edges of her mouth. She could hardly pull her eyes away from his, their dark depths flecked with gold reflecting the iron sea as it stretched into the distance, the sun lighting the tops of its waves.

'I shall be very grateful if you are able to deliver me alongside the cargo you are carrying,' she replied. He gave a shout of laughter before reaching into his shirt, pulling something from around his neck and passing it to her. She looked at what lay in her hand, a thin loop of leather on

29

which was threaded a smooth rounded pale brown stone, still warm from where it had lain against his body.

'It is a bezoar stone,' he explained. 'It is a charm to keep the wearer safe. Keep it until you are on dry land again. But I shall be seeking you out to return it.' He smiled, closing her fingers over it before a call from the other end of the boat drew his attention and with a brief bow he was gone, striding away, easily stepping with his long legs over the coarse hemp ropes lying on the deck. Freida slipped the charm around her neck where it rested on her chest, the warmth from him now transferring itself to her. He looked once back over his shoulder and, in that moment, she knew her heart had been caught.

Chapter Five

May 1580

The sound of Jacob crying reached down through the layers of Freida's sleep and wrenched her awake. In one fluid movement she was on her feet outside the heavy embroidered drapes hanging around her bed, bare feet cold on the rough strewings scattered across the floor. The lavender and rosemary she'd added when they'd been put down releasing soft, familiar scents.

She paused for a moment, her head on one side as she listened, before realising there was no crying. Creeping across the floor, lifting her feet up and placing them down carefully so as to avoid the floorboards she knew would creak, she made her way over to the wooden cradle in the corner of the room. Made of oak and carved with leaves and acorns, it was polished to a shining, burnished deep brown; it was her most favourite piece of furniture. And in it lay the most precious person in the world.

Her breath caught in her chest as she gazed down on

Jacob, his eyes tightly shut, his chest moving gently up and down as he slept. His soft linen sleeping cap was askew on his head and reaching out she carefully pulled it straight. He hadn't been crying; just like the numerous times previously she'd woken thinking she could hear him.

Her heartbeat slowly returned to normal as she nipped back across to her bed. A sharp, spiteful draught blew under the door, cutting into her ankles. She climbed up onto the impossibly high mattress stuffed with wool, brushing the pieces of rushes and dried herbs from the soles of her feet as she lay back down, curling herself around William's strong, warm back. She pressed her face against the fine lawn of his night-rail, inhaling the scent of pitch and burnt wood that never left him as she waited for sleep to envelop her again.

'My sweet wife, I must leave you for a week or two.' Willem was eating his breakfast as she drank a tisane of myrtle and honey whilst feeding pieces of soft white manchet bread soaked in milk to Jacob, who was sitting on her knee. Her head turned to him as she considered what he'd just said; her hand stopped in mid movement as she frowned at him. Jacob gave a shout and bent forwards to try and take the food still between her fingers in his mouth. She noticed Willem kept his eyes down, not meeting hers. He knew how she hated being left at home without him and with just their steward, Guy, to protect her and Jacob.

'I know I have not long returned from sea,' he continued, 'but my ship needs repairs to the rigging and I cannot have it done here in London. I am in danger enough hiding the *Windfly* at Wapping, hardly the best place given it is also the execution dock for those who are considered to be pirates. And those in power may accuse me of exactly that if they chose to.' He flashed his teeth at her. 'Thus, to have work done I must sail to the port at Norwich where they are more open to we Huguenots, the Strangers. Rest assured I will be as swift as I can possibly be.'

Freida nodded although she couldn't bring a smile to her face to match his own. Instinctively her arms tightened around Jacob until the small boy began to squirm and he let out a shout of indignation. Reaching across, Willem took him from her lap and, after kissing the top of his son's head, he passed him over to Nell, who was sitting beside the fire embroidering a delicate fine lawn shift for the small boy, careful blackwork around the edge of the sleeves. She clucked over him as she bore him away; there were no shortage of doting people in the household. Willem placed his large warm hands on Freida's upper arms, as always filling her with a feeling of security that only he could.

'Why not move next door and stay with Liskin whilst I am gone? She will be company for you in the evenings. You are safe, my love, I promise you. I would not consider going away if I did not believe that.' Freida gave him a shaky smile but she knew he'd be able to see the tell-tale tears hovering at the corners of her eyes.

'Yes, I will ask her later. I am sure she will not mind. When do you set sail?'

'On the tide tonight. The weather is fine at the moment so we shall slip away and hopefully back whilst the seas remain calm.'

'Then I must speak with Liskin now. And I have work I need to continue with. The map I am currently engraving for Abraham is almost complete and he tells me he has more

33

work, although he will wait whilst I paint the colours onto this one first. Emanuel told me this piece of work is the finest he has ever seen.' She tried to sound nonchalant but pride crept in to her voice.

'Naturally, my sweet,' Willem said. 'You carry the Ortelius name – one of the most famous cartography families in the world – and you are worthy of it. Your ability and skill inspire all those who are fortunate enough to witness that which you create.'

After the previous disturbance in the street, Freida had been too frightened to go near her workshop but she knew she needed to resume her work. Before she began, she visited her cousin to ask if she could stay whilst Willem was away.

'You are always welcome.' Liskin pulled Freida in close for a hug. She smelled of yeast and the sharp scent of rosemary and for a moment Freida relaxed into her. It dredged up memories of her mother making bread, adding herbs for flavouring. 'I will ask my steward to organise bringing your belongings and Jacob's crib today, and have your bed made up.'

'Thank you.' Freida smiled and kissed her goodbye before returning to her workshop.

As soon as she'd completed her work on the map, mixing pigments to a thin oil to create the paints, she hurried through to see Willem before he left for the *Windfly* and prepared to set sail. The sun was still high in the sky but she knew he'd be waiting and watching for the tide. Timing was everything. In the great hall she saw him talking with Emanuel.

'The postmaster has requested I sail to Amsterdam afterwards and collect some packages for him. A pouch of the much-desired sunflower seeds is waiting to be brought to England.'

Freida nodded, thinking of the tall plants with their incredible blooms as big and yellow as the sun they were named for. Her neighbours were all keen on the unusual flower and competed with each other to grow the tallest specimens. As she listened to Willem, she felt the familiar unease twist in her belly uncomfortably. She knew it was his life, his place in the world. When she'd first met him he'd been on exactly this journey, but it was never without danger. Nobody knew where or when the enemy may appear. If the Spanish were watching and waiting then there would be skirmishes or worse, and shots fired. And whilst his small ship was fast it didn't have the heavy guns his opponents did.

She opened her mouth to try and dissuade him but then closed it again, the words unsaid. It was not her place to berate or beg her husband in front of their neighbour. Outside the bells of Saint Dionis Backchurch tolled and she excused herself, leaving to go in search of Jacob.

Her son and it seemed most of her belongings, were already next door, carried across whilst she'd been working, and she hurried through Liskin's house to the solar off the great hall that her cousin mostly favoured. Indeed the room, hot from a blazing fire and the bodies of the occupants, had a stuffy atmosphere.

Jacob was being bounced on Nell's knee but he was red in the face and when he saw Freida his mouth opened and a loud wail filled the room. He held his arms out and she scooped him up, holding his sweaty body against hers. He was dressed in a long, quilted dress made of dark red velvet, which was no doubt contributing to his hot and sticky state, his cheeks tacky. She felt the flutter of a recurring panic vibrate in her chest. Was he ill?

'Excuse me.' She smiled at her companions and hurried out. A moment later she was aware of feet scuttling behind her and Nell caught up with her.

'Is everything well, Freida?' she asked.

'I am not sure. Jacob feels hot and I fear he may be sick.'

Once in her bedchamber she partially undressed Jacob until he was just in his long linen shift. Almost immediately he began to quieten down and his face returned to its usual colour. A few minutes later and his breathing slowed as he fell asleep. Freida was still sitting watching him when Willem came in to say goodbye. She tried to put a brave face on as her lower lip wobbled, but when he held her close to him, his big hand rubbing her back, she clung on as if she'd never let him go.

'Shall you go on to Amsterdam as Emanuel has asked?' Her voice was muffled where her face was squashed against his woollen cloak.

'I must. He is expecting various items to be ready for me to collect. Including, apparently, a dead Neapolitan tarantula from Abraham. It is said to be the biggest spider in the world. Do not worry, my lady, I shall be home before Midsummer's Day, and we can attend the pageant on the Strand and take Jacob to show him the puppets and performers.' Freida nodded, pushing herself away from him so she could look him in the eye.

'Just come back safely – that is all I ask,' she whispered. In his cradle Jacob stirred as if agreeing with her.

'You have my promise,' Willem answered, giving her a final kiss on her forehead before resting his fingertips briefly on Jacob's hair.

And then he was gone, just a breath of air gently stroking

her face as he swung out of the door. Freida sat on the bed, the ropes beneath the wool mattress sagging slightly and creaking under her weight. She gripped the edge to stop herself running after him, her knuckles white. She knew he had to leave, but every time he did a hard mass of fear lodged itself inside, making it hard for her to catch her breath.

'Calm waters, sweet husband,' she whispered, sinking to her knees to pray for his safe return.

Chapter Six

June 1580

Life resumed its normal routine within days of Willem leaving, Freida joining the family for meals but spending the majority of her time at her easel engraving. The glowing sheet of copperplate smooth and shining beneath her fingers as she leaned in close, carefully carving into it with her burins. The top of the burin was a smooth mushroom-shaped piece of walnut wood, which nestled in her palm and helped her to control the blade perfectly. The sharp metal shafts were cut to form a fine diamond-shaped point to engrave the surface before her. By pressing the edge with her fore-finger and thumb, she was able to angle the tip, altering the width and depth of the lines she made as she created the map in a mirror image ready for when it went to the printers later in the week.

She took Jacob with her everywhere and at the behest of the head of the household she was always accompanied outside of the house always by a journeyman who worked for Guy, a tall young lad called Christopher. She had a strong suspicion that Willem had laid out the conditions before he left.

Sometimes in the evenings she'd sit and play cards or embroider beside the fire in the solar after Jacob had gone to sleep, but most often she stayed alone in her room with just the crackling of the fire and the steady breathing of her son for company. She was locked into a world that felt as safe as she could make it. The incident with the city guards in the street had brought back fears she thought she had quashed and now she was on edge, the calm she had come to accept here in London feeling ragged around the edges.

After nine peaceful years in Antwerp, the arrival there of King Philip's soldiers under the Duke of Alba had brought back the horrors of her parents' murders and she'd fled to London, but now she wondered if she was even safe here.

Amongst the letters that arrived with Emanuel a few months previously had been one for Freida from Abraham. He was working on some new plates in order to add some pages to his famous atlas, and she was thrilled to have been asked to engrave a small addition to be included. It included the estuary at Kent and the Thames, and she knew she had all the information she'd need from the various maps she'd already worked on for the London surveyor Ralph Treswell. It would simply be a case of copying and amalgamating sections of plates she already had in her workshop.

Willem had been away ten days when Freida finished the map for her cousin. Christopher carried the copperplate, following her as they walked to Joan Jugge the printer on Paternoster Row, a widow who'd successfully taken over her late husband's business after his death. It was a part of

London she loved to visit, close to the bookbinders and printers at St Paul's. Here was a hustle and bustle of traders and street hawkers all trying to sell their pamphlets and bills declaring news and superstitions. Young apprentices, their skinny limbs sticking out of ill-fitting clothing, hurried through the crowds, heads down on urgent errands for their employers. Small barefoot children with grimy faces, hair moving with the lice that crawled there, watched for opportunities to snatch a purse or money pouch. Whilst the wealthy children of London were closeted and protected in opulent nurseries, the poor and abandoned children foraged for what they could to live. And sometimes failed to do so, with no one to mourn for them.

The churchyard at St Paul's was crowded with the city's goodwives and those who listened to those calling out prophecies, their voices colliding in a cacophony of sound, whilst sheds erected in the grounds of the great cathedral belched out smoke that filtered in to the nave of the cathedral through broken panes of glass. The great lightning strike of 1561, which had brought the steeple and bells crashing to the floor, had left a legacy that no one could afford to repair.

Mistress Jugge was the finest printer in the city and Freida was delighted when, three days later, the map was returned just as she'd hoped. It took many back-breaking hours colouring it with paints as she'd done so often before, followed by several evenings of stitching to attach it to a linen backing. Eventually she was happy it was complete and after wrapping it in oilcloth she walked along the street to visit Emanuel and ask him to send it with his next consignment. She was disappointed it hadn't been ready for her husband to have delivered it for her.

'I will send it on the next ship,' Emanuel promised, 'but first, may I see it please? I have been told of this outstanding map you have engraved for my uncle.'

'You may.' She smiled, a glow of warmth spreading down through her body at his enthusiasm. He bore more than a passing resemblance to Abraham and he always made her feel a little homesick for her cousin. After unrolling the packaging he reverently laid the map out across his desk. Seeing it as if through his eyes for the first time she felt a wash of pride flood through her. It was without doubt the best engraving she'd ever done, and she could tell Emanuel thought so too.

'This is magnificent,' he told her. 'The details are so fine. Exquisite.'

Freida felt her face flush at the pride she could not confess to. As she opened her mouth to demur, embarrassed to accept the compliment, they both turned as the door opened to reveal his steward followed in his wake by a stately-looking gentleman who swept in before inclining his head to them both. He scrutinised Freida at some length. She curtsied in response before smiling politely, wondering who this dour-looking gentleman was.

'Doctor Dee, how lovely to see you.' Emanuel greeted him as an old friend whilst Freida attempted to blend into the tapestries hung on the wall behind her. She had no desire for an introduction. Her natural reserve and continual worry for the safety of her family resulted in her trying to keep her circle of acquaintances as small as possible, but Emanuel held his arm out as if to draw her forwards. 'May I introduce Freida Ortelius? She is married to one of the ship's captains who deliver the post around Europe for me.'

Although Freida was now married, as was the custom in her homeland she continued to use her maiden name.

'My pleasure.' Dee inclined his head once again, adding, 'Please, call me John.' He smiled, his eyes creasing at the corners, and she felt her breath that she hadn't realised she was holding slowly ease. He was a slight man, impeccably dressed in a doublet and breeches of black grosgrain slashed to reveal a gold silk lining, his long white beard tapering to a neat point. On his head he wore a close-fitting plain black cap.

'John lives at Mortlake and has a library that surpasses all others in London, where he keeps a Mercator globe,' Emanuel explained. 'He is also advisor to Queen Elizabeth as court astronomer and is most learned in the subjects of alchemy. Often he visits our community to view any interesting artefacts or plants that have arrived.'

'And you seem to have something of interest today.' John indicated Freida's map, still laid out before them. He bent closer to examine it. 'I initially thought this had arrived from my old friend Abraham, but upon hearing that you are of the Ortelius family, my lady, I do not think that is the case. And looking closer I can see this is a detailed map of our own river Thames from the city down to the docks and then onwards to Kent and the sea. May I ask if you are the engraver?' He looked at Freida. Emanuel caught her eye and smiled encouragingly.

'Yes,' she whispered.

'Abraham was a cousin of Freida's late father and she grew up in his household. He commissioned this map to be added to a new atlas,' Emanuel explained.

'You have obviously inherited his expertise, and for a

42

lady to have your own atelier creating maps such as this is unheard of. You will be an inspiration for others to follow.' Dee pursed his lips, nodding slowly. 'I have had sight of one of Abraham's *Theatrum* atlases at court here in London. Our queen is most interested in maps and navigation, for she is constantly desiring to capture lands that may be claimed for England. Part of our magnificent empire. She would, I am sure, be delighted to meet such a talented relative of the most esteemed Abraham Ortelius, living here in London.' He paused as if an idea had suddenly occurred to him, and he lifted his hand, his eyes wide.

'May I borrow this?' He indicated the map. 'And take it to court? You should accompany me, for I would like to present it, and yourself, to the queen.' He looked at Freida, waiting for a response, his eyebrows raised. 'It is a great honour to be introduced to Her Majesty,' he added.

'No. No thank you, my lord,' Freida stammered. She knew she sounded impolite but she ploughed on regardless. 'Please do take the map. I shall have another one printed and commence the finishing again. It will be my pleasure, but I would prefer to not attend court myself.' She took a step backwards as if they were about to drag her away that very minute. Not understanding her reticence, Dee barely listened to her. Freida suspected he thought she was being modest as a lady should be, although secretly delighted at such honour. Everyone wanted to be presented to the queen. Everyone apart from her.

'I shall be present at the palace later this week. I have an audience promised and you may accompany me then. The queen loves curiosities and you and your map will be perfect. Now, Emanuel.' He turned away and Freida was forgotten as the two men left the room discussing a valuable book that Dee had recently acquired.

She sank into a chair beside the desk, pressing her hand against her heart, which was thumping painfully. Reaching out with the other, her fingers stroked the edge of the map. She resisted the urge to fling it into the fire that burned brightly in the stone fireplace. If she destroyed it, she'd just have to produce another. She could tell nothing would stop Doctor Dee in his quest to display it to the queen. If only he'd turned up another day. Or if he'd been even an hour later, the map wouldn't have been laid out on the desk. Now it was leading her into new places, into potential danger even though she couldn't articulate what she thought may happen, but she was being forced to expose herself to the English court. And she couldn't hide.

Liskin, however, was unashamedly excited when Emanuel told her about Freida's forthcoming presentation.

'Being presented to the queen – what an honour.' She breathed. 'To think that she may be interested in our family. Abraham will be so proud. I must write and tell him.' She looked around as if a quill and parchment would suddenly appear on the table beside her. Freida knew she'd been outmanoeuvred and there was no option but to accompany Dee. 'You must borrow one of my gowns,' Liskin added. 'Your clothes are good quality; however, not fine enough for court where the gowns are sumptuous. If we work together, we can add some extra embroidery. Or pearls . . .' She got up and left the room, still muttering to herself about ermine and feathers. On shaking legs Freida followed, suddenly desperate to find Jacob.

Chapter Seven

June 1580

Liskin's excitement about the forthcoming visit to court far eclipsed Freida's own emotions, which were churning in her chest, a snake trying to break free. She stood as if she were a manikin, stiff and upright, while a heavy saffron-yellow brocade gown decorated with tiny embroidered flowers the colour of fresh green spring leaves was fitted to her. Thankfully she and Liskin were approximately the same height but her older cousin was more ample around the waist and hips. They called a dressmaker in who spent hour after hour fitting it snugly to Freida's slight frame. In the evenings she felt obliged to join Liskin and Nell, sitting in the parlour sewing cuffs and hems by the light of what felt like a hundred candles glowing around the room, reflecting against the polished linen-fold wooden panels. But all Freida could see were the dark shadows of apprehension about her forthcoming visit lurking silently in the corners.

All too soon Friday arrived. She'd been hoping Willem

would arrive home early at least to accompany her, even if he had to wait outside the palace gatehouse. But it wasn't to be. At ten in the morning as promised, Dee could be heard downstairs. Freida felt the acid prickle of trepidation creep along her spine and her heart, which was already racing, sped up even further. The heavily starched ruff that had been fixed to her gown was harsh against her skin and prevented her from looking down at her feet, clad in soft leather slippers, which had been hastily made for her in the past few days. They were tight, and already pinching. She trusted the leather would stretch during the course of her visit or she'd soon be limping.

Downstairs Doctor Dee was also dressed up, wearing a luxurious doublet of burgundy brocade, his beard in its customary sharp point and his head covered yet again in a close-fitting black silk cap. Her own head was adorned with a simple pearl and gold comb in her hair, which was piled on top. He offered his arm to her and, placing her hand on it, she hoped he couldn't feel the trembling as they left Lime Street for Botolph's Wharf from where they could hire a boat to take them upriver.

Within minutes of leaving the house they were forced to pause, their passage halted by a flock of sheep. The animals bleated loudly, a cacophony of sound as if conscious they were on their final journey to Eastcheap and the slaughterhouses there. The noise they were making added to the general clamour of the city, church bells ringing and young apprentices shouting across the street to each other as they went about their business. The mess the animals left behind them made Freida screw her nose up as she attempted to sidestep the dung now in her path, conscious of her new slippers.

To her left, the great Tower of London loomed over the surrounding streets, its white imposing double walls and central imperious tower shadowing all that lay before it. There were rumours that the queen kept lions within the walls and for a moment Freida thought she heard a distant roar, curdling her already churning stomach. Freida had heard of the atrocities that went on inside the fortress – a stronghold of the monarchy – in the name of the security of the throne. And it now made her even more anxious as she stepped down into a wherry bound for court where the demands for torture were handed down. They were accompanied by Guy, for which Freida was very grateful. When she'd kissed Jacob goodbye the horrifying thought that she may never see him again skittered across her mind, even though she knew she was being ridiculous.

The Thames was as usual busy with numerous small craft moving between the larger ships, all vying for space together with the many swans who were a permanent hazard with their stately movement through the ever-swirling waters, as if aware of their royal ownership. Freida envied the boatmen going about their daily business. Not undertaking a journey for an audience that unlike most Englishmen she would do anything to avoid. So many spent their whole lives trying to climb the hierarchy and occupy the inner circle of the court, but it wasn't for her, a humble immigrant. In her hand she carried the oilcloth containing her map, and when they arrived at the landing stage at Greenwich Palace the boatman helped her up the steps. No green algae or slippery moss here, it was all very different from the other landing steps she'd used to board boats along the river. But nothing more than she'd expect at the palace.

Being a frequent visitor, Doctor Dee wasn't confronted

by the guards in their royal livery embroidered in stiff gold thread, and he and Freida followed one of them as they approached the heavy wooden gates that led to the palace. Around them immaculate lawns and flower beds rolled down to the river. To one side lay an extensive knot garden, the low box bushes intricately cut into looping designs, and she could smell the sweet scent of lavender. The new gatehouse built by the queen's father was, as had been described to Freida, a magnificent building, decorated with terracotta roundels containing busts of Roman emperors.

Once inside, the palace resembled nothing that she'd ever seen before and Freida forgot her nerves for a moment as she gazed around in awe. She was used to the houses on Lime Street, which were large, standing behind tall walls and high wooden gateways, surrounded by expansive gardens. Some, like Liskin's, had a tennis court as befitted the eminent society who lived there, but they were all a similar layout with a large central hall that everyone lived in. As well as her workshop, Freida had her small parlour at the back of the house, together with a dining chamber, and there were the usual kitchens and wash houses beyond that. But this was something else and truly a palace for royalty.

In front of her was the great hall, decorated with a black and white chequerboard floor, which led to a further porch, and beyond that the inner hall. Slowly turning on the spot Freida tilted her head back as far as she dared, placing one hand on Doctor Dee's arm to balance her as she looked up at the hammer-beam roof reputedly built to emulate the great hall at Westminster. In the centre was a vent to allow smoke to filter out from a now empty hearth in the middle of the room. This space was far more traditional than the other buildings in London Freida had been in, an ancient palace built for those anointed by God.

At the end of the room a tall bay window soared to the roof, lighting up a dais below, and opposite a grand stone archway led to a staircase laid with flagstones. Dee directed her across the hall to the staircase. Carefully lifting the front of her skirts whilst trying to not drop the map, Freida slowly walked up them. The grandiose interior of the palace was doing nothing for her nerves.

She found herself in a long gallery brightly lit by a wall of windows, sunlight pouring in. Opposite hung enormous tapestries depicting mythical battles, the threads in a myriad of brilliant colours shining as if they'd been polished. The ceiling was heavily gilded, adding to the brilliance of the room. She didn't know what to look at first as she gazed around. As she had feared, her new slippers were making her feet feel as if they were on fire and she was certain her heels were bleeding. Thankfully they were now walking on carpet, something she'd heard of but never experienced, and she was grateful for the softness beneath her soles.

Courtiers walked up and down, deep in conversation with each other or huddled in the corners where the light couldn't reach. There was an air of intrigue and conspiracy and Freida understood why the queen was so apprehensive of plots to assassinate her or remove her from the throne. She could feel the treachery, the passing of secrets, shifting around her.

Finally, they walked into an inner presence chamber more intimate than the gallery. Here there was the scent of juniper and cloves being burned on a dish in the fire. At the far end was a raised dais covered by a canopy and an ornate throne upon which was sat a slender woman with a pale face and the brightest red hair Freida had ever seen. It shone like the setting sun reflected on the river. The power and confidence emanating from her was palpable and Freida was relieved she had Dee to lean on as her knees began to tremble.

Around them people mingled, talking with each other, but all the time their eyes darted about watching those around them. Their elaborate clothing was colourful and Freida now understood why her cousin had been so insistent about what she wore. At least she could hold her head high as they advanced towards the end of the room where a small group of people were sitting or standing close to the throne.

As they approached, the queen – resplendent in a black gown heavily embroidered with gold thread – was talking to a tall dark-haired man beside her, but suddenly she turned towards them. Her eyes were narrow, her lips thin and straight and her countenance severe, every bit the ruler of a nation. Freida remembered the tales of the Tower and she shuddered. Abruptly Doctor Dee stopped and bowed low, and next to him Freida curtsied down on one knee and lowered her head. She was fervently wishing she were anywhere else but there. As Dee stood up, he allowed her to hold on to him as she got back to her feet. Freida's face burned as she felt the eyes of those in the queen's privy circle scrutinising her. Her hand holding the map was gripping so tightly she feared it would be ruined.

'Your Majesty.' Dee dipped his head once before continuing. 'I have brought a visitor with me who I believe you will be most interested to meet.' His elbow gave her the slightest nudge and, unsure of what she was expected to do, she gave a second curtsey as she heard Dee introduce her.

'Freida Ortelius lives with her cousin amongst the scientists and natural historians on Lime Street. You may recognise her name, Your Majesty, as being of the family of cartographers in the Low Countries.'

'Indeed I do, *Eyes*.' Freida had heard of this nickname the queen gave Dee, one of a number of pet names she used, but her attention was drawn to how deep her voice was, almost like a man's. 'As you know I possess a copy of Abraham Ortelius' *Theatrum*.' There was a pause as if they expected Freida to say something but she was struck dumb, her tongue stuck to the roof to her mouth.

'Abraham is cousin to Freida,' Dee explained. 'She worked alongside him for many years at his atelier in Antwerp, learning everything he could teach her.'

'A female apprentice?' the queen questioned. 'How original. And what are you carrying with you? Is it a gift for me?'

Freida opened her mouth to explain that it hadn't been made for her but then slowly closed it again. She stepped gingerly forwards, reached the throne and curtsied once more, offering up the map. This time thankfully she was able to get to her feet unaided and watched in silence as the queen unwrapped the package and sat staring at it for several minutes, her lips pursed. Freida was more certain than ever that Dr Dee had been mistaken in bringing her to court. Finally, the queen looked up and smiled at her, displaying surprisingly uneven and brown teeth.

'This is exquisite,' she announced, 'You have an admirable skill. I have rarely seen anything as fine as this. Come and sit beside me and explain how you have created this. Move.'

She flapped her hands at a woman sitting on a cushion at her feet who immediately stepped away to sit with a group of the ladies who were playing cards.

Freida spent the next twenty minutes explaining how she engraved the plate then took it to the printer before colouring and mounting it. She also admitted she'd worked on the colouring of the famous *Theatrum* atlas.

'I am impressed,' the queen said. 'And that does not happen often.' She looked around at her entourage and they dutifully laughed. 'I shall keep this for my collection of curiosities. You must return another day and I will show you some of them. Not just maps and atlases but also globes and navigational instruments to help my sailors. And we currently have at court my most favourite privateer, Francis Drake, lately back in England after sailing right around the world. You must be introduced to him, for I believe you will have a lot of shared interests.'

Freida's attention was caught by this; if this man was a privateer, then he had plenty in common with her husband and she would indeed be interested to meet with him. Even though she couldn't admit to the queen that she herself was the wife of a sailor, a Dutch *Sea Beggar*. Or pirate, as she suspected others saw him.

Whilst she was sitting beside the queen explaining, Freida could feel herself being watched, the hairs along the back of her neck prickling as if eyes were boring into her. She glanced up, expecting it to be John Dee keeping an eye on her. But instead, her eyes were met by another pair, dark and narrowed. The man who was staring at her was tall and stocky with black hair and beard, matching his eyes; he looked like a huge bear dressed in flamboyant lilac velvet.

'Señor Mendoza, are you wishing an audience with myself?' The queen addressed the man. 'As you can see, I am entertaining Mistress Ortelius who has lately arrived in London from Antwerp. The daughter of a cartographer, she then studied in order to follow her father's profession at the atelier of her cousin, the esteemed Abraham Ortelius. I was just explaining to her it is my wish that she is introduced to my especial sailor, Drake.' Freida could see that the queen had the slightest trace of a smirk around her mouth as if she were deliberately goading this man, whoever he was. Due to the fact that his fists were clenched and his face suffused with a dark red flush she suspected her assumption was correct.

'Your Majesty.' He gave a short bow. 'As you are well aware I do not accept that Drake is anything other than a pirate and a brigand who has stolen much treasure, which belongs to my king. I cannot imagine why you would wish to present Mistress Ortelius to him.' He had made his entire speech through gritted teeth.

'They have a lot in common because Drake has returned with much new information, which must be added to the great cartographers' works.' She turned to Freida and added, 'I shall send word when you may be introduced to Drake, and I will then show you some of the nautical instruments I have in my collection.'

'Thank you, I would dearly like to see those,' she replied as she stood up from the cushion and curtsied once more, walking backwards with Doctor Dee as they left the chamber until they were back in the gallery.

'Who is Señor Mendoza?' she couldn't help asking Dee the moment they were away from listening ears.

'Ah yes, our flamboyant Spanish friend.' At the word

'Spanish' Freida's head snapped round, her eyes wide; how could she have not realised where his heavy accent originated from? The word shot fear through her. 'Bernardino Mendoza is the Spanish ambassador to the English court. It is unfortunate our queen must endure a Catholic so close to the throne, and adjacent to the centre of this fair country's heartbeat with all the threats the Catholics are constantly plotting. But for diplomatic relations he must stay. In fact, I have heard it rumoured he fought beside the Duke of Alba in your native Holland.'

Freida stumbled and would have fallen if Dee hadn't caught her arm. The Duke of Alba. It was a name she'd frequently heard growing up. It had been Alba's troops who'd killed her parents. The queen may be the bee at the centre of the hive, but she was still harbouring enemies within. Just when Freida had hoped – nay believed – she was safe and that she'd escaped the war, there was someone watching her. Willem had promised her she was safe, but he was wrong.

She walked back through the gallery and halls beside Dee, breathing in great lungfuls of fresh air as they reached the palace gatehouse and the lawns flowing down to the river. She'd been so worried about the visit, and it had been every bit as frightening and overwhelming as she'd thought. And now, may God protect her, she was expected to go back. She could only hope the queen forgot about her. There was an atmosphere in the palace that was evil; she could taste it in the back of her throat.

As they stepped into a wherry to take them back to Lime Street, Freida looked up at the palace, the dark walls soaring up beside them, austere and foreboding. She was sure Mendoza was up there, watching her.

Chapter Eight

June 2022

Robyn was relieved the evening was fine, the sun setting behind the Brecon Beacons in the distance. Their majestic height threw deep blue shadows down into the valley where the Wye swirled and swept its way around the outskirts of the town. The fields and forest slumbered in the timeless twilight, ancient woodland that hadn't changed for thousands of years. The Beacons had watched over her as a child growing up, during her mother's funeral and then her own wedding at St Mary's, and her return to the town bowed under the weight of her sorrow almost seven years ago. Everyone was here for just a moment of time, a speck of dust in the universe, and above her the hills watched it all. And now they were sitting in judgement waiting – as her friends and family were – for her to undertake the hardest thing she would ever have to do.

She was on her way to the Three Tuns, her favourite pub, to meet a group of friends. A couple of whom had remained in Hay from their school days and others who'd arrived in the town to work or commute to Hereford. They all belonged to the local running club and often met up for drinks on a Friday evening.

The others were already sitting around a table in the corner, and after buying a round of drinks she joined them.

'Come and sit down.' Her friend Jenny patted the seat beside her. 'We're just discussing going to The Courtyard in Hereford next week to celebrate my birthday. They're showing *Psycho* as part of their Hitchcock season. Have you seen it?'

Robyn slid into her seat, her mind pausing momentarily as she wondered how to answer. Yes, she'd seen the film – such a classic. In fact, she'd probably seen every Hitchcock film that had been made. She and Nate had loved them. It was one of the first things they'd discovered they had in common. Whenever he was home they'd scour the internet looking for small independent cinemas – just like The Courtyard – who were showing one of the iconic films and they'd go out for the evening, dinner followed by the movie. She hadn't watched a single one since he'd gone. But going with her friends, an evening out – might that make it easier? She couldn't avoid the cinema forever.

'Of course. I'd love to come.' Her bright reply didn't fool Jenny, who narrowed her eyes. They'd known each other since their school days and although they weren't close, like everyone else in the town Jenny knew what had brought Robyn home.

'What's up?' she asked.

'Hitchcock films. They were something that Nate and I did together. We both loved them. I haven't been to the cinema since he disappeared.'

'Not at all? Not even to see a modern film?' Jenny's voice didn't disguise her surprise.

'Nope. I'd be remembering sitting in the dark with him, trying to help himself to my sweets because he'd already scoffed his own. Holding hands when it got to the scary parts. He was my soulmate and it just feels wrong going without him.'

'You can't stay away forever. Come with us. You can even hold my hand if you like. I promise not to snatch your popcorn.' Jenny nudged her shoulder against Robyn's, making her laugh despite the sombre mood of the conversation.

'I suppose I could,' she agreed. 'I do love that film. And it'll take my mind off other things.'

'Are you thinking about September?' Robyn had previously confided her torment and Jenny had never been one for beating about the bush.

'Yes, it's hurtling towards me now. I know I don't have to do anything immediately, but I can feel that everyone is waiting for that moment. Before this summer my dad rarely said anything, but more recently he's moved from a vague mention to telling me straight that I need to do it when we reach September. He says that I'm wasting my life, not following my career, but I can't imagine ever going back to all that: living in London and a high-flying career. That world has moved on without me. I can't sell our flat in Canary Wharf because it isn't yet legally mine, but I think I shall do it when the time comes. I'm sure Dad thinks everything will suddenly be fine once I've made the declaration. I just don't want to do it, though; I don't know if I'll ever be ready.'

'But Robyn, you're only in your thirties. You shouldn't be letting life leave you behind, you should be living every single moment . . .' Jenny's voice tailed off and her cheeks reddened.

'As if it's my last?' Robyn said. 'Is that what you were going to say?' She gave a wry grin but didn't attempt to hide the sadness in her voice.

'I wasn't going to say it, but yes. We live within the sight of those mountains.' She pointed to the window. 'They watch the world go past and we're here for a mere blink of an eye. I'm celebrating my thirty-sixth birthday next week, the years keep rolling on whether I like it or not. It's time to move on, declare Nate dead and start to live your life again.'

'As everyone keeps telling me,' Robyn told her. 'But it's not them who have to make the decision. And I've still got two months to the anniversary date so I'll decide when to do it, if I even want to do it, when the time comes. The fact he's never been found, and that when the seven-year anniversary arrives I'll have to declare him dead, makes me feel as if I am ending his life. I know there isn't any chance of him turning up, but with no body I suppose I've clung on to that hope all these years.'

Jenny squeezed her hand. 'You're allowed to feel sad for as long as you want to, you know,' she said. But it wasn't just the sadness haunting Robyn and she could only admit that to herself, her terrible guilty secret. What filled her inside, always there, twisting her guts and suffocating her, was the anger that Nate had chosen such a dangerous career, that he had opted to race a yacht sometimes in perilous, risky waters, which had ultimately taken him from her. That they'd argued about him undertaking the around the world race, the Vendée, renowned for its danger. Even on the last night before he left, she'd begged him to make it his last race but he refused. But as it turned out, it had indeed been his final one.

With everyone keen to see the film, they made arrangements to travel to Hereford the following week for a meal and the cinema. Robyn joined everyone outside in the warm evening air to sit at one of the outside tables.

Later she gave Jenny a hug goodbye before heading over the bridge towards home. Turning around she walked backwards. The mountains were barely visible now, dark against the night sky, which was covered in an uncountable number of stars. The moon was a sliver high in the sky. She was sure the peaks were observing her, judging her inability to move on from the hiatus she lived within and the anger she harboured, and she shuddered.

Chapter Nine

June 1580

Laughing, Freida leaned against an apple tree, holding her side as a stabbing pain reminded her she shouldn't be running about so soon after eating dinner. It was warm in the garden and from her workshop on the side of the house she'd heard the cook's two young daughters playing outside. Abandoning her work she'd wandered out to watch them. They were chasing each other around the orchard and before long Freida joined in. Nell was sitting beneath the shade of a mulberry tree with Jacob asleep on her lap, barely visible as she continued her never-ending sewing and embroidery, the piece of silk spread over him.

'Caught you!' Freida jumped out from the tree she was hiding behind and touched one of the girl's arms. They both shrieked before running away again. Neither of them was more than six years of age and they were already helping in the kitchen, but she encouraged Cook to allow them to use the garden for playing when the weather was fine, and not to make them work all day. She'd also been teaching them the rudiments of reading; Willem had warned her against interfering in how they were being raised by their parents, but she could see nothing wrong in what she was doing.

'Reading and writing are skills that benefit everyone,' she'd pointed out, her hands on her hips. 'And nobody else will teach them. I was taught while I helped out in my cousin's atelier. Abraham expected everyone to be able to read and write; he did not differentiate between the girls and boys, and neither will I. The competencies they learn now will help them later in life. When these girls are wives themselves, they will need to keep their husbands' accounts, and they can attract better husbands because of it. Besides, it helps me improve my English too. I know I can converse with the tradespeople and the servants with little problem—'

'And with the Queen of England,' Willem had interrupted.

'Yes indeed, but I still need to learn more. We only speak Dutch in the house between ourselves and also with Liskin and Emanuel; as Jacob gets older, he will need to speak perfect English so that he may learn a trade here.'

'Learn a trade? I intend for my son to follow his father on board the *Windfly*.'

Freida's mouth had fallen open. 'I will not allow that,' she'd started before she realised that Willem was laughing at her and she'd punched him playfully on the arm.

'I would rather he learned the art of cartography as you did,' he'd admitted and she was quick to agree. 'Your skills have introduced you to court. Who knows where Jacob could go when he is a man given he has such a talented mother?' Freida had nodded, although at the back of her mind was the tiny whisper of worry that court was a danger she didn't want her son to experience.

A week later, Freida was dismayed to receive another summons to wait on the queen. Her heart plummeted and the feeling of panic once again made her chest constrict. The previous visit had made her heart pound for hours after she'd returned home. She'd begun to believe that perhaps the queen had forgotten about her; after all, she had many dignitaries and courtiers visiting her all day long. But no, it seemed that Freida was a novelty not easily forgotten. And even now when she closed her eyes, she could see the Spanish ambassador looking at her, watching her with his dark, incalculable eyes. After Dee had told her about the man's past, she wanted to avoid him at all costs.

Willem had arrived home from his journey the previous day and she hurried to show him the letter from the palace the moment she received it.

'But this is a great honour, my love.' Willem put down his quill and paused in completing his ledger to pull her down onto his lap. 'To be invited by the queen herself. Who knows where this may lead? And you've brought this about because of the skills you possess. The ones your family are famous for. You should be proud of yourself.'

'I did not tell you everything though.' She paused for a moment. She hadn't been able to put her fears into words yet. 'There was a gentleman there called Bernardino Mendoza.' She went on to explain who he was, and how he'd made her feel. 'I could feel something sinister about him,' she whispered. 'I could feel it. He is not to be trusted; there was a wave of animosity pulsating from him. I do not understand if he knows who I am, whether he just hates all Dutch immigrants, or perhaps it was because the queen suggested she introduce me to Francis Drake. I do not wish to return there again. Are you able to accompany me?'

Willem gave a bark of laughter. 'Of course Mendoza does not like you. He will have recognised your name and thus know to whom you are wed. He has eyes everywhere and sees all things. The queen may not know, but rest assured Mendoza will. He is here at the command of King Philip. Since the *Sea Beggars* were banished from English waters after our skirmish with the Spanish in Plymouth, he will have been watchful for our return. In order to appease the ambassador, she cannot be seen to be supporting those who are at war with the Spanish throne, and thus the *Sea Beggars* are now exiled. I am surprised he has not discovered that the *Windfly* is hidden at Wapping; stealing in flying an English flag has, it seems, managed to deceive him. And I would not wonder at him knowing what I occasionally get up to whilst sailing the German Ocean.' He held his hand up as Freida opened her mouth to question what skirmishes he had omitted to tell her about. 'Unfortunately, I would be most unwelcome at court and would probably very quickly find myself deep in the bowels of the Tower, shackled to the walls. Did Doctor Dee mention who you are married to?'

'No.' Freida considered. 'As I recall, the fact that I am married was only mentioned in passing.'

'He would be aware what information is appropriate for the queen to know, certainly. And it is better for us if things stay that way. I will send Guy with you when you visit, but he will have to remain outside the palace walls. All will be fine, my heart; this can only be advantageous for you.'

Freida wished she could feel as enthusiastic as Willem obviously did. She put on her leather boots to go next door and consult yet again with Liskin about what she could wear, how she could alter the gown she'd worn previously so it looked different; it wouldn't do to attend in the same outfit, not at court where appearances were everything. But she did so with a heavy heart.

The days rushed past and Freida found it difficult to concentrate on anything else. She was occupied in her atelier for several hours each day, colouring a second copy of the map for Abraham after the queen had requisitioned the original one. And when she wasn't working, she spent as much time as she could with her husband and son, although increasingly she found herself being summoned by Liskin as new sleeves in a white silk embroidered with flowers in red to match her velvet stomacher and kirtle beneath were hastily stitched together.

On the day of the visit, Freida pushed her feet into the same leather slippers as before, this time thankfully feeling less tight. Outside it had rained continuously since the early hours, dripping off the clay tiles on their roof and pouring into the puddles that stretched from their garden wall to the houses opposite. A large hole where the cobbles in the street were lifted had filled up with the rainwater and now resembled a pond. She made a mental note to skirt around it when she left.

Willem had promised to come down to the wharf with her although he'd have to leave her there as she travelled upriver with only Guy to accompany her. He wrapped her in her black floor-length wool cloak to protect her as best he could from the weather and she fitted pattens, the wooden-soled protective shoes that tied on over her soft shoes to keep them clean from the inevitable mud underfoot. There was little she could do to shield the starched white coif on the back of her head. Her hair visible at the front soon stuck to her forehead. She would just have to hope she didn't look too bedraggled when she got to the palace.

The rain had eased slightly, reduced to a fine drizzle clinging in little droplets to Freida's clothes and skin like thousands of tiny diamonds. But the straw and animal waste on the streets stuck to her feet. All around them church bells struck the hour, a cacophony of noise exacerbated by the grating cries of rooks that lifted into the air from churchyards where they perched on gravestones as if awaiting the dead. Despite the inclement weather, the narrow paths carved between the dense buildings with their cantilevered floors reaching out to meet those opposite protected her from the worst of the rain. Shops and homes were full of people bustling around her, going about their business, heads down, hurrying. She was thankful Guy carried a sword with him whenever they were out of the house and she knew he wouldn't stop to think for a second to use it if she were ever in danger. And danger always lurked on the streets of London, brushing against them.

As she left Guy at the palace gatehouse and passed him her cloak and pattens, she was able to brush her damp hands down her reasonably dry skirts, the velvet comfortingly soft beneath her fingertips. Feeling more alone and vulnerable without John Dee to accompany her, Freida was relieved when a yeoman guard peeled away from the others at the gatehouse and walked slightly in front of her, leading her to the room where she'd previously been presented to the queen. This time, however, they traversed the room to a small gallery at the rear and beyond that the queen's privy chambers.

Freida couldn't pull the air into her lungs to breathe she was so in awe of everything laid out before her. To be invited to such a private area was the biggest honour – even she knew that. The small space was hot and stuffy, and several courtiers were milling around. Sconces on the walls held candles that flickered and danced as people moved around causing a draught and creating dark shadows that hid the faces of those who watched her. The windows were fogged, adding to the heaviness in the room, and a huge fire burned in the fireplace. Everyone turned briefly as she walked in before they returned to their whispering and gossiping, eyes darting towards her, a stranger in their midst. She half wondered if she could sneak back out, but as she considered it the group in front of her parted slightly and she was left standing alone, exposed, in the middle of the chamber.

'Mistress Ortelius.' The queen's demanding voice rang out and Freida felt dozens of eyes burning into her. She stepped forwards and curtsied deeply.

'As promised, I have someone for you to meet.' The queen beckoned her forwards and for the first time Freida noticed there was a dark-haired man with an auburn beard, his skin the same sun-browned leather as her husband's, seated on an elaborate carved chair adjacent to the queen.

He was leaning on the arm of the chair, relaxed, as if he belonged there. An amused smile twitched at the corners of his mouth. Could he smell her fear? Did he find it entertaining? Freida couldn't believe that anyone could be so composed in the company of such a frightening and powerful woman.

'This is Francis Drake, although to me he is just known as *Water*.' The queen continued, smiling at the gentleman. 'As you know, he has just returned from sailing right around the world. He found new lands to be claimed for the English crown and has returned with much gold, silver and jewels.'

Freida was relieved Her Majesty had no idea that her favourite Drake and Freida's husband were kindred spirits. All across London pamphlets passed from hand to hand announcing the return of the queen's esteemed sea captain from his circumnavigation of the world and her admiration for him, but she knew the queen would be enraged to discover Freida was married to one of the *Sea Beggars* and Willem was living with her in London.

'Francis has gifted me a map – the one he took on his journey around the world – and he has added lands that he has now discovered for the British Empire. I thought you may be interested to see it.'

'Thank you, Your Majesty.' Freida nodded. 'That would please me greatly.'

The queen rose to her feet and immediately every person in the room sank to the floor in reverence. Freida followed suit and remained where she was until she felt a hand under her elbow. She smiled at Drake as he helped her stand up and accompanied her to where the queen waited at the back of the room beside a table. For the first time since she arrived at the palace, Freida felt her shoulders relax just a little as she stood and looked at the map stretched out in front of her. Most of it looked familiar, the sort of thing she'd worked on in Antwerp with her cousin. But this had some interesting additions, and place names.

'It's quite magnificent,' Freida murmured, reaching out and feeling the rough parchment, creased and grubby beneath her fingertips. There were haphazard sketches of galleons in full sail on some of the seas. Drake caught her looking at them.

'Our Spanish friends.' He laughed. 'And they were carrying a goodly prize in gold and jewels taken for our monarch.' He smiled, his teeth white against his leathery skin as he nodded his head towards the queen who returned the smile, patting a heavy gold girdle, which hung around her waist. It was decorated with roughly cut emeralds that caught the candlelight and glowed with a deep red firelight blazing in their depths.

'Francis must return to his ship,' the queen explained. 'However, I am sure you will meet him at court again when he returns.'

'Indeed, Your Majesty,' Drake agreed. 'And before I depart, I must speak with Lord Burghley if you will give me your leave?' The queen nodded and he bowed before moving to the other side of the chamber where he started speaking animatedly and waving his arms about with the dour-faced Secretary of State, who was seated on a heavy oak chair beside the fire.

'I am pleased he has left us,' the queen said as she turned towards Freida and pulled her attention away from Drake, 'because I have a commission for you. I have seen how well you are able to engrave maps, and I wish you to produce one for me to gift to Francis. I would like him to remain in English waters, for every day I fear an invasion from the Spanish by sea, and he and his fellow sea captains could prevent King Philip from claiming our fair country for his own.'

Freida shuddered. Had she moved here simply to be hounded by the Catholics once more? It was beginning to feel that way. Perhaps she should remind the queen that the Dutch privateers could be a help to her if she hadn't banished them from England. These were not pirates with no regards to the ownership or country of origin of a ship, who attacked and plundered any vessel they encountered. Just as Francis Drake did, Willem and his fellow *Sea Beggars* carried letters of marque from their true monarch, the Prince of Orange, giving them permission to blockade the Spanish fleet. If they chose to steal whatever riches those ships held on board, that was their choice.

But without documents from the queen, whilst in English waters, Willem was considered an outlaw, a pirate. 'I would like a detailed map of the south coast, from Plymouth to Dover, the Thames and Anglia as far as Norwich. And the coast of the Low Countries. Every river, cove and bay where my navy may hide if needed. I've seen the exquisite detail you can create and it shall be a present for our famous sea captain.'

Freida knew there was no option but to accept, even though the task seemed monumental. And frightening. Supposing she couldn't do it or the queen was displeased, what would happen to her then? She had no choice though but to agree to the request.

'Thank you, Your Majesty. I would be delighted to create such a map for you.'

'Good.' The queen clapped her hands together in a childish gesture that surprised Freida. It gave her a tiny insight into the woman behind the crown, a woman who had the weight of ruling the country upon her shoulders but was still someone with a heart, and a capacity to show affection and pleasure. They were interrupted by Drake returning.

'I must make haste to Buckland Abbey to visit my wife, and from there to Plymouth so I may then sail the *Golden Hinde* to London. My horse and men are waiting. I have spoken with Lord Burghley and he is making arrangements for the treasure I brought to be stored at the Tower.'

'Of course, you must be on your way, and we look forward to your return. Godspeed, *Water*.' The queen turned away and Freida quickly curtsied, realising she too had been dismissed. Drake held his arm out and Freida laid her hand on it as he led her away, around the edge of the mingling courtiers as they all fluttered towards the queen, drawn back once more.

As they stepped into the gallery and headed towards the outer chamber, Freida heard a sudden noise, a sharp hiss on her right, and she turned to see what it was. Standing in the shadows, his face a vicious sneer, was Mendoza. He was staring straight at her.

Freida stopped for a second, rooted to the floor in shock, watching the ambassador as his eyes flicked between herself and Drake before stepping forward and placing his body between the two of them so she had to take a step back from him.

'Making friends I see, Mistress van Hoorn,' he said.

Her heart skipped a beat. Despite her use of the name Ortelius, Mendoza had still discovered to whom she was married. 'You will find yourself in danger if you remain in London. Your husband does not have the protection from the queen that Drake does.' The words were spat from between his thin lips, tiny droplets of saliva flying out. Emanating from him was the scent of myrrh, together with pungent spices she didn't recognise. For a moment she was rooted to the spot before she felt her arm being tugged slightly as she was pulled away and then they were outside the door in the outer chamber with the guards.

'I am sorry,' Drake said as he accompanied her through the corridors. 'It was unfortunate that Mendoza is at court today and he saw you with me. As Her Majesty said, I have had occasion to fight with the Spanish and naturally we will take any reward from their ships just as they would from us.'

'So the rumours are true? You are a privateer?' she asked. Drake inclined his head in acknowledgement.

'In my navigation to discover new lands it is inevitable I will meet others on the seas. But having heard to whom you are wed I believe that you know a little about the dangers for a privateer yourself? Is your husband Willem van Hoorn of the *Sea Beggars*?'

Freida could see no harm in admitting this, not now that Mendoza knew. 'He is indeed.' Her mouth quirked into a little smile as she thought of her husband.

'Does he live in your home country, estranged from you?'

Freida was unsure whether she should admit to this man she'd only just met how she and Willem were able to live as man and wife, but she felt she could trust him. There was something in his face that invited her confidence and she rarely saw that in anyone.

'He mostly lives here in London.' She dropped her voice to a whisper. 'But he keeps his ship hidden where it is docked. He brought me over from Antwerp when I left to escape the Spanish Inquisition. I am most afraid now that the ambassador knows of my family here in London.'

'Ah.' Drake stroked his beard as he nodded. 'This explains why you are here, a member of the renowned Ortelius family. But do not be afraid, fair lady, I am certain your husband will ensure you are always well protected.' By this point he had steered her through the numerous galleries and halls until they stepped outside where the rain had stopped, although the clouds still hung overhead, oppressive and grey.

Guy was leaning against a wall, his clay pipe clamped between his teeth and a cloud of blue smoke drifting around him. He looked surprised to see Freida on the arm of a gentleman but seeing her throw him a reassuring smile, he fell in behind them as they made their way down to the wharf. To her delight Drake had use of one of the queen's smaller barges and he took her back up the river in considerably more comfort than she'd arrived in. Her racing heart had returned to normal, and she knew it was due to the calm ambience of this man next to her. She wondered if the responsibility of other men's lives, of steering a ship through storms and battles, gave him such self-assurance, because she recognised the same aura in her husband. If only she could capture it herself and not feel so constantly afraid of who, or what, may be lurking around the corner to snatch away those she loved.

'I must leave you here,' Drake said as they stood on the quayside at London Bridge. 'But I would very much like to call on your husband if I may?'

Freida smiled and nodded. 'Of course,' she agreed before watching him weave away through the crowds and then turned to walk home with Guy. She was sure that she'd met someone who could be a good friend to them. And from her initial reluctance she began to feel pleased that she had the opportunity to draw a map to be given as a gift to him.

Chapter Ten

June 2022

Robyn carefully carried a plastic box in both hands as she made her way to Jenny's house where they'd agreed to meet up before leaving for the cinema. The contents of the box didn't look particularly special to anyone else, but to Robyn it was a huge achievement. When she'd first had the idea, she hadn't imagined she'd be able to go through with it, but here she was carrying a birthday cake – a *home-made* birthday cake – for Jenny.

Baking had always been a relaxing pastime, a way of winding down when work was stressful. When she'd spent weeks chasing someone through emails and phone calls to try and get a scoop on a story and it had all fizzled out. Or worse, that another publication had got there first. Then out would come the flour, sugar and eggs and the flat would begin to smell of warmth and love.

When Robyn began her married life, she was determined to create amazing offerings for Nate on his birthday each year, but it never turned out that way. On three consecutive years she'd tried a yacht cake, and each time although it tasted good, there was no resemblance to any sort of seafaring vessel whatsoever. Every cake had reduced them to tears of laughter when she revealed what she'd attempted. She'd insisted she was practising on him so that when the babies arrived, she could produce the same sort of confections she'd enjoyed growing up. Unicorns, dinosaurs, trains, their children would remember every birthday just as she had.

Except, it hadn't happened that way and since Nate had gone Robyn couldn't face any sort of baking. There wouldn't be any babies now to craft one of her masterpieces for. No laughing little faces, miniature replicas of Nate joining in his delight at another bizarrely shaped monstrosity with candles stuck in the top. So many of her dreams that now lay in tatters at the bottom of the Southern Ocean.

What she now carried wasn't one of her usual style. This was simply a Victoria sponge, no icing, no weird added pieces, in fact no candle as she couldn't find any in the kitchen. And yet it represented a huge hurdle for her – she had at least baked again. And if she could do that, what else could she do to repair her life and move on?

The trip to the cinema had been a success and Robyn caught herself singing under her breath as she walked downstairs to the shop the following morning, looking forward to beginning her research. But the shop was already busy and when she suggested that she hole herself up in the office and get started, her father pulled a face. One she knew of old.

'Sorry, not while we've got a rush.' He indicated the customers currently browsing the shelves. The early morning sun had heralded another fine day as coachloads of tourists filled the streets, most of them already carrying dusty old second-hand books. Someone was balancing a stack of Mills and Boons in one hand while she flipped through the stand of reproduction nineteenth-century maps of Europe with the other.

'This hardly constitutes a rush,' she muttered. 'Nobody's got their wallet out yet.'

As if he'd been overheard, a couple arrived at the counter with a tatty 1920s AA road map of Oxfordshire.

'Not a single motorway,' the buyer announced cheerfully. 'A far nicer era to have been driving around the UK.' He tapped his card on the reader and he and his wife left, poring over the book as they disappeared down the road.

'Go on then,' her father said. 'I can see how keen you are. And I must admit it is lovely to see you fired up like this. I haven't seen you so enthusiastic about . . .' he paused '. . . well anything since you came home.'

Robyn smiled as she left the shop, disappearing into the tunnels of maps and boxes to the office. She couldn't disagree with what he'd said. Her heart beat rapidly whenever she thought about the map. It had aroused an excitement that had been lacking for a long time. For too long she now realised, she'd shunned anything other than the mundane, too afraid to feel happy or excited. But this map had awakened something that she welcomed.

'What's the plan then? Have you discovered anything yet?' Her father had walked into the office behind her so quietly she hadn't realised he was there. Her body may be in the twenty-first century, but her head was buried in the sixteenth and she gave a start as he spoke, disturbing her concentration. He switched the kettle on and tipped some coffee into his mug.

'Nothing much,' she admitted. 'It's definitely in the style of the famous medieval cartographers. I can find images of maps of the era but it just isn't similar enough to any of them. We'll need to have the parchment authenticated when I take it out of the frame, but it does looks like the real deal. I have no idea why it's so detailed of the south and east of England though. That's very unusual; I can't find any other similar instances. And I need to determine how the map got here in the first place. You said that you didn't know it was here in the shop, but the Delisle, the French map that was on top of it in the box, was here when you bought the place so surely this item was on the inventory too, given it was buried beneath. Do you still have that documentation?'

'Well, yes I do. I'll dig it out for you.' Her father sounded doubtful she'd find anything. 'I don't have any firm ideas about the origin of this.' He slid into the chair beside her. 'And let's face it, I've seen an example of pretty much all eras of maps. This one is quite different to anything I've ever come across.'

'I like the thought that it may have been used. A sailor long ago held this to help him navigate.' Her voice caught as familiar tears filled her eyes. She used to think that eventually they'd dry up. That there would be none left, the hurt would lessen and fade away, but it hadn't happened. Anything could wound her, creep up and surprise her. That sharp realisation hit her that she had no closure. In those early days, Robyn almost obsessively watched the news every evening in case there was a report, an Englishman who'd been found on the other side of the world who'd had amnesia. A magical discovery by a visitor who recognised him from those initial news reports. Bloody, bloody man.

'Perhaps that's why it has arrived here, now,' her father replied. 'It's the right time for you. I can spare you from the shop for as long as you need. Go and discover who this sailor was and why he needed this map. Where it took him and the tales it may tell. But don't let it distract you from the arrangements you need to be thinking about. You can't use this map to escape from them.'

'I haven't forgotten.' Robyn turned away and got to her feet to have a sip of her coffee. 'How can I when you keep reminding me? I'll do it when I'm ready, Dad. And in the meantime I've been learning so much about cartography while I've been back home with you, I'd like to put that to good use.' Perhaps undertaking the investigation could help her mental state? Something needed to help her, even she acknowledged that.

Left alone with the map still laid out before her, Robyn pulled a notebook from the desk drawer and began to write a list of what she'd need to research and where she may find that information. A plan was always the first step. Even when she was working in journalism, that was where she started. She could do this; she knew she had the skills. Nothing would stop the weeks going by, just as they had for the past almost seven years, but perhaps she could finally still the countdown in her head, quieten the tick tock, tick tock. 'Okay, map,' she said, 'tell me your secrets.'

Robyn awoke with a shock, her heart thumping. Tipping her head on one side she listened for what she thought had wrenched her out of her slumbers. There it was again. The shriek of a gull of some sort, even though it was still dark outside. She checked her phone; it was only two-thirty in the morning, much too early for the birds to be awake. Perhaps something had disturbed it. She could hear it closer now. She plumped up her pillows and lay back down, but as she closed her eyes, she realised somewhere in the distance there was shouting and she sat up again. Was that what had disturbed the bird? Hay was not the sort of town where the pubs were open late, so middle-of-the-night revellers were virtually unheard of. Robyn cursed under her breath. She'd have to get up early in the morning and she wanted to go back to sleep, but now she was wide awake.

Lying with her eyes open and considering going down to the kitchen to make a cup of cocoa, the sounds she heard next had her sitting bolt upright. Gunfire. Or an explosion. The report had sounded like a rifle, but much harsher than the ones she'd heard when local farmers were culling rabbits. And she could still hear shouting.

Creeping silently downstairs to the kitchen, carrying her phone, she wondered whether to call the police. She was certain she wouldn't be the only person who'd have heard the noise and quite possibly someone living closer to wherever the crowd was had already reported it. The sound of gunfire made her uneasy though and she decided to nip down to the shop and double-check the doors were all locked. If there was a gunman in the town, she wanted to ensure they weren't able to enter her home.

The shop was in darkness. It was a thick blackness that enveloped everything, heavy and cloying. Was it usually this shadowy? She couldn't remember ever needing to come down in the middle of the night before; even in winter, the first strands of morning light were always filtering through by the time she opened the shop.

Deciding not to switch on the lights and alert whoever was out there, she tiptoed to the front door and checked the bolts were all across and the locks flicked down. Peering up and down the street she couldn't see anyone and the other shops and flats were in darkness. Surely she wasn't the only person who'd heard the commotion?

Walking through to the office, the bare floorboards cold against her feet, she checked the back door. Here the darkness felt close, suffocating and cold, much colder than in the shop. And the voices, although not close, were louder, more urgent, and she heard another blast of what was definitely a gun. There were more gulls calling now, a cacophony of angry shrieking. And that smell, what was it? It smelled like the Wye when the river burst its banks and the town's drainage was swamped: wet mud and rotting vegetation. But it hadn't been raining, not enough to cause that, so it must be the drains. She'd need to call a plumber in the morning.

Robyn shivered. She was now freezing and she didn't like the still, frigid atmosphere in the room. As if someone or something was in there with her. Standing motionless and invisible, they'd slipped into her time from another or were poised between the two, unseen. She shook her head. She knew she was on her own and even the shouting in the distance seemed to have abated, and all was silent.

Returning to the kitchen upstairs she made a hot chocolate and took it through to her bedroom. There was a trace, a tang of something acrid in the office that shouldn't have been there, something that didn't belong. The sour smell was redolent of what she'd noticed when she first opened the box containing the map. But that was in the safe and nothing could seep out of there.

After finishing her drink she lay on her back staring at the ceiling, but any hope of sleeping again was lost. Her head was a jumble of unanswered questions. She knew she hadn't imagined what she'd heard even though she had no rational explanation. The long slim fingers of dawn's light were starting to creep across the ceiling when she finally drifted into a fitful sleep.

The following morning at breakfast, Robyn asked her father if he'd heard any noise during the night, but he replied he hadn't. At her insistence, he called Alison and some of the other shopkeepers, but nobody else had heard anything. And there were no reports on the local radio. Robyn's stomach churned uncomfortably and she put her toast and jam back on her plate. She hadn't imagined the noises; she knew that. How could there have been gunfire that only she heard? And that eerie feeling downstairs. The shop wasn't haunted – she was certain of that – but there was a presence there she'd never encountered before.

Chapter Eleven

July 1580

As soon as she arrived home Freida relayed every detail of her visit, Willem making her repeat it all as the words spilled out over each other.

'Wait, wait.' He laughed and held his hand up. 'Speak a little slower please. You met that scoundrel Francis Drake and now the Queen of England has commanded you to create a map for him?'

'You know of him?' Freida was surprised.

'We have never been introduced, but of course I have heard his name mentioned many times. We are both rebels on the high seas protecting our countries from the Catholic curs.' He flashed his teeth at her and for a moment he looked every inch the pirate people supposed him to be.

'Word tells he has brought back many valuable jewels from his circumnavigation of the world. And I have heard rumours the Tower is full of gold, the queen now rich beyond belief. And she has asked you to produce a map for him? This is a huge honour, my love. Not just for you, but also the house of Ortelius. Your cousin will not mind waiting for his map when he discovers you have received such a demand from the Queen of England.'

'But I am not happy about how this may end,' Freida blurted out loudly. She rarely raised her voice and Willem took a step back in surprise. 'I do not want to visit court where there are dangers,' she added. 'I do not feel safe there. Everything about the place makes me feel uneasy. Being there makes me visible to Mendoza.'

'We all face dangers in our lives, every time I go to sea there are many risks but I always make sure I am safe as I can be. And so will you. You are stronger than you think.' He took her fingers in his big, warm hands and pulled her to her feet. He went to put his arms around her, but Freida placed her hands on his chest to stop him.

'You are in control of your ship and where she sails.' Her voice was wavering as she tried to explain. 'But I am not. I will be buffeted by the waves at court wherever they throw me. I am not able to make my own decisions as you do. It is not safe for me and yet now I cannot refuse; I have no choice. I am in a worrying situation not of my making, and I am very afraid.'

'You are perfectly safe, I promise you. Why would anyone wish you harm? It sounds to me as if you are the new pet of the queen.'

'Exactly. It makes me more noticeable, a target.' She tried to explain how Mendoza was watching her when she left with Drake.

'He frightens me. I could feel his animosity from across the room. Drake is ecstatic about the riches he has stolen from the Spanish and now, because of the map I have to draw, I have become embroiled in his notoriety. And as of yet nobody is aware I am married to another privateer. Nobody other than Mendoza and Drake. If he decides to make that common knowledge then I will be in even more danger, I am sure of it. Even the queen does not want you here. Once again, I am living my life trying to hide and yet now I am more exposed than ever.'

'No, my love, you are not. Nobody will hurt you I promise.' Willem glanced out of the window. 'I must leave the house for a short while. I am meeting a merchant at his warehouse. He has some samples of wool he wishes me to transport to Antwerp. The shadows are lengthening and I am already late. Go and see Jacob; he will calm your heart.' After kissing her gently, his cool lips there and then gone, he left the room and through her thin slippers she could feel the floor vibrating beneath his boots as he strode across the great hall, followed by the slam of the front door. It had swollen in the recent rain and no longer closed as easily as it once did. Something else to add to her feeling of unease, that someone could easily break in and take them away.

She ran upstairs to the nursery to find Jacob. Willem was sincere in his confidence that they were safe, but she knew better. She'd failed to protect those most precious to her before and she was sure if danger came calling, she'd fail them again. Imprinted into her eyelids was the menacing look Mendoza had given her. When she closed her eyes she could see him. Danger was lurking, she could feel it licking at her feet like the fire her visit to court had lit. Whether she wanted to or not – and if it were up to her the answer would be not – she had to start work on the map and hope she could do it justice. The queen had faith in her even if she didn't in herself.

As she sat in the nursery gently rocking the crib where her son was napping, an idea crept into her head and, despite her fears, she smiled to herself. If she was to engrave a map for Drake, she'd make a copy for Willem as a gift. It was good enough for the queen's favourite sailor so it was only right that her husband, her own particular favourite sailor, had the use of it as well. Leaving the nursery, she went to find parchment and quill to start a list of what she would need.

Chapter Twelve

July 2022

The more Robyn looked at the map, the more she discovered. The London houses were in such detail and each area of the city had illustrations to denote which trade was undertaken there. Leadenhall was named, illustrated with stone arcades around a courtyard, and behind it a narrow winding street named *'Lymme Streete'* with three houses drawn and the picture of what appeared to be the outline of a ship. Above the houses were engraved initials. Smithfield had tiny cattle and poultry with one extremely large goose, and clocks and minute scientific instruments were at Blackfriars opposite the imposing Baynard's Castle. Eastcheap had a flock of sheep wandering along, something Robyn could only smile at; it was now a busy throughfare close to Monument. All around St Paul's were shops decorated with books and papers. One establishment had tiny lettering on it and with the help of her father's eye loupe Robyn could just make out *'J. Jugge'*. She added that to her list of things she needed to research. After her initial investigations online and with her father's books, she had several places to search for leads.

Around the edges she could just make out some now faded clouds, and following on from the research she'd already done on other maps she knew that was quite a common decoration for the era she was increasingly certain this map was from. There was also a faint outline of what was possibly a nautical instrument although she had no idea which. Originally, she'd thought it was a compass rose but now she could see she was mistaken. She'd have to show her father and see if he had any ideas.

Continuing to work her way around the perimeter she reached the bottom right corner, where she suddenly stopped. Here, even though it was so faint she'd missed it previously, was what appeared to be a name. Was it a signature? Her heart began to thump. This could make all the difference to the provenance if they were able to decipher it. Pulling the loupe from her eye she looked again. Without the magnifying effect it was all but invisible, hidden by the stain spread across the corner. She breathed in and out slowly, biting her lip to stop herself squealing out loud. She ran through to the shop, which had thankfully just closed, asking her father to come and look.

'I think I may have just made a breakthrough.' She passed the loupe to her father. 'Look at the bottom of the map just here below Kent. It looks as if there's a signature, although it's not easy to read.'

He bent over with his face so close to the frame that his breath began to make it foggy. 'Yes, I can see it. Do you have some paper and a pen? I'll read out any letters I can decipher.'

'Right, let's look more closely.' Pushing the eye glass against his face he bent over once again. Robyn grabbed the notebook she'd been compiling her investigations in and told him she was ready to go.

'There's an F, then an R.' Slowly he read out the other letters. 'Freida? That's a female name. That can't be right – I've never heard of a female cartographer.'

'Does it give you any clues? Do you know of any cartographers with a similar name it could be, or could it be the name of the original owner?' she asked. She was disappointed he couldn't see any more of the letters.

'Nope, it means nothing. That's only the first name though. Let's see what the second name is – that may be more helpful.' He bent closer once again. 'Right, it starts with an O.' There was a long, drawn-out pause, and Robyn was about to ask if he was okay when he stood up and took the eyepiece from his face. He'd been holding it in so tightly it had left a red ring around his eye and with his hair sticking up from his head upside down, he looked like a mad professor. Quite unlike his usual debonair appearance.

'What?' she asked. 'What have you found?'

'Take a look yourself.' He passed her the loupe and ran his fingers through his hair making it sprout out even further. Robyn was puzzled and, after raising one eyebrow at him, she bent over to look once again.

'I can see the O,' she confirmed.

'And after that? What can you see after the O?'

'An R, I think. Then T. I can't make out the next letters though. Maybe a U, and the last letter is definitely an S.' She stood up again and looked at him. Her father had the biggest smile on his face and she thought he looked more excited than she'd ever seen. 'I don't understand,' she added. 'You look like you know something I don't.'

'Ortelius,' he announced as if he was the Master of Ceremonies at Buckingham Palace. 'I don't recognise the first name although just the fact it was engraved by a female is extremely surprising. In fact, amazing. The Ortelius family were famous cartographers in the Low Countries during the sixteenth century. Abraham Ortelius created the *Theatrum* atlas. They all intermarried frequently, so this would have been done by a member of his family. The Dutchwomen didn't take their husband's surname, so Freida wasn't an in-law. Which is useful for us now researching. This is a marvellous discovery. A genuine Ortelius here in the shop – it's beyond imagination. So now, as well as trying to trace the provenance of the document – without which it won't be nearly as valuable – you also need to discover what you can about Freida, then we can put a more conclusive date on it and quite possibly discover where it was engraved. This is brilliant, you clever girl. There's more of your old dad in you that I'd imagined.'

He gave her a hug and disappeared upstairs humming to himself, leaving Robyn to put the map away and switch out the light. Although the name of Ortelius meant very little to her, she'd come across it in general research books alongside that of Gerard Mercator and she knew that they were two of the foremost cartography empires during Tudor times. But a female mapmaker? That was unheard of. What sort of woman was doing a man's job five hundred years ago? Only one who was strong and independent. And yet here she was, in an era when it was expected of her to be equally strong, and she was struggling to find that within herself again. She needed to know how Freida had found that resilience.

'Hello, Wendy, how are you?' She sat up from where she'd slowly slumped down on the sofa as her phone began to ring. She loved Wendy and Dan, Nate's parents. Plenty of her friends complained about their in-laws but hers had always been kind and welcoming.

'We're both very well thank you. I'm just calling to see how you are, and to invite you over for Sunday lunch on the fourteenth of next month?' Wendy's roast dinners were legendary and Robyn could feel herself instantly salivating, but the date chosen was not lost on her. Nate's birthday. No wonder his parents wanted to spend it with the person who, apart from themselves, had been closest to him.

'That would be lovely. I'd be delighted to come, thank you.'

'Do you want to stay over? It's no trouble.' His parents had lived all their married life in Poole where Dan had taken over the family boat-building business; it was no surprise Nate had been so keen on boats and sailing. But after he went missing, Dan couldn't face working there and he sold the business before they both moved to Gloucestershire. It was as if they couldn't bear to even see the sea. Hiding in the country far removed from everything that had caused them so much pain.

'Thanks, but I'll probably come home afterwards. If I leave it until the evening, I'll miss any traffic.'

They agreed on a time and hung up. Robyn wasn't fooled by the invitation. Of course, she visited them whenever she could and they kept in contact by email, and it was Nate's birthday, but she knew why else they wanted to see her. To discover if she'd be making the declaration; it wasn't the sort of thing they'd ask in an email. Although they were as heartbroken as she, they'd accepted long ago Nate wasn't coming back. After a year, on the anniversary of his disappearance they'd held a memorial service in St Mary's where she and Nate had married, a form of partial closure she supposed. She'd attended the service even though she couldn't bring herself to participate in any way, a shadow shrouded in a voluminous black coat in the cold church, feeling detached from everything happening around her. Mentally she'd removed herself, only she knew that the sorrow she portrayed was a thin veil masking the anger and guilt – heavy, painfully chained to her. Impeding her life, stopping her moving on.

She hadn't been in the church since she'd walked out of it eight years previously on Nate's arm, her white rose wedding bouquet and an ivory silk sheath dress reflecting the sun that shone that day, lighting their faces. He'd worn silver cufflinks in the shape of tiny yachts. How different things were now.

Various friends and relatives had spoken that day. Including Sam, Nate's best friend who'd also been his best man at their wedding. He was a fellow sailor who'd crewed for Nate in numerous races. He too should have been participating in the same Vendée Globe race Nate was lost in, but with days to go before the start he'd broken his arm in a stupid drunken accident. He'd been angry at the time, but that sentiment had turned to devastation when the news broke that the support team had lost contact with Nate. He'd jumped in a taxi and raced across London to her flat and sat with her during the following days while they waited for updates, desperate to discover he'd been found and was okay.

But even Sam had eventually accepted Nate wasn't coming home. Only she refused to believe it. He'd stood up at that memorial service and talked about his memories of their friendship, their sailing days, his words going over her head. She was in a place so deep she couldn't find her way out.

She was almost surprised that Sam hadn't contacted her to remind her that the seven-year anniversary was fast approaching. Give him time, she thought. She wasn't even sure where he was in the world these days but he kept in touch sporadically and she was grateful his life had moved on. It was only hers that hadn't.

Chapter Thirteen

July 1580

Freida and Liskin were visiting Emanuel to deliver the replacement map to be sent to their cousin, together with a letter asking Abraham to send some paint pigments: ultramarine, goose-turd green and her especial favourite the dark grey called dead Spaniard. She needed the very best for this new commission. Emanuel was showing her some rhinoceros horn when they were interrupted as deep voices outside alerted them to visitors and in walked one of the very botanists they had been discussing, John Gerard, together with someone Freida instantly recognised, Francis Drake. He looked as debonair as he had done at court, dressed in a deep green velvet jacket and black breeches slashed to display a green silk lining. Seeing Freida his face crinkled up in pleasure.

'Mistress Ortelius.' He bowed low, pulling his cap with its jaunty white feather from his head. 'I was not expecting to meet you here.'

'Emanuel van Meteren is my cousin and my neighbour.' She inclined her head at his greeting. 'And may I introduce Liskin? She is the sister of Abraham Ortelius.' Freida could tell from the way Liskin was simpering she thought Drake was an attractive gentleman and he in turn was playing to that, his eyes locked on hers as he took her hand and bent to kiss it. From the short time she'd known him she suspected his behaviour and unabashed flirting was a reflection of a confident, flamboyant character.

'Ahem.' Behind him the gentleman he'd arrived with coughed.

'Of course, sorry.' Drake stepped to one side. 'I have come with another of your neighbours. I expect you are already acquainted?'

'We were just discussing you, Gerard.' Emanuel slapped him on the back, almost catapulting him across the room. 'I was telling the ladies about the herbal encyclopaedia you are currently compiling.'

'How fortuitous, for I have brought you something so surprising and new I had to show you immediately. Drake—' he tipped his head towards the man with a smile '—brought it back from the Straits of Magellan, one of the many places he visited on his voyage. I shall call it Drake's Root in his honour. But look, it resembles a little man.' He held it up triumphantly by the fleshy deep green leaves. The pale brown root below with fine hairy threads hanging from it was indeed the shape of human with tapering arms and legs from a thick coarse torso.

They all stared at it for a moment, Freida with her hand over her mouth. There was something compelling, disgusting about it. A tiny body grown in the ground. It resembled the form she'd been told a poppet took; a miniature representation of a person that supposedly witches used to cast spells. 'Is it really a plant?' she asked. Gerard moved closer with it and she leaned backwards in her chair. She didn't want it any closer. 'It looks like something used in witchcraft.'

'No, it is definitely a plant.' Drake laughed. 'Although I must admit I was astonished when I was shown one for the first time. I had to bring a sample back with me so we can grow them here in England. See, he has these bushy leaves for hair!'

Freida didn't want to see. The more she looked, the more it frightened her. She was sure she could see a face forming on it, an evil countenance. She tried – and failed – to pull her eyes away.

'I must go and plant him immediately.' Gerard laughed as he referred to the plant as a living being but Freida shuddered. She heaved a sigh of relief as finally he made his farewells and took the revolting object from the room. Beside her Liskin seemed oblivious to her horror and had even laughed at the strange object.

'Whilst I am here, I was wondering if I could discuss the map that you've been asked to draw for me. I know—' Drake held his hand up as Freida as she opened her mouth '—the queen wants it to be a secret so she can present it to me, but naturally someone in her inner circle told me. Despite her own beliefs, there are no secrets where Her Majesty is concerned. Don't worry, I will pretend that it is a surprise when I am given it.'

'Of course,' Freida replied getting to her feet and flicking her heavy skirts out. 'I am just returning home now. Would you care to accompany me?' Making her goodbyes to the gathered ensemble she walked along the street to her own house, which was looking magnificent in the afternoon sun. The lawns that surrounded it behind a dusty stone wall were starting to pale into the insipid straw of summer, patchy between the grass that still remained green. Builders and artists hurried along the winding street to slip down the alley just past her home leading to the Leaden Hall; soon there would be a pageant in the city to celebrate Midsummer's Day, and the props were being constructed there.

'And do you work here at your home?' Drake asked as they approached the front door.

'I do. I have an atelier in a room attached to the house with a door onto the street. It was built originally as an alehouse but we now brew ale in a room beyond the kitchen. Naturally I do not print my maps. The plates are taken to Mistress Jugge on Paternoster Row.'

As they walked in through the door, Freida was delighted to discover her husband standing in front of the fireplace, reading a letter. He looked up as he heard their voices.

'Hello.' Her face lit up. She never knew when he'd turn up so it was always a happy surprise when she found him there on her return, or heard his voice booming through the house. 'I did not know you were at home.'

'My work today did not take as long as I had thought so I have returned, and I see you have brought us a visitor?' He looked beyond her to Drake who was still standing in the doorway waiting to be invited in.

'Oh yes.' For a moment Freida had forgotten him. 'This is Francis Drake. We happened to meet at Emanuel's and he asked if we could discuss the map.'

'Francis Drake, I have of course heard many tales about you.' Willem bowed. 'Willem van Hoorn at your service.'

'A pleasure.' Drake returned the bow. 'Although I knew Mistress Ortelius is wed to yourself, I was not expecting to find you at home, my friend.'

Willem gave a bark of laughter. 'Most people in England and especially your queen would not call me a friend. Word tells that you are recently returned from sailing around the world. And bringing home a ship full of plunder if the rumours are true.' Willem raised his eyebrows waiting for confirmation.

'We met the *Cagafuego*, and yes we won the battle and took the spoils but my long voyage wasn't without a heavy price in my own fleet unfortunately. But this is what the protection of our country costs us. I am interested to see how skilled your wife is in her production of maps and I persuaded her to show me where she works, and to discuss if I can help her with any ledgers and maps to understand in more detail the intricacies of our home waters. We have agreed we will not divulge to the queen that I am already aware she is gifting me this precious map. Which I will treasure forever.' He tipped his shoulders and head to Freida who couldn't help a small smile of acknowledgement.

Willem called for wine and the two men were soon sitting, heads together, discussing the perils of their occupation. Excusing herself Freida went to the kitchen where she could hear the fractious cries of her young son whose flushed cheeks and chewing of his fists denoted the possible arrival of his first teeth. She scooped him up and took him through to her workshop with her.

Jiggling the baby in her arms, Freida pottered around. There was still the detritus of her day's work on the floor. She pushed it temporarily to one side with the edge of her foot, knowing that if she put Jacob down to sweep the room properly it would be filled with his plaintive wailing.

She'd just about tidied up to a reasonable degree, when she heard the voices of her husband and Drake as they walked through from the great hall to her atelier. Drake looked around the large space, his eyes opening wide as he nodded slowly.

'A suitable workspace for such a talented cartographer,' he remarked. Jacob gave a cry of frustration as Freida stopped rocking him and laughing Drake held his arms out towards the baby. 'Give him to me. I'm good with babies,' he said. Astonished, she passed Jacob over. Sure enough, Jacob immediately stopped crying and gazed up at this stranger, shocked into silence. 'So, tell me how you create your maps then,' Drake said, and tentatively Freida took him through each step and each piece of equipment. 'And will you be able to engrave what the queen is expecting?'

'I believe so. I have copies of maps of the coastline of the Low Countries and I also have access to maps of the English coastline created by your fellow countryman Christopher Saxton. I am confident I can combine the two and add further details as I learn more.'

'And how long will it take?' he asked.

Freida pursed her lips. 'It may take many months,' she admitted. 'It will need to be of the finest quality for Her Majesty.'

'And I am sure it will be.' Drake smiled as he handed Jacob, who was now quiet, back to her. 'But now unfortunately I must take my leave.' Addressing Willem he added, 'I hope that we may meet again soon.'

'You are always welcome in our home,' Willem replied as he accompanied their guest to the door.

Left with Jacob in the workshop, Freida felt a tiny spark of confidence in her skills. One that would need to be fanned many times before it would catch into a flame. Drake and her husband were both men of the seas and they had faith in her, so perhaps she should have a little in herself.

Chapter Fourteen

July 2022

Robyn placed the pile of paperwork carefully back into the file and laid it down on the desk. She'd believed her father when he said he was sure the map hadn't been in the original portfolio of the stock he'd bought with the shop, and it appeared he'd been right. She'd checked through all the lists to confirm whether it had been catalogued incorrectly, but it simply wasn't there. So where had it come from originally? The previous owner of the shop had died several years ago; she already knew that. Her father had stayed in touch with him and later attended his funeral. Originally he'd been a dealer in London in a little lane close to the Strand and had taken all of his stock with him when he relocated to Hay. Had the map come with him? But who had owned it before that? With no paperwork to give her a clue, she decided to start on her research of Freida Ortelius.

The family history of such world-renowned cartographers

was easy to piece together. Their home in Antwerp, the political background in Europe during the sixteenth century with the constant fighting between the Spanish Catholics and the Protestant Huguenots. The Inquisition, crawling through the population with their notorious brutal torture and murders. Blood had run in the streets. But this map must have been engraved in England, probably London given the detail of the streets and the names of the shops. Abraham hadn't lived in England, or at least it wasn't chronicled anywhere, but his nephew Emanuel van Meteren had done so, and he'd been living on Lime Street. From her scrutiny of the map already she knew that this particular street had more detail than any other. There had to be a connection between Emanuel and Freida.

Her research on Emanuel had uncovered letters between him and his uncle now stored at the Bodleian Library and she was eager to see them. She knew from her university days in Oxford that it wasn't easy for a member of public to request to see documents stored in the stacks, but thankfully her flatmate from those days, Martha, had continued studying and was now a professor of history of art at the university. She'd be able to arrange a visit and she picked up her phone and dialled Martha's number.

'Hello, you.' Robyn could feel the smile instantly bloom on her face. A chat with her best friend could always liven up a dull evening. 'How are you?'

'I'm very well thank you. Very well indeed. Your ears must've been burning because I was saying to Tom at dinner that I must call you and tell you our news, and now here you are.'

'News?' Robyn felt her heart begin to race and her face

burn, somehow certain before her friend spoke what she was going to say.

'I'm expecting. Eek!' Her voice tailed off into a squeal giving Robyn no doubts as to how she was feeling. 'Tom and I are having a baby. I'm already three months gone. I'm so excited. *We're* so excited. Tom is over the moon. Bit of a shock – we hadn't been trying but it's a happy surprise.' She paused for a moment in her nonstop chatter. 'Are you still there, Robyn?'

'Yes, yes of course I am. Congratulations to you both.' She could hear the brittle edge to her voice, which was an octave higher than usual. 'Such lovely news.'

They chatted for a few minutes before Robyn explained why she was calling, and Martha assured her she could organise a visit to the library to view the letters. She promised to let her know when it was arranged and whilst Robyn was very thankful, she couldn't get off the phone fast enough. Why hadn't she foreseen this? Martha and Tom had been married several years so of course they were going to want children at some point, and she should feel happy for them. Heck, she was happy for them, but she couldn't stop the falling feeling in her stomach as if it would sink too far and out of her body. It was only a matter of days since she'd been thinking about the fact that now she'd never have children. And Martha, her best friend, would be doing just that: bringing a new baby into the world, a tiny person who'd carry Martha and Tom's genes down the generations.

That longevity, permanence. A perpetual story being told through the decades. But now her story had halted. It didn't have to, she reminded herself. There was no physical reason she couldn't have a baby, although it would never be Nate's.

102

How much did she want a child of her own? A lot – she couldn't deny that. But even she knew it couldn't happen unless she moved on and met someone else. She stopped for a moment and considered what she'd just thought. She was so used to probing that pain like a sore tooth with her tongue but suddenly she realised that now it didn't hurt quite as much. Could she deny her heart? Perhaps the tick tock in her head was also that of her biological clock.

Outside it was still light, the sun now sitting close to the horizon and, pulling her trainers on, she decided to walk down to the river and visit their tree. To see if it would give her any answers.

The park was full of people, both holidaymakers and locals. Dog walkers, couples and many young families, playing with footballs and frisbees, pushing prams. Suddenly it felt like the whole world was having children and leaving her behind. Above her young buzzards called with their high-pitched screams carrying to each other as they circled on the warm thermals, dark flecks against the ultramarine of the summer sky. Reaching their tree, she placed her hand on the trunk, feeling the warmth within it, soaked up from the sun during the day. Storing it as energy for survival over the winter and for new growth the following spring. New babies, new growth, the world kept turning like a carousel even though she'd got off.

'Hey, Nate,' she whispered, conscious that unlike her early morning visits she may be interrupted by others, 'it's just me again. Are you still listening to me from wherever you are now? Or have you moved on to wherever you had to go? All of life keeps dancing on, doesn't it? Martha and Tom are having a baby. They're going to be a family. Just as we promised ourselves when the time was right. We never got to that time though, did we? But now I'm thinking that perhaps I'm getting there, except you aren't here anymore. I don't want to make the wrong decision, Nate. In fact, I don't want to make any decision, but perhaps I'm going to have to.'

Chapter Fifteen

August 1580

Freida picked up her willow charcoal and laid it down again. The task ahead seemed so huge, so daunting, she was too afraid to start. It was just an initial sketch, she reminded herself and there would be many more before she began to engrave it. But so much was at stake. This time she would gift it to the queen and it had to be perfect. Better than perfect, if that were possible.

She turned again to the ledgers and maps both Francis and Willem had loaned to her. They were an additional help to the maps she already had to work from, ones she'd brought with her from Antwerp. But would they collectively hold enough information for the item she needed to produce? The ramifications of creating something finer than she'd ever done before filled her with dismay. It could potentially propel her further into prominence at court. She wished, not for the first time, she hadn't met Doctor Dee that day. It started a series of consequences and now she was going to have to continue to visit the queen whenever she was summoned. And she wasn't sure if it would be expected of her to take in her work as it progressed, so she needed to make a start because she had no idea when that invitation would arrive.

Every visit to the palace was shadowed further by the fact that she may encounter the Spanish ambassador there. Her heart thumped when she thought of him and the way he'd watched her, haunting her every waking moment.

She heard the giggles of her baby son approaching, and looking up she watched as Willem walked in, Jacob's face wreathed in smiles as he chuckled, his father tickling him.

'I have a visitor for you,' he announced as he passed Jacob to her. 'I have to go to the *Windfly* and ensure some repairs have been completed. I will need to take her out later this week to confirm the new rigging is satisfactory, and Emanuel has just called in to ask if I can take some samples to Antwerp so I will combine the two tasks.' As usual Freida felt the plummet of her heart at the thought of Willem being away. She missed the warmth of his body next to hers in their bed but even more than that she missed the feeling of security she had when he was at home. Even staying next door wouldn't curtail the worry about him not returning. How could she prevent something awful happening to him when he was so far from home?

'You must go away again so soon?' She could hear the plaintive note in her voice but she couldn't stop it.

'It is my trade, to ensure that post and samples can reach our shores safely. Just as I did with you, the most precious cargo of all. But I have come to find you not simply to tell you that I have to go away soon, but to invite you to sail with me. To see our shores from the sea will surely help with the map that you must engrave for the queen.' He looked around the room. 'I see that you are ready to start.'

'I am,' she agreed, bouncing Jacob up and down on her knee. 'I am much feared though that I shall not do it well enough for the queen.'

'You are able to draw a map that pleases your cousin Abraham, one of the greatest cartographers this world has ever seen,' Willem reminded her. 'You definitely have the skill to produce one that the queen will be happy to present to Drake. What say you? Will you come sailing with your husband?'

'And Jacob?' She ruffled the pale silky hair on the baby's head. 'If I come, will we take him too?'

'No, my love, that is not possible. I expect fair weather but I cannot guarantee it and I do not want to worry about anyone other than you whilst I am sailing the *Windfly*. Jacob will have to remain at home.'

'But how can I keep him safe if he is not with me?' Freida's voice began to rise. 'I cannot protect him if we are many miles away.' In her head all she could see was the sneering face of Mendoza, his hot breath laced with wine brushing against her face as he whispered his threats of what may occur if they remained in London. But going home to Antwerp would be just as, if not more dangerous, and she wasn't going to run away again. It was as if he knew the fear he twisted within her chest, as though he could see into her soul and all that she kept close was laid bare. Because of who she was married to and her friendship with Francis Drake.

'We will leave him with Liskin. Their house is very well protected and they have more servants than we do. Jacob will be perfectly safe, I promise you.' Freida pressed her lips against her baby's face as she considered Willem's suggestion. Every sinew in her body strained in mutiny against leaving Jacob and being so far from him. Supposing Mendoza discovered she wasn't there and his men came calling? He seemed to know everything that went on in London. But she had to agree with Willem – it would be extremely helpful if she could experience being out on the sea. Between the two nations she called home. And perhaps on this voyage she wouldn't have to spend quite so much time in the cabin as her first sailing to London. But there was always a risk they wouldn't return at all despite the reassurances Willem had given her; many ships lay at the bottom of the seas after a battle with either the weather, or their enemy.

'We have to leave him at some point,' Willem reminded her, 'and he is not a small baby anymore. This is probably the safest it will ever be.'

Freida swallowed hard and tried to blank Mendoza from her mind.

'You are right,' she eventually agreed, 'and coming with you is an opportunity I cannot miss. Yes, my husband, I will accompany you. How many days do we have before we leave?'

'The tides will be just right on Friday, so you have three days in which to make your preparations. And now I must away to the *Windfly*.' He bent down to kiss her, his familiar musky scent making her heart beat faster as she reached her arms up to wind around his neck, and then he was gone.

'Come, Jacob,' she whispered to the baby now nestled against her neck, the smell of his own warmth filling her nostrils and making her squeeze him tighter as if she would never let him go. 'Let us go and find Liskin and make arrangements.'

Her legs were trembling as Freida stepped into the small craft, the pinnace bobbing gently up and down on the Thames. It belonged to Willem and sailed with him on the *Windfly* secured on the deck so he could always reach shore even if rocks prevented him sailing close to land. A brisk wind beneath a blue sky whipped up tiny peaks of white foam, dancing across the surface of the water, making her cheeks sting. Above the city streets grey clouds were beginning to gather. Sitting down she pushed her shaking hands between her knees so Willem couldn't see how afraid she was. She knew if he guessed at even half of her dread, he'd insist she returned home. And a large part of her would have been delighted to do so, but she had to do this or she'd be letting him down.

Willem placed the small chest containing her belongings into the boat, making it rock slightly from side to side before he climbed in and sat beside her. 'Are you excited?' he asked, taking her hand in his.

'Yes.' She nodded, hoping he couldn't hear the uncertainty in her voice. He had a lot to concentrate on when they were on board the *Windfly*; worrying about her would just add to his concerns. 'Although it is just a little cool here on the river.' She wanted him to think that was what was making her hands shake, and sure enough it seemed to have worked as he started to rub them between his own as two of his crew began to row upriver to Wapping. All around her the boatmen called to each other, hailing fellow scullers across the murky river. The wind made her eyes water as she dabbed at them with her embroidered handkerchief, a gift from Nell the previous new year. It was disguising the fact that she had tears of apprehension there too.

'And your concerns about Jacob fussing that we are not home are unfounded. He was happy and laughing when we left him, and he has a whole raft of maids waiting to look after him. Guy and Christopher are perfectly capable of helping Liskin's steward keep the household safe just as they have always done.' She wasn't as confident as him though he hadn't experienced what she had. She'd left her vulnerable son behind and she wouldn't be able to relax until she was home.

As the small craft bumped against the bow of the ship Willem helped Freida to her feet and she climbed the stairs to the quay, treading carefully at the bottom where the steps were covered at high tide and were consequently thick with slimy green algae. She'd had the forethought to wear a modest kirtle of plain wool with a simple shift underneath so that as much as possible her skirts didn't impede her walking. She'd have preferred to be wearing the close-fitting breeches of the men, but it wasn't seemly so she wore the next best thing.

Keeping her eyes on her feet, Freida averted her eyes from the docks around them. Adjacent was the popular Prospect of Whitby tavern and alongside hanging in cages was the grisly sight of executed pirates and mutineers, their bodies bloated and starting to fragment. Willem had explained to her how the bodies were kept there until they had been covered by the tides three times and she didn't want to see anything more than she had to. The gusting wind carried a rotting stench and she tried to tell herself it wasn't their disintegrating flesh.

The deck was clean and scrubbed, the wood pale from the salt water and sun that bleached them, and the crew stood to one side in deference as Willem and Freida boarded. He took her luggage to their cabin; she'd been pleased when she realised that unlike her previous voyage with him, this time she'd be able to share her bed with him, which would be a comfort to her when she woke in the night and listened for the breathing of her baby that wouldn't come. Willem had warned her they'd need to set sail immediately. He'd been on board the previous day ensuring everything was prepared and ready. And sure enough with a shout she felt a juddering beneath her feet as the anchor was hauled up and the oarsmen started to pull the ship away from the dock. She stood beside Willem, his big strong hands gripping the whipstaff, an extension to the tiller, which helped him steer in narrow channels. Steadily they moved down the river while she watched the scenery as they passed.

She could see the tall brick kilns at Limehouse, which had originally given their street its name, and in the distance the village of Rotherhithe, clusters of ramshackle houses perched on dry ground amongst the marshes, desolate and as grey as the clouds that had steadily been gathering above her as if they had sunk down to claim the earth. On both sides of the river villages huddled in the distance, unsteady houses with the pall of smoke being tugged away from rooftops in the strengthening wind. On the common land surrounding the villages, sheep and cattle grazed. Closer to the river stood taverns to entice in sailors who were aboard the many ships berthed on the riverbank as they waited for the docks at Mansion House to be free. There they would unload their cargo upon their return, where the customs men would assess the tax before it was sold to the many merchants with warehouses along the Thames.

As they sailed past Greenwich where the queen was currently residing, Freida wanted to hide behind the barrels sitting on deck. She knew she couldn't be seen but there was still the underlying uneasiness the queen would discover to whom she was married and they'd all be executed. Then she would have led them into the same death as her parents. High on the mainmast where the crow's nest stood, an English flag cracked and snapped in the wind. A deception of not only her queen, but also the Spanish. She knew they'd run up the Dutch flag as they approached Amsterdam, alerting any other ships as to their nationality and where their allegiance lay.

'How do you know which way to steer us once we reach the open sea, if you do not have the sun or the moon?' she asked Willem, looking up at the sullen clouds now heavier than before. She could feel fine spray occasionally stroke against her face and she couldn't decide if it was from the water they were now slicing through or the skies that were threatening to unleash their fury upon them. 'Even I know the maps that I draw can only help when you are steering the correct course.'

'Have you heard of an astrolabe?' he asked. 'The scientists and instrument makers of Thames Street are producing instruments to assist we sailors in new ways that we have not had before. Every time I visit them, mostly our fellow countrymen, I see new things. So now, as well as my charts—' he waved his hands across the battered papers that were scattered across a wooden chest standing beside the tiller '—I have my astrolabe. This new one is brass and far superior to my previous wooden one. It helps me navigate across the seas. Even sailing over to Amsterdam, a route I take frequently, it will be advantageous. See here?' He lifted a brass ring up. 'This is the alidade and I look through it to the sun, or the Polaris star at night. Then I can read the latitude and I am able to navigate with it. It is most beneficial when the seas are calm but less so in rough weather. Then I must get one of my officers to use a second one to improve our accuracy. Now, turn around.'

Letting go of the tiller he took her shoulders in his hands, strong and brown and rough from the manual work his sailing necessitated, and he pointed. 'And look at England as we leave. You need to remember all of this.'

Freida remembered why she'd agreed to come on this trip, and running to their cabin she snatched up the sheets of parchment she'd sewn into a crude sketchbook, together with her charcoal, to start some drawings that would be useful details on her final map. She'd been so busy taking everything in she had forgotten the purpose of her voyage and quickly she began to make amends.

Chapter Sixteen

July 2022

Robyn carefully lifted the map from its box and placed it on the desk. She turned it over and examined the back of the frame. So far she'd been concentrating on the map itself, but she also needed to understand its history, how it had arrived in her father's shop. If she knew that, she may be able to discover why it had been made, learn its story. Her heart beat a little faster. She'd forgotten how much she enjoyed the detective side of investigating; it was like old times. As if she had been transported back in time and she was in her former life. Perhaps she could pursue this as a career? It was worth considering. A new life. Not as shiny as before – it would never be that – but if she made the declaration she could move on. The future hung tantalisingly in front of her, out of reach.

Bending closer to the frame she could just about make out some numbers. She'd discounted the faded marks previously, more intent on the map itself, but could this tell her anything about its journey?

'I've just closed up.' Her father's voice jolted her back to the present. 'I'll do the cashing up and then start dinner. Have you made any breakthrough here?'

'You know how it works, Dad.' Robyn laughed. 'I'm unlikely to make some sort of magical discovery. I just need to remove each layer like an onion, each clue hopefully leading to the next one. I'm wondering about these numbers stamped here on the frame. Have you any idea what they could be? They're obviously a much later addition. I'm guessing nineteenth or twentieth century.'

'Let's have a look.' Her father picked it up and held it tilted to one side to capture the best of the sunlight. 'B231,' he said. 'This is the stamp of an auction house. Braithwaites of Norwich. They're probably the foremost auctioneers of maps, atlases, globes – anything to do with cartography really. They sell etchings and also the plates. I've had a lot of dealing with them over the years, which is how I recognised this stamp. If you call them, with a bit of luck they'll still have records or the catalogue of this item. They should be able to trace it with the number. What a stroke of luck eh?' He patted her on the shoulder and disappeared back to the shop.

Robyn pressed her hands against her mouth. She knew that occasionally a tiny sliver of good fortune could open a search right up, and perhaps this was exactly that.

The following day she called Braithwaites the moment her watch said nine o'clock and managed to speak to one of the senior specialists about the map. She was relieved her father's name immediately gave her a status she didn't consider she deserved, and after a quick explanation the gentleman assured her he'd look in the archives and call back. She hoped he wouldn't take too long. And in the meantime, she wondered how Martha was getting on organising her visit to Oxford.

She opened the browser on her laptop to send her friend an email to enquire about progress, and she found waiting for her an email from Sam.

Hi Robyn,
Just checking in to say hello, hope you're doing well. How's life in book city?

Robyn smiled. He always referred to Hay-on-Wye that way.

I'm just at Rouen at the moment doing a couple of urgent repairs to the boat and then I'll be heading for Plymouth. I'll be back in the UK for a couple of months. Can we have a meet-up? It's been too long since we last saw each other. Love, Sam

Robyn clicked the reply button. She always enjoyed catching up with him, someone who really understood her husband and was happy to chat and reminisce about him, not changing the subject as most others did.

Hey!
Great to hear from you and that you're so close to home. I'd love to see you – I'm currently involved in a project I think you may be interested in; when we get together, I'll explain all! Give me a call when you're back in Plymouth and we can make some arrangements. LY Robyn xx

She returned to her research but a small smile remained on her lips. She was looking forward to sharing the map and everything she was trying to discover about it, with him.

The call from Sam came a week later. 'I'm travelling up from Plymouth on Monday. I have to meet my sponsors in London on Thursday so I have a few days free, if you're able to meet up?'

'That would be great. I'd love that. D'you want to come here? You know the spare room is always available and Dad will be happy to see you.'

'If you're sure I won't be in the way? I don't want to take you away from work, but you know how much I like being out in the sticks, some good country air to clear the salt from my lungs.'

'Of course you won't be in the way, and I'm sure Dad will happily spare me from the shop. Anyway, remember I told you I have something amazing – well potentially amazing – to show you, and it needs to be kept here in our safe. So come and stay and we can have a proper catch-up.'

After arranging that Sam would be with her late afternoon on the following Monday, they hung up. Robyn slumped back in her chair, her work temporarily forgotten. The mention of sponsors had made Robyn's heart thump hard in her chest, her hairs along her arms standing up. Nate had had several sponsors and that relationship had been a constant in the background of their lives. She'd forgotten about how he was often in meetings and having promotional photographs taken and for a moment she felt tears well up. Was she starting to forget him too? Would he fade into the shadows of her heart as time marched on? Tick tock, tick tock, she could still hear it but it wasn't as loud as before. Looking down she kept her eyes averted from the calendar above her.

On Monday morning, Robyn was up early making the spare bed and humming to herself under her breath. She was looking forward to seeing Sam for a catch-up, despite most of his conversation usually being centred on what had happened during his most recent race or trip, which always hurt a little; although not as much as it once did. But she also wanted to share the map with him. She knew he'd be as fascinated as she was. She put some fresh towels on the end of the bed and headed downstairs to open the shop. She wasn't going to be a lot of help over the next three days so the least she could do was start early today.

By mid-afternoon, the dull steely grey skies that had hung overhead all day without moving thickened into a heavy blanket, bowing down towards the earth as if to suffocate it, and a deluge of heavy rain swept in like a curtain, running down the streets and sending the tourists into cafés or back to their hotels. Robyn had stationed herself at the shop counter and the shining empty pavements looked forlorn without the summer visitors, so she was delighted to see someone hurrying down the other side of the street, because immediately she recognised who it was. Just like Nate, Sam had a way of walking even on dry land as if he was still at sea. He couldn't lose the gait that was essential for balance when he was hopping about on the deck of a yacht. The shop door opened and he burst in, carrying a kit bag over his shoulder.

'Typical English weather – why did I come home?' He ruffled his short red hair spraying droplets onto his shoulders and it stood up on end, shining with beads of rain. As Robyn came out from behind the counter, he swept her up into a bear hug and she wrapped her arms around him, feeling his strong warm torso through the wet of his shirt, smelling the sea on his skin, a brackish trace embedded in his pores.

'It's so good to see you,' she said when he finally let her go of her. 'I did try and organise some nice weather but obviously the email went astray.'

'I don't mind really; it wouldn't be home without some rain. And it's great to see you too.'

'Let me just tell Dad you're here and we can go upstairs. You can dump your bag and I'll make us a hot drink.'

By the time Robyn had made him a sandwich and a pot of coffee, they'd both caught up with each other's news. Sam's yacht needed several repairs and updates to the GPS so he'd be in the UK for a couple of weeks at least, which suited Robyn. His presence always made her days a bit brighter. Even when it was raining he brought the sunshine with him, and the warmth sank into her bones. Life felt more relaxed when Sam was there. Although he'd be visiting his family, hopefully he'd have a sizeable length of time when he may be kicking his heels so she could get him involved in her quest.

She explained about the map and her current research, and at his request she took him downstairs to the office and got it out of the safe. The strange feeling she'd had in the office that night a few weeks previously hadn't left her but she'd pushed it to the corner of her mind and nothing like it had happened again. And there had been no mention amongst their neighbours of the shouting she'd heard.

'Can you smell it?' she asked as she laid it out on the desk. The briny scent she'd initially smelled was now more pungent and there was something else, something smoky and metallic. Sam breathed in slowly.

'Nope, nothing. What can you smell then?'

'I'm not sure, but it's a bit like the sea. Salty and similar to seaweed, and there's just a trace of hot tar. Perhaps it was used on a ship?' She didn't mention that she could smell burning and the sharp scent of gunpowder, as if a residue of Guy Fawkes Night. That had only appeared more recently.

'It does look really old.' He bent close to it, slowly examining it. 'And this frame is quite deep. Is there something else behind it?'

'I don't think so, but my next step is to take it out. Dad will have to help me with that though; it needs a specialist. The map is almost certainly printed onto parchment and looking at the texture and density of it I think it's medieval, but it possibly has something backing it. And then there's this stain all across the bottom here. I suspect it may be blood, but I can't be certain until I can examine it closer.' Sam bent down to where she indicated and nodded.

'And what have you found out about it so far?'

Robyn explained about the signature she'd found, and the auctioneer's stamp on the back of the frame.

'A female cartographer from such a renowned family is unheard of. This will be a huge breakthrough if I can establish its provenance and discover why she was engraving such an unusual map. I've looked online and the Bodleian have a collection of letters between the cartographers in mainland Europe and those in London. Mercator, Abraham Ortelius – all very famous in their day. And there's correspondence between Ortelius and his nephew in London, someone called Emanuel van Meteren. We do know a bit about him and he lived in the sort of era that this map may have been produced. I'm hoping to go and view the letters.'

'And what happens after that? Where are you heading to for more research? A trip to Holland to investigate from that side of the North Sea perhaps?'

Robyn laughed. 'That isn't on my list. Well not just yet, anyway.'

If she'd thought Sam's silence regarding Nate was an indication to how his visit would continue, Robyn was wrong. Although she suggested she cook dinner for them, Sam insisted they went out to eat and after an enjoyable pizza they stopped off at the pub for a nightcap.

'Ahh.' Sam drank down half of his pint in a single gulp. 'I love my job but I do miss good old proper British ale. You can't get beer like this anywhere in the world.' Robyn smiled at the pale froth now attached to his upper lip as she sipped her own half-pint. She'd chosen a craft beer with a significantly lower alcohol percentage; she wasn't going to risk any strange middle-of-the-night noises again. 'And talking of my job,' Sam continued. Robyn's heart sank. She'd been naive to think she wasn't going to get pressure from him too.

'Please don't,' she implored. 'I know what you're going to say.'

'I know you don't want to hear it, Robyn, but it needs to be said. I have to say it. Surely now you must acknowledge that he's gone? That for some reason we'll never know, he wasn't clipped on and went overboard? It's almost seven years and you need to move on with your life before you waste it all. Go and make the declaration and accept closure. Wendy and Dan need to have it done too. Do it for them?'

Robyn put her glass down on the table, sliding it slowly in the pool of condensation that had formed there as she thought about her response.

'I know how many years it is in September. Seven years, eighty-four months, two thousand five hundred days, or thereabouts,' she replied. 'Every single one of those days have been a living hell where I have to wake up and for a moment think he'll be there beside me before I remember he won't. Grief is supposed to lessen in time; at least that's what the counsellor said. Nate's backing team insisted I went to see her when I was still living in London but they wasted their money. The raw grief is not as harsh as it once was – she was right there. Now it's just a permanent dull ache lodged in my chest. But the anger? That just won't go away and I can't imagine even now it ever will. Nate chose to have a career that put him in huge amounts of danger; he was a selfish bastard and now I can't forgive him for that. He could have just done safer races. Nobody told him to do the Vendée, to sail around the world on his own. He left me. I can't forgive him as much as I want to, because I hate him for what he's done to me And then I feel guilty for having those thoughts about him when I still love him. Until I get past that I can't go and officially, legally, end his life. Just because the magic seven-years milestone is approaching is immaterial.'

Sam caught hold of her fingers in his. They were cold from his beer, the glass now empty in front of him.

'You can't run away forever, Robyn.' His voice was husky and he sounded on the verge of tears. 'We all loved Nate but now we need to let him go.'

Robyn held his hand tightly, feeling the calluses that shaped them warm against her skin. The same rough and damaged skin that Nate had. She'd be in a worse place without Sam who was always there for her; even when he was away he was at the end of an email or the phone. His strength and friendship had helped her through the darkest of her days and she valued him more than she could express in words. She knew that he, just like her father, only wanted the best for her. That she could somehow repair her heart, her soul, and begin to live again.

Chapter Seventeen

August 1580

The sea soon became choppy and the salt-laden spray coming over the bow stung Freida's face, drying to a harsh grit and making her skin sore. Willem brought a jar of lanolin and he gently smeared it over her cheeks.

'It may not smell very nice,' he admitted, as she wrinkled her nose, 'but the salt can rip the skin from your face. You are far more delicate than I.' He indicated his own weathered skin that had been exposed to the sun and wind and sea water for years.

'I must take my papers to our cabin,' Freida said. 'They will become too wet out here. I shall do more work on them later.' After wrapping them in a leather binder she collected her drawing implements and returned them all to her chest. Here the smell of the sea and also that of the galley below deck could not penetrate. The wood of the panels around the walls smelled of beeswax where it shone with a warm glow from the polish that had been liberally applied. She was certain it didn't have this level of preparation when it was just Willem occupying it, even though he was the captain.

Once they were clear of the Thames estuary, Willem took his astrolabe out and handed it to Freida. A watery sun was trying to break through the clouds and it reflected on the polished brass of the instrument. As she took it, she almost let it slip from her hands.

'It's heavy!' she exclaimed.

'Of course – it needs to be sturdy to survive being on board. See how these dials move around? I can measure the height of the sun or the pole star and from that I consult my charts and tables and find out my latitude. Then I have a better idea of where we are going.'

'And when the sun is not shining? How does it work then?'

'Less successfully, I must admit. Thankfully today I can work out where it is, so let me show you how the instrument works.'

Standing close to him Freida watched in amazement as he looked between his chart – the lines criss-crossing it across the seas, linking England with the rest of Europe – and the astrolabe several times and then called a command to one of his deckhands who began to roll out the smaller lateen sail on the short mizzenmast near the bow. The ship started to bank to the left, the wind catching in the mainsails as they whipped and cracked, the sea starting to bubble up around the bow as they picked up speed. She could feel the strong breeze pulling at the simple coif she wore on her head, threatening to tug it off as she held it down with one hand. Willem had suggested a simple tied piece of linen would be more effective when she was packing at home and she could see why now. When she'd travelled to London she hadn't been on the deck whilst they were sailing at speed, clipping the waves as they were now, so she hadn't realised how fast they would go. She was loath to go inside though when there was so much to see.

They'd now moved further out into the open sea and above them shearwaters with their wings outstretched blew along with the wind, whilst gulls turned and pirouetted, their screams torn away by the weather. Beside the ship porpoises curled up out of the water, as if trying to race against them. The land receded in the distance until it was a dark line on the horizon. She didn't want to miss a thing. Although she couldn't stop the constant panic clawing at the back of her mind reminding her she'd left her precious son behind where she couldn't protect him, she could see now that Willem had been right and it wouldn't have been practical to have him on board.

'We will travel a little further up the coast and then sail closer so you can see all the river inlets leading into the sea along the coast here. At the moment we are passing Essex, and we will drop anchor tonight close to St Osyth. We have enough supplies to take us to Norwich and there we will sail up the Yare to collect bales of wool to deliver to Amsterdam.'

The novelty of being on board with Willem eventually began to pall. The bed in his cabin was only made for one and extremely narrow so there was no chance of them sharing it. She slept there fitfully whilst Willem slept on deck with the crew or below on the orlop deck, and lying in the dark listening to the water slapping against the side of the ship filled her head with every dreaded scenario she had ever imagined. Were the Spanish lying out there watching them and waiting for the right moment to come aboard and slash their throats as they slept? Although the night watchman was sitting up top with his lantern and a telescope, she knew how easy it would be to slip silently, darkly, alongside them and then it would be too late to sound the alarm.

Daylight brought a brief amnesty to her worries and she sat for hours sketching as they sailed as close to the coast as they dared, whilst avoiding treacherous rocks, Willem knew exactly where he needed to steer the *Windfly*, his hands strong and steady on the tiller. She could see villages in the distance and, as they sailed past Suffolk, the dwellings became longhouses in a deep pink below heavy rush-thatched roofs sitting amongst open fields dotted with many sheep grazing below the wide, open skies. She saw the Orwell and Ore where they flowed into the sea and the *Windfly* was often accompanied by seals, their shining smooth heads appearing from the sea beside the ship.

The fare was very simple and not particularly appetising, Willem had warned her about this before they left London. The fresh vegetables soon ran out and once the chickens they had brought with them were slaughtered and the salted beef eaten, then the almost constant fish making up the bulk of their meals became monotonous. The bread they'd brought became stale and dry and began to be flecked with green and Freida mostly ate the cheese and apples, now soft and wrinkled, which she'd put in her own chest, pleased Liskin had suggested it. She noticed the seals appeared when the cook threw the fish innards overboard and they were accompanied by the seagulls swooping down to snatch anything they could. The only thing that didn't seem to be in short supply were the beer and spirits, which were considerably stronger than Freida was used to.

'The crew need something to cheer themselves up,' Willem explained when she almost spat out the beer he gave her, it didn't taste like the regular small ale of home that was much weaker in comparison. 'Sometimes we may be at sea for many weeks, and our beer and rum will remain in a state to be drunk for a long time. And it makes everything feel a bit better when the seas are rough and the food is rougher and it has been many weeks since we have seen dry land, let alone set foot on it.'

Finishing her beaker of beer, Freida could understand why the sailors preferred it as the horizon tilted slightly. She closed her eyes and the familiar rocking of the wooden deck below her feet felt intensified. She made a mental note to drink only small amounts when she was really thirsty, and not gulp down a large cupful as she'd just done.

'I'm just going for a little lie-down.' She belched slightly as she stood up from the barrel she was propped against, waiting for a moment for her head to settle. As she walked tentatively away towards the after deck, she heard the rumble of Willem's deep laugh behind her.

The landscape in Norfolk as they sailed up the Yare was flatter even than Suffolk and she could see a lot of other waterways snaking into the distance reflecting the blue sky above them, flashes of sunlight sparkling off them like the silk ribbons she bought from the peddlers who walked along

Lime Street. All around her, to the straight line of the horizon in the distance, lay verdant green fields alongside heavy marshes, the reeds swaying as if a pale green sea. Freida spent hours sketching so she could capture this landscape that reminded her of her homeland. A stab of homesickness cut into her. She could barely remember the home where she'd spent the first nine years of her life; however, she missed her friends and cousins at the atelier in Antwerp. Her life was in London now with Willem and Jacob but without her relations in the Low Countries she wouldn't have the skills to be where she was now. She wondered if Abraham had yet received the letter she'd written telling him of the commission from the queen.

When they reached Norwich they docked at the busy port, the ship shuddering as the hawser slowly lowered the anchor. Freida hopped from foot to foot as she waited impatiently for the gangplank to be lowered across to the jetty. She was delighted to be back on solid ground. From miles away she'd spotted the spire of the cathedral and the pale sandstone of the castle perched on a hill overlooking the city, nestling within the walls that protected them. She walked slowly as she weaved from side to side, thanking Willem for warning her that after adjusting her balance on the ship she'd need to reassess it when she was on dry land again.

Before long the ship was loaded with bundles of coarse wool woven by the Strangers in Norwich – Huguenots like herself who'd escaped the fighting and persecution in their own land, hounded by the Catholics. She had heard tell they'd found a new safe home with the people of Norwich, assembling the looms they'd brought with them and now weaving top quality wool, which was then dyed in Antwerp where it sold for a good price.

'Now we set sail for the Netherlands,' Willem said, 'where we will collect plants for John Gerard. He wished me to purchase bulbs for some new varieties of the most sought-after tulips the Dutch have grown. They fetch huge prices and all the botanists of Lime Street want to grow them. After that I must take some letters to Brielle where we shall unload the wool. Then we will be ready to set sail for home. Soon it will be possible to see the coast of the Low Countries, so have your parchment and charcoal ready.'

His eyes were alight with excitement, his mouth open in a huge grin as he called out orders to the crew and held the tiller tight in his hands. His hair lifted in the strong breeze and his back was straight, his head held high, and Freida could see how much he loved being aboard the *Windfly*. It was his life and his love. She had long suspected that she came second in his affections and here was the evidence. She knew he enjoyed being with her and Jacob in their home, but this was where his heart lay and she understood she could never ask him to give this up.

Willem was right and soon Freida was sketching and making notes as they sailed along the coast first to Amsterdam and then to Brielle where the buildings with their distinct architecture looked familiar, making her yearn for her child-hood home. Her eyes skittered across the quay, expecting to see Spanish soldiers there waiting for her, the image of Mendoza's face lurking around the corner of every building. Her hands shook violently as Willem handed her up to their pilot who had jumped across onto the public jetty as soon as the anchor was down. Unlike Norwich where she'd felt safe and couldn't wait to explore the city nestling beneath the imposing castle, here she wanted them to be on their way as soon as possible. She was relieved when they only stayed a matter of hours and were soon lifting the anchor. The now familiar pull of the oars below her feet moved them slowly out of the harbour.

Finally, they were on their way again. The cook had restocked with fresh food, so their diet improved considerably as they left Brielle, and to Freida's relief Willem had plotted their course and they were heading for home. As the days passed, her arms felt heavy with longing to hold her baby son and, now more than ever, she yearned to be back in their home. Above them the clouds were the deep purple of fresh bruises, and on the horizon she could see the edges scattering like loose embroidery threads as the rain began to fall. She felt the hairs on her neck and along her arms stand up; she feared they were in for bad weather. The wind that had been a brisk breeze an hour ago was now blowing hard, strands of her hair escaping her coif and whipping against her face while waves were crashing against the side of the ship, splashing onto the deck before running away through the gunwales.

Willem called to her to go below deck as the waves started to tower up beside them and the *Windfly* suddenly dipped steeply to one side. Freida grabbed hold of a barrel beside her as she almost lost her footing and she didn't need telling twice: she'd rather feel sick in a dark cabin than risk being washed overboard and drowning. Willem had lost a man the previous year and before they'd left London she'd promised to always do as he told her while they were on board. Just as his crew did.

During the night that followed Freida couldn't sleep as she sat on the small chair nailed to the floor, gripping the arms of it, her knuckles white as the ship was flung from side to side. Her feet in their sturdy boots were placed hard against the floor to try and keep her balance. From above she could occasionally hear her husband shouting instructions; other times his words were caught by the storm and thrown to the wind. All around her was a thick, viscous black, darker than she'd imagined possible and she didn't dare light a lamp in case with a sudden lurch of the ship, the flame caught on something and set the cabin alight.

At one point she fell to the floor onto her knees and began to murmur every prayer she could think of, wishing she had brought her Bible with her. Not that she could see it anyway. There was a small porthole covered in thick glass behind her and the sea continually crashed against it, huge grey waves demanding entry. She was thankful the contents of the deck were stored in cupboards or chests that couldn't move or she'd have been buried beneath them.

Eventually the pitching of the ship lessened a little and she was able to sit down on the edge of a bunk, pulling her legs in, bracing herself against the side. Laying her head down, she waited for the mercy of sleep to envelop her.

'Freida?' She awoke to daylight and the face of her husband who looked exhausted, dark rings beneath his eyes and his beard, usually so neat and tidy, squashed against one side of his face. 'Are you all right, my love?'

'I am, but are you?' She pushed herself up onto one arm, running her hand through his hair, which was knotted and stiff with salt, her fingers catching in the tangles. 'You look so tired.'

132

'It was not the worst storm we have been in, and we have got through it without any injuries or damage and for that we must give thanks to God. I will fetch you some water in which to wash and then come up on deck and have something to eat. With a fair wind we only have about one and a half days sailing to reach home.'

Despite so little sleep overnight, Freida suggested Willem took the bunk in his cabin to rest for a few hours and after a quick splash of her face and hands she pulled her boots on, tied a wool shawl around her shoulders and went up on deck. Here she could see evidence of the storm, pools of stagnant water on the wooden planks, scattered with clumps of shining green seaweed like crawling sea monsters. Rigging lay in untidy piles, making her lift her feet to avoid tripping on them, and the pinnace had come free from its securing in the middle of the ship. One of the crew was busy mending a piece of canvas, with the biggest needle she'd ever seen, together with waxed twine. She looked around for somewhere to sit without being in anyone's way as they tidied up, but before she could do so a shout from the crow's nest brought everyone's eyes to the horizon on which they could see the outline of another ship. The young boy up top, swaying with the motion of the ship, removed the telescope from his eye.

'Tis the Spanish,' he shouted. 'I can see their cannons and they are coming this way!' Freida felt her world tilt as if they'd hit a big wave and she grabbed hold of the foremast beside her for a moment as her vision swam. The Spanish were coming for her just as she knew that one day they would, and the *Windfly*, with her smaller guns, was no match for a big ship's imposing cannon.

Chapter Eighteen

August 2022

The tourist season was at its zenith and Robyn felt frustrated that she hadn't any spare time to devote to the map with the shop constantly busy. Hay was a town that encouraged browsing and spending the whole day drifting around the shops and cafés, which was great for the economy but not for her.

Finally, she had an email from Braithwaites and she scanned the contents quickly, clapping her hands in delight before taking her laptop through to the shop counter to show her father. She was relieved to see that just for once there were no customers and she could have his undivided attention.

'Look, Braithwaites have come up trumps. They've found our map in their catalogue just as you said they might. It was sold to the previous owner of this shop in 1950 and came from a big house sale in Norfolk. They can't tell me who it was but they have offered to mediate with the current members of the family.' She had summarised the email so succinctly he didn't need to continue reading.

'You haven't lost any of your investigation skills,' he told her, giving her a brief hug. 'I knew you could do it. It's as if I'm seeing the old Robyn slowly emerge from her shell.'

After picking her laptop back up, she took it back through the office, ruminating on what her father had just said, realising with a shock that he was right; she was beginning to feel more like her old self, a tiny insight into how her life could be, moving forwards. It was up to her to take the necessary steps.

Placing the map back into the safe, for a moment the air around her trembled and once again she had the strangest sensation, instantly surrounded by the familiar vegetation scent of seaweed and around her the room swayed slightly as if she were stood on the deck of a boat. Somewhere outside a seagull shrieked and she was reminded of the night she'd ventured downstairs, hearing the shouting and what she was still convinced was the sound of gunfire. She'd tried to put it to the back of her mind but it still lurked there. Never before had she come across something she just couldn't explain, and the memory haunted her. The gull screamed again and she shook her head, telling herself she was being silly. They frequently had gulls inland and undoubtedly it was one of those she'd heard. And anyone would feel light-headed after skipping lunch and making do with another very strong coffee.

After flicking out the light she stood for a moment in the gloom, acknowledging that despite trying to convince herself otherwise, something was happening that she couldn't rationalise. The cold, sharp atmosphere that accompanied the map every time she got it out had softened a little, almost as if someone with her was exhaling slowly. Perhaps it was relief that she was starting to unravel the mystery.

'Please wait,' she whispered. 'I'm getting closer.'

With her newfound information Robyn now had more avenues to research. She started with the Ortelius family and their history, which then led like a series of expanding tunnels through to the other prominent cartography families as the tangled intermarriages between the families tied her in knots. Eventually she found a sheet of A3 paper and attempted to draw a tree of the interwoven relationships. It made her own family tree suddenly look poor in comparison, a mere sapling. Just her and her father and now with Nate gone, no grandchildren either. And what would happen to the shop when she wasn't there to manage it? She'd always assumed as she lived her busy, full life in London that when her father retired it would be sold. There had been nothing in her life plan about returning to Hay full time. She'd had everything mapped out. And now that map was in tatters, in worse condition that the one she was now investigating.

It had been her intention to have a family; children to inherit everything and who may have even wanted to take over from her father, and now that wouldn't happen. All that she should have had, the life they should have built, swam before her eyes and she felt them burn with futile tears. Bloody grief, just when she thought she was on top of it another wave would come from nowhere and swamp her like one had supposedly done to Nate's yacht. And bloody Nate – she hit her palm on the table – leaving her without the future they had planned. The clock in her head was suddenly ticking louder than ever.

She rubbed her eyes with the heels of her hands and then turned to her laptop and typed *'Dutch Revolt'* into the search engine. It was an area of history she knew little about, not even touched upon in her history lessons at school. But as it covered the era during which she suspected her map had been made, and given that half the map was of the Low Countries, she wanted to know as much as she could about the religious turmoil and the fight between the rightful ruler William, Prince of Orange, and the Spanish King Philip.

Behind her she could hear her dad chatting with Alison who'd arrived with takeaway coffee and cakes thirty minutes previously. She smiled to herself as she considered that despite the signs in the window forbidding customers from bringing food and drink into the shop, when presented with a hot cappuccino and a cinnamon bun, his principles slid through the floorboards. She suspected the surprise breakfast would be secreted beneath the shop counter in case customers came in. And the longer Alison kept him talking, the more time she had for research.

She was so involved as she read account after account of the appalling treatment of the Huguenots, the killing by the Spanish of thousands of soldiers and innocent people, she barely noticed the time passing. The blood ran in the streets as religion battled religion, much the same as it had in England during the time of Mary Tudor. Had her map been drawn against the background of this? Or, as it was now in England had it been created here? The more she read, the more she was certain the two countries' histories were intertwined.

'Can you come and help in the shop please?' Her father's voice carrying into the office from the end of the passageway reminded Robyn that it was a normal Wednesday morning in August, at the height of holiday season. He sounded tetchy and she couldn't really blame him; she needed to be earning her wages, and becoming caught up in her investigations, she'd forgotten about her day job.

'On my way,' she shouted back, reluctantly closing down her laptop and tidying up her books and notes. She'd be back there as soon as customers allowed, the map was beginning to consume her every waking moment, pulling her in, imploring her to unravel its secrets.

But another busy day in the shop meant that after she'd cooked dinner whilst her father was cashing up and tidying downstairs, it was almost eight o'clock before Robyn could return to her studies. Spreading her paperwork across their dining table she tried to work out what was useful and what wasn't.

Her father put a cup of tea on the table beside her and leaned over the table, picking up various pieces of paper and looked at them, frowning.

'All I've got is lots of information that doesn't tell me about this particular map. I was hoping to find some sort of pointer towards who Freida was, and why our map is so unusual. But I've found nothing, so although I know more about the Ortelius family and the other cartographers, I'm not sure where our map fits into all this and where I need to go to next. I'm going to visit Martha tomorrow and see the letters in the Bodleian. I'm hoping they may give me some more leads to follow.'

The fine weather broke as Robyn drove to Oxford. Her good mood at the thought of an evening out in the nightlife of a vibrant city instead of the country pub in Hay where everyone knew her plummeted as she switched on her windscreen wipers. She slowed down as the traffic on the A40 began to crawl along, puddles forming immediately as a curtain of rain bounced off her bonnet and the ground. The sky above her was a deep foreboding purple, which stopped abruptly on the horizon where a stripe of sunlight bled into the green fields and promised better weather. The lights of the cars coming in the opposite direction were making her head hurt.

After pulling up outside Martha's house, she waited in the car for a moment as if the rain that had followed her doggedly along the remainder of her journey and was still hammering on the car roof may suddenly abate. Eventually Martha appeared at the front door and Robyn grabbed her overnight bag from the passenger seat and made a dash for it.

Despite the bad weather they ventured out to a nearby pub. Robyn had been expecting her friend to have a small baby bump, but Martha pulled her T-shirt tight against her jeans to demonstrate that her stomach remained completely flat.

'I keep checking in case it suddenly pops out overnight. I really want to look pregnant.' Martha turned the edges of her mouth down. 'But so far there's nothing. If I hadn't had a scan and seen the baby waving at me, I wouldn't believe that there was anything in there.'

The pub was small, and despite there being no students in the city it still seemed to be full of young people. Robyn managed to grab a table in the corner while Martha was at the bar and she reappeared with a glass of wine for Robyn and an orange juice for herself.

'Now then tell me what you've discovered so far about the map,' She said.

'I think I know who engraved it.' Robyn went on to explain how she and her father had deciphered the signature. 'But I'm no further on with why it's such a detailed area. I'm hoping the letters tomorrow will give me some sort of lead.'

'I've booked us in for ten o'clock so we can't sit in here until last orders. And how's your other project going?'

For a moment Robyn stared at her, her eyebrows furrowed before she rolled her eyes at her friend. 'You mean about Nate? Honestly it seems that everyone I know only has one subject to talk about. Did my dad call you?'

'No.' Martha laughed. 'Although I expect if he'd thought of it, he would've done. We're all just worried about you and want you to be able to move on. It's been long enough. Too long.'

'I know, I know, it's all I keep hearing. When I'm ready I'll do it. Not when everyone else has bullied me into it.'

'Okay, I promise not to mention it again. At least on this visit.' Martha smiled to soften her words passing her a copy of the menu, and they decided what to eat.

Robyn slept fitfully, unused to the noise as cars on the street outside the house; she hadn't realised just how quiet it was at home. In the morning, despite her disturbed night, she was up early and waiting impatiently for Martha whose morning routine was not hurried.

'Right, I have your ticket. You'll need to take the Bodleian Oath as it's your first visit.'

'Oath?'

'Yes, it's a bit old-fashioned now but it's usual that one of the librarians will ask you to make it because it's "tradition".' She made quote marks with her fingers before picking up her handbag and leading the way to the bus stop.

When they arrived at the illustrious Oxford library, Robyn left her backpack in a locker and, carrying her phone, she followed an assistant librarian upstairs as he took them to his office. She'd have liked to have sat at one of the long tables in the reading room. Robyn was awed by the almost ecclesiastical atmosphere of the historic building, the thick silence of centuries of learned academics increasing their understanding of the world hung heavily in the dark room, a suffocating mood of learning. The filtered light from the leaded windows reflected off the acres of polished wooden desks and bookcases. There was an overriding smell of beeswax polish and musty, ancient books capturing a hundred thousand souls within their covers. But she knew that for items as fragile and old as the ones she'd come to view they'd need to be somewhere more exclusive, so she was confined to a modern office instead.

The librarian disappeared again and Robyn gave Martha a nervous smile. She'd been told she could use the camera on her phone to take photographs and her friend already had a colleague lined up who'd agreed to translate the ancient words. She had no idea if this was going to be helpful in her quest, but it was worth a try. She was certain Abraham Ortelius was somehow connected to Freida and she hoped fervently that she'd learn something more from these letters.

The door opened and the librarian returned with several grey conservation boxes. Martha had requested them from the stacks a few days previously. The first document was

141

laid out on a foam rest cushion and long strings of beads covered in cloth were laid over the corners to gently keep the letter in place.

'Snakes.' Martha smiled as she pointed to the beads. 'That's what they're called here.'

Robyn held her breath as she leaned as close and dared to look at the tiny letters. It meant nothing to her, but around her the air stirred and shifted. The sharp tangy smell, the one that surrounded her when she looked at Freida's map, was there in the room: age, fear and the sea. The letter continued onto a further page and when she'd photographed the first sheet the librarian stepped forward and replaced the piece of parchment with the next one.

'Isn't it amazing?' She turned to Martha. 'A letter from Abraham Ortelius. I can't find a lot online about Emanuel except that he was a nephew who'd moved to London for safety. But they were obviously close.' She turned to the librarian asking, 'May I see the next one please?'

For the following hour Robyn pored over and photographed each of the letters, praying silently that one of them would give her some sort of clue to help her learn about Freida, and understand the map. She had no idea how difficult the translating would be, but she was impatient to know what they said and hoped it wouldn't take too long.

Eventually Robyn was finished and after thanking the librarian they went back downstairs where she handed in her reader's ticket and collected her backpack. The sunshine outside felt harsh and bright after the hallowed halls she'd just been in, the spell she'd been under shattered abruptly. For a moment she'd been there in the sixteenth century but now she was here, now – firmly in the present day – and it was a shock.

'What happens next?' she asked Martha. 'Do you have the details of your contact who can translate them for me?'

'Yes, I've already warned Geoff.' Martha steered her across the road towards a coffee shop. 'I'll send you his email address. He's expecting to hear from you. Don't forget, though, he also has his usual work to do.'

'Honestly anything he can tell me would be brilliant. Tell him there's a crate of beer in it for him.'

'That will definitely help.' Martha laughed as they went to order some hot drinks.

Chapter Nineteen

August 1580

Freida felt her bowels turn to liquid as she heard the shout from above and, looking to the horizon, she could see even without the aid of a telescope a Spanish galleon heading towards them, its sails full of wind. Reaching behind her she clung onto the mast, collapsing against it before her legs gave way.

The ship's boy had climbed down from the crow's nest at the top of the mainmast so quickly, she couldn't bear to watch in case he fell. Now he was ringing on a brass bell placed in the forecastle at the bow. At the sound of its ominous tolling the deck was suddenly full of crew, Willem appearing immediately and running to where his second in command was already shouting orders to men rushing about in a well-practised drill. On the gun deck gunwales were opened and the small brass cannons were wheeled forward from where they'd been lashed to the deck as the shot was lifted from chests. One of the crew lit the linstock in readiness to light the gunpowder, the Spanish approaching them at an alarming rate.

Willem appeared in front of Freida. 'You must go below deck again,' he told her roughly, putting his arm around her and ushering her towards the door leading to the ladder. 'It is not safe for you to be up here.'

'You told me that we would not see the Spanish, and we would be safe,' she hissed. 'Why are they here now?'

'I can never guarantee things,' he snapped, 'but we have been blown off course by the storm last night and I suspect that they have also. There is not any reason why they are so close to the English coast if they are delivering to their soldiers. It is unfortunate they have seen us but we are fast, very fast, and our guns may be smaller but they are accurate. Go down below and wait until we have seen them off.'

Doing as she was told, Freida returned to the orlop deck where the low ceiling brushed the top of her cap. No wonder so many of the crew walked with hunched backs if they spent half of their life stooped over. This was where the stock and provisions were stored – other than the heaviest items, which were kept beneath her feet in the hold – but she was too nervous to sit down, walking back and forth, back and forth in the confined space. Why had she agreed to come on this trip? Her greatest fear, the Spanish, were out there and advancing quickly and she was trapped in a ship with nowhere to run. Thankful now that Jacob hadn't accompanied them, she sank to her knees and curled herself up in a ball as she had in the cupboard all those years ago.

Above her the shouts of the men were almost drowned out by the sound of the guns being fired, the acrid scent of smoke and gunpowder drifting into the cabin. The ship shook every time the cannon shot its ammunition as if it were about to break apart, and in the distance she heard the boom of the other ship returning fire. Was she about to meet her maker at the bottom of the roiling sea around them?

Still crouching on the floor with her eyes tightly shut, she knew the moment the *Windfly* was hit, her head jerking up. There was no doubting what had happened. A splintering sound had been followed by an almighty crack as the screams from above her head were joined by her husband's booming voice shouting for calm and telling them to continue priming the guns. Looking around, she expected to see water gushing through the wall or rising through the floor but at least for the present she was dry. She couldn't bear being down in the cabin and not knowing what was happening.

Getting to her feet, she defied Willem's orders and crept along the passageway, slowly climbing the ladder and pushing open the trap door to poke her head out. Her view was hampered by the blue smoke enveloping the ship as if a cloud had fallen from the sky, catching in the back of her throat and making her cough. She could barely make out the movement of boots as men ran up and down. Thankfully the cannon roar seemed to have stopped and as she couldn't see anything burning, she continued climbing until she was up on deck.

Instantly she could see where the ship had been hit, one of the small masts lay across the deck, its sail caught around the base, rigging tangled, the men having to scramble over it. Looking out to sea the Spanish ship had smoke rising from it and it appeared to no longer be gaining on them. She looked around for Willem and spotted him standing at the stern shouting instructions. Around them the wind whipped hair around faces and pulled words away before anyone heard them.

Lifting her skirts, Freida climbed over the mast and went to her husband, grabbing hold of his arm to attract his attention.

'Are we to be saved?' she asked.

'God willing yes, we can outrun their larger ship, which does not have the speed we do. And we managed at least two direct hits. That will keep them busy for a while.' He grinned at her and she realised with horror that he was enjoying himself. That, despite promising her there wouldn't be any chance of fighting, in fact when he'd seen the Spanish galleon on the horizon he had been delighted. 'We have taken a hit ourselves.' He indicated the mast now lying on the deck, its splintered edges sharp and dangerous where it had been blasted apart. 'It will need repairing of course but it is nothing to be concerned about.'

'Well I was worried,' she shouted. 'And you certainly do not appear so. You promised me we would be safe when I consented to come sailing with you. I was a fool to agree.'

'That is not true.' He wrapped his arms around her so she was pinned to him. 'I said it was extremely unlikely we would meet a galleon at this time of year and on the route we took. I could not have foreseen the storm that blew us both off course. But look, she is sturdy and as quick as the wind; that is why she's called the *Windfly*. You were never in danger. And now we can see the Essex coast.' He pointed to a thin strip of land in the distance. 'The men are about to lower our Dutch flag and run up the English one. By high tide tomorrow we will be docked at Wapping once more and then we can return home to Jacob.'

Chapter Twenty

August 1580

Within days Freida began to feel calmer although she couldn't bear to even go into her workshop for a while. She spent her waking hours as if glued to her son, not leaving him for a moment, even when he was asleep. Finally though, with the constant reminder of the map that the queen was expecting nagging at her every thought, she found her way back there. The relaxing ambience of the room and the quiet concentration slowly began to soothe her. The smooth glowing copperplate had been delivered and was ready on its stand, her tools laid out on the bench. She now knew every inch of the map she'd drawn onto the parchment first, committing it to memory until she was dreaming about it. She just needed to add everything she'd learned on her voyage and she would be ready to start.

Fitting the mushroom-shaped smooth wood of her burin onto the palm of her hand, she mused that it held the warm familiarity of an old friend. Pressing her thumb and forefinger against the wedge-shaped blade that would produce V-shaped lines, each tapering to a point, she gently placed it against the plate. It wasn't a case of simply copying the series of drawings she had been undertaking for weeks, they all needed to be engraved in reverse, so they'd be correct when they were printed. She was so used to adjusting to this, her mind could switch to this view as naturally as looking at something the normal way.

Her eyes darted back and forth between her sketches and her engraving, adding layers of detail to the coastline as it crawled up to the busy port of Norwich and carving fine cross-hatched lines to shade the flat barren marshlands of East Anglia. She included every inlet, every tiny dip in the coastline, where the dark sea reached up the stark sheer cliff face soaring to the sky above and where clutches of houses clung to the edge of the land as the sea lapped at their doors. The rivers and coves she'd seen, and those she'd taken from the charts she'd borrowed were captured in her heart; especially those of her homeland. On her trip with Willem, she'd seen it all. The houses in Holland were different in style to those in London, although still using the same cantilevered upper floors to gain extra floor space, but wherever they were, they were all homes where people lived, laughed, cried and died. She wanted to include it all on this map. To tell those people's stories of living so close to the fierce waves. To show this English queen that her home country was as important as England.

The more she engraved, the more of her soul was being buried in the lines she cut. What had begun as a simple commission was becoming a part of her, every house or building, every street was important to her in some way.

This was beginning to be a part of her, her life flowing down the blade of her tool and into the copperplate.

Freida's whole body was shaking and she'd been stabbed with pins on several occasions.

'Keep still,' Liskin admonished as she stood to one side observing and offering suggestions. Freida had already seen the seamstress's mouth tighten when another criticism floated through the air and she had a large amount of sympathy for the poor woman. This was no ordinary ensemble, not a simple day gown – if those could be described as simple – to wear to the palace. Two weeks previously, she'd received a command to attend Richmond Palace where an extravagant banquet was to be held to celebrate Drake's safe return, and there had followed a huge commotion about what she'd wear and how to behave, who to try and speak to in order to further the cause of the scientist and botanist community she lived within. Wasn't being invited by Her Majesty enough?

Somewhere at her feet the hemming of the gown continued, the thick layers of embroidered taffeta the colour of the cypress tree standing in their garden, a deep luxurious green that fell like a waterfall over her skirts beneath, shimmering in the firelight as she walked. And moving wasn't easy in such a voluminous dress, the stomacher in pale green silk embroidered with tiny golden-centred saffron crocuses was tight against her, making it difficult to breathe. How would she be able to spend an entire evening – longer even given the rumours of the queen's entertainment – so trussed up?

Her nerves were exacerbated by the fact she had no option but to attend on her own. Apart from Doctor Dee, and she could only hope he'd be in attendance, the only other person she knew was Drake, and he'd be employed paying court to the queen and conversing with the most eminent guests present, those closest to the throne. With any luck she'd be able to hide at the edges of the room in the dark corners until she was able to escape. And there was always the fear that the Spanish ambassador may be present. He always seemed to be wherever the queen was, a spectre at the feast.

The gown had been delivered an hour before she needed to leave and reluctantly she'd allowed the maids to lace her into it, under Liskin's instructions. Her hair was piled onto her head with pearls wound into the curls and coils. Another new white ruff scratched at her jawline and the matching linen pleated cuffs almost hid her hands. The ring Willem had given her on the occasion of their marriage caught the firelight and shone, the green and red stones amidst the heavy gold shining brightly, glowing from within. Tonight, she needed the comfort it gave her more than ever and she constantly rubbed the pad of her thumb against the stones like a talisman.

A shout from downstairs alerted her to the carriage arriving. It was a rare sight in London and she'd never been in one, but Willem had insisted. She couldn't risk walking through the city to find a boat in her finery. He'd travel with her to the palace, and he'd promised that he and Guy would wait all evening at the gatehouse for her to ensure she'd get home safely. The two of them were more than a match for any cut-throats who may stop the carriage as it moved through the dark streets of London.

As she arrived downstairs, Liskin handed her something wrapped in a scrap of embroidered linen. Opening it she saw that it contained a fine gold filigree pomander, and lifting it to her nose she inhaled the soft scent of damask rose and verdigris, reminiscent of warm summer days and less worrying times.

'Thank you, I will take care of it,' she promised.

'It is yours now. You are visiting court and you need to emulate the other ladies, to be appropriately attired.' They kissed briefly and then laying her arm on Willem's outstretched one, she walked with him out of the house, her deportment belying her trembling legs and fast beating heart.

The journey went far too quickly for Freida's liking, and she alighted at the gatehouse alongside the river beside many other guests. She was now grateful for the fuss and effort Liskin had insisted on as, looking around, she could see that she easily matched everyone else in grandeur and fashion and would be able to blend in. As agreed, Willem and Guy accompanied her to the gatehouse where a clutch of other personal guards were already congregating. Both the men removed their clay pipes from their jerkin pockets and settled on the ground, leaning against the palace wall. Willem smiled and mouthed, *'I love you, pirate's wife,'* using his pet name for her. Feeling as if he'd wrapped her in a fur-lined cloak of safety she followed the other guests towards the palace gates, trying to move out of the way of the numerous riders that were passing through, their horses buffeting people on foot if they accidentally wandered into their path.

Inside the great banqueting hall, the light from a thousand candles stacked in tall gold candlesticks shone, turning the room into a brightness more dazzling than midday when the summer sun was overhead. With two blazing fires in fireplaces the size of a small chamber a fine layer of smoke hung high in the vaulted ceilings over the revellers, streaked in misty threads across the elaborately decorated ceiling its plasterwork, the carved oak beams barely visible. It was already dusk outside but you wouldn't have believed it when standing in that room, the gilding on elaborate carvings reflecting the candlelight as if on fire. Rows of tables with polished shining goblets and vast silver dishes awaiting the feast were set out whilst all around her groups of chattering nobility meant the noise was deafening.

The temporary confidence she'd arrived with drained through her body to her feet and disappeared into a puddle on the floor. Other guests pushed around her until she felt like a piece of flotsam being dragged back and forth on the dark waves of the sea she'd recently sailed upon. Hastily she gathered up her skirts and moved to a wall where she could stand against an enormous brightly coloured tapestry depicting a scene from the Bible, and hope she wouldn't be seen.

The chattering around her stopped abruptly as a loud fanfare from a quartet of trumpeters dressed in the red and azure tabards of the royal livery heralded the arrival of the queen and her especial guest Francis Drake. As the noise rang out, Freida along with everyone in the hall knelt down in reverence. She remained there watching and waiting, her head lowered until she was conscious of those around her standing up again and she could follow suit.

The queen was now perched on a large red and gold throne placed on a dais at the far end of the hall where she was visible to all, with Drake sitting on one side and Lord Burghley on the other. She was dressed in a gown of deep black velvet, covered in embroidered flowers of both red and white and scattered with a myriad of pearls and glittering rubies. The cuffs of her sleeves were edged in heavy gold threaded lace, which matched the edging of the stiff white ruff around her neck. Pearls were entwined in her hair, covering her head in an elaborate design. The skirt spread out so far it appeared to pin both Drake and Lord Burghley against their chairs. It glinted and danced with the tiny jewels sewn onto the fabric, and even from a distance Freida could see that the queen's fingers were laden with rings heavy with jewels. Around her neck lay a heavy carcanet of shining gold, intricately interspersed with sparkling diamonds and fat, crudely faceted rubies. Freida had never seen jewels so striking. In one corner of the room on a low stage musicians started to play the virginal, lute and harp, their music barely audible above the babble of voices.

Following others to sit at one of the tables and carefully positioning herself at the back of the room, she listened in to the gossip that carried on around her. Everyone was talking about the queen's privateer sitting next to her looking very dashing in a black doublet the slashes in the upper sleeves displaying the gold lining pulled through. His hair was shorter than was fashionable, his beard was clipped and tidy. The women around her were giving him admiring glances whilst discussing indiscreetly how he was considered dangerous and because of that, extremely attractive. Some of the talk, however, wasn't complimentary as his elevated status stoked jealousy amongst other courtiers who all hoped for the same.

Freida smiled to herself remembering how he was now a friend to her husband, who was far more handsome than Drake. She was so fortuitous to have him in her life, even though she wished he didn't have to go away on the *Windfly* and face the unavoidable dangers he did. Ones she herself had witnessed when she'd been foolhardy enough to agree to sail with him. Although they'd resolved their differences after their argument on board, she'd never set foot on his ship again; of that she was certain.

If Freida had hoped that hiding at the back of the room would render her invisible, she was mistaken. A tug at her elbow made her turn to see a young page, his hair cut in the fashionable smooth cap, bow before her before, saying, 'Her Majesty requests your company.' With her heart sinking, Freida followed him across the hall as other guests turned to watch, finally noticing her.

'Pray come forth and sit beside me,' the queen patted a small stool almost at her feet and Burghley left his chair and disappeared through a door behind the throne. It was panelled to exactly match the rest of the room and Freida hadn't even noticed it was there.

The queen was smiling, her brown teeth just visible through thin lips, red against the white lead paste that covered the royal skin. It didn't disguise where the pox had damaged her though, nor detract from a shimmer of anger shining in her eyes. Swallowing hard, Freida stepped forward and perched on the settle, arranging her skirts around her to mimic how the other ladies around the queen were sitting. Her previous pleasant connection with the queen seemed to have disappeared and she was uncertain as to what she'd done wrong.

Chapter Twenty-One

August 2022

Robyn woke with a familiar painful ache in her chest. As if someone were sitting on her, stifling her breathing. Slowly she filled her lungs and let the air out slowly. She didn't need to look at the calendar today to know what date it was as she dropped from a great height into a dark well of sadness. Nate's birthday. He was such a kid when it came to birthdays. She'd always teased him about it, how being an only child had turned him into a spoiled brat. But he hadn't been spoiled, just cherished as a surprise late baby and he deserved it all.

On the desk in the corner of her room, balanced on top of her notebook now filling up with notes she'd made whilst researching the map, was a birthday card. Exactly like the last seven years, lovingly chosen, written in, sealed down. But no one to give it to. It would be put with the others, and the silly things she'd bought him, daft bits she'd seen and thought, 'Nate would love that' – buying it even though she couldn't give it to him.

And today she would go and visit his parents. It wouldn't be a sad occasion; they could always think of memories to make them laugh. She and Nate had enjoyed some amazing birthday celebrations over the years, always topped off with her appalling attempts at a cake, which had been their hilarious highlight of the day. One year she'd visited him when he was at port in Cape Verde and once when they'd been able to have a few days together in Mexico while his yacht was in for an overhaul. Such happy memories, she smiled to herself. Those were the ones to cling on to today.

Downstairs Alison was already stationed behind the counter even though it was barely nine o'clock. During the summer months they stayed open on Sundays to make the most of the tourist trade, although that balanced out from November to Easter when they took two days off and enjoyed the slightly slower pace of life. It really was the wrong time of year for her to be researching a map that took her away from work. Alison smiled brightly as Robyn opened the door at the bottom of the stairs and slipped through. Ever since she had banged it wide open and almost knocked a customer flying, she'd been more circumspect when arriving on the shop floor.

'Morning, love,' Alison greeted her. 'I've escaped from my shop; I think my son and his wife have had an argument because I could sense a strained atmosphere. The last thing they need today is me hanging around getting in their way. I suspect they can't wait for me to retire and get rid of me permanently.' She laughed, before adding, 'Malcolm's just in the office by the way, apparently doing a deal with someone in Tokyo.' She dropped her voice to a whisper. 'I think he just wanted a cup of coffee in peace but don't tell him I told you that.' They giggled together and Robyn felt a pang of guilt that she was still playing gooseberry in their love life. She was certain that without her living there Alison and her father would already be married and Alison could properly let the next generation start run her own shop the way they wanted to but in deference to Robyn's grief they'd all put their own plans on hold. She wasn't being fair to them, any of them. Her evasion of what she needed to do was having an effect on more than just her life, the ripples from her pebble in the pond spiralling out, touching others.

'I won't disturb him,' she said taking her car keys from her bag. 'Tell him I'll be home later tonight. I'll text him when I leave Wendy and Dan's.' She may be in her thirties but her father still worried about her driving long distances and she could understand that, so she always did as he asked. Waving her hand goodbye, she walked round to the back alley where they and the other shop owners on Castle Street parked behind their premises.

The journey down to the village in Gloucestershire where her in-laws lived was enjoyable. Putting the date and the reason for visiting out of her mind for an hour or two, the country-side she passed was at its prime. The leaves on the trees were still full and verdant like frothy skirts on an overly enthusiastic ice-green bridesmaid dress. The hedgerows she drove past slapped against the side of the car where they'd grown out of control, leaving damp petals and grass seeds stuck to the bonnet and windscreen. The combination of an English summer, sun and rain in equal measures had served its purpose and the countryside was running riot. She may be paused in one place, stalled in life, but everything else, seasons and Mother Nature carried on. As if to prove her point, a buzzard flew low over the hedge ahead of her, a small rabbit clutched in its talons.

'Hello, Robyn, how lovely that you could come!' Wendy was on the drive before she'd even switched off the engine and the moment she stepped out of the car, collecting up a bunch of yellow roses she'd stopped to buy on the journey down, she was enveloped in a bear hug. The familiar scent of Chanel No.5 mixing with the roses that were being crushed between them.

'Come on in and have a drink.' Wendy ushered her inside. It had always been the same with Nate's parents; they moved through life at a hurried pace, sweeping up all before them. She wondered how on earth they'd adjusted to retirement, but she suspected they hadn't slowed down at all, merely exchanged work for golf and a hectic social life.

Inside the smell of roast beef assailed her nostrils, making her stomach growl. Deliberately skipping breakfast knowing she'd be eating a big delicious dinner she could already tell she wasn't going to be disappointed. In the kitchen Dan was pouring huge gin and tonics.

'Not for me, thank you.' She laughed, waving her car keys. 'I need to drive later. I'd better stick to a soft drink.'

Dinner was served half an hour later. As she'd suspected enormous dishes full of vegetables had appeared, all glistening with melted butter, and Dan confirmed he'd grown them in the garden. Several slabs of pink beef and the biggest Yorkshire pudding she'd ever seen balanced on her plate. There was barely any space to pour the gravy without it flooding over the edge and onto the pale washed tablecloth decorated with sprigs of forget-me-nots. Very appropriate for the day, Robyn thought. They talked about the garden, a holiday Wendy and Dan had taken in Tuscany, and Robyn told them about the map and the research rabbit holes she'd fallen down trying to discover where it had originated from. By the time they'd finished the bowls of trifle Wendy had produced, even while Robyn was half-heartedly protesting that she couldn't eat another thing, the dishes were whisked away into the kitchen and Wendy suggested they had coffee in the living room.

They drank coffee and reminisced about birthdays Nate had enjoyed as a child, the first dinghy he'd been given when he was seven, the year the family dog had eaten half of the birthday cake whilst they were enjoying a party in the garden. These were all stories Robyn had heard before but she let them tell her again, allowing them to wallow for a few hours.

'Well, Robyn, have you given any thought to September? Nate's seven years? I know over the years you've had difficulty accepting what happened, but now I'm sure you can see you need to declare him dead and lay him to rest?' She'd been expecting it; she'd even prepared her answers but she still felt a dart of shock at Dan's question. She pushed the ticking in her head deep into its recesses so she couldn't hear it.

'I know we're only weeks away from that day.' Her voice wavered as she remembered the day he was announced as missing. The day that had started normally but ended by changing her life forever, just another number on the calendar yet now this awful date that carried such significance. 'But I haven't really made any decision about when I'll do it. I mean, I know I can do it on that date but it doesn't have to be then, does it? I can do it any time afterwards.' She realised with a start as she said the words that she was beginning to accept she would at some point do what was needed.

'You could of course,' he agreed, 'but you need to move on with your life. You're still young and you may meet someone else, have a family. You'll always be like a daughter to us but don't let your future be stolen from you.. Nate would never have wanted that for you.'

'Just suppose for a minute that he isn't dead though?' It was an old argument they'd heard her express many times in the early days after his disappearance as she tried to deny the inevitable to herself. 'We've never had proof; nobody's ever found him.' Her old excuse was beginning to sound futile even to her.

'If he turns up nobody will be happier than us sitting here today. And he'd just laugh that he'd been declared dead. He'd put his death certificate in a frame on the wall. He wouldn't begrudge you having moved on. You know all he wanted in life was for you to be happy. And it's what he'd want in death too.'

'Well anyway I can't do anything yet. It's too early. And when the right time comes of course I'll let you know first. No one loved him more than we three sitting here now. I know you've made peace with it, so now it's up to me to do so as well.' Robyn tried to steer the conversation onto something she was more comfortable with. 'Now, are you going to take me on a tour of your garden while it's looking its best?' She gave them a smile that told them the subject of Nate was closed and nodding in acceptance they all got to their feet to go outside.

★　★　★

It was dark by the time Robyn arrived home from Nate's parents' and she was relieved to find the flat empty and a note from her dad explaining he and Alison were eating at the local Italian restaurant and afterwards he'd be spending the night at her home. He reminded Robyn to send him a text when she was home and she did so, then she made a mug of hot chocolate and took it to bed.

It was always a sad time having to see Nate's parents despite how much she loved them. Each visit was a reminder of that which all three of them had lost. The cord binding them together was frayed, tiny threads flickering in the wind, and yet they were still inextricably tied. It hurt even more that Nate wasn't there with them, laughing and winding his mother up, looking on indulgently while he teased her. His place at the table was an empty void, a hole that could never be filled.

Chapter Twenty-Two

September 1580

'Word has come that you went to sea recently?' Despite the noise around the hall, the babble of hundreds of voices, Freida could hear the queen perfectly. Around her the air felt echoey, as it had been in the hall at her own home when she and Willem had just moved in and it was empty, no furniture or tapestries in there. Every whispered word could be heard in each corner of the room. She was certain that all the guests were listening in to what was being said.

'Yes, Your Majesty.' Freida's words stuttered slightly as she pleated the rich taffeta of her gown between her shaking fingers. 'In order to assist with my assembly of the map you requested, so that I may see for myself how the rivers and ports are situated along the east coast.'

'How studious of you.' The queen inclined her head. 'And pray tell me upon which vessel did you sail?'

Freida's thumping heart began to speed up even further. She was being led into divulging information that would harm her. There was no doubt the queen knew the answer to her question, and that she was merely waiting for Freida to speak it out loud and tighten the noose around her own neck. Taking a deep breath, she tried to steady herself, her heart beating rapidly in her chest. She knew what Her Majesty thought about her husband and his compatriots even though they only did what Drake, her favourite, did.

'I . . . I was on the *Windfly*, which is my husband's ship,' she whispered. In the silence that followed, her fingers now gripping the folds of her dress so they cut into her skin, she waited for the angry deluge to fall down on her. She hadn't yet witnessed it but she'd heard from more than one source about the ability of the queen to turn from being friendly to exploding in anger at a second's notice. And she suspected she was about the witness it. Her hand fluttered to her neck, pulling at the ruff, which suddenly felt tight and constricting.

'Your husband, Willem van Hoorn?'

Her intuition was correct. The queen already knew all of this, so why had she brought Freida to question her? In order to accuse her of not telling the truth when she gave her name as Ortelius? It hadn't been a lie; it had simply been fortuitous that in her homeland the women kept their maiden names. This was it then. She'd escaped her persecutors in her homeland to end her days somewhere in the bowels of the earth beneath the Tower of London. An image of Jacob that morning, his soft cheeks and his shining eyes of the deepest grey flashed into her mind and was gone. Her eyes filled with tears, wondering if she'd seen him for the final time.

'Indeed, Your Majesty, that is he.'

'And is it true as I have been told that he is one of the Dutch *Sea Beggars*?'

'He is.' Freida's voice by this point could barely be heard. 'But he only sails between England and the Low Countries to deliver post, samples and curiosities to the scientists and botanists on Lime Street. He does not pursue the Spanish galleons to attack them.' She didn't mention that he would, however, fight back when needed. 'He is a peaceful man.'

'Ah yes, Emanuel van Meteren, the postmaster of the Republic of Letters. A distant cousin of yours, I believe?'

Was there nothing she did not know? Full marks to Walsingham and his spies. 'Yes, he is a nephew of Abraham Ortelius, who is a cousin of mine on my father's side.'

'Are your parents still living?' Finally, something she hadn't managed to discover. Freida explained about how her father had been a cartographer but her parents had been killed by the Spanish when she was a young child and so she'd eventually ended up working in the atelier alongside her cousin.

'I do not like to have people I have banished from my kingdom slipping in under the English flag.'

Freida's eyes widened; even that information about how Willem managed to dock in London was known.

'However, Drake speaks very highly of your husband and I trust your own judgement, so I will allow him to continue to visit our shores and keep the safe passage of the papers and samples that assist our own countrymen in discovering new plants and interesting scientific and mathematic discoveries.'

'Thank you, Your Majesty.' From where she was sitting Freida bowed her head and discreetly wiped her sweating hands down her gown.

'Your hatred of the Spanish matches my own I imagine?' the queen suggested quietly, and Freida looked up, nodding.

'That is correct, Your Majesty. They loathe the Huguenots. We were persecuted and thousands of my kinsmen were slaughtered. They are still being killed.'

'Yes, we have reports coming from Antwerp and Amsterdam which tell us this, and England is also in a precarious position. My sister was married to the King of Spain and he would dearly love to invade our shores and put a Catholic ruler on the throne. I prefer to keep Drake and his fellow sea captains here at home so they can protect us should Spain send an armada. I have told *Water* he is to go nowhere without my express permission.'

'But, Your Majesty, why do you have the Spanish ambassador at your court if they are the enemy?'

'Because it is politically the sensible and correct thing to do, to appease King Philip. I do not enjoy having him here. Walsingham watches him at all times, he is not to be trusted. I am certain that he is in correspondence with my cousin, Queen Mary, and is a conduit between her and my enemies across the water in Paris. You are lucky to have cousins who mean you no harm or who would take what is rightfully yours. So you have encountered our friend Mendoza?'

Freida explained about their previous meetings.

'Watch him always and remember what I say about him, for he is a dangerous man. But he will not get the better of me, the Queen of England.' The queen smiled at her and Freida felt a surge of admiration for this woman who lived a precarious life, and yet possessed an extraordinary inner strength.

'And do you think you will ever find a husband to share your throne?' she asked, wondering at her own daring, but her confidence growing.

'I do not. There is a steady stream of suitors, foreign princes and kings, but why would I risk handing over my power to a man? If I married, he would be the king, and I merely his consort. I was not born to that. This throne is my rightful place and no man may take it from me. I will rule this kingdom as is God's will until I die.' She turned away to speak with Drake who was still seated on her other side, and gratefully Freida rose to her feet and stepped away to return to the darkest corners of the room.

Chapter Twenty-Three

September 1580

The dinner courses, of which there were so many that Freida lost count, followed one after another. Roasted goose, beef, veal, lampreys and strong-smelling rich venison pies, decorative salads with vegetables cut into elaborate shapes mixed with almonds and raisins were followed by pies with plums, figs and cherries, cheese tarts, custards, gingerbread and fritters. It was finer than any feast Freida had ever tasted and although she kept thinking that she couldn't eat another morsel, as the next course arrived she found herself taking a selection of whatever was on offer.

Eventually stunning cakes covered in marchpane and decorated with coloured comfits were brought out and Freida helped herself along with everyone else marvelling as the sweetness melted on her tongue. Sugar was a luxury even in her own household and this was beyond anything she'd ever eaten. No wonder it was the queen's favourite. Washing it all down with a thick, fragrant claret followed by sweet spicy hippocras she started to feel light-headed and the perimeter of the room began to recede slightly as if she were sitting on an island. It was hot amongst the hundreds of other bodies so to cool herself down she poured herself more wine.

The music was becoming louder and dancing had begun as couples stood around the centre of a cleared area in front of the dais. In the centre the queen danced with Francis Drake as the gathered ensemble moved away to watch the couple. Freida watched from a distance, now standing in the shadows. Her slippers were starting to hurt her feet but there would be no chance to sit down and also no way of leaving until the queen did, and that could be many, many hours. She'd more than had enough and the candles and pressing bodies were making her feel overwhelmingly hot. And not just her, as the acrid smell of other revellers' sweat made her feel slightly sick.

Soon other people began to dance or moved away to find more wine and help themselves to the honey-coated nuts and sugared plums now placed along the table. Standing once again as close as she could to the tapestry, this time she leaned back slightly to take the weight off her feet and stop the room spinning. Freida suddenly realised that others around her were turning to look and moving to create an opening to allow someone through. Her heart began to race. Was the queen passing close by? She wasn't sure if she could curtsey without falling inelegantly to the floor. With a sigh of relief, she saw it was Francis Drake, who smiled wide as he arrived in front of her.

'Mistress Ortelius, I am delighted to see you this evening. I trust you and your family are well?' He bowed to her and she managed a small dip before resting her hand on the wall behind her to balance herself.

'We are, thank you,' she replied before adding in a whisper, her head down, 'I would wish my husband were here beside me, but as you know, he is not welcome at court.' She was fond of Drake because he was a friend of Willem's and she felt an affinity with who he was and how he lived his life, but she preferred not to be associated with him in company. He commanded a visibility she tried to shun. All around them courtiers watched them closely.

'No indeed, his kind are not popular with Her Majesty. Does she know your husband's past?'

Freida pursed her lips. 'She does indeed. She spoke with me earlier about him, although I do not know how she became privy to this information. Willem is waiting for me outside the gatehouse at this moment; I would like to leave, but I have been told I cannot until the queen has retired for the night.'

'That is true. Come and dance with me. That will while away some time.' Before she could argue or even explain about her spinning head and sore feet, Drake took her hand and laid it on his arm, accompanying her to where the other dancers moved sedately in a pavane in time to the music being played by a quartet of musicians in the corner. Before long they too were circling around the floor until she began to feel distinctly nauseous. She managed to tell Drake she needed to sit down and he delivered her to a bench.

'Stay there. I will fetch you some small ale. The wine at dinner was very potent.' He disappeared again and the revellers standing close by turned to stare at her like a flock of pigeons all moving at the same time. She knew any one of the other guests would be preening and delighted to be the centre of attention but, embarrassed, she kept her head lowered and waited for Drake to return with the ale.

'I must return to pay court to Her Majesty,' Drake apologised, handing her a silver beaker. 'I suggest you slip out quietly and return to Willem so he may take you home. I will pass on your apologies to the queen.'

'I will, thank you.' Freida nodded and took a long draught of the ale. She needed to be outside in the cooler evening air. Watching him make his way back to the throne where the queen was laughing with the Earl of Northumberland whilst her eyes constantly scanned her guests, noticing everything. Like the hawks that she and her noblemen took hunting, she missed nothing.

After she'd finished her ale, Freida placed the cup on the table behind her and got unsteadily to her feet. Around her the revelling was becoming rowdier, brightly garbed jesters weaving their way amongst the crowd juggling and tumbling across the floor, whilst the queen's fool, a young girl that Dee had told her was called Tomasin de Paris, cavorted in front of the throne. A group of mummers dressed in animal costumes ran amongst the courtiers and the laughter and chatter increased. The rushes on the floor were tacky with spilled drink. She could feel the soles of her slippers sticking to them as she tried to push her way between the dancing guests. As she twisted from side to side attempting to make her way towards the door, she felt an arm snake around her waist. Pushing it away forcefully, she hurried faster.

Suddenly she was stopped by a hand gripping her upper arm and instinctively she tried to shake it off but it tightened. Turning to see who was impeding her exit she was horrified to be face to face with the olive skin and dark eyes of Mendoza. Bile burned at the back of her throat and she swallowed hard.

'Mistress Ortelius, the pirate's wife who is recognised by the Queen of England – what a pleasant surprise.' It came out as a whisper, a hiss of fury as he pressed his face close to hers. A waft of leeks and stale wine made her wince.

'Remove your hand please.' Freida could hear the fear in her wavering voice and she silently cursed herself for her lack of courage.

'I will, presently—' his smile didn't reach his eyes '—but first I wish to have a little discussion with you and nobody will miss us if we just step outside the hall.' As her eyes roved around the room he added, 'It is of no use looking around for Drake – he is paying court to your queen. Nobody here will miss you.' He pulled her arm sharply so she had to take a step forward to avoid falling over and his arm tight around her waist like a vice holding her to his body. She tried to recoil but he was clutching her too forcefully as he marched her out of the room to a smaller gallery. Here other guests who had spilled out of the banqueting hall milled around, couples enjoying the darker corners where the candlelight didn't reach. Freida felt herself being pulled into one such pool of darkness and slammed against the wall. The panelling dug into her back and her tongue was stuck to the roof of her mouth.

'Leave me alone. I have nothing to say to you,' she uttered through gritted teeth. Mendoza pressed against her so she could barely breathe and she realised that anyone passing them would assume they were in a tryst, just as others were in many dark corners during such festivities.

'Not yet. I see that you are now good friends with that thief and murderer Drake. The pirate who kills the Spanish and steals our gold. You have not chosen your friends wisely, despite my warnings; although what else could be expected from one of your kind? Heathens.'

'Kills and steal? Like you yourself did when the Catholics invaded my homeland? *Whose house is of glass, should not throw stones at another.* Do you not know Chaucer, Señor Mendoza?' Freida didn't even know where her words had come from but she felt a strength grow from her anger, spreading through her body. Her audience with the queen earlier had imbued her with a confidence she hadn't felt before. He sneered at her, ignoring her question.

'Remember, I know who your husband is too. And where his ship is docked. And I know where you live and that you have a son called Jacob. I could take them both from you like that—' he clicked his fingers in her face '—if I chose. I have eyes everywhere. You are not safe here unless you stay away from Drake and your husband leaves these shores and never comes back. Heed my words or else pay the consequences.'

Freida was shaking, but by that point she didn't know if it was fear or anger. Once again the Spanish were threatening her, warning how she could lose everything she held dear for the second time. She wouldn't let that happen. As his hands loosened slightly on her upper arms she placed both hands on his chest and pushed as hard as she could, propelling him into two courtiers who were staggering past, and she ran for the door, which led to a wide brick entrance and in the distance, the gatehouse. Her head cleared slightly in the balmy night air where a light breeze blew against her face, cooling it. She hurried as fast as her heavy skirts allowed until she reached the huge oak doors at the gate where she found Willem and Guy now sitting on the grass, playing cards and sharing a flask of wine. Her husband jumped to his feet as he saw her.

'Are you all right, my sweet?' He caught her arms and she winced where they were bruised from Mendoza gripping them so tightly. She shook her head whilst looking behind her to ensure she hadn't been followed.

'May we leave please?' she asked, her voice breathless. 'I will explain when we are away from here.' She could tell by Willem and Guy's puzzled faces they didn't understand her haste, but she wasn't going to elucidate until they were at home and safe.

Thankfully their carriage awaited them at the palace gates and once they were inside, Freida was able to lean into Willem, her breath coming out in a ragged exhalation that seemed to last forever, as if she had been holding it all in since the moment she'd stepped into the palace.

'Now tell me what happened. Did someone hurt you?' Willem asked.

'It was Mendoza – he was there. I didn't realise he was watching me. He saw me talking with the queen. Who incidentally knows I am wed to you and who you are. I danced with Francis, but when he returned to sit with Her Majesty, Mendoza accosted me. He threatened me. Us. That we must not convene or correspond with Francis; otherwise we are not safe. And you must take the *Windfly* and leave, never to return to London. Ever.' At this point the tears that had been subdued by the adrenalin coursing through her body burst out of her and her shoulders heaved as she sobbed. 'I cannot lose you both. But what can we do? The Spanish are still fighting at home and they are now after us here; nowhere is secure. And how can I avoid Drake if the queen invites me to court?'

'We will be safe, I assure you with my hand on my heart.' She could hear the anger in Willem's voice. 'Nothing will harm us. I promised you the Spanish cannot touch you here and I do not lie.'

He hugged her close to him so she could feel his heart beating through his leather jerkin, which smelled of smoke, burning tar and the sea, where the salty brine in the air had made it faded and rough. She knew he meant everything he'd just said, but he couldn't be with her all the time, not when she was at the royal palaces or he was on a voyage for Emanuel; then she and Jacob were vulnerable. The moment that Doctor Dee had seen her map he had unintentionally started a series of events that were now beyond her control. As their carriage rattled into their courtyard and she alighted, she could feel the darkness closing in on her and the lamp Guy carried couldn't light away her demons.

Chapter Twenty-Four

October 1580

It took many days before Freida felt well enough to enter her workshop again and she had a lot of work to catch up on. The day after the banquet the pain in her head was appalling and she spent half the morning in bed with a wet cloth laid across her forehead. She could hear Jacob playing somewhere in the house but she was too ill to go and see him. By dinner time, however, she began to feel a little brighter and after eating some beef pottage her headache receded. But the fingerprint-sized bruises on her upper arms and the pain inside her chest still remained. She had regressed to being nine years old, escaping from her village, not properly understanding why the Spanish had killed her parents simply for not following the same church. In truth she still didn't understand their animosity.

Finally she picked up a fine burin and continued with the outline of East Anglia, gouging clear, sharp furrows; adding the majestic Norwich Castle, which from its vantage point on top of the hill stared out over the city, watching all that happened beneath its walls. Freida had to stand up so that she could reach it properly, and she'd dressed in a simple light kirtle of green kendall over a linen smock, so she could move about easily. It was far more comfortable than the extravagant gowns she was required to wear when going out and the items she was required to wear to court. The bones in the stomacher she'd worn to the banquet had dug in so much they had left deep red marks against her skin.

Once she was involved in her work she forgot all time, and every evening for a week a servant was sent to come and find her when it was suppertime. She was completely immersed in her undertaking. It was going to take several months to add all the detail she had planned and she was determined this was going to be the finest map any cartographer had ever created. But it was going to take a lot of hard work and already her fingertips were sore and damaged, her thumb blistered from the tools as sliver by sliver the fine V-shaped lines tapering to a point continued to shape the lands beneath her hands. She etched long flowing strokes of the rivers winding their way across the land, and short intricate parings eating away at the shoreline.

The pain in her hand was simply the price she had to pay. She was used to it and it would be worth everything to produce something the Queen of England would accept as perfect. The pride she felt in her work gave her a silent strength, every line engraved was also cut into her soul. She was the map; the map was her.

Chapter Twenty-Five

November 1580

'I think these are the sheets you will be most interested in.' Lord Burghley turned the pages of the atlas until he reached a map of Kent. 'You will need to include the great port of Dover. And here on the previous page is the Thames, and Essex.'

'Indeed.' Freida bent close to examine the print. 'Mr Saxton is every bit as skilled as he is reputed to be. If I could sketch some of these details, my lord, it will help me greatly with my own work.' She had been delighted to receive an invitation to visit the Lord Chancellor at his home on the Strand to view his valuable bound atlas of maps of all the English counties by the famous English cartographer. Willem was once again across the sea collecting packages from the Low Countries and the chance to visit this house was much welcomed.

'Indeed, of course you may. Let me call for some wine. I have some papers I need to attend to at my desk.' He indicated behind him to the vast dark wood desk piled high with documents in scrolls and sealed with wax. Others lay open, ribbons cast to one side and held down at the edges to stop them curling up with a variety of weighted objects. Freida could identify a jewelled ink pot, sticks of red wax beside a candle and a small brass weighing scale. Weighing up the lives and fortunes of those at court. The workplace of a man who sat alongside the queen and who did her every bidding, whilst subtly steering her in political directions and discreetly advising her.

They were in Burghley House on the north side of the Strand. It was an area of the city that Freida had frequented with Ralph Treswell as she assisted with his surveys. Whilst doing so she'd sketched the gargoyles fixed along the top of the pale stone walls, cowering beneath the eaves, screaming silently at those who dared to walk beneath them. She'd been interested to see the majesty within, and she hadn't been disappointed. Walls were painted with fleur-de-lys in red and green and hung with portraits of dour-looking Burghley family members. A large mirror in the first hall was set between alabaster columns. Alongside the artworks were tapestries of mythical battles in a myriad of colours. A beautiful gold-painted lute lay on a side table as if it had been cast aside just before she arrived. Lord Burghley had offered to show her the Saxton atlas and she was sure the diagrams of the English counties he was famous for would help her.

Although she had already started the engraving, any extra details she could add to give Drake – and therefore Willem – an advantage when fighting the Spanish in the German Ocean were worth having. Picking up her sketch-book and charcoal she began to work, the soft grazes of her strokes on the parchment being matched by the scratching of Burghley's quill on the vellum he was working on, pausing every few seconds to dip into the inkpot and tap it on the edge before continuing. The fire crackled and a trace of applewood smoke mixed with the scent of hot wax.

Two hours passed in the peaceful ambience, Freida doing what she loved most, absorbed in her drawing. A beaker of wine and a platter of sweetmeats had appeared on a small table behind her, but they remained untouched. The candles around her continued burning down, the wax pooling on the chest as it dripped from the pewter sticks. Eventually behind her, Burghley cleared his throat, startling her out of her concentration.

'So, Mistress Ortelius, tell me your thoughts on creating such a special map for our queen. Have you considered that it may put you in danger? Every day I sit at my desk here and deal with the miscreants of folly and those who would upset the crown. There are those at court who do not want your map to be completed.'

'You speak of the Spanish ambassador?' Freida looked over her shoulder at him as he placed his quill on the desk and nodded.

'You could surely not have imagined when you came to live in London amongst your fellow Huguenots that you would be called upon to use your skills in this way?'

'No indeed, and as I am sure you are aware my husband's profession accentuates the need to keep myself and my family from public eye, and yet this is such an honour I no longer wish to hide myself away. To be so afraid of the might and violence of the Spanish – I have wasted too many years of my life doing that. I have already been threatened and told not to persist, but that is not an option, even if I wished to. I am determined to continue; this is more than just a map to me, it is a piece of art. It is engraved on my heart as much as my soul is engraved within the lines I etch. No one will stop me from completing it.'

'Brave words, mistress.' Burghley's face was grave. 'Yet even at this moment your husband meets with the Prince of Orange who is mustering forces to remove King Philip and his Spanish soldiers forever from your homeland and put the prince once more upon his throne. His actions put you in great danger. Those who have defied Mendoza have met their end in a pool of blood.'

Freida's eyes grew wide, her mouth opening and closing with no sound coming out. She had no answer, no idea that Willem was so closely involved with the political turmoil in Holland and that he had deliberately kept it from her. And if Burghley knew of what he was doing in their home country, then she had no doubts that Mendoza did too.

I have witnessed the actions of the Spanish,' she acknowledged, 'and it coloured my life. It brought me running to England for safety and yet now that I am in danger again, I find myself turning to face my opponent. I will flee no longer.' Although her heart was beating fast, she could feel a shaft of steel as sharp and fierce as her burin blade buried deep within her, strengthening her spine.

'Good.' Burghley nodded, his lips pursed. 'I believe you have the forte to complete the commission. And Drake will need everything he can place his hands on in his fight with the Spanish in years to come; I am certain of that. They will not stop until they have sent an armada to our shores. Now—' he got to his feet '—I have other treasures as well

181

as Saxton's maps. Let me show you. These will be of great interest, I am sure.' He led the way from the room and, after placing her charcoal down, Freida followed.

They walked down dark, dimly lit corridors panelled in wainscotting that was dull and dusty, and Freida pulled her skirts away in an attempt to stop them becoming dirty. Here, where guests didn't usually venture, the splendour of the public rooms was not evident. There was very little light, just an occasional sconce on the wall containing a single candle, and the light did not venture as far as the floor where the sparsely scattered rushes appeared to move. Freida wondered what was occupying the passageway with them; Lord Burghley would benefit from some vermin-catching cats. She'd heard that his family resided at his seat in Lincolnshire and his wife never ventured to London, which explained why only his office showed any signs of cleanliness.

'In here.' Burghley opened a set of double doors and stood to one side. Freida gasped at what lay before her. Here, the room was lit by tall leaded windows, each diamond-shaped pane throwing a shaft of sparkling brilliance onto the cabinets standing in serried ranks of military cases around the walls, displaying a collection of curiosities to rival any that she had seen before.

'I collect all of the new navigational instruments,' he explained. 'I expect you know the quadrant and astrolabe—' he pointed into a case at the familiar triangular shape of the quadrant and the circular dials of the astrolabe '—given your husband's occupation. But also here I have a new item, a "volvelle" or "nocturnal" with which the ships can navigate at night. By looking at the pole star through the hole in the centre and then lining up this small lever with the constellation of Ursa Major, a sailor can estimate the time on this smaller dial, the volvelle. The notches around it can be felt and counted in the dark. By knowing the time it is possible to calculate the tides, which gives the ability to dock at night.' Freida bent closer, looking at the discs, the centre one with its serrated dial engraved with the hours of the day. 'And here look, a compendium with both lunar and solar volvelles, calendar, sundial and small simple theodolite. This is one of my particular favourites amongst my collection.'

Freida was fascinated by the volvelle. After experiencing how difficult it had been to creep into the port of Brielle at night so as to avoid being seen by the Spanish, she could understand that owning one of these would be very beneficial to Willem; it may protect him when he was at sea. Was that why Burghley was showing her? Considering that Doctor Dee was most likely person to know where she could source one from, she made a mental note to write to him and ask.

Eventually, after examining all of the cabinets, she admitted that she should return home. Guy had been waiting in the street quite long enough. They returned to the office so she could collect her sketchpad and roll of charcoal pieces, and as she did so she heard voices approaching. Burghley looked at her and held his hand up to indicate to her to keep quiet, but before he could step outside the room and prevent his guest from entering, the door opened and in marched Mendoza with two of his guards. Burghley's steward was behind them, looking apologetic.

'Lord Burghley.' Mendoza's voice was sharp. 'Forgive my intrusion but information has been brought to my attention that requires urgent clarification. I have been told today that your soldiers have been in the Spanish Embassy without my permission. This shall not be tolerated.'

'I am sure they had good reason. I shall call for the commander of my men and ask. Please wait here.'

As Burghley moved to the corner of the room where his steward was waiting, Mendoza turned and noticed Freida who was standing as still as she could, her breath held tight in her chest.

'Mistress van Hoorn, I did not expect to find you here.' His words were clipped, no disguise of his dislike of her. His eyes flicked towards the atlas on the table behind her, his lips stretched thinly and tight over his teeth. 'Still continuing with your map?' he asked. His contempt of her was blatant and his attitude fired a bolt of heat as if from a crossbow into her chest.

'Of course. I have a commission to complete.' She tilted her head up and maintained eye contact.

'I find myself unsurprised that you are yet again involved in matters that do not concern you. At the home of the Lord Chancellor, despite my suggestion that to complete the map would be most unwise. And I have reason to believe that your husband is currently assisting enemies of the Spanish across the waters. I warned you previously I will not allow this to continue. Keep your doors locked tight day and night. You will receive a visit to ensure your husband knows to remain at home and protect his own family before he attempts to defend his homeland.' His voice was so low she wondered if she'd even heard him correctly.

Freida looked across to Burghley who had heard nothing; Mendoza was too careful for that. But he'd heard her sharp intake of breath, and perhaps guessing she was in distress he moved swiftly across the room to stand in front of Mendoza, calling for his guards as he did so. Almost immediately the room was crowded by thick-set men wearing pewter breast plates and carrying pikestaffs. Freida hadn't even noticed any soldiers when she had arrived; however, it seemed that whilst discreet, they were in close quarters.

'The Spanish ambassador is leaving,' Burghley told them and with one final glare at Freida, Mendoza left the room, the guards close behind. 'Are you unharmed?' he asked Freida when they were alone in the room again. 'Shall I call for some more wine?'

'Thank you, but I am just shaken. I have heard these threats before.' She clasped her hands tight around the oilcloth now containing her sketchbook.

'You should take heed though,' he warned. 'Do not dismiss them. I have seen too many bodies pulled from the Thames, slit from throat to groin by a sharp Spanish blade. I would not wish that for you. Did you come here today with guards?'

'No, just my steward. We live a quiet life on Lime Street; we have no need for guards.'

'Perhaps not before, but now, mistress, I implore you to consider it.'

Freida inclined her head in acknowledgement of the suggestion and, after bidding him farewell, she followed his servant to the street where Guy was waiting, his face pinched and pale in the cold. He smiled and inclined his head when he saw her arrive and together, they walked down to the jetty as Freida explained what had happened. He needed to know the danger Willem was putting the household in. He didn't seem surprised when she explained that apparently her husband was meeting with William of Orange.

'I will look into employing some guards, mistress,' he reassured her. 'They will be with you at all times to keep you safe.'

'And Jacob?' she asked.

'And Jacob,' he confirmed.

Chapter Twenty-Six

August 2022

Robyn had just put dinner on the table when her phone rang. She glanced across at her father who raised his eyebrows silently. She knew his opinion on phones at the dinner table, but she'd already seen the caller display and was desperate to know what information may be forthcoming.

'Sorry,' she mouthed at him before pressing the answer button.

'Hi, Geoff, good to hear from you. Do you have news?' She couldn't hide the anticipation in her voice.

'Hello, Robyn, I won't keep you but yes; I've just emailed the translations of the letters to you.'

'Brilliant, thank you so much!' She gave her father a thumbs up. 'I wasn't expecting you to have finished them so quickly.'

'I did have to call in a few favours; you owe me several slabs of beer. Anyway, I think you're going to be very excited when you discover what they say. Call me back if you need anything clarified when you've read them.' They said their goodbyes and Robyn placed her phone back on the table. Now she needed to eat dinner, even though every fibre in her body wanted to open her laptop and see what Geoff had sent. She relayed the conversation to her father.

'That sounds like it may be an important breakthrough,' he replied. 'It'll keep you busy this evening. I'm amazed at how much you've been able to unearth about the map. When I first discovered it, I honestly thought you'd hit a brick wall, it's so unusual. You were right to suggest I let you investigate it; you've learned more than I realised since you arrived here. I'm really proud of you. It feels as though the map has started opening your world up again.'

Robyn reached across and squeezed his hand, her eyes filling with unexpected tears at his words. She looked down at the back of his hand. Despite his work to keep trim and remain youthful, the skin here belied his age, lined and creased with the passage of time, sandy-coloured spots beginning to develop. He wasn't getting any younger. She realised that he'd put his own life on hold seven years ago when she'd arrived home and she wasn't being fair to him. Not him or Alison. They had a chance for a new life together; was she stopping them fulfilling their dreams?

The rest of the meal was eaten in silence as Robyn considered what she'd recognised, that her living in the flat and how it affected all those around her wasn't something that was just going to go away. But first she needed to know what her letters had divulged, and the moment they both finished eating she dropped her plate in the sink and booted up her laptop.

'Leave the dishes. I'll do them later,' she said, drumming her fingers on the arm of the sofa, waiting for the computer to boot up. It had never seemed so slow. Finally, she opened her inbox and double-clicked on the email. There were two documents, each titled with the original Latin of the letters she'd seen in Oxford.

The first one dated in 1578 was from Abraham Ortelius to Emanuel van Meteren and described how he was sending his young cousin, Freida, to Lime Street to escape the fighting in Antwerp and said that she was to live with his sister Liskin. Robyn exhaled slowly. Now she knew why Freida was in London when she engraved the map. The next letter was dated almost two years later and was from Emanuel back to his uncle. This was even more exciting; Robyn could hardly believe what she was reading. It referred again to Freida, and this time mentioned her husband Willem – a *Sea Beggar* – and their young son. It also spoke of a commission by Queen Elizabeth.

And now, cousin, I must inform you about a very special map that our dear friend and relative Freida is engraving for the queen's favourite, he who sails and discovers new lands. The queen is still much afraid of the Spanish and their threats to invade these shores and she desires to keep Drake close by to protect England. Freida was invited to court by my acquaintance Doctor Dee, who is scryer to Her Majesty. This map shall be more detailed than any other ever to have been engraved, and it is a great honour for our cousin to have been thus commissioned.

Freida had been asked by none other than Queen Elizabeth I to engrave a map for Sir Francis Drake. These were names known to everyone in England. She'd come from one of

189

the most respected cartography families in Europe and ended up at the English court. And somehow married to one of the Dutch seafarers – a privateer just as Drake had been. These letters were almost all the proof she needed. She wasn't certain yet that hers was the map described in the letter, but if it was it had belonged to Drake, a gift from his queen, and judging by the dates on the letters not long after he'd arrived home from his circumnavigation of the world.

But why was the map stained with what she still thought was blood, and why was it so detailed of not only the south of England but also Holland and Belgium, when Drake wasn't a native of those countries and to her knowledge nor did he visit them? Her next task was to remove the map from the frame and have the stain chemically tested. She may need Martha or Geoff's help again for that. There was something missing from the puzzle, but she was certain she was getting closer. Perhaps her lead with Braithwaites would be able to shed more light. And it appeared Freida was caught up with suspected Elizabethan pirates. Now the supposed bloodstain on the map began to make sense. She was living in dangerous times.

Chapter Twenty-Seven

December 1580 – January 1581

Christmas and New Year on Lime Street was a merry affair. It had been cold for weeks, the pale sun barely climbing into the sky and providing no warmth. Then the bitterly cold nights scattered a layer of harsh white frost that didn't disappear during the day before another night's worth whipped across the city, making the streets and paths slippery. On her walk to St Paul's with Guy in search of new charcoal and paints, Freida saw a horse slide over on the icy cobbles. She could hear its screams long after they'd hurried away as fast as they dared with fine hemp ropes tied around their pattens to prevent themselves from suffering the same fate.

Finally on New Year's Day heavy, muted clouds blotted out the pale blue sky of the previous week, the grey lined with muddy yellow as they gathered overhead ominously and began to drop ragged flakes of snow, tumbling to the frozen ground and lying like a soft carpet across the gardens and streets. This day was the highlight of the festivities, even more important than Christmas, which had centred on a church service in the morning and a feast at dinner, followed by a travelling group of mummers who'd entertained them all at Liskin's house since it was the largest on the street. But New Year's Day was a day to give gifts and the food would be elaborate as it appeared continuously on the tables set up in the great hall.

Willem had gifted Freida a length of shining gold silk and she was already planning a new gown to be created from it. In return she'd given him a pair of heavy leather gauntlets to protect his hands whilst he was at sea, but in her mind all she could think about was the day when she could present him with a copy of the magnificent map she was creating. As time went on it was growing into something exquisite, the most unique thing she'd ever made and secretly she was immensely proud of it.

However, the enjoyment of the celebrations was overshadowed for Freida, with the knowledge that the following day she had to attend a New Year's party at the palace. She'd been invited by Doctor Dee to accompany him, which allayed her worries slightly. Hopefully this time she wouldn't be on her own attempting to make herself invisible, but the memory of what had happened when Mendoza threatened her at Richmond was still uppermost in her mind. She'd ensure she was close to Dee at all times.

The queen was observing the festivities at Westminster and thankfully the trip along the river was short as the sharp, icy air caught at the back of Freida's throat. It was difficult to talk and she'd wrapped a woollen scarf around her mouth to stop her lips from becoming chapped and sore, so the journey was quiet, the rhythmic splash of the oars in the churning water calming her racing heart. People were out and about enjoying the festivities, the Thames full of tiny craft bobbing about and occasionally bumping into each other, provoking shouting. Doctor Dee had hired a tilt boat with its canopy giving her a little shelter, and she hoped the Thames would still be flowing when they were ready to return home; it was known to freeze over when the weather was very bad.

They entered the palace at the queen's bridge, where the royal coat of arms was displayed and four huge posts were topped with tall heraldic beasts: a dragon, a lion, a greyhound and finally a tiger holding a gilded vane. All around banners and bunting in red, gold and deep blue now had a topping of sparkling white snow. Ladies in wide, full gowns swept up towards the gatehouse, the bottoms of their dresses brushing the top of the snow where it lay thick each side of the path, leaving a covering like ermine fur to their hems.

Freida tried to keep her balance as she slipped about and secretly wished she could have worn her practical pattens instead of the necessary leather slippers, which would be fine for dancing if she was denied the opportunity to decline but were of no use for the inclement weather. She grabbed Dee's arm and almost pulled his slight frame over as she slipped once again. She saw him frown but he politely managed to not snatch his arm away.

Inside the great banqueting hall, it was overwhelmingly hot, full of courtiers and nobles pressed together despite the enormous space. Already the queen was seated at the end of the room and instinctively Freida dropped down to one knee. Looking again towards the queen she was not shocked as she recognised who was sat on her left; once again, that rogue Francis Drake. Despite the large crowd milling around, immediately he caught her eye and raised his eyebrows as he grinned at her, inclining his head slightly. She felt herself colour as she hastily looked down at the floor.

'Have you seen what Her Majesty wears on her head?' Dee whispered in her ear.

Freida nodded, she could hardly miss it: an ornate and heavy-looking gold crown studded with numerous clear green emeralds that shone in the candlelight.

'It is truly magnificent,' she agreed. 'A gift for New Year perhaps?'

'Indeed, the court rumours say it was presented to her by Drake. No wonder he is sitting up there next to her. Bought himself a seat at the top table.' He sounded bitter and Freida was surprised, wondering if he was jealous. It was no secret that the courtiers who were allowed at court were all intent on becoming intimate with the queen and consequently the means to great riches and power.

'Are you sure it is from him?' she asked.

'I am indeed, and I have heard tell that is a Spanish crown stolen in a skirmish off the coast of Mexico whilst he was on his circumnavigation of the world. He is bringing grave danger to our shores and presenting it to the queen to flaunt before those who will be angered by her actions. I heard tell she was advised to return the Spanish plunder, but both Drake and Lord Burghley persuaded her to keep it, and it now lies in the Tower armouries. Apart from a great deal of gold coin, reputed to be in the region of one hundred thousand pounds, which appears to have gone missing. No surprises to whom that has gone – his attire is suddenly even more peacock-like than most other visitors at court.'

'Who is insisting she returns it? Surely it was won in a just battle?' Freida was thinking about the treasure she knew her husband had previously taken from galleons, which he considered fair gain, just as the Spanish did when they invaded Holland and took all they could lay their hands on. The spoils of war.

'Walsingham says we should not keep it knowing it deliberately antagonises the Spanish, but Her Majesty cannot resist any jewels and the riches that increase her wealth. What Drake has brought home for her has cancelled all of England's debt. I suspect that none of it will be returned, neither the gold and silver coin, nor the jewellery. And speak of the devil . . .' He pointed across the floor as heads turned to watch the subject of their discussion walking towards them, his familiar confident smile and closely clipped dark beard making him indeed look like the devil. Danger followed him like a fine wool cloak billowing out behind as he walked along, settling on the shoulders of those around him like the snow outside, wherever he stopped.

'Mistress Ortelius.' He bowed from the waist although his eyes never left hers and as decorum dictated, she curtsied in return. 'I was hoping you might attend the festivities.' Turning to Dee he added, 'Doctor Dee, how delightful to meet you once again. I see you have finished your wine. If you wish to replenish your cup then please go ahead. I shall look after our good friend in your absence.'

Dee paused, looking between the two of them for a moment. Willem had given him strict instructions to not abandon Freida for any reason, but Drake was staring him in the eye, daring him to refuse. After a moment where Dee's indecision was evident on his face, he gave a curt nod of his head, turned on his heel and went to look for a servant with a flask of wine.

'A happy New Year to you,' Drake said the moment they were on their own. 'Did you enjoy the revels over Christmas?'

'We did, thank you,' she replied, smiling as she thought of the feasting and jollities that Jacob had been delighted with even though he was still too young at ten months to understand what they were celebrating.

'And was your husband able to join you?'

Freida knew that Drake was mostly interested in whether Willem was out at sea goading the Spanish but was unable to be as blunt as he'd like to in a crowded hall when every word he said was being listened to. Anyone who could gain a step towards being one of the queen's inner circle was looking for any way in which they could do that. And Drake was very popular with her.

'He was. The current weather precludes any visits elsewhere.' She kept her tone as neutral as she was able to, knowing that he'd understand. Drake nodded.

'And now,' he announced with a flourish, 'I have a New Year gift for you.' From behind him and until that point unseen, a page stepped forwards with a velvet cushion in deep blue with thick embroidered whirls and leaves decorating it, upon which was perched an ornately carved wooden box. Opening it, Drake took out a large gold brooch decorated with emeralds and diamonds. 'May I?' he asked, and before she could reply he had pinned it to her gown. It was so heavy it pulled the fabric down a little.

'But, Francis—' she put her hand up to try and stop him, using his first name as she did when they were at her home

'—I cannot accept such a bauble; it is too much. Surely you should have given this to Her Majesty?'

'It is a part of an ensemble that matches the crown she now wears, but she has enough riches from me. It is my decision to whom I gift it, and I choose to give it to a talented woman who is currently engraving a map for me. Call it an acknowledgement of my thanks, if you wish.'

An uncomfortable feeling began to crawl over her. 'My lord, was this, and the crown the queen wears, brought home from your recent voyage?'

'They were indeed, although their origin need not be of any worry to you. The queen is not concerned either.'

He'd told her everything she needed to know. 'Please, I cannot accept it. I thank you for your kindness, but please take it back.' She fumbled with the catch, trying to remove it and scratching her finger on it. She put her finger in her mouth to stop the blood dripping on her clothes and marking them.

'Nonsense,' he admonished. 'It is mine to present to whom-ever I wish and it looks beautiful on you. I shall not take it back. And now I must return to sit with our sovereign, who I can see grows impatient and shrewish; she desires to be attended by her favourites at all times.' He gave a wry smile and bowing again he took her hand and kissed the back of it, before being swallowed up by the crowds around them, leaving her standing on her own and still being watched by the people close to her. She looked around for Doctor Dee but he was nowhere to be seen. Unsure of what to do and trying to quell the feeling of panic at being on her own and feeling vulnerable, she began to make her way towards the edge of the room, following the path she'd seen Dee take earlier.

Her finger was starting to hurt and the blood wouldn't stop, so she pulled her tiny linen handkerchief from the drawstring purse hanging from her girdle and wrapped it round, watching the red seep through the fabric and onto the lace, which she'd sewn on herself. It would be ruined and she was disappointed. She was not a great seamstress and her embroidery was often poor; the time and effort this had taken would now be of no point as it was spoiled.

'You have hurt yourself, Mistress van Hoorn?' An insidious voice in her ear, instantly recognisable, slithered like a snake into her head. The Spanish ambassador was the only person who'd refer to her using her husband's name. Nobody else at the banquet other than Dee, Drake and the queen knew to whom she was married. She turned to face him, trying to summon a polite smile to hide the quiver of fear that rooted her to the spot.

'Ambassador, I am surprised to see you here. Do you invite yourself to every occasion at the palace?' She was astonished at her own bravery, the dislike of him sparking an anger that had slowly been brewing over the months. 'But please do not concern yourself; it is simply a scratch. I am waiting for Doctor Dee to return with a drink for me.' She hoped that by indicating she wasn't there on her own he would move on to bully someone else. But he was no longer engaged in conversation instead he was staring at the jewel that now adorned her chest.

'Where did you get that brooch from?' His voice snapped out so sharply that her head jerked back as if he'd slapped her.

'It . . . it was a New Year gift,' she stuttered, her momentary self-confidence beginning to slip away, dripping from her like the blood that leaked from her hand.

'From that pirate Drake I suppose? I observed him speaking with you, as did most of the guests here. That jewel is part of the collection which the queen also wears, stolen from the *Señora de la Conceptión*, one of Spain's finest galleons until she was sunk by that pirate. The jewel you wear is Spanish and belongs to King Philip, and I demand that you return it to me, as his representative at Queen Elizabeth's court, forthwith.' He held his hand out as if expecting her to remove it immediately at his behest.

'I will not.' She recovered her composure and defied him. 'It was a gift to me, and I shall keep it. If you feel that this, and indeed the queen's crown, belong to your king then go and ask the queen to return it.' Her brave speech was cut off as his hand whipped out and grabbed hold of her hand, which was now wrapped in the bloody handkerchief, and held it up in front of her.

'Mistress—' his face was pressed close to hers, the spices that he smelled of heavy around them, his breath hot against her cheek '—this will not be the only blood shed by yourself or your family. I have been crossed once too often by these brazen, lawless privateers, and now someone will pay the price. Blood will be spilled, of that I can promise you. It will pool on the floor of your home and the stench will never leave you.'

His words made her flush with nausea. He wasn't to know she already carried the reek of lost blood always with her. To her immense relief she heard Dee's voice somewhere to her left and after stepping backwards away from Mendoza, she turned towards where she'd heard him, pushing through the crowd to him and the elderly man he was talking with. They both turned as she arrived and bowed to her.

'Mistress Ortelius, I was just talking about you to my learned friend Edward Kelley.' He inclined his head towards a man wearing a black silk cap close to his head. 'I was saying that you are creating a map to rival anything he or I have ever seen before. We are hoping we will be able to view it when it is complete.'

'Indeed, gentlemen, I am sure the queen will be delighted for everyone to see it once I have presented it to her. The engraving is coming along well now and I shall have it completed by the time winter is over.' She suddenly realised that just as Mendoza had, Dee was now staring at her new brooch.

'A new bauble, mistress?' he asked.

'Yes,' she replied finding it difficult to hide the irritation in her voice as yet again she had to defend herself for accepting it. 'A New Year gift from Francis Drake. It has not been received well by the Spanish ambassador though.' Her emotions threatened to overwhelm her and her voice broke a little.

'Do not worry about him,' Dee reassured her. 'He cannot do anything whilst he is here at Her Majesty's invitation. But make sure you do not meet him or his men when you are away from the palace and on your own if he is displeased with you. Many a man has become a headless corpse floating down the Thames.'

Freida shuddered. In future she'd be taking Guy or Christopher with her everywhere she went. And she'd be reminding Guy about his previous suggestion to hire guards outside their door for extra protection. Now was the time she needed them.

'I would like to go home please, if you do not mind.' Not giving Dee a chance to argue she began making her way through the heavy crowds milling around in the hope that the queen would not notice them leave. Freida had had enough and with a heavy weight of despondency in her heart, as leaden as the brooch that adorned her chest, she could only think of getting back to the safety of her home, and her husband. The threat of Mendoza and the warning Dee had given sickened her, bile burning at the back of her throat.

Chapter Twenty-Eight

February 1581

Willem reassured Freida he'd hire guards if she wished him to, but that Guy and Christopher were more than capable of preventing anyone from entering their home unless they'd been invited. And they had loyal neighbours who could be called upon if needed when Willem was away at sea. Freida wasn't convinced. He hadn't been privy to the way she'd been threatened, nor was he present when Mendoza told her what he'd have done to her, to Jacob. When she'd relayed what had happened at the New Year party, Willem had just shouted with laughter. She knew he didn't take the ambassador seriously, but Freida had felt the venom emanating from him and she'd been left in no doubt as to how serious he'd been. She would have to place her faith in Guy and the other servants, although they didn't inspire her with confidence.

With London still gripped by freezing weather, Willem remained at home for the next six weeks and Freida ensconced herself in her atelier to continue with the map. She was fast approaching the final parts and every day the floor was covered in fine shavings of copper as she added subtle details. Around the edge she engraved clouds and across the water she etched tiny Dutch houses in both Amsterdam and Hoorn, a town north of the city where she knew her husband had originally come from and where his family still lived, with buildings similar in style to those in Antwerp.

As the map began to reach its conclusion the weather finally started to improve and the muddy slush that had lined the streets for weeks, piling up in the gullies at the edges, began to flow down towards the Thames as it melted. Out in the garden tiny shoots of fresh green leaves began to appear on the mulberry and rowan trees, bringing the promise of spring.

Freida breathed a sigh of relief that Jacob had survived the winter without succumbing to any chills, as small children often did. Now that he was able to sit up on his own and was taking a few tentative steps, she played with him in the solar, the floor scattered with his carved wooden toys that Willem had made for their son during his confinement as the hard winter prevented him sailing. But the moment the weak sun began to touch them with delicate fingertips of warmth, barely there but bringing hope, Willem was throwing the items he needed for a voyage into his chest. Freida could not disguise her disappointment.

'I will be sad to see you go.' She pulled a face at him as she perched on the bed, watching him place his charts and instruments into the heavy oak box alongside his clothes and the boots he only wore on deck. Finally, his velvet cap went on top and he shut the lid.

'And so shall I, my sweet.' He sat down beside her and

wrapped his arms around her. 'But you know I cannot stay away from the sea for long. It is in my blood. I need to feel the deck rolling beneath my feet, the spray of the saltwater making my hair stiff and my skin burnt.' Freida nodded. She knew how much happier he was when he was steering the *Windfly* through the waves, in control of her huge bulk and the men who sailed on her.

'And will you be visiting the prince again?' she asked. The argument that had ensued when she had confronted him about his visit to Holland previously had continued for days, sharp spats of accusations followed by long pauses of silence. They had never spoken harsh words to each other during their marriage and it had left Freida shaken. And disappointed because although he hadn't denied who he was meeting up with, nor the fact he had been doing it for years, he refused to stop. Freeing their homeland meant everything to him.

'I do not wish to talk of this again. You know that I must do whatever he asks of me. We will not agree on this matter. I must follow my heart and my love of our homeland.' His face shut down and she knew she would not dissuade him. 'However, I will remind Guy to hire some guards for while I am away to allay your fears.'

'Thank you.' Stretching up she kissed him, his short beard a little scratchy against her fair skin. Hers was as pale as his was brown, the whites of his eyes and the deep grey irises – the colour of the sea he sailed – a sharp contrast. Jacob had inherited his father's eyes and it made her smile when she looked into them to see his father looking back at her.

*   *   *

Within two days, Willem was gone. Freida prayed on her knees every night that he would return unscathed and she attended church every day. It was all she could do to protect him and keep him safe so far from home. However, she did at least now have two burly men, both appearing capable of seeing off any unwelcome guests, and their presence did make her feel somewhat safer. She disappeared each morning together with Jacob to her atelier, to complete the engraving of her map.

She was worried to hear that Drake was apparently not at court and immediately her thoughts went to whether he was sailing in a fleet with Willem. If it was true then everyone at court would know she was on her own at home. And 'everyone' meant the Spanish ambassador who seemed to have knowledge of all that happened in London; he must have as many spies as Walsingham did.

As the light began to fall one evening, Freida laboured in her workshop, adding the final details to the map. She knew she needed to make a decision soon when to accept it was complete so she could take it to Mistress Jugge to be printed, but she wanted it to be perfect and it wasn't quite that yet. At her feet Jacob slept on a thick quilt he'd been playing on, and she hummed to herself contentedly. She could hear the sounds of the rest of the house preparing for supper, the clanging of pewter and laughing in the big hall. She'd noticed that a kitchen maid was sweet on one of the new guards, and judging by the whispering and giggling from the end of the long dining trestle table at dinner that day, the affection was returned. It did her heart good that people in the house were happy, spring was approaching and the sap was rising.

A sudden sharp splintering sound behind her made her turn as a door that led to the garden disintegrated. An axe, which was now wedged in the middle, was removed before it reappeared, a large hole rent in the wood. Two men, their faces covered with pieces of hessian sacking, pushed through into her workshop and she couldn't even utter a sound, so shocked was she. The guards were always stationed outside the door which opened onto the street beyond, but the intruders had arrived through a door opening onto the garden. They must have scaled the wall. She had no idea why the guards had not come running and her throat was so dry she couldn't shout out for them.

The moment the intruders, both with huge shoulders and thick-set torsos, were in the room one of them snatched Jacob off the floor. Freida saw the flash of a small silver blade whip out from a sleeve and held up against Jacob's face. Immediately, the cold metal and sudden movement woke him up and, mouth open wide, he began to scream.

'Give him back.' Freida took a step forward to take him. 'Give him to me please.' Her voice wobbled as she pleaded.

'Be quiet and listen to what I tell you,' the other man growled. Despite the face coverings she could see their dark eyes narrowed at her, their distinctive Spanish accents a giveaway as to who had sent them.

'We're here to remind you of what you were told before. Advice you have not heeded. Stop engraving the map; you were warned of the consequences. And, we have been sent to retrieve the bauble you were given at New Year. Where is it?' He looked around the room as if he was expecting it to be lying on a velvet pillow on her workbench.

'Give me my baby back. The guards will be here in a

moment.' Freida's voice was starting to rise and suddenly – moving so quickly she didn't see him coming – the thug who wasn't holding Jacob whipped across the room and pulled her arms behind her back. Jacob had redoubled his screams and Freida wished that just for once one of the servants would come through to see why he was so upset, but they were used to his tantrums – he was as feisty as his father. And where had being married to Willem led her? Here, right now, her arms pushed so far up her back that she cried out in pain. Because hiding in a cupboard hadn't saved anyone but herself, and now she was going to allow it to happen all over again.

'I do not understand why Mendoza cares about what I am creating for Francis. It's just a map – there are very many of these in the world.'

'Because he believes it will give an advantage to that rogue Drake whilst attacking our ships.' While one of the thugs replied, they were both attempting to overturn the copperplate, hampered by the fact that one of them had his arms gripped around her and the other was holding a screaming, squirming Jacob. Eventually the thug held Jacob over one arm and with the other he began to sweep everything off her workbench onto the floor, stamping on it with his heavy boots, crushing her tools beneath him.

Her drawings followed. Before she could even explain the brooch was in a casket in her bedroom and that if they gave her Jacob she would run and retrieve it, one of them took a spill from the fire and lit the pile of parchment on the floor, placing Jacob back on his mat. The man holding Freida threw her to the floor before bending over and pressing his face to hers.

'Next time we come, your baby's blood with be splashed on every surface until there is none left in his body,' he hissed, 'and you will be so mutilated, your robbing *Sea Beggar* husband won't recognise you.' And with that they were gone.

Freida crawled across the floor to snatch up Jacob before getting to her feet and trying to stamp out the fire as it licked her skirts. Running to the door, she screamed for help as loudly as she could and, to her relief, she heard the pounding of feet as the servants in the kitchen came running. Including the two guards, bearing matching horrified expressions on their faces.

With six heavy stamps from their booted feet the fire was out and they kicked the glowing shards into the fireplace. Behind them Nell ran across to take Jacob who was still crying loudly. Freida, unable to remain standing any longer sank back down onto the floor.

'Mistress, what happened?' Guy had just arrived, looking around at the mayhem in the room, the pall of blue smoke hanging over everything.

'Mendoza's men.' Freida had started coughing and now couldn't stop. A beaker of ale was thrust into her hands and she took a large gulp. With his hand under her elbow Guy helped her stand up and guided her into the big hall, sitting her in the chair she usually occupied beside the fire.

Crouching down on his haunches beside her he said, 'Tell me what happened.'

Haltingly she told him everything she could remember. 'It all happened so fast. Where's Jacob?' She began to look around. 'I cannot hear him.'

'Do not worry he is with Nell. She said his leg is grazed

208

a little but otherwise he is unhurt. He's having some milk with honey and has stopped crying. He will soon forget. But you, mistress, are you hurt?'

'I fear I may have some bruises where I was thrown on the floor before they fled, but otherwise I am all right.'

'Who was it? What did they want? Master Willem told me before he left that you were frightened because of the threats, hence why I hired the guards. Except they were of no use, hanging around the kitchen maids and not doing what they are paid to do. I wonder if they were bribed to leave you on your own. Rest assured, mistress, they will be gone forthwith. If my master finds them, he will run them through with a cutlass.' Taking her cup, he added, 'I will fetch you more ale, and send Mistress Liskin to you.'

Guy disappeared into the kitchen and she could hear his voice shouting. He wasn't a tall man, but he could be ferocious when he needed to be. She wouldn't want to cross him and she imagined that the two fools he'd employed would be quailing at the onslaught on his anger. They'd be gone from the house before supper was served; that was for sure. Had they taken money from the thugs to be elsewhere when they arrived? She guessed she'd never know. It put her off employing anyone else but she'd leave the final decision to Guy who, in her husband's absence, was in charge of the household.

Liskin appeared at the door and hurried over. Her linen coif was half hanging off her head where she'd run across the gardens from next door.

'One of the kitchen boys just ran over to tell us.' She knelt on the rushes beside Freida's chair. 'Are you hurt?'

She shook her head as the initial shock of the attack began

to wear off and she felt hot tears start to course down her face and drip off her chin.

'They had Jacob and I could not stop them,' she sobbed. 'They had a knife and might have killed him if they so chose.'

'What did they want though? How could you be a threat to anyone?'

'Not me, but Willem and Drake are. And in order to try and stop them attacking the Spanish galleons they showed how vulnerable both Jacob and I are. They also wanted the brooch Drake gave to me, and I was told to stop engraving the map because of the advantage it may give to Drake. They tried to damage the plate I have spent so long working on although they did not manage to. As soon as it is complete, I shall take it to Mistress Jugge; I shall ensure it is done in the next three days. I do not want it here a moment longer than it needs to be.'

'Some of my men are currently improving the locks on the doors under Guy's supervision. And they will bring your work in here. You must work in the hall in future so that it is impossible for anyone to reach you without going past your servants first. You will not have any need for guards by the time we have finished.'

From the kitchen a maid staggered across the hall with a heavy leather bucket that steamed and smelled of rosemary.

'Come and see with your own eyes that Jacob is now happy and unharmed. He has a small scratch on his leg. And I have requested that your bath is filled upstairs. Go and rest in that. Do you have some comfrey for any bruising?'

Nodding, Freida got stiffly to her feet and made her way to the kitchen to find Jacob holding court. The young kitchen boy had left his post turning the spit to act the fool and make the little boy laugh, his previous upset forgotten. Nell was holding a poultice to his chubby leg and taking a quick look Freida could see that it would heal cleanly, God willing. It could have been so much worse – it didn't bear thinking about.

Mutely Freida walked up to her chamber where Liskin helped her disrobe and she sank into the small wooden bathtub placed in front of the fire, steaming with hot water. She hadn't realised the knife that the thug was carrying had nicked the back of her arm but as she sank beneath the hot water, the scent of rosemary as it steeped soothing her, the water began to turn pink and a sharp stinging pain caught her breath.

She didn't take a bath very often – it was not a simple thing to organise – but as she closed her eyes she waited for the worry of the past hour to leach out into the water. But it went nowhere, her shoulders still rigid with tension, her stomach knotted so tightly it might never unravel. She'd escaped from Antwerp to be safe from the Spanish and yet every step she took steered her towards the danger she cowered from as she found herself embroiled in the court of Queen Elizabeth. Falling in love with Willem who was now caught up with Drake, being introduced as a fine cartographer to the queen. All of this had led her to this point – in just as much danger as before. She'd come full circle and was still at the mercy of King Philip's men. How could she break this cycle? Or was she destined to be caught in it forever until they had taken everything from her?

Chapter Twenty-Nine

March 1581

'Mistress Ortelius, word has come that you were attacked in your own home. This makes me very disturbed.' Doctor Dee sat beside the fire in the great hall when Freida descended the following morning. She'd insisted on having Jacob sleep in her bed for the night but with his leg still sore, he kept waking and he proceeded to cry and kick and subsequently she got very little sleep. It was past ten o'clock by the time she was washed and dressed, her hair just tidied and hidden beneath a linen cap as she'd hurried downstairs to greet Dee.

'Doctor Dee, I apologise. I did not know you were waiting for me.' She hurried forward and bobbed a small curtsey, her body feeling as if it were covered in bruises as he got to his feet and bowed.

'The apologies are all mine,' he protested. 'I should have returned later but I was so worried when I visited Emanuel and he relayed the events of yesterday evening I felt I must see for myself that you are not injured, or whether in fact I should fetch a physician.'

'It would seem my household have been quick to spread the bad news—' she gave a wry smile '—but rest assured both Jacob and I are shaken but unhurt. The intruders came from the Spanish ambassador, hoping to retrieve the brooch Drake gave me at New Year. And to yet again try and persuade me to stop making the map that the queen has requested of me.'

'This I can believe of the Spanish cur. But your husband? Is he not at home?'

'No, he is presently at sea. I doubt those men would have come calling unless they knew he was not at home. He had hired two guards but they were not at their post when the henchmen broke in. I was working in my atelier; they have ruined all that I kept in there although thankfully they were unable to damage my etching, which is now almost complete. I shall have to replace the burins I use; they were burned and are now useless. Perhaps you can direct me to a workshop who may be able to help me?'

'Of course. I know all the finest workmen in the city. For the most part they are your compatriots, immigrants from across the water, and they will be able to craft you some excellent replacement tools. Come.' He got to his feet. 'Let us go now. You cannot allow Mendoza and his men to frighten you, nor dissuade you from continuing your craft.' He smiled encouragingly. She nodded and returned his smile then went to check on Jacob before finding her boots and asking Guy to accompany them. She would go nowhere now without protection of some sort. Doctor Dee was not built for fighting and neither was she.

Blackfriars – the area of the city to which Dee now took her – was familiar to Freida. She'd previously travelled to St Paul's and Paternoster Row when visiting the printers or buying more ink and paper, and this was an area she'd walked with Treswell, assisting with sketches of the layouts of houses. Walking north from Blackfriars they cut along Ludgate and from there to the Strand. As well as being the home of the mansions of Essex, Burghley and Somerset, this was the realm of the silversmiths and the scientists, the instrument makers and the fine craftsmen. All around were cranes renovating the monasteries that had fallen derelict and turning them into tenement housing; there was no inch of space in the city that wouldn't be built upon to accommodate the growing population.

Dee steered her into a premises with a wide window, the panes of glass in differing thicknesses letting light filter in, illuminating dust motes hanging suspended in the room. Immediately she could smell smoke and hot metal and there was a ringing from somewhere beyond the rear of the shop, a sound of metal on metal. They walked through to a courtyard where a smelting oven burned in the centre of the space, and a man was perched on a stool, bent over something he was sharpening, running it over and over down the length of a whetstone.

In the far corner of the yard two small children played with a group of pebbles, their faces turning to scrutinise the visitors. They were both dressed in linen shifts, russet britches and scuffed leather boots. Freida could tell that unlike a lot of the young boys she'd passed on the streets between her home and this establishment, these two with their clean faces and sturdy bodies were well cared for. Far too many children in London had to beg for food, or steal it. Such a huge gap between them and the overindulgence she observed at court.

'Isaac Stow,' Dee introduced the man who laid down what he was working on and stood to bow at Freida. 'This lady is in need of some burins and I have assured her you are the very best craftsman in London.'

'Indeed, goodwife, I can provide you with whatever you need.' He held his arm out to indicate she should precede him into the workshop, which took up two sides of the courtyard. Despite his name sounding English she could tell immediately from his accent that he hailed from the same side of the German Ocean as she did.

Inside the light was dim; however, she could make out a piece of crinkled velvet laid out on a trestle table upon which was a selection of tools with wooden handles similar to the ones that had been broken or thrown on the fire. Stepping forward she picked them up one by one, weighing them in her hand and after taking her glove off, she wrapped her fingers around the smooth wood. They needed to fit perfectly in the palm of her hand, just like the ones she'd brought from Antwerp, which she had been using since the age of twelve. They were specialist tools and needed to be precise and true.

'These are just samples,' Isaac explained. 'I will make the handles to precisely fit your hands, so they are simply an extension of your fingers.' Freida smiled and nodded. That was exactly how she needed them to be. When she was engraving, she barely noticed she was using a tool, it was so much a part of her. Isaac took each of her hands and with a piece of tape he measured her palms and the length of her fingers, marking on the tape each measurement.

'I would like one of each of these please.' She moved three burins to one side and removed her purse from where she had stowed it deep inside the folds of her kirtle. They agreed a price and she handed over two crowns. It was a fair sum if they were perfect, and in truth she didn't mind how much they cost if they were the right tools for her. After saying their goodbyes and agreeing Guy would return to collect her purchases a week later, she followed Doctor Dee back through to the shop, quickly slipping a groat to each of the small children who were in the courtyard. Their faces lit up and she smiled at how delighted they were.

Dee steered her around a body that lay in the pathway in front of them. Freida looked at it as they walked past, the filthy breeches torn along one seam and showing white flesh beneath, whilst the linen shirt was brown and grey with dirt and unpleasant-looking stains.

'Is he dead?' She turned to ask Guy who was always one step behind her.

'I do not believe so.' He shook his head. 'I suspect he is merely inebriated.' He stepped back and none too gently pushed the body with the toe of his boot, which resulted in a long groan from the man on the ground. Guy looked at Freida and nodded and they quickly followed Dee who was darting between the city's goodwives and merchants, and tiny lithe children always looking for purses to steal or running errands for their masters who filled the narrow streets of London. Unlike Lime Street, here there was no fresh air or tennis courts, nor gardens full of the much-cherished tulips or the tall sunflowers with huge golden heads swaying in the wind. No sunlight that filtered through small leaded lights to warm floors and release the scent of myrtle and rosemary hiding amongst the rushes beneath her feet.

Here the houses stood cheek by jowl with each other, clustered together as if for protection from the weather and who knew what else. There was very little light – just a perpetual twilight and, in the gloom, Freida imagined that any number of crimes could be committed and go unnoticed. This was where the darkest and poorest members of society hid. There was a smell in these streets and alleyways, one of cooking vegetables, bread, wet mud and horse manure, often together with the stench in warm weather from the Fleet ditch, and it wasn't pleasant. Wrinkling her nose, Freida pulled the hem of her skirts away from the cobbled streets and held her breath until they reached Cheapside, one of the main thoroughfares through London.

Now they could see the sky and feel the sun, finally giving forth some warmth on their faces, and Freida breathed a little more easily. The conduit in the centre of the street poured out clean water suitable for using in the house. Around it women stood chatting as they filled jugs and leather buckets. The air was full of noise. Street vendors called out to entice customers; cages of squawking chickens and other birds were piled high, threatening to topple over and spill their contents. Between the vendors were women carrying baskets of oranges on their heads, whilst others had trays hung about their necks full of assorted items.

Freida spotted some buttons she thought Nell may like and a comb she would have purchased, but she was hurried along by Guy who was ever mindful of the young grubby street urchins darting between the adults looking for purses to snatch.

The street was also filled with stalls selling every type of food imaginable and her mouth watered as the scent of hot pasties and warm bread filled her nose. She watched Guy look longingly as they walked past a pie seller, but she knew he'd consider it beneath his station to eat one walking along the street whilst accompanying her. She could tell by where the sun hung in the sky that it was dinnertime, her own stomach gurgling in recognition, and she hoped that the last establishment they were heading for was not far away.

Dee steered them along Cornhill towards Austin Friars where he explained that the huge mansion in front of them, its heraldic shields sitting high along the top of the walls set around three courtyards, had once been a monastery, and subsequently belonged to a man called Thomas Cromwell, but was now the Drapers' Hall. He cheerily told her how Cromwell had engineered the downfall of the queen's mother but had eventually been beheaded by the king who had once lauded him. Freida was fascinated by everything she could see; these streets appeared to be the centre of the scientific instrument trade. Around her she heard familiar words from her childhood being called across the street.

'Is this a Huguenot community?' she asked Dee. Her eyes lit up with delight. 'I can understand what they are saying.'

'Indeed.' He nodded. 'These craftsmen came from your homeland to escape the Spanish, just as you did. You have something in common with them. In fact, more than one thing, because they are creating navigational tools amongst other items. I thought you may like to be introduced to a friend of mine, Humfrey Cole. He makes instruments for many sailors including Drake, and even the queen possesses a selection. Come, let us go and meet with him.'

'Yes, I have viewed the collection belonging to Lord Burghley,' Freida replied. 'I would love to meet him.'

They continued walking until they reached a small shop. The door was wedged open to let the light in, the small window not doing a good enough job. A man sitting behind a workbench jumped up as he saw Dee, bowing to the three of them before clasping the hand of his friend.

'John Dee, how delightful to see you once again. And you have brought some guests too? Let me fetch some drinks for us.' He hurried through a curtain at the rear of the shop before returning with a tray containing four cups of wine and some small biscuits. Freida had taken the chance whilst he was away from the shop to wander around, picking up and putting down various pieces of brass and gold, an astrolabe that she recognised and several that she didn't.

Once they were all seated on stools, Cole drank his cup of wine in one large swig and then asked, 'To what do I owe the delight of this visit?'

Dee introduced Freida, adding that she was married to Willem van Hoorn. Immediately their host's eyebrows shot up so far they disappeared into his hairline.

'An Ortelius?' he repeated. 'Are you related to the great Abraham Ortelius? And married to van Hoorn? I know of him, of course. All of Saint Bartholomew Lane knows about the *Sea Beggar* who hides here in London in plain sight beneath the castle walls of a queen who once banished him

...s fellow privateers. Whilst allowing Drake to do exactly ... same pillaging in her name. Slightly hypocritical ...ethinks.'

'Abraham is my relative, a distant cousin. I learned my craft first with my father, also an Ortelius, and then later at Abraham's atelier in Antwerp. And now I engrave maps in my own workshop behind our home in Lime Street. And it seems that my husband, Willem, requires no introduction.' She smiled, pleased that he was so well renowned even if it was for his less than lawful activities across the sea in Europe. And it was true what Cole had just said: Willem was only doing what Drake did, protecting their countries from invasion. She knew the queen was very afraid of the Spanish finding some way, some door to open and take her throne, just as they had in Holland.

'Indeed, a neighbour of mine made him a quadrant a few years ago.'

'I have seen this item; it is very fine.' Freida nodded. 'But around your shop I see many other instruments. Can you explain these to me please?'

'I would be delighted to.' Cole's face lit up at the chance to talk about his work. He got to his feet and took something from a shelf. 'This is a theodolite,' he explained. 'See how it enlarges items that are across the street?' Freida barely had a chance to properly examine it, with its shining engraved planes and the interlocked cogs, before the next one and then another one was placed in front of her and a further explanation started.

After one shelf had been cleared and the contents were laid out across the workbench, Cole went and collected what he had been working on as they arrived.

'This is new,' he explained. 'I have not made many. A volvelle. Or I believe the sea captains call it a "nocturnal". With it they can tell the time and subsequently the tides and sail into port at night, just by using the stars. Very useful for those who need to arrive somewhere without being seen.' His eyes slid sideways to her as he gave her a wry smile.

Freida picked it up, turning it in her hands. It was still warm from the friction of the tools where Cole had been filing it when they had arrived at the shop.

'Will this piece be for sale, or is it a commission?' she asked, her head on one side as she thought.

'It is not owned by anyone yet,' Cole told her. 'If you would be interested in purchasing it I am sure we could come to an agreement on a price.'

Guy cleared his throat. 'Mistress, it would not be seemly for you to negotiate a financial arrangement; I shall return and do that for you.'

'No.' She put her hand on Guy's arm. 'I can and will discuss this with Mr Cole myself. I do not need you to speak for me.' She straightened her back and fixed him with a stare from beneath her straight brows. She didn't need a man to speak for her – hadn't the queen told her that? And shown and proven it.

They agreed a price and Cole promised to deliver it within the month. Freida was delighted and intended giving it as a gift to her husband when he returned from his current voyage. She knew from the time she'd sailed with him that entering a port under the cover of darkness so as not to alert the enemy was a matter of immense peril. This nocturnal would be of great help to him she was sure, and she was impatient to give it to him.

On leaving the workshop, they walked back towards Lime Street. Deep grey clouds were starting to build in the sky and an icy cold wind sliced across Freida's face, making her huddle further into her cloak. The tentative warmth of spring from earlier had gone and nature was showing them that winter wasn't done with them yet. Bad weather made her worry even more for Willem somewhere out in the cold seas. What if the worst happened? She'd probably never know unless someone survived to tell her. He'd be lying at the bottom of the ocean swilling about in a watery grave, being pulled and pushed by the tides, never to return.

She gave herself a mental shake. There was nothing she could do, but the feeling of apprehension hung across her shoulders constantly. When she was in her atelier, when she was watching Jacob sleeping at night, so young and innocent, his face smooth and unlined; always in her heart was the fear, the dread that the man she loved wouldn't come back. And there was nothing she could do to stop it, nor stop him.

Chapter Thirty

August 2022

The dappled shade from the leaves above her flickered against Robyn's eyelids as she lay on the mossy ground. Beneath her, sharp twigs dug into her skin through the thin T-shirt she was wearing, but she couldn't be bothered to sit up and brush them away. Her mind was whirring and this was the place, as always, where she could think things out. Lay all the pieces out in the expanse of her mind like a jigsaw puzzle and try and put them in the right order. If there was one, when so often there wasn't.

That morning yet again the subject of her declaration had been raised as she and her father had been eating breakfast. It had been triggered by a report on the news about a huge yacht, a millionaire's plaything, which had gone missing.

'Have you given it any more thought?' her father interrupted her reverie.

'Sorry, what?' She began to spoon jam onto her toast and

acted as if she had no idea what he was referring to. She knew he wasn't fooled though.

'You know what.' His voice was sharp and she looked up in surprise. He rarely raised his voice. 'You said you'd go and find out what you need to do over the summer, ready to make the declaration in September. Have you actually done anything about it yet? We're already in August and now you're only weeks away from the anniversary.'

'I know, Dad, I know. I see the weeks racing past, just like the months and years from when I last saw him. My final memory, standing on the quayside at Les Sables d'Olonne, Nate shielding his eyes against the sun as he gave one final wave. That's the last thing I have to hold on to and by declaring him dead, that's all I'll ever have to remember him by.'

'Nonsense. You have a hundred thousand memories of him. Happy memories. Your wedding day, holidays, fun nights out in London. You'll always have those. Remember him then, laughing, playing the fool. He was always looking for the next daft thing to do, wasn't he? Those are the memories to cling on to.'

'Oh yes he was constantly looking for some silly prank.' Robyn couldn't help chuckling despite the serious tone of the conversation. 'Remember when he set up that water obstacle course in the garden in Poole? He always had to go to extremes. Anyone else would have been happy with a slide into the pool, only Nate had to add the trampoline and his childhood swing. I think he'd have been first in the queue to enter *Ninja Warrior* given how competitive he was. And it was no surprise he romped around his mad garden Olympic course while the rest of us were very wet and bruised by the end. For Nate there was no point doing something unless he was pushing himself into realms that made it dangerous or risky even if we were in the back garden supposedly having a barbecue and relaxing . . .'

Her voice tailed off as she realised what she'd said. Her father could obviously tell she'd arrived at the same place he was because, patting her shoulder, he got to his feet and disappeared into the bathroom leaving her sitting at the table staring into space. Because what she'd just said was true. Nate was an adrenalin junkie; he never took the easy safe route. And she was aware of the niggling realisation that had dogged her all summer – that her father only wanted what was best for her when reminding her about the declaration. He was trying to gently steer her to where she needed to be, so it became clearer, more resolute.

All day she'd mulled over the conversation in her head as she served customers and tidied shelves until now when she finally had some peace and could come to their tree and talk to Nate. Below her the river flowed silently past, just the occasional squawk from a duck or the plop of some other river dweller disappearing under the water. She preferred not to think of anything that was alive being under the water.

'Nate, why can't you tell me what to do? You were always my sounding board; we discussed everything. Now I have to make the biggest decision of my life – well of your life as well – and you aren't here to advise me. Because you lived your life doing what you were compelled to do, living on a knife edge of danger.' Only silence greeted her. Wherever he was, he couldn't hear her. Perhaps now was the time to go and make that declaration.

★   ★   ★

Spurred on by her thoughts, before she went to bed that night she emailed the solicitor they'd used in London. Nate had insisted he wrote a will as soon as they were married. Neither of them had expected it to be needed until they were both old and grey, but he'd assured her it was standard practice because his profession was dangerous so she'd gone along with it. And now she'd need to make an appointment for when the time finally came to have his will executed. She didn't even have any idea whether Andrew Pointer, the original solicitor, was still working there, but she'd soon find out. Before she had time to talk herself out of it, she hit 'send' on her request for an appointment.

Robyn checked her phone every fifteen minutes the following day, waiting for a response to her enquiry, and was finally rewarded mid-afternoon when a reply arrived from Andrew's secretary confirming he did indeed still work there and suggesting Robyn called to arrange a visit to his office. There was no question asking why she wanted to see him and Robyn wondered if he'd guessed. Her surname and her face had been on the news and in documentaries over the years but for the past couple of years her husband's fate had slipped from the public's interest.

Before she could think of a reason not to do it, she called the number on the bottom of the email and arranged an appointment for the following week. After finishing the call, she put her phone down, a wave of nausea washing over her. She'd started putting the wheels into motion and already she was regretting it. She went to find her father and tell him; at least one of them would be happy with the decision.

'It does mean abandoning you and the shop again,' she admitted, 'so if you'd rather I wait until past the actual anniversary I can? There's nothing I can do at this point. All Andrew can explain is the process and if he's prepared do it for me, take on all the legalities.'

'Don't you worry about the shop.' He flapped his hand at her. 'It's far more important that you get this underway. And maybe you can do some more map research while you're in London?'

Robyn nodded. She wasn't sure what she needed to investigate next, but if she could find something, she could use that as a legitimate reason to be up in London – as if denying why she was going to be there, pushing it into the cupboard in her mind where she hid everything she didn't want to think about.

A sudden storm cleared the streets of customers as they all piled into the many local cafés. After pushing the door shut to prevent the rain blowing in, Robyn's father came to find her in the office. With his help the previous day she had opened the frame and removed the map and it was now laid on sheets of acid-free tissue on the desk. As they'd suspected, it was backed with a thick linen fabric, carefully stitched around the edges of the map to the parchment.

'What's this?' He pointed to something very pale in the top right-hand corner.

'It's almost faded to nothing,' she replied. 'I couldn't see it before; it was covered by the edge of the frame. Originally, I thought it was just a compass rose like other maps of the era, but I'm beginning to think it isn't. Have you any idea what it is?'

'I'm not sure. It appears to be an engraved dial and what looks like a clock hand.' He rummaged in the desk drawer

227

and removed two eye loupes, passing one to Robyn, and together they held them to their faces and bent closer.

'I think you may be right,' she said slowly. 'What on earth can it be?'

'It's so bleached it's difficult to see. Pass me a piece of paper and a pencil and I'll try and sketch it, then we'll do some research.' Pulling a notebook and a pencil from the desk drawer she passed them over. Behind them the shop doorbell rang out.

'You carry on.' Robyn jumped to her feet, not wanting to interrupt his concentration. 'I'll go and see to the customers.'

As the rain outside slowly abated she began to get busier again and it wasn't until she shut the shop ninety minutes later that Robyn was able to return to the office.

'Well?' she asked. 'I was expecting you back in the shop to give me an update.'

'I've been doing some research of my own. I'd forgotten what fun it is − like a detective through the centuries, a time traveller. Here, look at this.' He passed the notebook he'd been drawing in. 'It's only a quick drawing from the bits I could see.'

'I still have no idea what it could be though. Has it been engraved on or added afterwards like the signature we found?'

'It's true engravings were altered and added to over the years as more information about countries around the world was discovered, but I think this was painted on at the same time as the map was created. It isn't raised as the other lines are, which is why it has faded so much. And I've been online looking at things too.' He swung the laptop, which was open beside him, so she could see the screen. 'I think

228

it's a maritime instrument. These navigation tools were just starting to be used more widely when this map would have been created. I've been trying to see if I can identify it.'

Robyn leaned in closer to see what he was showing her. 'What are these then?'

'This is an astrolabe, but I don't think it looks very similar to my sketch.' He held it up against the screen. 'My thoughts are that it is a volvelle. See here how it would have had a hand to move around? A bit like a slide rule really. And look, there are serrated edges all around the inner dial.'

'Mmm, you may be right. What did they use a volvelle for?'

'There were two kinds according to what I've just read. Ones to use with the sun, and also ones to use with the moon. Both would have been used to calculate the time in order to navigate.' He went on to explain what he'd discovered. 'These days the likes of Sam and Nate have everything done for them on a computer – no using the sun and the moon and stars. Anyway—' he got to his feet '—I'm going to cash up the till and then start dinner. You carry on if you want to down here. I'll give you a shout when it's ready.'

Robyn nodded, her eyes already glued to the screen as she entered 'volvelle' into Google to see what else she could discover.

The items that came up drew her into a rabbit hole of information as she examined image after image along with descriptions of how the instrument worked. One link took her to a surviving piece in the British Museum and this then led to its maker, a man called Humfrey Cole. His dates put him firmly in London around the time her map may have been created, but she couldn't find an immediate connection and admitted to herself it was highly unlikely there was one. However, as she was going to London in just a few days, it was the perfect opportunity to go and have a look at it in person.

Chapter Thirty-One

April 1581

A young messenger boy arrived at the house on Lime Street. Freida was sitting down at the table breaking her fast, passing small pieces of white manchet bread to Jacob who was mostly throwing them on the floor with great shouts of delight, making his mother and Nell both smile at him indulgently. He'd already eaten a bowl of porridge sweetened with honey and it was stuck to his round cheeks.

A knock at the door made her look up as her heart jumped. Since the intrusion of Mendoza's men and knowing the brooch was still sitting in a small wooden casket at the back of a press in her bedroom, she was always on edge they'd return. Although it was a different tactic if they were emboldened enough to simply arrive at the street door. Guy appeared from somewhere inside the house and went to open it. There was a pause while he took something from the visitor and handed over a groat before approaching Freida, holding out a letter.

'For you, mistress.' He handed it to her but waited for

a moment. Raising her eyebrows, she turned it over to open it, recognising immediately the now familiar seal of Queen Elizabeth pressed into the deep red wax. After pulling it apart, she quickly scanned the contents, praying she wasn't yet bid to take the map to the queen. It was close to being finished but she still needed one final day and then it needed to go to the printer, and to be backed with linen stiffened with the starch made from boiled arrowroot, which was used to make her ruffs so crisp, to make it more robust. She probably needed another two weeks.

'It is an invitation—' she put her hand on her heart, waiting for it to stop racing '—to view Drake's ship, the *Golden Hinde*, which is now moored at the docks in Deptford. I am bid to be in the queen's entourage.'

'A great honour, mistress,' Guy replied, but she could see the concern in his eyes.

'What worries you?' Freida put her hand on his arm. 'I can see you are not happy about this?'

'I cannot accompany you, and the master was explicit in his instruction for me to be with you at all times unless you are at home or within the royal palace. Here you will be on the royal barge and we do not know who will also be there.'

'Nobody will be able to attack me in plain sight, surely?' Freida said. 'I am sure I will be safe. And, more importantly, I have no choice but to go. May you be waiting at the jetty when I return? That would make me feel safer.'

'Of course. I shall send Christopher to watch out for sight of the boat returning and then he can run to warn me. There will be plenty of time for me to get to the jetty. The queen's boat moves extremely slowly so the city folk can see her in all her glory as she passes.'

Freida nodded her acquiescence; it sounded a sensible plan and she felt a little more reassured that she'd be safe.

'I must go and speak with Liskin about my attire for this event as it is only a week away.'

The new burins arrived two days later. Holding them in her hand, Freida was delighted. As promised, they fitted perfectly into her palm, turning her fingers into artist tools. The soft, smooth wood warmed as she held them until she could barely discern where her hand finished and the tools began. The metal shone and she pushed the blade into the plate on the easel, marvelling at how it sliced through like her dinner knife cut into butter. She ran it down her finger in admiration but to her horror immediately beads of blood began to well out of a fine slice of her skin. She hadn't expected it to be so sharp and before she could prevent it, blood dripped down the plate. Hastily she wrapped a rag around her finger and with another one she wiped the engraving clean. They were certainly sharp and despite her scratch, she was delighted with them.

She was even more pleased when, just two days later, the volvelle arrived from Mr Cole. Its fresh brass shone as it caught the candlelight in her workshop, the dial inscribed around it feeling rough beneath her fingertips as she ran them over the grooves. She picked up one of her new tools and carefully engraved their two initials in it. W and F, always together even when they couldn't be in person before putting it away in the chest with her tools for when Willem came home.

★ ★ ★

Thankfully the cut had almost healed by the following Saturday as Freida travelled to Drake's ship. Every day she hoped Willem would return. She'd have felt safer if he were there and she knew he'd have found a way of following her, even though he wouldn't have been invited aboard. She sincerely hoped Doctor Dee would also be present. Drake was hosting the queen and would probably not notice Freida was in attendance.

After her previous visits to court, Liskin had insisted Freida expanded her wardrobe to accommodate any further occasions and prevent the previous panic of finding something suitable to wear. After organising a suitable selection of gowns, she left it to her cousin to decide what she should wear for this auspicious event. The one that was picked out was made of heavy blue brocade with a matching cloak trimmed with coney fur, together with an elaborate headdress.

'It will be cold on the river,' Liskin explained when Freida had questioned her choice. 'It was snowing only two days ago. The sun may be shining now but you know how quickly the weather can turn. Believe me, you will be thankful of your warm gown.' Freida suspected she was correct so she closed her mouth and allowed Liskin and her dresser to lace her into the outfit, layer by layer, feeling hotter and increasingly weighed down as each item was added. Finally Liskin pinned the brooch, the cause of so many worries, to the centre of her bodice.

'No, I cannot wear this,' she protested, but Liskin put her hand up to quieten her.

'It will be expected,' she insisted. 'Drake will look to see if you are wearing his gift, and no doubt the queen will too. You cannot risk the displeasure of Her Majesty, however much you may wish to; you have no choice.'

In truth Freida knew her friend was correct in her interpretation of the situation she now found herself in, and she felt the weight of duty and tradition heavy upon her. The dresser handed over her gloves, a small purse and her gold pomander to attach to her girdle. It knocked against her thigh as she walked, a sliver of comfort – a small action reminding her of home, safety and her daily life.

She walked down to the river with Guy, chattering on in her nervousness about nothing in particular. She didn't enjoy her visits to the palace and this was far worse. They needed to walk further than Botolph's Wharf, its slippery narrow steps down to the water too precarious in her big gown. She required a bigger craft and easier access so they walked through the city to London Bridge where Guy found a tilt boat, its canopy and cushioned seating more suitable.

Sitting opposite Guy, she watched the other craft filling the river and making it difficult to navigate a straight path to where the royal barge could be seen waiting, pennants in red and gold fluttering in the breeze in anticipation. Freida wished she could feel the excitement everyone else seemed to be experiencing, instead of wishing fervently that she was back at home engraving her map. If it hadn't been for her cartography and her illustrious family name, she wouldn't have come before the queen and subsequently been introduced to Francis Drake. Which had ultimately resulted in the renewed threat of danger from the Spanish ambassador, the fear of him making her insides hurt. She hadn't eaten since the invitation had arrived.

'See here,' Guy said cheerfully, 'the queen's barge is

looking very fine. You will have a smooth travail along the river to Deptford and everyone will be able to see you. It is a great honour to accompany Her Majesty. Who would have thought that the wife of a *Sea Beggar* would be accepted at court with the courtiers and nobility.' Freida wasn't sure she had been accepted at all. She nodded mutely.

Once they disembarked at the landing stage, she was required to wait with the other ladies until the queen arrived and was seated on her throne at the bow. Freida stood to one side with Guy, away from the crowd.

'There are not many people here,' she said hopefully, 'maybe this is just a small party?'

'I expect this is just a select few,' Guy replied. 'Others will make their own way to the ship.' His words did not comfort her.

Finally, the queen arrived surrounded by her entourage and accompanied by Lord Burghley. They boarded the barge and once the queen was settled everyone else followed. Guy gave Freida a gentle push on the small of her back and smiled encouragingly.

'You will have a wonderful day,' he reassured her. She returned his smile and nodded, but she suspected it did not reach her eyes. Joining the last few guests, within minutes she was seated on a banquette near the back of the boat. The cushion was padded and covered in rich red velvet, soft and thick between her fingertips as she buried them into the fabric. The oarsmen between where she was sitting and the queen pulled the boat smoothly and slowly out into the centre of the river to commence the journey.

Beside her one of the queen's favourites, Henry Percy, lounged at the other end of the seat and mostly ignored her, instead waving to the crowds on the riverbanks who, as Guy had predicted, had gathered to hail the queen. Freida let the steady movement of the boat as the oars swept through the water, slowly drawing them forwards, relax her. The fact that Mendoza wasn't on board with the queen's select party gave her hope he would not be attending at all. She should be safe, at least for today.

Chapter Thirty-Two

August 2022

Robyn was delighted to discover Sam would also be in London on the day she was due to meet Andrew Pointer, and she booked a train ticket for six in the morning so she could spend a few hours with him prior to her appointment. Despite the feeling of strength she'd had when calling and arranging to see the solicitor, her courage slowly seeped away during the intervening days and she felt less resolved in her decision to be setting the process into action. Her father had assured her that once the appointment was made, she'd feel more conviction, but she was still waiting for it.

'Good to see you, country girl,' Sam greeted her as she walked through the barriers at Paddington station. She immediately felt a rush of sheer joy to see him. He'd never know how much she valued his friendship and how unwittingly he had helped her in her long journey to accept what had happened to Nate. No one else knew the danger of being out in treacherous seas without a single person for hundreds of miles, the fear that Nate would have gone through. Only Sam understood.

'Hello.' She threw her arms around him, holding him tight, relaxing against him as he hugged her back. She put the afternoon's appointment to the back of her mind, intent on enjoying her time with him.

'So where first?' he asked. 'Coffee? You can explain what this is that you want to investigate.'

'Sounds good to me.' She patted the backpack slung over her shoulder. 'I've got loads of notes I've been making. I'll take you through them while we have a drink. In fact, we may need several coffees – there's a lot of information.'

They were soon sitting at the back of a café, two steaming flat whites on the table, the rest of the space taken up with pages of Robyn's notes, arrows drawn to other sheets and circles around some names. Occasionally she'd move one of the pages or add a scribbled comment along a margin.

'I still don't understand it all,' Sam admitted. 'How have you got from the map you decided to investigate to all of this?' He swept his hand across the table.

'Because one thing seems to lead to another and I have disappeared into a rabbit hole of cartography research.' She laughed at herself but she could tell from Sam's reaction that her glow of enjoyment at what she was doing was showing on her face. Her father had been right when he'd suggested that doing this would help to take her mind off everything else. Of course she still thought about Nate every day, but now, finally, something else was sharing the space in her head.

'It's funny to think they sailed in those days with nothing more than a sheet of parchment with a map, which may or may not have been correct, and possibly an astrolabe or another instrument if they were lucky. Drake managed to circumnavigate the world like that,' Sam said. 'Incredible really. I feel like maybe I cheat a bit with my banks of computers and GPS these days.'

'Actually, it's the instruments they used that have brought me to London early today because Dad thinks the diagram in the top corner of the map – one I'd originally thought was a traditional compass rose – is actually a rare type of instrument called a volvelle. And there's one in the British Museum, which I really want to go and see. Apparently, they also have some ledgers that belonged to a chap called Humfrey Cole – he was an instrument maker in Elizabethan England. It's definitely a similar era to my map.'

'We'd better make a move then, because you've got a meeting with your solicitor today haven't you?'

Robyn regretted telling him her real reason for visiting London. She wanted to enjoy her trip to the museum and her time with him without the dark cloud of what she would be doing later hanging over her. To push it to the back of her head just for a few hours. 'Yes, but it's not until later this afternoon,' she explained, 'so plenty of time for us to go and have a rummage around the antiquities of old London town.' Collecting together her paperwork, she pushed it all back into her backpack before carrying their empty cups to the counter and following Sam out into the sunshine and the dusty street.

The road was full of cars sitting nose to tail, going nowhere, and the fumes that filled her lungs made Robyn screw her nose up. She'd loved living in the capital with Nate; the frenetic pace of life had suited them. But now, after so many years in the quiet of Hay-on-Wye with just a few months of the year when people filled the town, London was chaotic. The noise of traffic roared in her ears and she felt overwhelmed and longed for Hay, where the clear air and the surrounding hills would fill her with a sense of calm and comfort. Whatever happened over the next few months, she couldn't imagine ever living anywhere else; perhaps now was the time to start looking in estate agent windows for a place of her own. To give her father and Alison the space they deserved.

After coming out of the underground station Robyn and Sam wandered along Great Russell Street discussing the buildings they walked past, looking for the familiar blue plaques that hung on some of the walls. At the entrance of the museum a crowd of noisy school children milled around, a constant moving wave. Three teachers attempted to count heads, becoming more and more exasperated as children swapped places in the crocodile or ran across the courtyard, as a peaked cap blew away on a gust of wind. Robyn couldn't help smiling at them, their excitement at a day that wasn't spent in school palpable.

Standing in the huge, light-filled atrium with its distinctive triangular design on the domed roof Robyn and Sam searched in the guide for any collection that may hold what they were looking for.

'Here?' Robyn pointed. 'Room forty-six?'

'Let's try,' he agreed and they walked back through the imposing dark entrance, a distinct contrast to the atrium. Here tall columns lent the space the ambience of a Greek temple.

Upstairs they navigated their way through the maze of rooms until they finally reached where they wanted to be.

Once inside it took them a while to find the section they needed, but as soon as they were there Robyn was engrossed as she made her way around the cabinets looking at the items on display. Despite the fact that the museum had been modernised many times over the years, the musty scent of centuries of valuable objects hung in the air. A thousand ghosts standing guard over their precious belongings.

In the far corner Robyn found what she'd been searching for in a cabinet of complex brass nautical instruments.

'There, look.' She pointed to the rear of the cabinet. 'A volvelle, made by Humfrey Cole.' She read the card, 'And engraved on the rear with initials F and W.' Her voice tailed off as she turned to Sam. 'Could that be Freida and Willem do you think? Or is my imagination just thinking what I want to be true?' She was holding her hands together under her chin, a wide smile on her face. 'Somehow I need to discover if this did indeed belong to Freida. And whether my map is the one in Van Meteren's letter to Abraham, as well as why it covers such an unusual area.'

'And why it has a bloodstain across one corner?'

'I'm not sure I'll ever know that.' Robyn shrugged her shoulders. 'It's unlikely to have been noted anywhere.'

'And did you say they have the ledgers here? Can we take a look at those?'

'They're in the museum archives, but not on show. I'll see what I can find online.' She followed him back out of the room, turning to take one last look at the volvelle, a tangible connection to her map.

'I need to go and run a few errands,' Sam explained once they were outside again. Yet another school party waited impatiently, almost identical to the ones who'd been there when they arrived, only the colour of the school jumpers differing. 'I'd really like to continue this with you, but I have a meeting I need to go to. And you have an appointment too.'

Robyn nodded, the excitement that was making her heart race dissipating, and her mood plummeted.

'Thanks for all your help.' She plastered a big smile on her face and hoped he wouldn't be able to tell exactly how false it was. 'I'll let you know if I discover anything else. I really want to know more about Freida. A woman doing a man's job in the sixteenth century. It hardly seems possible and yet with every stone we turn over, there's more evidence that she was doing exactly that. What a remarkable woman.' It was as though Freida's poise and assurance was reaching out to Robyn through the map and starting to permeate her with a strength of her own.

'Yes, keep me updated please.' After kissing her on the cheek and wrapping her in a big bear hug, Sam walked away, turning for one last wave as he disappeared down the street. Robyn watched him go as if trying to imprint his image on her brain. She had forty-five minutes before her appointment. She'd already checked and knew she needed to be close to Sloane Square and she slowly walked towards the tube, following in Sam's footsteps.

On the train to London she'd already managed to talk herself out of attending this appointment, and yet after what she had discovered that day in the museum and the truth about Freida that she continued to discover she realised that perhaps she could take this first step. She couldn't do anything final today, anyway.

Arriving at the right place, she approached the door of Pointer and Pointer. Robyn stood on the pavement at the bottom of the steps that led up to the front door, her legs shaky and weak as she held on to the black-painted railings beside her. The last time she'd been standing on that spot, Nate held her hand. They were happy and chatting and just going through the motions of writing a will because they were getting married. Never imagining she'd actually have to ask for it to be executed. And that couldn't happen until she'd told the world he was dead.

'Come on, Robyn, you can do this,' she whispered before walking up the steps and opening the door.

Chapter Thirty-Three

April 1581

The journey along the Thames to Deptford filled Freida with wonder, her worries about Mendoza now forgotten. The other craft that permanently sculled the water crowded close to the barge, the occupants hoping to catch the eye of the queen, and from her seat at the back away from the royal inner circle, Freida watched the people waving from the shore. The coloured pennants cracked in the wind and at one point Freida held her hand to her ornate headdress to stop the breeze whipping it from her head. Despite Liskin's ministrations, she wasn't convinced there were enough of the sharp pins in her hair to secure it.

Once they'd gone beyond the city walls, the scenery changed noticeably. Small villages sitting away from the riverbank, groups of houses huddled close together with squat churches keeping watch over them. Moored alongside were the ships carrying spices and silks from foreign·lands, waiting for their turn to enter the docks at Customs House and unload their cargo. The officers there worked long hours ensuring that the relevant taxes were paid by the merchants awaiting the goods to fill their warehouses. Everyone, whoever they were, was expected to hand over their dues to fill the crown's coffers.

Freida knew Willem occasionally moored along this part of the river close to Rotherhithe and she gave a silent prayer of thanks he was currently away. She was certain the queen would recognise his ship with its English flag yet also with a distinct Dutch style. Now that Her Majesty knew Willem was mooring on the Thames she'd grudgingly agreed to his being allowed to continue because of her fondness of Freida, she was prepared to look the other way and pretend she didn't know he was there. At least for the time being.

And what would happen when the map was finished? She'd be taking it to the printers within days and then it would just need backing and it was ready to present. Finally the reason for her visiting court would be finished and she fervently hoped she'd never need to return. That the queen would forget about her, a simple Dutch cartographer from a famous family, and she'd never see Mendoza again. If Drake embarked on another long voyage, then his connection with Willem would be cleaved and life could return to normal; they could live quietly in Lime Street as they'd always intended. She suspected, however, it was unlikely. She'd overheard more than one courtier discussing the queen's fear of the Spanish invading and the constant danger of her cousin, Mary Stuart, who was known to be in contact with those on the continent, and also of her desire to protect England's shores with her navy, which included Drake.

The cheers and shouting along the riverbank increased until the air was so full they drowned out the cries of the gulls that swooped above them and were thrown about in the breeze, grey scraps of cloth at the mercy of the weather. Freida realised that they'd reached the *Golden Hinde* as the barge headed into the quay. The planks beneath her feet creaked as the oarsmen turned the heavy craft towards the wharf where a wooden jetty had been assembled for the queen and her party to board the ship. Everywhere was decorated with yet more pennants and banners and the crowds here were so loud that Freida wanted to put her hands over her ears.

She waited until the queen's inner circle had disembarked, attempting to make herself invisible amongst the other courtiers and ladies present as they all moved along the quayside to board the *Golden Hinde*. Above her, Freida could hear the snapping of the furled sails as the wind blew against the masts and she felt a surge of melancholy for Willem. These were the sounds that she'd woken to when she'd sailed with him on the *Windfly*, and she imagined him at that moment walking the deck, his boots pounding the pale boards bleached white with salt. The sea was in his blood just as mapmaking was in hers, both of them dedicated to their calling.

A yeoman guard in his red and gold livery helped her step aboard, and immediately her eyes scanned for somewhere she could view the proceedings without being noticed. On the poop deck Drake was greeting the queen, down on one knee with his short black cloak sweeping the planks, an elaborate floppy hat in dark green with a long white feather almost obliterating his face. She couldn't help a small smile at his flamboyant attire.

Taking a step backwards Freida stumbled as she bumped into someone and she turned to apologise. The words froze on her lips as she came face to face with the one person she'd fervently hoped was not attending, his black eyes burning with his disgust and hatred of her. She was so shocked to see him that she immediately took a step back, almost tripping on a coil of rigging on the deck. Mendoza's hand shot out to steady her but then didn't let go, gripping her upper arm tightly.

'Pray, remove your hand please.' Freida's voice was gruff as her mouth instantly dried. She tried to swallow but her throat was blocked by a large lump of fear, her previous confidence seeming to have deserted her.

'Mistress Ortelius,' he sneered. 'I did not think your station at court warranted an attendance at such an occasion, given that you must be most accustomed to being aboard a privateer's ship. Although I have heard tell your husband's vessel is not as illustrious as this one. They both deserve to be at the bottom of the ocean though, and I intend to ensure that happens.' Freida opened her mouth to remonstrate but before she could say anything, Mendoza's other hand grabbed the brooch she hadn't wanted to wear, pulling her cloak towards him and forcing her to take a step forwards. She knew it had been a mistake; she should have protested louder when Liskin had insisted. It was as if she had a premonition of this moment. His eyes narrowed until they were slits, his black lashes barely concealing the anger, which still managed to crawl out of every pore on his face.

'This does not belong to you,' he spat. 'Spanish plunder. Thieved by pirates in the employ of your monarch who is herself a usurper and not the true claimant to the crown. I demand you give it back this instant.' His hand tightened, pulling the cloak towards him as Freida tried to step away, stretching the fabric between them as if it would tear at any moment.

'Unhand me.' Her voice wobbled as she raised it slightly, hoping to draw the attention of the others milling about close by. She could see now that her intention of hiding away from the celebrations had been an error, simply giving her enemy the chance to single her out and threaten her.

'My lady, are you in need of assistance?' A deep voice beside her made Mendoza let her go and step backwards. She turned to see one of the queen's guards at her elbow. She'd never been so pleased to see the shining pewter of his plate armour.

'Thank you,' she replied. 'I believe that perhaps the Spanish ambassador has confused me with someone else. I shall go and watch the proceedings a little closer to ensure I do not miss anything.' Her eyes met the guard's and she held them for a moment until he gave the merest nod in acknowledgement. As she lifted the front of her gown to move away she heard the guard, his voice menacing, telling the Spanish ambassador he should remain where he was. She felt assured she wouldn't be bothered by him again that day, but her heart was still racing, her palms clammy. Mendoza was insidious, appearing whenever she wasn't expecting him, always reminding her she was in constant danger.

Ahead of her something appeared to be happening. The queen's entourage who'd been watching a troop of Miwok warriors from New Albion – whom Drake had brought back to England – performing a tribal dance suddenly moved away from where they were perched on velvet-covered benches arranged around the throne. It was very different to being on board the *Windfly* where the only comfortable seating was in Willem's cabin. She could imagine the days of preparation that had been made for this visit, ensuring that the deck of the Hinde was transformed from a working, seafaring vessel to a situation where the queen may be comfortable. Two complete opposites.

Abruptly Drake was on his knee in front of the French envoy who was currently petitioning for a marriage between his king and Queen Elizabeth, whilst Lord Burghley handed him a sword. He placed it carefully on each of Drake's shoulders before everyone on board began to cheer and clap. The queen's strident voice carried across the heads of the crowd. 'Arise, Sir Francis Drake.'

The applause rose to a crescendo as Drake swept his hat off his head and bowed low first to the queen and then to the rest of the party, which just made everyone shout and cheer loudly in delight. Despite her experience earlier, Freida couldn't help turning a little to see Mendoza's response. She smiled to herself as she saw his face contorted in fury. Her day had improved a little.

'A glass of wine, my lady?' A voice at her elbow made Freida turn to find a cup being proffered to her by a servant, accompanied by Lord Burghley.

'Thank you.' She inclined her head as she took the cup from him. 'How lovely to see you again, my lord.'

'A fine spectacle today, is it not?' He indicated the queen and Drake now sitting beside each other talking animatedly.

'Indeed,' she replied. Instinctively her hand moved to the brooch, checking it was still attached to her cloak.

'I saw our Spanish friend with you earlier,' he continued, 'so I sent one of the guards over to intervene. Now I can see what has upset him. Is that not part of the consignment of jewels brought back by Drake?'

'It is,' she agreed. 'I would have preferred not to wear it, but my cousin insisted that I would have offended Drake, and potentially the queen, had I not. Unfortunately, it was seen by the Spanish ambassador earlier and he was most displeased. As you observed.'

'Yes, the look of black thunder that adorns his face is so often there I fear it is now a permanent part of his countenance.'

They were interrupted by Drake who'd left the royal party enjoying the banquet that had been brought aboard early that morning, and he was now making his way around the ship greeting the guests. Freida had already seen him ignore Mendoza as he walked past, as if the ambassador were simply not there. Standing in front of them now, he bowed to her and then to Burghley.

'Good day, my friends,' he said, his eyes sparkling. 'I see you are wearing my New Year's gift.' His eyes strayed to her brooch. 'I trust that our friend Mendoza hasn't seen it?'

'Unfortunately he already has. The man has eyes like a magpie when it comes to searching out any bauble he believes belongs to his king.' Burghley spoke before Freida had a chance to. 'Luckily I noticed him antagonising our young cartographer friend here so was able to instruct a guard to intervene. It would seem he has already met with Walsingham to demand that the spoils of war should be returned. However, Her Majesty disagrees and thus for the present, everything remains in the Tower.'

'I agree with Her Majesty,' Drake replied, his teeth flashing as he smiled. 'I lost some of my men together with my brother, and my ship was almost sunk to claim that treasure for the queen. I have no intention of allowing it to return to King Philip. And Mistress Ortelius knows as well as anyone here how hard won any battle is with the Spanish, given that her fellow countrymen in the Low Countries must live under their tyranny and control. Her own husband sails that way even now.'

Freida turned to look at him. Willem had assured her that this time he was only taking his usual packages and samples to Calais before returning with similar items and letters for the inhabitants of Lime Street. Did Drake know something she didn't? Her hands prickled with sweat as she curled her fingers in her soft leather gloves. Drake raised his eyebrows at her as if answering her unspoken questions and she wondered when, or if, Willem would return.

Chapter Thirty-Four

April 1581

Despite constantly moving around the ship to ensure Mendoza couldn't approach her again, Freida felt his eyes watching her and she silently cursed the wretched brooch once again. She hadn't wanted it in the first place and now it seemed to torment her. She'd love nothing better than to pull it from her cloak and throw it over the side of the ship into the river to sink out of reach forever.

Eventually the queen and the newly knighted Sir Francis Drake boarded the royal barge and set off together back towards Westminster palace, leaving the other guests who'd travelled upriver with the royal party, Freida included, to find alternative craft. As she hesitated, unsure of how she was going to get home, she was ushered from the ship to the quay where other ladies of the court were boarding a smaller version of the queen's barge and she hastily followed, hoping they'd also be returning to the palace, as that was where Christopher and Guy would be waiting for her. All the while she kept looking out for Mendoza, breathing a sigh of relief as the boat moved off and he wasn't on it with them.

The return journey wasn't as joyful as the outgoing one, the crowds on the riverbank and the festivities now dispersed, the earlier sunshine replaced by a fast-falling, thick, damp fog as the temperature cooled. Sitting under the awning on the craft did nothing to protect the passengers and Freida was soon sodden, the wetness clinging to her clothes like a mould blooming on them. It became impossible to see the bank as they reached the quay and as she alighted, she looked around for Guy who'd assured her he'd be there by the time she returned. There were various lamps burning as other servants and guards waited for their mistresses to arrive, but of her steward there was no sign. Where could he have gone? Guy had been very firm that Christopher would run to alert him. Had the fog prevented her arrival from being seen in good time?

Standing on the quayside in the shelter of the palace's towering stone walls, which disappeared into the fog, she eventually decided she had no option than to attract the attention of one of the boatmen and hire him to take her back to Botolph's Wharf, from where she could walk home. Her teeth were gritted and her shoulders hunched. This was not a good situation for a lone woman to be in. There were a hundred cut-throats on the streets of London and it was murky and dank. Never had the city been so uninviting.

She managed to hire a small craft. As they slipped out into the silence of the river, the fog enveloping them and muting all other noise, for a moment she thought she could hear the plop of another pair of oars close by but she could see no ripples on the water indicating anything was there, and she told herself it was doubtless simply a swan. They frequently got in the way of the smaller boats especially when it was such low visibility.

The chill from the river didn't help her mood as she sat in the bow of the boat and invented a hundred different tortures for Christopher who appeared to have left his post for whatever reason. Then she reminded herself that she wouldn't need to deal with him; his apprenticeship in the household would be terminated immediately when Willem was informed of what had happened. That was if Guy even allowed him to remain in the house until her husband returned home.

Finally, after what felt like an age, they pulled up at the steps to the wharf and she paid the boatman before carefully climbing up the steps, holding on to the damp and slimy wall with one hand and lifting the front of her gown with her other one. Her new gloves would undoubtedly be ruined but it couldn't be helped. Walking up Botolph's Lane she attempted to get her bearings as to which way to walk next. She'd never been this far from Lime Street on her own. She was always accompanied by someone else; Liskin, together with a servant as protection, or Guy. And she'd never been out in such dense fog.

As she arrived at Fenchurch Street, giving wide berth to a man who was sprawled on the ground, she heard a slight scuffle behind her. Turning, she didn't catch sight of who it was before she felt a sharp blow to her head and she screamed, falling to the ground. Then a shout from somewhere up ahead, before she blacked out.

When she came to, she could see a light bobbing somewhere above her head and someone had a hand under her arm trying to pull her into a sitting position. Looking around, she could see she still appeared to be in Fenchurch Street but the back of her head was throbbing, her arm soaked from where she'd fallen in a puddle.

'What happened? Did I slip?' She got slowly to her feet, almost falling again as her foot became tangled in her skirts.

'No, mistress,' came a gruff reply from the man holding the lantern that was swinging beside her. Turning carefully, she drew her breath in sharply as the stab of pain in her head made her feel nauseous. The gentleman standing before her, a look of concern on his face, was well dressed, a merchant possibly guessing from his embroidered doublet in taffeta topped with a stiff starched white ruff. The feather in his cap drooped down while the damp fog swirled around them.

'I believe that you were set upon. I heard the footsteps of people running away as I arrived. You are lucky I happened to be walking along the street and heard you cry out. This fog makes it difficult to see anything, and some scoundrels will take advantage of that.'

Immediately Freida's hand went to her purse attached to her girdle but it was still there, the coins kept within heavy in her palm. Then she lifted her hand to the clasp of her cloak and she realised her brooch was missing. It may have just been a coincidence that a criminal had seen it and taken a chance, but she'd put the contents of her purse on it having been taken by one of Mendoza's henchmen.

'Do you require some assistance in getting home?' She realised that her rescuer was talking again.

'Thank you, I would be most grateful,' she replied. 'I accompanied the queen to Deptford and then when I returned the journeyman who had been instructed to wait for me was not in attendance. I was trying to make my way home alone but I am unfamiliar with the streets in the fog and I fear I am now lost.' As she explained she began to wonder if Christopher had been disposed of by Mendoza's men to ensure she would then be on her own. Initially she had been cross that he wasn't where he should have been, but now she was very worried as to what fate may have befallen him.

The gentleman introduced himself, explaining he was a goldsmith with a workshop at the Royal Exchange and that he was on his way home to his wife and six children. Feeling safer she leaned her arm on his proffered one and he walked with her to Lime Street. It was merely half a mile away, had she but known which direction she needed to be going in. As the house loomed into view, she felt tears well up in relief.

'Do come in and have a cup of ale,' she said, 'and something to eat. I am most grateful for your assistance today.'

'Thank you, my lady, but I will not. I must return to my home. I am delighted to have made your acquaintance and might I suggest you do not venture out again on your own in such inclement weather?' There was no danger of that and she reassured him before banging with her fist on the front door of her house, almost falling in as Guy opened it.

'Mistress?' he questioned as he stepped to one side and guided her in. Her head and shoulder where she'd fallen were by this time burning with pain but she hadn't liked to mention it to her good Samaritan. Now she was home she couldn't prevent the tears from welling up and running down her face. 'Mistress where is Christopher? He was told to wait for sight of you and come and collect me. And you have blood on your collar.' Immediately he called for a servant, sending one of the kitchen boys for a rosemary infusion from the stillroom and instructing another to get the physician. He helped Freida to one of the chairs beside the fire and stepped to one side as Nell helped her take her boots, cloak and gloves off.

'I do not know where he is,' she told Guy who was standing to one side, a concerned look on his face. 'When we returned to the palace he was nowhere to be seen. It was extremely foggy at the riverside and I did not wish to wait there on my own, unsure of whether he was coming back, so I decided to try to walk home.' A sharp intake of breath told her what Guy thought of that decision but even after what had happened, she couldn't see any other option. 'I was on Fenchurch Street and I felt something hit the back on my head and I fell,' she continued although even as she was saying it, she was wondering if she was remembering correctly. Perhaps she had just hit her head *after* she'd fallen?

'Were you robbed?' Guy continued questioning her, even though the physician had now arrived and was investigating the wound on the back of her head. Nell had dabbed some ointment of rosemary on it, and it was now stinging worse than it had been before.

'Not my coins—' she held her purse away from her girdle to show him '—but my brooch has gone.' She pointed to her cloak, which was now slung across a bench. By this point Liskin had arrived and she picked up the discarded cloak to check.

'You are right; it is missing. Whoever attacked you must have taken it. Have you no idea who it could have been?'

'I'm not certain, but I do remember a very distinctive smell. Myrrh and also a sharp spice such as turmeric, one that I have smelled before when those thugs broke into my atelier, and also on Mendoza. And he was at the festivities on board the *Golden Hinde*. He approached me but Lord Burghley's guards intervened. Do you think he followed me when we arrived back? He wasn't on the barge that I returned on. I didn't see which one he travelled in but I did wait a little while on the quayside, wondering where you were, or even Christopher, before I hired a boat to bring me to Botolph's Wharf. I do not imagine he pursued me, but I can believe he may have sent one of his men.'

'That would not surprise me at all,' Guy replied. He opened his mouth as if to continue but he was interrupted by noise and banging at the door. Freida sank into herself, trying to hide. Supposing it was Mendoza intending on finishing what he had started?

The door opened and instead of her enemy it was Willem who strode into the room, his tall ship's captain's leather boots ringing against the flagstone flooring.

'What is going on here?' he asked staring at the group assembled beside the fire.

'Mistress Freida has been set upon whilst out in the city.' Guy explained what had happened. Willem marched over to examine the wound on her head, wrapping his arms around her and almost lifting her from the chair.

'Someone had better explain to me why my wife was out alone in the city.' Willem spoke slowly, his voice cold and controlled and only Freida could tell how angry he was.

To her, however, he was tender as he ran his fingertips down her cheek. 'Thankfully it does not look too deep or serious,' he murmured looking at the physician who'd just arrived for agreement.

'You are correct; there is no danger here,' the doctor replied. 'See the apothecary for a honey poultice and all will be well.' Guy slipped some coins into his hand and showed him to the door.

'We were not expecting you yet, husband.' Freida laid her hand on Willem's arm as he settled on the chair beside her. 'You are usually gone longer than this.'

'I did not think to be home so soon either,' he replied, 'but I have been sent home and tasked by he who has my loyalty, he whom I will always stand beside, with an undertaking. One that with all my heart I do not wish to do, and yet I have no option. I have returned to carry out what I must. But now—' he smiled at her although she could see it didn't reach his eyes '—you should divest yourself of that heavy gown, which sadly is spoiled with blood from the wound on the back of your head.' He lifted her to her feet and Nell moved to help her upstairs. But the darkness of what Willem had just said clung to her. He hadn't elucidated on whatever he had been asked to do but it was something serious; she could tell from the look on his face, a sickening countenance lodged there. Her stomach churned and she felt a wave of nausea rise up from her gut. She was beginning to realise that danger followed her husband about like a multitude of ghosts, waiting to claim him for their own.

Chapter Thirty-Five

August 2022

'Hello, may I speak with Robyn please?' She hadn't recognised the number on her phone display, but the rounded deep voice of the caller didn't sound like a scam call, so cautiously she explained she was Robyn. 'Brilliant. My name is Margaret Cordwell and I've been given your details by a chap at Braithwaites' Auctioneers in Norwich. I believe you're in the possession of a map that used to belong to my family and were after any details I can give you?'

'Oh goodness yes, thank you so much for calling me,' Robyn replied. 'The map belongs to my father who's a dealer. We also have a shop in Hay-on-Wye. I've been doing some research on it. I traced it back to Braithwaites but all they could tell me was that they sold on behalf of someone in your family. Are you able to tell me anything more?' Robyn sat down on the sofa, a frisson of excitement fizzing inside her. Could this be the clue she needed to discover the story of how the map ended up at the shop?

'I'm happy to tell you what I know, but I have very little information about how we came to have it. It was sold in 1950 by my father because of the crippling inheritance tax when my grandfather died. We have a family estate here in Norfolk with a small manor house and several pieces of art, furniture and artefacts had to be sold, including your map. My father is no longer with us so I can't ask him why he decided on that particular piece to go, but I do remember him telling me there were rooms they hardly went into, filled with pieces nobody looked at, so that may well be why it was included.' Robyn felt her heart sink. It sounded as though Margaret didn't have any useful information.

'I do think, however, that some of my family history may help you,' Margaret continued, 'because a lot of the art and furniture was brought to our house by a chap called Henry in the seventeenth century. He married the eldest Cordwell daughter and moved here taking her surname. Apparently because she was the eldest child and due to inherit, her father had made it a condition of the marriage, to ensure the family name carried on. Which of course it did, because here I am, also a Cordwell.' She had a tinkly laugh that made Robyn smile.

'Thank you,' she said. 'I can try and research Henry. Do you have any other information about him?'

'Sadly not. I have a family tree one of my daughters drew up, but I don't know anything else about him. She's due home from travelling around Australia in the next couple of weeks. I can ask her if she knows anything else and get her to call you if she does?'

'Oh yes please, anything she knows could be just the clue I need.' They said their goodbyes and Robyn put her phone down. The map was laid out on the desk in front of her. She imagined she was walking along those narrow winding streets, smelling the bread, vegetables and hot meat being sold by traders on the streets, listening to their shouts encouraging buyers, and hooves clattering on cobbles. Feeling the constriction of clothing that was not designed for comfort: heavy and hot, skirts impeding progress. All manner of medieval London life was there, static on the parchment. And the ships sailing majestically on the seas, their sails full of wind, looked so peaceful and safe. If only. She could picture it all.

Her eyes drifted down to the bloodstain across the bottom. Had Henry had some sort of accident whilst bringing it with his worldly goods to his new bride's home? She wondered if she'd ever know.

'How was your trip to London?' Her father arrived in the shop five minutes after she'd unlocked the door. She'd put the map away again and was in the office with her laptop, several tabs open as she tried to research Cole's ledgers to see if she could find out any more details of Freida's possible commission whilst simultaneously trying to uncover a lead for Henry Cordwell. She was already clicking on links to try and find some sort of evidence that pointed to the volvelle at the British Museum belonging to Freida Ortelius, determined to prove the instrument on her map was indeed the one she'd viewed the previous day.

'I've got loads to tell you.' She wrapped her arms around her waist and tapped her foot on the floor, unable to keep still. 'I've just had a call from the daughter of the chap who put the map into the auction, so I have more leads to follow.'

She went on to explain what they'd discovered in London. 'If I can find an entry for the sale of the volvelle then I'll be far more certain the two items are definitely connected.' She bent closer to the screen as she scrolled through the lists, hoping her father would wander back out to the shop.

'And . . .' he cleared his throat '. . . how did you get on with Andrew Pointer? Have you a plan of action ready for next month?'

'It went fine, Dad, but before you ask, I didn't tell him I wanted to go ahead with the declaration. I just couldn't, but I did agree to him transferring the paperwork to a local solicitor who can handle everything for me. I know it isn't what you want to hear but it's a start isn't it?'

She blurted it out quickly then waited as the silence stretched out, second by second. To her surprise he said nothing and eventually she looked up from her laptop at him.

'I suppose it is,' he agreed. He sounded so tired and worn down, she felt a stab of guilt behind her breastbone. 'I thought you were beginning to move on. To stop watching your life flow away year after year. These past few weeks you've seemed more animated than I've seen you for a long time and I'd hoped it was the first steps of your recovery. I want you to live every minute of your life in technicolour, not black and grey. You deserve happiness, love, a family, the works. Don't waste it, my darling, because you're only here once.' He squeezed her hands and Robyn thought she heard a cracking in his voice. She knew she wasn't the only person who was suffering by her prevaricating.

'I know, Dad. I'm feeling better than I have in the past seven years. I know I need to do it but I keep thinking that it's so final. In my wedding vows I promised to love him forever, under any circumstances.'

'And so you will. Doing this won't diminish how you feel about Nate, how you'll always feel about him. But he's gone, Robyn, and you need to accept that and move on. I've got a business card somewhere for James Salcrest; he's a solicitor here in Hay. I've met him at a couple of business events. Give him a call and go and see him; get the paperwork transferred from London.'

'Then you'd have someone else to get on my case more locally, eh?' She smiled as she said it, but she knew that despite her attempts to appear positive and accepting of the situation on the outside, it wasn't quashing her pain deep inside. She recognised though that her father only wanted what was best, and that was why he kept encouraging her.

'That's not why I suggested him.' He returned her smile. 'I'm just trying to offer ideas to help in any way I can – you know that don't you?'

'Of course, and you're right. I promise I'll give him a call and put the wheels in motion.'

'Thank you.' Her father's voice was so quiet she barely heard him. Patting her on the shoulder her father turned at the sound of the shop bell ringing and once again she was on her own in the office. Picking up her phone she looked up the number of James Salcrest's office and scribbled it on the corner of her notebook. She'd walked past his office hundreds of times as they were around the corner from the old cinema and yet she'd never really noticed it. But she knew that now she was ready to go and speak with him. A call from the shop alerted her to the need to be helping her father out and she left her laptop to go and assist with the customers.

She didn't get back to her research until much later in the day after a wave of tourists who'd arrived on coaches filled the streets and pleasingly also filled the tills with cash. She'd sold several atlases, two facsimile globes and some of their unframed prints of the Mappa Mundi, an exquisitely illustrated medieval map of the world. She overheard one couple discussing how they were moving on to visit Hereford and she wondered if they realised they'd have the opportunity to view the largest and most complete version in existence at the cathedral, which somewhat eclipsed the prints just purchased.

Her father had put a lasagne in the oven and after a welcome shower Robyn settled down on the sofa to continue her investigations. She switched on the angle-poise lamp behind her as she slowly read through the ledger information.

Just at the point when she thought she couldn't look at the screen any longer she spotted it. For a moment she wondered if she was hallucinating after looking for so long, but there it was in black and white. An order by Freida Ortelius for a volvelle, for which she paid ten gold nobles. There was no mention of it being engraved, but perhaps he'd just decided to do it, or maybe she asked him later so it wasn't entered in the ledger. Everything was slowly beginning to make sense, as the pieces of the puzzle slipped into place.

Chapter Thirty-Six

April 1581

The mystery of Christopher's disappearance was solved three days later when his body was pulled from beneath London Bridge where the swirling, churning waters of the great river threw up everything that had drifted downstream. Guy went to arrange his burial. On his return he grimly informed Freida and Willem that the young man had met a violent death.

'His head was barely on his neck.' He held the back of his hand to his mouth as if he were about to vomit. 'His throat was slit, ear to ear, and his guts were spilled from his belly.' Freida sank down onto the chair behind her. She was certain there was only one person who would have arranged such a killing, another reminder that no one in the household was safe. Wherever she lived she attracted danger and death.

A pall of sadness lay over the household and everyone felt nervous; Freida could see it in their eyes. She'd inadvertently invited this into their home. Once again there were guards at every external door. Despondently she spent her days finishing the final lines on the map to her satisfaction and prepared it to be printed. Then she went to find Willem and gave him the gift she'd been hiding.

'I have heard of these,' he told her, unwrapping the velvet wrapped around it and turning the shining brass instrument in his fingers. His delight was palpable. The fine lines at his eyes crinkled up as he smiled. Where he had been sailing and squinting into the sun his face was a deep brown, the white lines fanning across to his hairline where the furrows hadn't tanned. She smiled as she ran her fingertips along them. 'But I have never seen one. Can you show me how it works?'

'It will be my pleasure,' she answered, so pleased to see his obvious delight and knowing that it would help him in future sailings. With the aid of several pieces of parchment on which she drew diagrams, she explained how it would help him.

Since he'd let slip that he'd been asked to undertake a job he was unhappy about, she'd noticed he was preoccupied all of the time and often disappeared for hours at a time, or was hidden away with Guy in the parlour with the door locked. She'd asked both Guy and Emanuel what this secret was that was taking so much of her husband's time, but they had both apologised and refused to tell her anything. The parlour door was suddenly locked all the time, even when he was inside. She'd resorted to listening at the door when she heard him talking, but she could hear nothing bar a deep muffled murmuring of his voice through the thick oak. Nell had caught her on one occasion, raising her eyebrows and saying nothing as she swept past. Freida didn't care what anyone else thought. Something was being planned and there was a tense atmosphere in the house, which had never been there before. Her shoulders were permanently stiff, her jaw clenched as she tried to discover what the secrecy was about.

Later the same day, Willem accompanied her to the printers whilst two servants carried the precious plate of her map through the city streets. It was wrapped in a large piece of fustian cloth and constantly Freida's eyes darted around, watching the shadows between the houses and shops for Mendoza's men. Any sudden movement or shout from one of the many people who crowded the streets and jostled against them made her head twist around, eyes wide with fear. Willem had one arm around her and the other holding the hilt of his sword at all times but she still couldn't stop her heart from racing.

Where they lived amongst the quiet scientists and naturalists there was no requirement for a sword when out walking, although she knew that he kept a dagger permanently hidden in his boots. And it was beside him at night, inside the drapes where he could snatch it out at a moment's notice and sink it into another man's flesh. She couldn't be squeamish about it; she knew that his battles at sea involved the killing of men before his enemies got the chance to do it to him. It was his life and she'd married him knowing who and what he was.

Whilst the map was being printed, Freida started to clean up her workshop. She was accompanied by Jacob, happily sweeping with a small version of the broom she was using, made for him by Guy. Since the incident with Mendoza's henchmen, she didn't let the boy out of her sight when she was at home. The threats the ambassador's henchman had dripped into her ears months before haunted her dreams. And having experienced how stealthy and silent those rogues could be, she was endlessly vigilant.

Two weeks after Willem's return, Freida was surprised to find him dressing one morning in an elaborate velvet doublet of deep burgundy with flashes of gold in the slashes at the tops of the sleeves, similar to the embroidery around the bindings. It matched a pair of puffed breeches with the same gold lining, and white silk hose. At his neck a snowy white ruff splayed out.

'Willem, you are looking extraordinarily elegant this morning,' she commented, running her hand down the soft cloth stretched across his broad back. 'I have never seen you wearing clothes such as these. You would not be amiss at the English court . . .' Her voice tailed off as she realised what she'd said. 'Are you going to court, my love? You know Her Majesty has said she does not wish to ever see you there. She merely tolerates you by refusing to acknowledge to whom I am wed.'

'Do not worry,' he replied. 'Although I am going to the palace at Westminster, I am not going to pay court to the queen and there is no reason for her to know that I have been there. She is, I am reliably informed, residing at Greenwich at present. I am going to visit Sir Francis Walsingham.'

'The queen's spymaster? For what reason would you wish to visit him?'

'I cannot divulge, but I promise you that if I could think of a way to avoid what is going to take place then with all

270

my heart and prayers to the Lord Almighty, I would. But these trials are above us, outside our control. I will explain everything to you when the time is right and I shall allow no danger to come knocking at our door.' With a chaste and brief kiss on her lips he was gone, his heavy boots hitting the floor and making it vibrate under her velvet slippers.

Her heart was beating fast as she pleated the fabric of her skirts between her fingers. His comment regarding danger had not comforted her at all, merely heightening her unease that something was very wrong if Walsingham wanted to see Willem. She couldn't help the thought that the crisp white linen of his ruff would be stained scarlet with his blood if this was some sort of trap.

With her fears crawling through her body, making her head ring with panic, she could do nothing but pace the floor and await his return. She held tightly to Jacob for a while, but eventually he became tired of his mother's rigid grip and no number of cuddles would stop his fractious cries so she passed him to Nell and continued walking around the great hall on her own, one ear permanently attuned to the sound of horses coming along the street. Willem had taken Guy with him, and she could always tell the particular dancing trot of her husband's palfrey on the cobbles outside.

The familiar austere framed portraits on the walls against the glossy polished wood of the panelling became her acquaintances as she traversed the room, and she found herself making up stories of their lives in her head to try to divert her uneasiness. It didn't work though, and she carried on pacing even when dinner was laid on the table in the dining chamber and the rest of the household gathered to eat the roast pork, beef and vegetables that were laid out.

Finally, Nell came to her, her face creased with worry. 'Freida, whatever is the matter?' She pulled her gently to a chair beside the fire and placed a cup of wine in her hand. 'Has something happened?'

Turning to her friend, Freida had tears in her eyes. 'I do not know.' She took a mouthful of wine and felt its warmth steal down inside, further and further down. 'Willem has gone to meet with Walsingham. He took Guy and they have been gone for hours. I know something is wrong, terribly wrong. Willem tried to warn me but said he could not tell me more. I can feel trepidation in the air; it is rough and scratchy when I breathe in and out, catching in my throat and threatening to suffocate me. There is no reason why Willem would be summoned to the palace unless something awful had happened. Or is going to happen. I am greatly afeared he is not coming back and that the queen has arranged this meeting to be rid of my husband forever.'

'You are thinking too much of it,' Nell said sharply, lifting her hand as if to slap it down on Freida's own, which twisted and turned together in her lap, then lowering it slowly. 'You are behaving like the people on stage at the playhouse, with much overacting to make the audience excitable. There is nothing to worry about, and yet you are determined that there shall be. Take another cup of wine and I will sit and wait with you until Willem returns.'

Freida was not pleased with the comparison between herself and the players at the theatre who were often crude and loud, but she nodded and remained in her chair drinking wine and staring into the fire. All the time though her whole body listened to the sounds on the street outside the door, and as twilight began to fall and the servants lit the candles

272

around the hall, she finally heard the hooves she'd been waiting for. She thrust her cup at Nell who was sitting quietly humming as she played cards. She ran to the door, wrenching it open.

Jumping from his horse, Willem threw the reins at a stable boy, as did Guy, and together they walked in, the steward immediately slipping away into the shadows at the corners of the room on his way to the kitchen.

'Now will you tell me what is going on?' The relief that Freida felt at the sight of her husband arriving home was replaced by a red-hot anger. One that had been building up over the preceding weeks and that she could no longer suppress. She wouldn't be ignored by him any longer. Her hands on her hips she stood in front of her husband, preventing him from moving further into the hall.

'Naturally I will, my love.' He smiled, but it didn't reach his eyes where she could see uneasiness as he looked around the hall and not at her. 'First though I must eat and drink. Despite the opulence of the palace, there was very little offered in way of victuals – save some ale, plums and cheese – which does not stop a man from starving over the course of a day.'

Frustrated, Freida couldn't wait for a servant to bring something, instead running into the kitchen where she saw Guy standing at the table with a dish piled with the remains of dinner. Grabbing a pewter charger from the top of a chest, she piled it with bread before snatching up the last of the cold pork from the table, some apples and ginger cake, balancing it on one hand in order to carry a large beaker of ale in the other. Backing out of the door and opening it with her bottom, she hurried back to the fire where Willem was waiting.

Eventually he finished eating, refusing to engage in conversation until he'd quite finished, wiping the back of his hand across his mouth. He placed the platter and his cup on the small table placed beside his chair.

'You will not like what I have to tell you.' His voice was grave as he kept his eyes locked on hers. 'But you must trust me when I tell you that we have no choice in this matter and I will never allow harm to come to our son.' Freida grabbed his hands in hers and held them tight.

'Look at me, Willem,' she whispered, 'and tell me what you speak of.'

Chapter Thirty-Seven

September 2022

Robyn put the lid down on her laptop, tapping her fingertips on her teeth as she stared out of the window. She'd reached a dead end in her investigation and she needed a new path to head down. She was so close to proving this was the map made for Drake but there were holes in her research, and without closing the gap, the provenance simply wasn't good enough. The tale wasn't yet told and she was desperate to learn the rest of Freida's story, but she was worried her trail had petered out.

She was still sitting and musing when there was a light tap on the office door and, looking up, she saw the smiling face of Sam peering around the edge.

'Surprise.' He grinned. 'I've got a couple of days off and I wanted to see how you're getting on with your map. I hope I'm not disturbing you. Your dad sent me through, but he said he's a bit busy so can you go and help him?'

'Oh, of course.' She hastily kissed Sam on the cheek as

she hurried past. She was so absorbed in her research that she kept forgetting her day job during the busiest time of the year.

It was lunchtime before she was able to join Sam again in the office.

'I hope this is okay, me arriving without invitation? After our trip to the British Museum, I wanted to know what else you've discovered. I know I could have just called, but here I am anyway.' He pulled an apologetic face and she laughed.

'You're welcome any time; you know that.' She wagged her finger but couldn't help grinning at him. 'I have got a little further with my search, although I've reached a dead end now.' She explained everything she'd found out about the volvelle and also about Henry Cordwell. 'There's the possibility that Margaret's daughter may have other information about him. I'll have to wait and see if she calls me. I think my next task is to see if I can unearth any Ortelius descendants who are alive now. I know that isn't likely but I need to have tried everything. I'm beginning to understand Freida's story but what I still don't know is why this map is so different to others done at the time. A female cartographer would surely be the sort of ancestor that would be talked about, or that they may have some record of? I need to start a new line of enquiry. Ha, the old investigative journalist is back on course. I knew I hadn't lost it. I blew enough scandals wide open over the years with my tenacity, and I'm determined to follow this to the end.' Another piece of the shroud that had veiled her fell away as the old Robyn shone through brightly, the shadows of the past seven years beginning to fade. Pulling her laptop in front of her she began to type.

'Shall I go to the café and get some sandwiches?' Sam suggested. 'This may take a long time and we're going to need to keep our energy levels up.'

Between spells of serving in the shop, Robyn and Sam tried googling every search term they could think of to discover anyone who may be related to Freida's family. Sam had found the marriage of an infamous army captain who'd been decorated in the Napoleonic Wars to a girl with the surname Ortel in the early nineteenth century.

'It says Ortelius in brackets afterwards so it appears she may have shortened her name. Could she be a descendant of Freida do you think?' he asked. 'There aren't many details about her; most of this article is about him and the number of soldiers he killed. Her name was Johanna.'

Robyn quickly entered 'Johanna Ortelius' into her search engine, her fingers shaking slightly and her breath held as she typed. 'I can see the same article as you have about the chap she was married to—' she scrolled down further '—and she had seven children. Oh.' She turned her mouth down at the edges and looked across at Sam. 'Only two of them survived after a big typhoid outbreak in 1836. How awful.'

'Does it say the names of the children?' Sam asked.

'Nope. Damn, I thought we were onto something there. I'm not giving up now. I'll try searching for Ortel as a surname; perhaps it was shortened at some point over the years.' Robyn scrolled down her screen. 'Bingo! Well, possibly. Look, there are three people on Facebook with the surname Ortel. I'm going to message them all and see what happens.' Before she could change her mind, she sent each of them a quick message explaining that she was doing some research into the Ortelius family and enquiring whether they were related. She kept it vague; she had no intention of mentioning the map just yet.

By mid-afternoon the following day she'd received replies from two of them. One explained it was her married name and her husband said he had no idea of any Ortelius connection, but the other response sounded more promising. An Annemieke Ortel living north of Amsterdam who confirmed she was indeed descended from the Ortelius family line.

'As you know, I didn't mention the map in my initial enquiry,' Robyn explained to Sam, 'but she and her father have an antique map sales business in Amsterdam. Spooky, eh? It has to be more than a coincidence.'

'I agree. Surely they must be descendants of the Ortelius family,' he replied.

'She's invited me to visit if I'm ever over there.' Robyn pulled a face. 'So I'm hoping to go as part of my "research".' She made quote marks with her fingers. 'I'll head over there as soon as I can organise it and meet up with her.'

'I have an idea.' Sam got to his feet adding, 'Do you want a coffee?'

'That sounds good,' she answered. 'Shall we go out and get one?' Nodding his agreement Sam pulled his shoes and coat on whilst Robyn quickly found her handbag and led the way through to the shop where Alison was helping her father. They worked together so well, happy to spend all day with each other and once again Robyn was reminded that her days of living upstairs needed to end, to allow her father and Alison to fully live their lives as they wished. The flat would be too small for three of them, but now finally moving out didn't feel the impossible situation it once did.

The weather had turned during the past week and it appeared summer was over. In the next few days, the children would be going back to school and the autumnal chills were already knocking at the door demanding to be let in, but the café at the end of the street was steamy and warm. There were still plenty of customers enjoying afternoon tea, their cake stands piled high with sandwiches and tiny scones. Robyn ordered two coffees and some chocolate brownies, smiling at the waitress, a girl she recognised as one of a cohort of university students who spent their summer breaks helping out in local businesses.

'When were you thinking of visiting Holland?' Sam asked. 'Can your dad spare you?'

'I mentioned it in passing earlier, and he's fine. There are only a couple of weeks left of tourist season left now so trade is starting to slow down.'

'In that case I have an idea that may just work for you. I have to take the yacht for a test run after the recent repairs, so I could sail her over to The Hague and moor up there. If you fancy coming along, we could go and meet your Dutch connection and see what else we can find out? When are you thinking of going?'

'As soon as possible!' Robyn grinned. 'Thank you, that would be amazing.'

'There is something to do first.' He looked down at his fingers laced within each other and paused. Robyn wondered if he was about to do 'Here's the Church' with his fingers.

'What?' she prompted after the silence stretched into several seconds; although she knew what he was going to say.

'You need to go and sign the paperwork at the solicitors to start the process for Nate. I know what you're going to say.' He held his hand up to stop her interrupting. He was right; she was already opening her mouth. 'That this is blackmail, but I promise it isn't. I'm making you go and do what's best for you because I care about you. You've been skirting around the issue all summer despite your dad, Martha, Wendy and Dan, all of us asking you to make the declaration when the time comes. You can't run forever, Robyn, and now you've reached the end of the road. Autumn is just around the corner. Go and see that chap your dad suggested and give him the information he needs. Then we'll sail to Amsterdam and try to find the final piece to the puzzle of your map.' He pushed his chair back and stood up, bending to kiss the top of her head. 'I need to go to Cherbourg and prepare to leave. Meet the solicitor and follow me down next week. I can stop off at Dover and collect you. Bring warm clothes; it'll be cold off the east coast.'

She sat on her chair not moving, even when she heard the door close quietly behind her and she knew he'd gone. Sam had been her stalwart, her rock over the past seven years and especially over the summer as she battled everyone and her own inner demons to stop time and prevent the inevitable as the date drew closer and closer. But now he'd drawn a red line and, in her heart, she knew he was right. She wanted him to take her to Holland and try to discover why Freida Ortelius had drawn such a map for Queen Elizabeth and also perhaps find out why it had what she still suspected to be a large bloodstain. And why it was decorated with an instrument that now lay in the British Museum. Now she needed to be brave and go and see the solicitor.

Freida had pushed herself to become a strong woman, one worthy of her commission in an era when women had to fight for any sort of recognition. She was an inspiration now, nearly four hundred and fifty years later, her strength helping Robyn to see that she could also do something that for years she had thought she couldn't. The day had come and she accepted it was time to let Nate go. Everyone was right. She was ready.

Tuesday dawned bright, the sun a red ball on the horizon. Robyn had been lying awake since the first birds had started the dawn chorus after a restless night. Knowing she wouldn't be able to sleep again she pulled on a pair of jogging trousers and a hoodie. It was noticeably cooler in the mornings; Sam was right that she'd need warm clothes on the yacht. She slipped out of the flat and down onto the street, which was empty apart from the occasional pigeon and seagull that flew up into the air shrieking at her disturbing their peace as they picked at rubbish left in the gutter.

Without even thinking about it, Robyn knew where she was going, her feet finding their way down the paths towards the river. She needed to be with Nate, to tell him what she was about to do, and there was only one place she could do that.

In the copse it was gloomy, the sun not yet high enough in the sky to break through the canopy of leaves. Reaching their tree, she leaned against it and slid to the ground, the rough bark scratching against her spine despite her sweatshirt. She'd lost weight over the summer, the pressure of what was to come making regular meals seem unnecessary.

The world was following its cycle. Year after year it kept

revolving as the seasons carried on turning. But Nate wasn't there to watch them. She'd never have his children to run around catching the leaves as they drifted to the ground. He wasn't coming back; and now she had to move on with her life. To finally end this limbo of wanting and waiting. Today was the day she started the end to this torture. So why did it feel like her heart was breaking all over again? Tears ran slowly down her cheeks to drip off her chin, her forehead resting on her knees.

She picked up a yellow leaf from the ground beside her and pushed it into the front pocket of her hoodie. A small heart already dying and turning gold, heralding the end of the season, of its growing year. A final blaze of glory before it fell to the earth to turn into mulch and provide the nutrients for next year's growth.

'The autumn leaves are turning, Nate,' she whispered. 'I can't wait any longer for you to come home and dance in them. You'll never stop dancing in my heart but the time has come to say goodbye. To tell the world you're never coming home.'

Chapter Thirty-Eight

September 2022

Despite her father's insistence she should dress smartly to visit James, she ignored him and wearing her jeans and the same hoodie she'd worn earlier she set off to the solicitor's office. Her heart was thumping so hard she could feel it pulsing in her neck. She pulled up the hood of her sweat-shirt, trying to find comfort in the dark enclosed interior; it had worked before, but this time it failed her.

As she approached the office, her feet started to slow down but she kept on putting one foot in front of the other. She pushed the door open and gave her name to the smiling receptionist and despite the suggestion that she take a seat, Robyn paced up and down waiting for her name to be called. It was only a few minutes but it felt like hours and she clenched her fists with the effort of not walking back out of the door.

'Robyn, how lovely to see you.' James was standing outside his office, a welcoming smile on his face. She'd seen him around town as they both went about their business and she'd wave a hand if he passed the shop, but she'd never met up with him in his professional status. He'd handled the legalities when her mother had passed away and she knew her father's will was lodged with him. Ushering her into his office he closed the door behind her. Sliding into the seat he proffered she tried to smile, but she could feel how tight and false it was. She sat on her hands.

'So, how can I help you today?' he asked. Robyn opened her mouth to explain and then shut it again. Could she actually get the words out? Now she was here, every part of her was desperate to not say the words out loud. It was almost as if she physically couldn't say them.

'My husband, Nate. He went missing during a yacht race,' she blurted out. Her eyes filled with tears and she cursed herself out loud. Just for once she needed to explain what had happened to him without crying. Wordlessly he pushed a box of tissues across the desk towards her and gratefully she pulled three out and blew her nose noisily. He was obviously prepared for near-hysterical clients.

'I did hear about that,' he replied. 'I recall it being in the paper and someone mentioned that he was related to the owner of the map shop. How very sad for you.'

'It is, yes.' Robyn nodded. 'And it'll be the seven-year anniversary the week after next. I have to declare him dead so our assets can be put in order and I need a death certificate for various agencies.' She took a deep breath before continuing, 'I've been blocking it from my mind for years but now the date is almost upon me and I can't put it off any longer.'

'Of course.' He nodded as he scribbled notes on a yellow lined pad. 'You can go online and make the declaration yourself if you wish. There's a government website and it'll take you through every step, or I can do it for you. We'll need to advertise it in the *London Gazette* and there are various other legalities to go through but they're straight-forward. And then you can inform everyone who needs to know.'

'I'd rather you did it. If it's left to me, I'll never do it. I can't bring myself to fill in his details and submit the form. The solicitor we used in London for our wills has said he will forward everything that he has if you contact him.' She passed Andrew Pointer's business card across the desk, relieved that she'd remembered to push it into her back pocket. 'And when it's done, I need to sort out our flat in London and decide what I want to do with it, whether I want to move back there and pick up where my life paused but never restarted.' She looked out of the window where the trees swayed in a brisk wind. 'Or whether I find a house and live here permanently. I don't think my dad and Alison really imagined that I'd be here playing gooseberry for the rest of their days.'

'Of course. You don't need to make up your mind just yet though – all of this will take a couple of months. I'll send you an email with the details of the procedure and my fees and if you're happy with it all then just let me know and I'll start the process.' He smiled at her and she realised the meeting was over. Getting to her feet she shook his hand and then left the office.

'I'm sorry, Nate,' she whispered. 'You'll always be in my heart but I cannot stop it happening, not now.' Everyone had told her she'd feel like a great weight had been lifted when she finally did what needed to be done, but it hadn't happened. Not yet. But that day would come; she was sure of it. Her hand closed around the dead leaf in her pocket, squeezing it between her fingers like the constriction around her heart.

Chapter Thirty-Nine

May 1581

'I have something very grave to tell you,' Willem began. Freida felt her stomach roll as if it was about to expel the wine she'd drunk earlier. Her legs began to shake and she pushed her hands onto her knees as if to stop them. She could tell by the grey pallor beneath the brown of his face, the lines etched into his skin, that he was about to divulge something terrible.

'When I told you of my visit to Amsterdam, I did not tell you the whole truth, and for that I apologise. Whilst I was there I met with the Prince of Orange and he asked of me an assignment, a task I cannot refuse. It has been arranged with the help of our friend Walsingham because he controls all security at the Spanish Embassy, and today I was told the full extent of what I must do.'

'The Spanish Embassy?' She repeated what he had said, unable to grasp what he was saying. Why would he have anything to do with the people who'd been threatening her, their family, their servants for months? Had he forgotten Christopher had been murdered the night she'd been attacked? Slowly she closed her mouth from where it hung open. 'Sorry, my love, but I do not understand what you are saying to me. I am confused. You met again with William of Orange, despite my entreaties to not do so? That was reckless and dangerous.'

'Freida.' He took hold of her hand and with his fingers under her chin he tilted her face so that she was looking at him. 'Everything I do is reckless and dangerous. I sail the seas between England and the Low Countries, fighting with the Spanish when I am required to do so. Meeting with the prince is no worse than that. Although that which he and Walsingham have asked me to do is of the greatest peril we will ever face.'

'Please tell me, what have they asked of you?' she whispered.

'The prince wishes to double cross the Spanish ambassador. To make him believe I am prepared to accept a bribe and enter a conspiracy to surprise the English garrison housed at Flushing who now hold the port for England. Then we will hide our ships along the coast and attack the Spanish fleet when it arrives, using the map you have made for Drake to assist us.'

'I do not understand. He has asked you to deceive the Spanish ambassador in this most perilous of ways whilst he stays hidden and safe in Holland? And to use the help of Francis to do so? I trust you told him that you will not accept this request; we cannot bring any more danger to our door.'

'I am unable to deny what he has asked of me. He is very close to finally ridding our homeland of the Spanish

288

and this could be the turning point – if I can persuade Mendoza I am sincere in what I am proposing.'

'Willem, this is sheer foolishness! He will not believe a word you say. You are a *Sea Beggar*, most hated by the Spanish. You will be killed and probably the rest of us too, once you are dispensed with.' Her horrified words were tumbling out one over the other in her haste to stop him from even considering such a plot.

'That is precisely why it is more likely to succeed,' he explained, keeping his voice calm, the antithesis of how Freida was speaking. 'Because we are sworn enemies, I will approach Mendoza and tell him he has won. That I fear for my family and am therefore offering a solution so we might stop the feud once and for all, and he may leave us alone. I am due to visit him tomorrow. I met with Walsingham today because his spies had informed him that the ambassador is currently out of the city so I would not be seen. And I was dressed as a courtier so blended in well with the others who walk the corridors of the royal palaces.'

'I cannot listen to any more of this.' Freida got to her feet, brushing her hands down her skirts. 'I forbid you to continue with this proposal.'

'Unfortunately it is not you who decides. I have no choice if I wish to support my prince. And that I will do.' His statement fell into the silence in the room as the door to Freida's atelier banged in the distance.

Chapter Forty

May 1581

'The bait has been laid,' Willem said, looking around the table where Emanuel and Guy were sitting. Freida had joined them even though Willem had told her to remain in the solar. With a strength and resolve that was growing every day, she ignored him and sat down with the men. 'I have accepted a bribe of one thousand ducats to enter into a conspiracy with him to surprise the English at Flushing. It went even better than I had thought, or that Walsingham and the Prince of Orange had hoped it might. We were not expecting Mendoza to think it was his own idea, but it appears he will pay me to be a turncoat and sink his own ships.' He roared with laughter, his white teeth flashing in his bronzed face. Emanuel and Guy joined in his obvious delight. 'There is, however, a difficulty with the plan—' his voice became serious again '—some danger I had not predicted, although it is nothing that I cannot overcome.' At this point he looked across at Freida, his face no longer full of laughter.

'What sort of problem?' she asked. 'What could be even more dangerous?' The air in the room crackled with a foreboding that had not been there before and a beat of fear trembled in her chest.

'It will be necessary,' he began, 'nay it has been agreed, that I will provide a hostage for Mendoza. A guarantee he will not be deceived and my intentions are honourable. I am sorry, my love, that I must do this but I promise you with all my heart that no harm will come to him. He will be well looked after.'

Freida looked between Willem and Emanuel, who both now looked incredibly guilty. Whilst Willem did at least have the courage to look her in the face, Emanuel was now looking down at his hands on the table, his long fingers locked together.

'I do not understand.' Her voice wavered. 'Who will be safe? What do you mean a guarantee? You have already admitted that you do indeed propose to mislead him as he suspects. The plot is extremely dangerous so what else has been agreed?' In the pause that followed she added in a quiet voice, 'Tell me now, Willem.'

'It is Jacob. We must let Mendoza have Jacob as a hostage until he is certain we are not fooling him. But have no fear because there are plans afoot to ensure he will be snatched back from the embassy.'

'Jacob?' Her voice, usually demure and quietly spoken, screeched out so loudly that even her own ears rang with the sound. It was immediately followed by the pounding of feet as various servants close by came running. 'Why are you speaking of our precious son?' Her voice hadn't lowered at all but Willem quickly waved away the servants.

'Hush.' He got up from his seat and held on to Freida's

shoulders as he crouched down so his face was level with hers. 'Let me explain and you will see you have nothing to fear.' Pulling up a stool he sat down next to her, holding both her hands in his as if she may flee at any moment.

'This is the final act of war I will undertake for the prince, I promise. You will need to pack our belongings, for we shall escape home to Amsterdam as soon as my mission is complete.'

'But what if you fail?' she replied. 'Mendoza will kill our boy. He may do it anyway – he's threatened enough times. I cannot allow you to do this. Send me as hostage instead. Or I shall take Jacob and hide with him, somewhere you cannot find us.'

'He will not harm a hair on Jacob's head. I have given you my promise.'

Freida turned to Emanuel. 'Cousin, surely you can explain to my husband what a terrible plan this is?'

'It is not my place,' he admitted. 'It is my greatest wish that our homeland is ruled by our prince, and Willem is to be a part of the device that finally makes it happen. I have to support him. And I firmly believe our friend Walsingham will ensure the safety of your child, for it was I who went to him to avail him of the plot. You can be assured there are many of Walsingham's men within the Spanish embassy, and the security within is under his jurisdiction; he will appoint the staff who care for Jacob and the guards who watch over him night and day. Your son will be as safe there as he is here. If not more so.'

'How can he be? I am here to make sure he is safe, his own mother. You are sending him into the middle of the enemy's camp.'

'As we speak the prince's man Christiaen the Elder is on a ship sailing to England at the invitation of Walsingham. He will be secreted in Emanuel's home until the time comes when he will infiltrate the embassy to coordinate the rescue of our boy.'

'What do you mean, rescue? The more you tell me the more outrageous your claims become! You told me he will be in no danger and now you talk of rescuing him, which would not be required unless he is going to be exactly that, in extreme peril! Did you leave your senses behind with your prince?'

'There is no point shouting about it, my love.' Willem held his arms out to the sides in appeal. 'I have no choice in the matter. I agreed to do this task and I must fulfil my promise.'

'When?' Freida spoke through gritted teeth. She could taste blood in her mouth where she had bitten the inside of her cheek. 'When is this happening?'

'We have about a week,' Willem admitted. 'I must await Christiaen's arrival and then the plan will be carried out, and we will be on our way home to Amsterdam.'

'Except that once Mendoza discovers you have fooled him, we will all be dead, starting with our son. He has said he wants Jacob because he does not trust you. And rightly so.'

'I believe he does now have faith in me. I have led him to think that I will sell my allegiance for the gold. It is not difficult to fool someone like him; he only sees in others a reflection of himself. You must complete your map for the queen and deliver it as promised so Mendoza does not suspect anything, then pack up all of our belongings. I will have them taken to the *Windfly* under the cover of darkness and when Christiaen has rescued Jacob we will sail before Mendoza even realises our son is taken.'

Freida knew at that moment nothing she could say or do would deter Willem from this perilous mission. He had given his word and he would not go back on that. She could only think of one person who could intervene, one person who could tell Walsingham who it seemed was co-ordinating everything from his safe home at Mortlake to prevent the murder of her son. The queen.

Freida wouldn't let Jacob out of her sight. Where she went, he went. If Nell was confused, she didn't say anything, just bringing her sewing, stitching a new night-rail for the little boy and sitting wordlessly, her head over the tiny stitches and keeping quiet. Freida knew she wouldn't be able to take Nell back home with her if Willem's plan went ahead, and she'd been sworn to secrecy so couldn't tell her companion what was troubling her. Although she'd shortly be breaking that vow. She had to try something to stop Mendoza taking her child.

The day after Willem had spoken to her, the two copies of her map were returned, together with her plate, which was now resting again on its wooden easel. Freida gently ran her fingertips across the beauty of the finished piece. The printers had used a thick, viscous oil-based ink, which was spread liberally across the plate before being pressed in with a starched piece of cheesecloth. It was essential it went into every tiny crevice and reservoir or the map wouldn't be complete when printed. Every undulation, each line was now slightly raised from the parchment and as she stroked it, she imagined she was feeling her own fingerprints in the contours upon the map. She had placed a part of herself in it, something unique and distinctive that would always connect them together.

After sending out for a length of heavy linen she immediately began backing each map with three pieces of the fabric, pushing her needle through the stiff layers methodically as her mind constantly turned over the task ahead of her. If she couldn't persuade the queen to intervene then she'd fail in all that she had tasked herself with, her lifelong responsibility. To protect her son, her husband. Her family. This time she was going to stop the Spanish from killing her family.

With the maps finally completed, Freida carefully wrote her name across the bottom of each, before adding a diagram of his volvelle to Willem's. She was proud of what she'd achieved over the months since she'd been given the commission.

She went next door to find Liskin. If her cousin and friend was surprised to see Jacob toddling beside her, she said nothing. Freida wondered how much she knew but she'd been warned to say nothing and in this she was in agreement. The fewer of her family who knew the better; they were less likely to also be in danger. She was determined to protect them all with her life, as she would do for Jacob and Willem.

'I have to attend court tomorrow,' she explained. 'The map the queen requested for Drake is now complete and I have had word she will receive me after dinner. Could you please come and assist me in dressing once more? None of the maids attend my hair as you do, nor does Nell see the correct colours to wear.'

'Of course I will,' Liskin assured her. 'I enjoy doing it. I do not have the opportunity to see the fine spectacle of the queen's court for myself so I must await your tales when you return.'

Freida smiled at her, but inside her heart was beating erratically with what she was going to try and do when speaking with the queen.

As promised Liskin was with Freida late morning the following day, to begin the laborious task of dressing her: shift, petticoat, bum roll, stomacher, kirtle and finally her gown, the sleeves requiring attaching with ribbons through the eyelets at the top. At Liskin's suggestion Freida was wearing her gold silk gown made with the fabric Willem had given to her as a New Year's gift, the spring having suddenly caught everyone unawares with a burst of heat. The gowns she'd worn to the palace over the winter, the damask and velvet, would be far too warm, and the smell that often emanated from others in the queen's circle of nobilities was a sign of how inappropriate clothing could be unpleasant. Her sleeves were cream silk set with seed pearls caught in gathers, and embroidered cuffs, with the stiff linen ruff at her neck in a creamy colour to match. As before, Liskin piled her hair up on her head and fixed a small jewelled headdress on the back of her head.

When she could put it off no longer, Freida wrapped the map in a piece of oilcloth and walked with Guy and Willem to the river. She was still finding it hard to speak to her husband, giving him monosyllabic curt answers when he spoke to her. The love she had held for him close to her heart was now wavering and threatening to turn to hate. She was thankful he'd wait for her at the gatehouse as he

296

had previously but given his betrayal of her – his family – she wondered if he'd still be there when she left. She couldn't trust him anymore and in the long dark hours of the night as she lay awake, she wondered if she ever would again.

The sun was marking deep shadows from the headstones that stood in the graveyard at St Andrew Undershaft as the clock tower rang out for two o'clock. She'd become used to the sound of it ringing every hour day and night, the backdrop of sounds as she conducted her life in London. It would never be the same again. Now it sounded as if it were tolling for the dead. She shuddered. As they approached the river she could smell the drains that flowed into it, the waste from the city's inhabitants running down the streets and into the water. The sudden warm weather created a stench that made her pull her pomander to her nose to try and mask it. The scent of lavender did not completely get rid of it, but the sweetness gave her something to concentrate on.

Once they were in a wherry on the river the smell lessened a little as a cool breeze blew across and the air was clearer as she alighted on the quay below the palace. She ignored the arm Willem proffered and walked with her back straight and in silence to the gatehouse.

'We will wait here,' Willem told her and she inclined her head in acknowledgement before following the guards in front of her. For the first time she wasn't frightened about meeting Mendoza whilst she was there. This time she was going to petition the queen to intervene and risk the potential of Willem's fury. She'd never felt it turned on herself; however, she'd witnessed it after the attack on her the day of her visit to the *Golden Hinde*. And it was frightening even when she wasn't the recipient.

As she followed the guards through the palace rooms, the panelling beside her glowing beneath the burning candles in the sconces on the wall, the thick tapestries of biblical scenes added a splash of colour to the otherwise severe interior. Freida looked around wondering if it would be the final time she'd walk through these spaces, which held the ghosts of deceased royals drifting mournfully from room to room. When she'd first arrived at the palace everything seemed huge and frightening and yet now, she just accepted it for what it was: the seat of power. Wherever the queen was, there beat the heart of England.

Finally, she was shown into the gallery where she'd first met with the queen the previous year. It seemed a lifetime ago when she'd reluctantly accompanied Doctor Dee to the palace. She'd cursed him privately many times since then for pulling her into the world of the court, making her visible to Mendoza. If that chain of events hadn't occurred, she wouldn't now be facing the possible murder of her son. Her eyes darted around, left and right, but she couldn't see her enemy. Probably because he was too busy planning the demise of her family.

The courtiers around her moved to one side and the guards stopped and bowed their heads as they neared the throne. Freida sank onto one knee holding tight to the oilcloth in her hand until she stood up and realised the queen was beckoning her forward and holding her hand out. Freida handed the map over and held her breath, hoping the queen would approve.

As directed, she moved forward and perched on the edge of a chair placed close to the throne and watched as it was revealed. The silence stretched onwards.

'This is exactly as I had envisaged,' the queen finally said, a rare smile on her face. 'You are indeed as talented as had been told to me and you should be proud of this. I know Drake will be a pleased recipient. You have upheld your family name and your cousin Abraham will receive a missive from me congratulating him on such a worthy holder of the great Ortelius name. And I shall tell Lord Burghley to recompense you with gold. You are truly a skilled woman.'

'Thank you.' Freida's voice came out in a croak and she dipped her head at the compliment. Her whole body was shaking. If she didn't broach the subject she knew she needed to speak of now, it would be too late. She cleared her throat. 'If it pleases you, Your Majesty, may I speak with you on a private matter?' She glanced up from under her brows at the queen who was frowning, looking displeased at the unusual request. She glanced around but most of her ladies were playing cards at a table several feet away. Waving away the two guards who stood behind the throne, she turned her attention to Freida. It was now or never; Freida knew she had but a minute whilst she wasn't overheard.

'Your Majesty, your spymaster Walsingham has become embroiled in a plot concocted by the Prince of Orange to fool the Spanish ambassador. They intend to deceive him and prevent an attack on the English at Flushing, in my home country.'

'This sounds an admirable plan, although I am unsure why it concerns you, Mistress Ortelius?'

'I have become involved because the person who will be at the centre of the ruse is my husband, and even worse, my young son who is but fourteen months old is to be used as a pawn in the plan, and kept as a hostage by Mendoza.

Your Majesty—' her voice began to break '—one word from you could stop this foolishness. I sincerely believe the ambassador will slaughter my child when he realises, as he will do, that he has been deceived. I have lived my life in fear that I cannot protect those I love and now all that I dread is coming to pass.'

'Your husband the *Sea Beggar* intends to fool Mendoza?' Instead of looking angry at what she had been told, instead the queen was smiling as she nodded her head. 'It is fitting that a privateer who has previously ransacked Spanish galleons and risked his life traversing the sea between here and the Low Countries should now hoodwink the Spanish ambassador.'

'But my son . . .' Freida's eyes welled up as she couldn't hide her true feelings from the queen anymore. She may be a queen but she was also a woman; surely she understood even though she didn't have children of her own.

'Mistress, you need to call on the inner strength that I know you possess,' the queen told her. 'That we, the weaker sex are required to nurture and grow throughout our existence. I have the hardest of lives, not just one child to protect, instead a whole nation of children and yet I do it with my head held high. Let no man believe that he can best me. And you too can do this. You are protecting your child and your husband by worrying and caring about them and being brave enough to ask me to intervene. But I cannot; that is not my place. You will save them from harm, Mistress Ortelius. Harness the strength you have within and fight for what is yours. Just as I fight every day for what is mine, my crown.'

The conversation came to an abrupt end as the queen turned away to speak with a messenger with a letter and standing up from the chair Freida curtsied before walking backwards towards the door. She knew she'd been dismissed and that her plea to the queen to intervene had failed. Now she had no choice but to do what the queen had told her to. To save her family herself. Perhaps she did have the strength to fight after all. Standing up straight, her head held high and backbone solid, she turned and swept out of the room.

Chapter Forty-One

June 1581

With no knowledge of when Willem's plan would come to fruition, Freida tried to keep herself busy during the following days. When she wasn't packing up their belongings into crates and chests to be stored on the *Windfly*, she spent time in the garden playing with Jacob. The warm weather continued and new leaves in sharp pastel green began to unfurl as nature awoke. The apple tree displayed its frothy pale pink blossom with pride. Beneath it Freida chased Jacob around the trunk as the petals drifted down to graze against their heads while he giggled until he fell on his knees. He was still a little unsteady on his feet but he loved being outside and Freida found herself wondering how their life would be if they survived to return to Holland.

Here in London had been everything she'd sought for a short while. She'd enjoyed a peaceful existence and it was almost beyond comprehension how it was about to fall apart.

There was no point in dwelling on the chain of events; she'd done that every night as she lay awake, turning over in her mind the peril Jacob would be in. She knew Willem was also putting himself in danger all for the cause of their homeland that he loved, where her parents had met their end, but this time she wouldn't let that happen. This time, they would all be saved.

Ten days later Emanuel sent a message asking her to call at his house. There she found a man she didn't know but immediately guessed his identity. When he stood and bowed to introduce himself, she managed to arrange her features into that of polite welcome.

'Christiaen the Elder, I believe you are expecting me. Our mutual friend here—' he indicated Emanuel seated beside the fire '—has fully updated me as to the predicament your husband finds himself in and the situation that has been insisted upon by the Spanish ambassador.'

'Then you will already be acquainted with my own views on this matter,' Freida replied shortly. 'It is wrong of the prince to ask this of Willem and my husband was a fool to agree to the terms laid out. To put our son in mortal danger whilst he himself sits in the centre of a plot to help the Huguenots defeat the Catholics. Always so much blood spilled in the name of our Lord. I watched it happen to my parents; I will not let it happen to my son. Nor my husband.'

'Goodwife Ortelius, I have travelled to London to ensure it does not. The plan is that Jacob will be snatched back from the embassy and I am here to guarantee that this comes to pass. Sir Francis Walsingham has supplied a map of the building for me—' he smiled at her '—an item you yourself will be familiar with, given your name. I shall know exactly where to find your son when the time comes. It has been organised with meticulous precision.'

'But how will you have access to the embassy?' If Christiaen had thought that she would happily accept this explanation he was sadly mistaken. 'You are Dutch and an enemy of the Spanish. I cannot see that you will be welcomed with open arms.'

'Indeed, this is true. I shall need to find another way to enter but this is where Walsingham's map will help. Nothing will go wrong, mistress.' He smiled at her again.

'I wish I had your confidence—' she didn't return his smile '—because it is *my* child who will be in danger, not yours.'

'But Christiaen is risking his own life to help to snatch Jacob back,' Emanuel interrupted, getting to his feet and holding his arms out in appeal towards Freida.

'Yes,' she agreed, and he has chosen to do so. Did anyone ask me if I am happy for Jacob to be put in this position? No of course they did not because you all know I would have refused. The prince should have found another way to fool the Spanish.' She looked at the two faces in front of her. She could read the sympathy in their eyes, but she knew no amount of arguing was going to change anyone's minds. They were prepared to use her son as collateral in their constant fight against the Spanish. Her past was crouched on her shoulder, coming back to haunt her.

As she turned to leave the room, an idea was already forming in her head, spinning around, sparking more plans as it began to come together as a whole. Christiaen had a map. If there was one person who could read a map as well as she could read the lines on the palm of her hand, it was herself. She had complete confidence in her ability; all she needed was a minute and she would be able to find her son herself. She didn't need any of the Prince of Orange's men to do what was needed.

It was easy to decide she needed sight of Walsingham's floor layout of the Spanish Embassy, but first she needed to find it, and that wasn't going to be easy.

Christiaen was staying with Liskin and James, Emanuel's house with his brood of noisy children running through his home considered unsuitable. Liskin's was a house that Freida was familiar with, and on a quiet afternoon when Willem was away from home – Freida had no idea where; he no longer told her – she slipped next door.

A passing servant told her that the mistress was on Newgate Street buying meat for supper. Freida felt her pulse quicken; this was the best opportunity she may get and mentioning some embroidery threads she needed to borrow she hurried upstairs heading towards the solar. Standing in the entrance to the room she paused, her head tilted on one side. If anyone approached, she could enter and pretend to be looking for the threads she knew would be kept in there, but all was quiet. Where would Christiaen be given rooms? The family slept in chambers on this floor and the one that she herself used when staying was down a short passageway at the end of the building overlooking the courtyard. Would Liskin have put him in the same room?

Slowly she made her way along the corridor, picking each foot up and slowly placing it gently on the floor, her skirts lifted away from the rushes that whispered with every sweep of movement against them. And how had she not noticed the way the floorboards in this house creaked and moaned with every step? Probably because she'd never needed to be so secretive before. Not since she'd been hidden beneath the eaves of a house all those years ago. The memory of that time – now smudged with age – curdled in her stomach, which was already churning with anxiety and ready to erupt at any moment. That time she'd hidden from the Spanish to save herself, but this time she would confront them to save her child. She hurried the last couple of steps and eased the door open.

She had assumed that even if this was his room, Christiaen would be out somewhere, but in case he was at home she already had an excuse of looking for a pearl encrusted hair pin missing since she had last stayed with Liskin. So many excuses ready on her lips if required. She hadn't needed to worry though; the room was empty. Looking around she stepped inside, frowning as she checked the space around her. She wasn't certain now if this was the room she needed. It was completely clear of any personal possessions. The top of the press and the chests were bare, the polished wood unadorned, and Freida cursed under her breath. If he wasn't in here, where was he sleeping? She was just about to slip back out of the room and look in some others when she noticed a quill abandoned on the windowsill. Perhaps the room was occupied after all. Pushing the door open properly she tiptoed in; it appeared that Christiaen was simply a much tidier house guest than herself. When she stayed, the detritus of her life scattered on every surface.

She opened the doors on the press and it revealed neatly laid out a comb, velvet cap, two new quills and inkpot and a pair of lambskin gloves. But no map. Moving to the chest closest to the bed she lifted the lid. A sudden shout in the street outside made her hurry to the window to see if it was her neighbour returning, but thankfully it was just the apothecary opposite hailing one of his customers. Heaving a sigh of relief she returned to the chest where, laid on top of a bundle of clothes was a large scrolled-up piece of parchment. The ends were slightly crushed and bent as if it had been handled, unfurled and rolled up many times. She pulled it open herself and then laid it on top of the quilt on the bed.

She could see immediately this was a sketch of the floor plan of a house, and some rooms had been labelled. Was this the map she needed? She had to be quick before anyone returned, and she was relieved when she spotted that the street outside the floor plan had been labelled. Water Lane. This, she had overheard Emanuel mention, was where the embassy was located, its rear gardens backing onto the river so the ambassador could leave or he could bring in guests, all without the prying eyes of those who watched him. No wonder Walsingham insisted on overseeing security so he could keep an eye on the comings and goings.

Quickly she scanned the diagram in front of her, committing it to memory. She'd been promised that Jacob would be kept in the nursery and with no other information to assist her, this was where she would be going. She could only hope she was correct. It was in a wing at the rear of the house, which was a stroke of luck as it would be easier to enter the house there. After one final look she rolled it up again and replaced it in the same position in the chest before stealing from the room again and going back downstairs. She sent a prayer to her Lord in heaven that she didn't meet with any of the household as she moved through the house and out of the side door that led to the kitchen garden, and from there to her own physic garden.

Once back in her workshop she picked up her sketchbook and drew a quick reproduction of what she'd just scrutinised. The first part of her plan was in place.

Chapter Forty-Two

June 1581

Slowly the chests and presses she'd filled with their belongings began to leave the house. Subtly and often under the cover of darkness a cart would pull up outside the gates and a piece of furniture would be loaded on before the wheels rattled away down the uneven street towards the Thames. The *Windfly* was moored as usual at Wapping and if they were caught in the act of retrieving Jacob it would be a long way to run whilst being chased by soldiers. Her easel and plates were also packaged alongside the contents of her atelier, but at the last moment she'd snatched back the map she'd made for Willem and her new steel burins. They were too precious and would travel with her.

The atmosphere in the house was stiff with fear and anticipation. Only three people actually knew what was happening but their anxiety and fear had spread across the rest of the household. Willem had insisted Nell was sent away because they couldn't risk involving anyone else who may chatter with others. Fortunately, Emanuel's wife, Ester, had just given birth to their fifth son, and Freida asked Nell to move to their home and help out in the household. She had a lump in her throat as she said goodbye, knowing they wouldn't be there when she returned. And that they may not be alive, any of them.

Eventually the day came she'd been dreading. Each morning she awoke wondering if that day would be the one when it happened and at night she'd lie down with Jacob in the bed beside her, watching his soft sleeping features, his tiny pursed lips blowing out a little with each breath he exhaled. Willem seemed to have abandoned the marriage bed. She had no idea where he was sleeping and she cared not one bit. She could barely look at him despite the many times he'd attempted to explain that none of the events that were about to unfold had been his idea.

She was sitting beside the fire in the nursery. A cold squally wind had blown away all vestiges of the early spring warmth. Jacob was by her feet playing with some wooden blocks Liskin had given him to celebrate his saint's day. Gazing out of the window, its thick buckled glass distorting her view of Leaden Hall behind the houses adjacent to her own, she imagined the merchants inside, measuring and weighing lengths of silk and wool to sell on to their customers. All going about their daily existence, lives that were calm and orderly. And closer, men hurrying into the Pewterers Company guildhall opposite, sheafs of papers under their arms. Beyond that a burial was taking place in the churchyard of St Andrew Undershaft. Small people in mourning attire stood together with the silhouette of the pastor as he moved around the grave, a dark gaping crevice in the earth. Was that where they would all be by the end of the week?

The sound of heavy feet on the boards outside the room attracted her attention and seeing the look on Willem's face as he entered with both Emanuel and Guy, she guessed immediately why they were there. Jumping to her feet, the sewing she had been pretending to do fell to the floor.

'No, Willem, I implore you. Let us leave now on the *Windfly* and find somewhere we can hide and live the rest of our lives quietly.'

Willem gripped her arms firmly and looked into her eyes. She could see sadness in his but didn't know if it was just a reflection of her own. 'My love, you know I cannot do that. I must carry out this mission for our prince and the good of our homeland. It will all be over soon. We shall leave with our son and not spend the rest of our lives running from those who would hunt us down.'

'Just as Mendoza will when he discovers he has been tricked?'

'By then we will be back in Amsterdam, and safe.' He let go of her arms, holding her for a moment within his own before he left the room. The nursery was empty; whilst he'd been attempting to reassure her, Guy and Emanuel had taken Jacob.

Freida sank down onto her chair, her head buried in her hands as she sobbed, her face shiny from her eyes and nose streaming, howling so loudly it brought Liskin – who'd just been informed of what was happening – running from the hall below where she had just arrived.

'Hush, cousin,' she soothed, rocking Freida's huddled form. 'What Willem has agreed to is reckless, but you must trust him. Christiaen and Emanuel will ensure Jacob is unharmed. Do not forget Sir Francis Walsingham is a very clever man and he has spies and men working for him everywhere. Come, let us go to church and pray for a quick resolution to this plan.'

Freida remembered what she'd just been watching at the church through her window and shook her head. She wanted to go nowhere where the cloak of death hung so heavy.

Chapter Forty-Three

September 2022

Robyn lay on her back, her eyes open and staring at the ceiling. She'd been awake for hours watching as the night slowly receded, drifting away, and the sun broke through the darkness. She just wanted the day to go away, so that she could skip this date. But it wasn't to be. There was no way of avoiding it. Even if she stayed in bed all day it wouldn't change a thing. The time on her phone confirmed her suspicion; it was barely four o'clock, too early to go out for a run. And she didn't think she could bring herself to visit their tree, not today. Rolling onto her side, she curled up in a ball, pulling the covers over her head as she tried to block out the world.

'You've got a visitor.' Her father smiled at her as he popped his head around the office door. Without a word being said he'd accepted that she wanted to spend the day quietly.

She'd been reading a book, trying to stop her mind from wandering, and she gave a start as he spoke.

'A visitor? Who is it? Hang on a moment and I'll come out to the shop.'

'No, it's fine – I'll send him to you. It's James Salcrest.' Robyn's heart sank as she nodded. She hadn't expected to hear from him today, and yet today of all days it was surely the most predictable thing.

'Hello.' His face appeared around the doorframe. 'I hadn't realised how far this shop went back. I thought I was going to get lost amongst the book-lined passages.'

'Yes, it is a bit of a maze.' She smiled even though it felt as though her mouth could barely move. As though it may split the rigid facade she'd fixed to her face that morning.

'Come in.' She indicated the chair on the other side of the table. James stepped into the room and sat down. Robyn noticed that instead of the sombre suit he'd been wearing in the office when she went to visit him, he was wearing chinos and a T-shirt.

'Day off?' she asked.

'Not really, but on days I don't have any client meetings I tend to dress down. One of the perks of being the boss.'

'Open a bookshop,' she told him smiling, 'then you can dress down every day.'

'I know nothing about books despite living in Hay,' he admitted. 'I'll stick to what I know.' Pulling at the knees of his trousers he sat down opposite her. Then his cheery countenance slid off his face and he looked more like the serious solicitor he'd been a couple of weeks previously.

'I expect you can guess why I'm here.' He cleared his

throat. 'I didn't want to just email or phone you; I thought this needed to be said in person.'

Robyn nodded. She didn't want to hear it, nor discuss it. If she just sat in silence hopefully it would all be over quickly. Like a visit to the dentist but far, far worse.

'Since your visit to my office I've compiled everything I need to submit the declaration and I've received your husband's will from your previous solicitor.' Thank goodness he hadn't said her late husband. 'Although we cannot execute the will until the declaration is complete. And I've come here in person to say that when you're ready you only have to say the word and I'll put the wheels in motion.'

'Yes. Thank you.' Robyn looked down at her hands, twisting together under the table. 'I'll let you know then?' She looked up and managed another tight smile. She wondered if he was expecting her to tell him to go ahead at that very moment.

'Of course, of course.' He nodded and got to his feet. 'The ball's in your court now, but only when you're sure it's time.' He held his hand up to wave goodbye and then he was gone, leaving her once again with her dusty old books and her memories.

At five o'clock her father appeared again at the office door. 'I've closed for the day,' he told her. 'It's been fairly quiet anyway. These came for you.' Stepping into the room he held out a box containing a bouquet of white roses, every bloom perfect, not a blemish on them. Robyn felt tears prick at her eyes. She'd kept them at bay all day but her barriers were starting to crumble. She pulled the flowers towards her and removed the card although she knew who they were from, who'd send her blooms just like her wedding day bouquet.

Thinking of you today. With our love always, W&D

Today must be just as difficult for them as it was for her and they must be wondering whether she'd submitted the forms now that the date had arrived. She picked up her mobile to call and thank them.

'Hello, Wendy.' The phone had been answered instantly as if she'd been sitting beside it waiting for it to ring. 'I've just called to say thank you for the lovely flowers. You really didn't need to, but they're gorgeous.'

'You're very welcome. I just wanted you to know we're thinking of you.'

'It's definitely harder this year,' Robyn admitted. 'My solicitor has everything ready to go now, so I only have to give him the nod. I promise I'll do it soon.'

'Don't you worry – you take care of yourself in the meantime.' They said their goodbyes and Robyn slipped the phone in her pocket. The stage was set now and there was nothing left to do but say her lines.

Chapter Forty-Four

June 1581

At Lime Street, the house echoed with a never-ending silence. No thumping of small feet as Jacob toddled through the upstairs rooms or his laughter as he slid on his bottom down the polished oak stairs. No giggling or shouting, the sound of him calling 'Mama' across the great hall if she appeared when he was there. Even Guy's dog lay morosely beside the fire, no food thrown on the floor by chubby hands.

At night Freida lay awake, the space where her little boy had slept beside her a telling sign, cold to the touch. Willem had returned to their bed after Jacob had been taken to the embassy, but she'd turned away from him. She'd trusted him with her life, with Jacob's life, and she'd been wrong to do so. She couldn't rely on someone else's strength; she needed to depend on her own. What the queen had told her was true: she was the might she needed, not anyone else. It was her role in life. What happened to her parents wasn't her fault – she'd been but a young child. Had she

317

made a sound that day and alerted the soldiers to their hiding place? Maybe, or maybe not. But she was no longer a child and now she'd protect her own. She only had one person reliant on her protection, not an entire nation. Her shoulders were wide enough.

Entering her room, her eyes scanned the furniture and she wondered if she could find what she was going to need. She went to the chest at the end of the bed that Willem used when he was at home, and she lifted the heavy lid. It creaked loudly and she held her breath. She didn't want anyone entering the room whilst she searched it. All of their belongings were on the ship now but surely there was something left, something not worth taking?

After ransacking all the storage in the room she put her bounty on the bed, smiling to herself. There was a torn and dirty shirt of Willem's that she wouldn't need, but the pair of old breeches and some hose with a large hole in them would be useful. The only jerkin that hadn't been packed, still awaiting a long rent in the back to be sewn up by herself was too large, her husband being far broader-shouldered than her. After stuffing the clothes under the coverlet she left the room quietly, her head on one side as she listened to the noises throughout the house. Dinner was being laid out on the table. She could smell the hot roasting fat of the goose that had spent the morning slowly turning on the spit, mixing with a dish of stewed leeks and a new vegetable recently being cultivated in London. Shiny and purple and almost bigger than her hand, it was reputed to be a *mad apple* and was already one of her favourites. She had no doubt that cook had prepared them deliberately for her.

To not appear at dinner would simply result in someone being sent to look for her and she couldn't risk that, so she slowly walked downstairs and sat at the head of the table as she always did, saying grace before helping herself from the dishes before her. To her relief all members of the household were present, including Guy. Their dear, loyal steward who'd been as kind and faithful to herself as he was to her husband. She felt a pang of guilt at what she was about to do but she squashed it down, knowing she didn't have a choice. She ate slowly, every mouthful sticking in her throat as she tried to swallow it, taking several gulps of ale to help wash the food down. After picking at a few pieces of meat and some of the strong salty cheese, she took an apple and stood up to leave the table. As the servants got to their feet, she waved at them to sit back down. She needed everyone to continue with their meal and thankfully they did so, Guy included.

Walking over to the staircase she glanced back over her shoulder at the table. Everyone was engaged in conversation, in helping themselves to food; it was the most robust meal of the day and they'd need to ensure they were completely full to keep them going as long as possible. Supper was always a small repast before bed, and often the servants didn't break their fast at all in the morning although she always insisted that cook put out some bread and cheese or frumenty in the mornings for those who wanted it. After slipping down beside the staircase she entered the corridor that led to the servants' dormitories. And Guy's chamber. As steward he was not expected to share with everyone else.

She paused outside his door to check if she could hear anyone coming but the voices were still drifting from the great hall, so she lifted the latch and slipped inside. Her eyes skimmed around the room, looking for anywhere that seemed likely, before tiptoeing across and opening a large rough pine chest. It was empty. Biting her lower lip, she looked inside a press and smiled to herself as her hand darted inside and snatched the jerkin laid on top of a small pile of clothes. It smelled of tobacco and body sweat but that couldn't be helped. Beside the pile of clothes was a worn moleskin cap and she grabbed that too before slipping back out of the room.

Returning to the hall she could see dinner was now over and Guy was talking to cook so she hurried upstairs to stow the clothes under her coverlet with the others. Without access to any long boots, she'd have to wear her own leather winter boots that had been made for her the previous year. The stage was set. She'd be riding into more danger than she had since that day so long ago when she was just nine years old. She had failed then, but this time it would be different.

Two days after Jacob had been taken to the embassy, Emanuel arrived. Freida was sitting in the solar, his toys at her feet in a carved oak chest that had been a first birthday gift from Willem, waiting for him to return and pick them up again.

'You dare show your face, cousin?' If he was surprised at her harsh tone, he didn't articulate it. He couldn't hide the shame in his eyes though.

'I have come to tell you what I know,' he told her, sitting down beside her. 'I do not blame you for being displeased with me, but if anyone was going to take Jacob to the embassy, I wanted it to be someone he knows and trusts.'

'You use the word "trust" too loosely,' Freida replied. 'There is nobody in this whole appalling situation who can be trusted. Please tell me what you know and then you may leave.'

'Jacob is safe and happy. As far as we understand Mendoza has not been near him once. He is looked after by a Spanish maid in the nursery with the other children. He has come to no harm. Tomorrow night, Christiaen will snatch him back and you will all be leaving. It will be dangerous – we cannot deny that – but he will approach the embassy from the river, land at Buckland stairs and crawl silently up Water Lane to a gate in the garden wall. Walsingham has apprised him of the way to enter the building without being seen. You must be ready to go, Freida. It will happen very quickly; there will be no time to lose.'

'I will get my baby back tomorrow?' she whispered.

'You will,' he confirmed, patting the back of her hand. 'But be prepared. Guy will accompany you to the *Windfly* where you must wait for Jacob and Willem, before you set sail. I am sure the volvelle you gifted to Willem will be of great help in your escape.'

'Thank you for coming to tell me,' she acknowledged. 'I must make my final preparations to leave.'

Following the sound of Liskin's voice she found her cousin in the kitchen with Cook discussing meals for the next few days. Did she see a fleeting look of guilt dart between the two of them?

'Can I help with anything?' she asked, a smile plastered on her face. She saw Liskin's shoulders slump and, taking Freida's arm, she guided her out of the room and back into the great hall.

'I know Emanuel came to tell you that tonight Christiaen

will snatch Jacob and you will all leave for Holland. I have faith that soon our prince will rule our homeland and we can travel there safely and live in peace. I will miss you greatly, cousin, and Willem and Jacob too. I was arranging with Cook about the food that will be on board for your journey. He has been preparing a haunch of venison, some pies and custards and comfits for Jacob. We do not know what he will have been fed at the embassy and he may be ailing. I have also put together a box of medications and ointments for any eventuality. Come, let me give that to you now.'

She led the way across to her own house where as promised a small chest that would not take up much room in Willem's cramped cabin was waiting. 'See here, rosemary and myrtle, comfrey, and also feverfew, and here, pennyroyal. I have sent for saffron from Gerard too.'

'Thank you.' Freida put her arms around Liskin and hugged her tightly. Whilst she had been spending days worrying about Jacob, her ever-practical cousin had been considering what they needed for the voyage.

'Do you know what time I am to leave?' she asked, trying to keep her voice steady but sure that the sound of her heart pounding could be heard echoing around the hall.

'Did Emanuel not tell you? He told me earlier the snatch will happen at nine o'clock tonight when darkness has fallen. They will need to avoid the night watchmen as they escape. I believe you are to be escorted to the ship by Guy at eight o'clock so you are waiting for them. A horse will be made ready so you can both travel with haste.'

Freida nodded slowly as if agreeing with the plot, even though her mind was whirring with how she would need to sneak away before eight o'clock. The horse would be very useful to her, as her plans began to form.

'Will you have supper with me this evening?' Liskin asked. 'The last time before we all meet again in our homeland?'

'Of course,' Freida agreed. 'I shall come to your home at five o'clock.' She hugged her cousin before walking sedately upstairs, her steady steps belying the shaking legs beneath her skirts. She continued the farce until she arrived in her bedchamber where she flopped down on the bed before her legs gave way.

Chapter Forty-Five

June 1581

Supper with Liskin was a sad affair. They'd lived almost in one another's houses in the two years since Freida arrived, and she'd miss her cousin. She had so little family left after the raids of her childhood that she clung to her Ortelius relatives and yet now she must leave them. She hoped one day to be reunited with both Liskin and Emanuel, just as she hoped to see her cousin Abraham again. After a mostly silent meal she got to her feet and enveloped her friend and relative in her arms, holding her tight. She desperately wanted to tell her what she had planned, but she knew to do so would invoke Emanuel and Guy intervening to prevent her. She had one last thing to do before she left, and after saying her goodbyes she returned to her house via the stables. To her relief only the stable boy was there; the rest of the servants at supper.

'You have a horse for me for tonight I believe?' she asked.

'Yes, mistress, she's here. A fine jennet – would you like to see her?'

'I would, thank you.' She smiled at him before following him to the stall where over the gate a grey head welcomed them. She stroked the soft nose, making a mental note to bring some apples with her later. 'I would like to take her around the yard outside before we leave later, so that she is used to me. Could you have her saddled up at seven o'clock please? I will return then. Do not forget or I will be most displeased.'

Thankfully the lad didn't question her, agreeing immediately. Another piece of the plan slotted into place. When she returned to the great hall it was empty, supper having been eaten and the household dispersed to their various activities. Collecting a couple of apples from a bowl left on the table she glanced at the clock on the wall. She was aware that it wasn't accurate and that Guy could easily come for her earlier than she was expecting but she doubted he'd be a whole hour early. Nevertheless, it was time to get out of her gown – it wouldn't be easy on her own – and dress in the clothes she needed to wear when she set off. The hour was fast approaching.

With much wriggling she managed to get out of her clothes and then it was easy enough to remove her kirtle and stomacher and bum roll, followed by her petticoat, until she was stood in just her smock and stockings. She pulled Willem's thicker old stockings on over the top of her own. The night would be cold and she needed as many layers as she could. Next the breeches were slipped on. They were too large around the waist but she'd been expecting them to be and she retrieved an old partlet and tied it tightly around her middle. Guy's jerkin was, as she suspected, a little too large across the shoulders, but after wrapping a woollen shawl across her chest first it fitted better. Finally, after pulling on her stout boots, she slipped her cloak over her clothes and pulled Guy's cap on.

She didn't have a mirror to admire herself in but looking down she was certain that under the cover of dark, which was now falling fast outside, twilight tapping at the window, she could easily be mistaken for a young lad. Inside the jerkin she pushed the map she'd made for Willem and her burins she'd collected from her atelier earlier and secreted in her room.

Creeping downstairs, she paused on the dog leg of the stairs to listen for voices but apart from cook shouting at one of the kitchen lads, all was quiet. It was now or never, and she ran down the corridor beside her atelier and out of the door through which Mendoza's henchmen had burst so many months ago. Now she was going to get her revenge.

After running around the outside of the house she entered the yard where, just as promised, her horse was waiting, huffing in the cold night air, its breath visible puffing out of its soft grey nose. Freida would have liked to give the stable boy a groat as thanks but she had no time to find him and offering the horse one of the apples she led her to the mounting block, gathering the reins in her hands and climbing on. Pressing her hand against her chest, she felt the familiar lump of the bezoar stone Willem had given her on board the *Windfly* the first time she met him. For luck he had told her that day. He'd never asked for its return, and she was relieved because now it needed to bring her luck and protect her in a way she wouldn't ever have imagined.

It was the oddest sensation riding astride for the first time but after a couple of paces around the yard she began to feel the rhythm of the beast moving beneath her. Kicking into a trot she left behind the home she'd been so happy in, where she'd created her maps, given birth to her baby and laughed with her husband and family. Now she was going to get Jacob back and begin a new adventure. The queen's words, *'You will save them from harm, Mistress Ortelius. Harness the strength you have within and fight for what is yours,'* rang in her ears as the thud of hooves hit the cobbles beneath her, dancing in time to her erratic heartbeat.

The streets were quiet and she knew she needed to keep going and not look to either side in case someone took a shine to her horse. Although she looked like a young man she wouldn't stand a chance if someone tried to pull her from the saddle. She vaguely knew the directions to reach the embassy, smiling to herself as she headed for London Bridge. If someone who'd helped create maps of London couldn't find the way to go, then she wasn't the cartographer she thought she was.

Her horse's hooves clattered on the cobbles beneath them, the sound only becoming muffled when they galloped along the softer mud streets. On London Bridge, its gate decorated with the decomposing heads of executed traitors, Nonsuch House towered over her as she flew past whilst the shops with their shutters closed against the night stood close together with no space between, not even for a piece of parchment to slip between them. Floor upon floor stretching out across the street far above her head were all shuttered and closed as she rode beneath but she could see candlelight glowing through cracks in wood and for a moment she wished she was sitting beside the fire in the solar with Willem opposite her and Jacob asleep in the nursery above them. She mourned the life she used to have, knowing it would never be the same. But now all that mattered was getting Jacob back and them all to safety across the water before Mendoza discovered he'd been deceived by her husband.

Pausing for a moment as she reached the other side of the bridge she turned her horse left, trotting a little slower as she negotiated the narrower streets around the riverbank until she arrived at Water Lane. Then ahead of her, she could see the embassy. She'd seen it once before when visiting the city with Doctor Dee and she recognised it right away – guards wearing the Spanish livery of King Philip standing tall outside the gates, which were locked and bolted. Was Christiaen already inside? She needed to find the back entrance she'd seen on the map.

Sliding down from the saddle, she held the reins in her hand as she crept slowly towards the building, intending to try and listen for any sounds that might give away if her husband and his accomplices were already there. A soft misty rain was beginning to fall, which would mute any noise. Useful for Willem, but not for herself. She needed to intercept them because Guy wasn't going to find her at home to take her to the *Windfly* and if she missed them here, she'd find herself left behind. There would be no time to change the arrangements.

She stole along the side of the building, keeping her back against the wall until she reached what she assumed were the kitchens at the rear. She could hear voices in a language she recognised from both the soldiers fighting in Holland and more recently the ambassador and his men and she knew this was the right building; nobody else would have

Spanish servants, and she could smell burnt fat and a spice she was unfamiliar with, mixed with cabbage and the heady scent of yeast and hops. The alehouse where they brewed the beer for the embassy must be close by.

A door further along the building opened and a young girl staggered out with a heavy bucket in each hand. She disappeared into the gloomy night and, taking her opportunity, Freida scurried along the back of the building, keeping in the dark edges beyond the candlelight at the windows. She slipped in through the door, which was still wedged open.

Inside it was dark but she couldn't risk lighting a candle. She'd brought a stump of one in her pocket but it was only in case of a dire emergency. From her map she was certain that the corridor she was standing in led to the scullery and beyond that, the servants' hall. The nursery was above but the only way to access it was up a flight of stairs on the other side of the hall. If someone was in there and she was stopped, it would be the end. Her life, Jacob's life.

Not for the first time she wondered if she was doing the right thing, whether her stubbornness and reckless attitude had lured her into a wildly dangerous situation. But it was too late to back out now even if she wanted to; she had to save her child. And was Christiaen also here, creeping along dark corridors? It hadn't occurred to her what may happen if he got to the nursery first and Jacob was already gone. It was a flaw in her plan but she was too far in to worry now.

Turning a corner in the corridor she could see the flickering light from an open doorway ahead and she crept towards it hoping that, like her own home, the servants started to retire for the night as soon as they had eaten supper and finished their chores. She could hear voices somewhere in the house but they were muffled and seemed to be far from where she was standing.

There was just one young maid in the hall sweeping the floor beneath the long trestle table, assisted by a large hairy hound who was intent on pouncing upon any pieces of food her broom missed. Neither of them looked up as Freida walked through, keeping her steps steady, trying to look far more confident and at home than she felt and the strange clothing didn't help. As soon as her foot was on the bottom step she shakily let her breath out and skipped up the stairs quickly until she was standing in the dark of the room above. This was an empty echoing hall with several doors leading from it, and she knew which one she needed. What she didn't know was what she'd find behind it.

Keeping away from the window to ensure her silhouette wouldn't be seen from outside, she hurried across to the far corner where the shadows collected. Pressing her ear against the heavy wood she could hear nothing on the other side. Would Mendoza have placed guards in the room in case of a rescue mission? Or was he too arrogant to believe they would do such a thing?

She put her hand on the door latch to try and muffle the click as she pushed it down and slowly pulled the door open. She held her breath but all she could hear was the slow steady breathing of sleep and she stepped into the room. A single candle burned in a sconce on the wall and in the barely there light she could see four small truckle beds around the edge of the room, together with a cradle and a larger bed that she guessed belonged to the nursery maid and was currently empty. She needed to be quick and hope that Jacob would not be discovered missing until she was away from the building.

The children sleeping in the beds closest to the door were too old to be Jacob, but as she approached the third bed she recognised the small and perfect features of her sleeping son. Bending down and resisting the urge to pause and check he was unharmed she scooped him up into her arms. Immediately he nestled sleepily against her, even in sleep recognising his mother's touch, and as she smelled his unique baby scent, she felt her eyes swell up with relief. She turned towards the door to retrace her steps back to the garden and make her escape but standing silently in the aperture was the outline of another person, watching her.

Freida froze as she held Jacob closer to her. This was it. She'd escaped from the Spanish once before, but now she'd taken a step too far. Instinctively she took a step backwards but before she could move any further the other person was suddenly beside her, and in the murky half-light she recognised Christiaen's profile and she heaved a sigh of relief. Her racing heart began to slow down, the sweat that was prickling across her forehead cooling. She saw the flash of a blade as he slipped a dagger into his boot, covered by his long woollen cloak. His expression was one of shock but neither of them had time to discuss why Freida was there in the embassy, dressed as a boy.

Pulling his cloak around them all he hurried her back the way she'd come. At the bottom of the stairs, however, he ushered her through a door she hadn't seen on the map and suddenly they were outside the building in the cool night air, further along than where she had entered it. With his arm still across her back Christiaen hurried her down the lawns to where she could hear the splash of the river, smell the wet vegetation and feel a breeze on her skin. She began to breathe a little more easily as she realised she had rescued her son from the Spanish.

As she reached the water two people loomed up in the dark and she tried to stop running but the momentum of Christiaen kept her moving. As they drew up closer one of them lit a lamp and held it up and Freida recognised Willem's face just at the same moment that he saw who was carrying Jacob. His face suffused with anger, his brows low and his mouth thin and straight. She felt the vice-like grip of his hand grab her arm and the warmth of his breath against the side of her face.

'I do not understand why you would come here in the dark and somehow have Jacob in your arms,' he whispered close to her ear, 'but right now there is no time to find out. Have you come here on horseback? We need to ride to London Bridge as if the streets are on fire and then along the banks to the *Windfly*. Where you should have been waiting.' Freida nodded and explained where she had left her mount beside the building, and Emanuel slipped away, returning thirty seconds later leading her horse.

'I will give you a hand up on your horse now, and you will ride in front of Emanuel so he can see you at all times. Do you understand me?'

Freida nodded silently. She knew in her heart why she'd felt compelled to come but she could see from Willem's eyes just how unwise she'd been, and for the first time she felt a dart of guilt at the added danger she had placed on her husband's shoulders. Willem swung onto his horse and leaned down to take Jacob, sitting him across his saddle in front and holding on to him with one arm, the other gripping the reins as he turned his horse around and began to gallop across the lawn to the street, followed closely behind by Christiaen.

Wordlessly she walked to her horse and lifted her left leg at the knee, feeling Emanuel's hand cup her shin before lifting her effortlessly into the saddle. Emanuel slapped the back of her horse and she kicked it hard. She couldn't afford to lose sight of them or she'd be left; she was sure of it. Behind her she heard shouting and she stood up in the saddle urging the horse to go faster, the wind whipping strands of hair that had escaped her hat against her face, the rain catching the soft skin of her face and making it burn.

It wasn't far to the bridge, but still a mile or more further to Wapping, and Freida was surprised when Willem suddenly pulled his horse to a stop and slid off. She had no option but to do the same as both Emanuel and Christiaen followed suit. Now that their own horses had stopped, she could hear the shouts of guards running along the streets somewhere behind them and it wouldn't be hard to work out that they would come to the river. Where else would a *Sea Beggar* go but to water? Freida was desperate to check that Jacob was unharmed but Willem kept a tight grip on him.

'We must leave the horses here and continue on foot,' he told them. 'We will creep along the bank here just above the water. Thankfully it is low tide. It will be muddy and slippery, and if anyone goes into the river, we shall not have time to come back and get them. One false move and you are dead.' He looked straight at Freida as he said it and the enormity of what she'd done finally hit home. But she knew that if she had to do it all again, she would. She wouldn't rest until her son and her husband were safe. She gave a curt nod as his eyes met hers and then she scrambled down the bank with Emanuel behind her. The noises from behind were getting louder, the guards advancing ever closer.

The mud along the riverbank smelled so bad that Freida felt her stomach lurch and she had to swallow quickly before she vomited. A mix of rotting vegetation and effluence and what smelled like a decomposing carcase. The water lapped at her boots, her stockings inside now sodden as she carried on silently, pulling her feet out from where they sank in and stepping forward, trying to stand in the voids left by Christiaen's feet in front of her. They squelched with each movement and more than once she wobbled and would have fallen into the Thames had it not been for her cousin's arm shooting out to steady her.

She'd never been so grateful to have him there with her, but a moment later as the crack of a flintlock gun ruptured the air something whistled past her head and fell into the river ahead of them, shortly followed by a shout from Emanuel and a splash in the water.

Chapter Forty-Six

September 2022

With her suitcase stowed in the boot of her car, Robyn hugged her father goodbye. It was a long drive to Dover and she wanted to leave with plenty of time to spare.

'Are you sure it's okay for me to be away for a week or so? I don't know how long the investigations in Holland are going to take.'

'Of course it's fine,' he reassured her, 'and I want to discover the end of the story of the map as much as you do. If you can uncover anything about Freida and her husband that'll be brilliant. And it will make the map worth more, which benefits us both if we're able to prove its provenance, especially if it transpires to be the one Queen Elizabeth the First had made especially for Francis Drake. So, take as much time as you need. Besides I think you probably need to get away from here for a while. You did a very brave thing going to see James and I'm proud of you. Life will get better, I promise you. Now you can start to move forward.'

Robyn nodded. But first, she had something else very important to do, to finally discover the missing pieces of Freida's life. Another woman in another time who'd demonstrated an incredible strength.

When she arrived at Dover, she called Sam who directed her to where he was moored. She couldn't help a frisson of excitement seeing the shining catamaran sat in the water. This wasn't going to be a gentle sail across the sea; she realised that now. 'We're all ready to go,' he told her. 'The shipping forecast is looking good so come aboard and we can set off. Have you got the map with you?'

'I do,' she confirmed. 'Dad wasn't happy about me bringing it but I feel as if it needs to be with us. As if it's returning to its rightful home after being lost. I've got it safely packed though in a conservation box. He did make sure of that.'

Once she'd stowed her bag in the small cabin below, which smelt of varnish and fresh paint, she returned to the deck where Sam was preparing to cast off. She'd sailed several times with Nate over the years but this was the first time in over seven years she'd been on board a boat. The rocking beneath her feet felt familiar and she realised that, despite worrying about it, this was a big step she was taking towards her freedom. Out of the jail that she'd built around herself.

The sun had warmed the deck and she slipped her shoes off for a moment. She knew Sam wouldn't let her keep them off once they were moving, but while he was busy she sat down and turned her face up to the warmth, enjoying it soaking into her bones. There wouldn't be many more balmy summer days. All around she could hear the singing of rigging striking against masts across the marina, playing a tune of the sea. A happy sound or a sailor's lament, who knew?

Beneath her feet the boat vibrated as Sam fired up the engine to power them away from the mooring and out into the Channel. He'd shown her on the computer in the control room their route and he expected to be in Amsterdam by nightfall, which she was pleased about. She'd never enjoyed the loneliness and silence of the open sea at night. It was full of unknowns. And she couldn't help associating it with the fact that it was thought probable Nate had gone missing during the dark hours. He used to check in once a day, but his support crew had told her that if he'd been in trouble during waking hours, he'd have possibly messaged them earlier. They'd come to the conclusion something had occurred during the darkest hours of the night before he could get to his VHS radio. Now they'd never know.

'Ready to go, cabin boy?' Sam's voice interrupted her musing.

'Oi, less of the cabin boy if you don't mind!' she laughed as she answered. 'I'll be first mate thank you. But yes, I'm ready. Let's go and discover if this really is Freida's map.'

Sam slipped the lines from the dock and they slowly made their way towards the Channel. It would be sluggish moving amongst the other craft, which made it the busiest shipping lane in the world, but once they were into the North Sea, they'd be able to raise the main sail and the proper journey would begin. Leaning back against a mast she watched the world go by. She could still see the English shore on the horizon and knew that somewhere to her right lay France.

It was peaceful with just the calling of the petrels that followed them skimming along the surface of the water, together with an occasional cormorant, its black wings against the blue sky like scraps of burning paper rising from a fire, buffeted by the wind now stronger out on the open water.

Before long the jib and spinnaker were raised, the water spraying against Robyn's face as they sliced through the waves. They surfed across the tops of the waves, the boat barely dipping as it flew over the dark sea. She watched Sam, a grin on his face as he hopped across the bridge between the two hulls, constantly checking things before jumping back into the cabin to ensure the autopilot was keeping them on track. She'd never seen him happier and she smiled at him, as suddenly she realised what she'd been missing all along. It was such a shock that she held her hands to her mouth, her breath caught in her lungs. This was where Sam was happiest, doing what he loved; and it had been the same for Nate.

Even though Nate was sad to be leaving her each time he went away, she'd always sensed a shift in his mindset as a race start approached. He loved it, every minute of it. 'It's just me against the waves and the weather,' he'd told her once, his eyes alight. It was his life, and ultimately his death, but he'd died doing something he loved. For so long she'd been angry with him for having such a dangerous profession but now, like the sunlight cutting through the clouds above them, a shaft of golden light that lit the tops of the surf beside her, she knew that she hadn't seen what was there the whole time. She'd been blind. All along she'd been wrong to feel angry Nate had chosen such a dangerous career, one that took him from her. To think how selfish he'd been.

Because he'd been living his life the way he needed to. She couldn't have stopped him doing what he loved, and nor would she have wanted to. So how could she be angry with him for following his heart? It was time to let him go.

As promised before nightfall the skyline of Amsterdam came into view. The clouds hanging on the horizon on their journey now crowded about them, grey and menacing.

'I'm glad that we're arriving now,' Sam admitted indicating the heavy sky above them as tiny spots of cold rain scattered across them. 'I wouldn't want to be out at sea when this hits.' Firing up the engine he took down the sails and steered them into port where he'd previously organised a mooring for the week. Neither of them knew how long their mission would take, but seven days were all he could spare.

Robyn was pleased to be back on dry land, stretching her legs and stamping her feet to rid them of the slight wobbly feeling, even after just a day on board.

'Dinner?' Sam asked, and she nodded enthusiastically. She hadn't thought about lunch before they left and was disappointed to discover that the small fridge on board only contained two pork pies and a bottle of orange juice. Sam had confessed he'd already eaten two of the pies before she'd arrived. Now she was ravenous and eager to find somewhere to eat.

'Lead the way,' she agreed, following him through immigration. He'd suggested they found somewhere to stay in Amsterdam to stay in for a few days and given the tiny cabin space on the yacht she'd readily agreed, booking them into a small hotel.

Stopping at the first restaurant they found, they both ordered steak and chips. It wasn't the local food Robyn liked to eat on visits abroad, always preferring to try new things. But she was starving and as soon as it arrived, she fell on it, eating the chips so quickly they burned her mouth. They both ordered tall glasses of beer and felt considerably better by the time they'd finished. Robyn insisted on paying the bill.

'It's the least I can do as you're over here helping me.' She put her hand up to stop any arguments. She knew Sam too well.

They found their hotel overlooking a wide canal with little problem. Robyn couldn't stop marvelling at the unique architecture and more than once Sam had to stop walking and wait for her to catch up as she took out her phone to snap photos. Tall, narrow buildings with row upon row of large windows to let in the light were topped with ornate gables standing sentry along the canals. Everywhere cyclists wove in and out of traffic and around pedestrians and across the numerous bridges.

Once booked in they agreed they'd meet up in the hotel bar in an hour for a quick nightcap and to discuss the meeting the following day with Annemieke, which Robyn had organised before leaving Hay. She carefully unpacked the map box, laying it in a drawer beneath her clothes. It was too big to fit in the tiny safe in the bottom of her wardrobe but she was loath to leave it anywhere it may be discovered, even though nobody knew that she was travelling with such a valuable piece of art.

'So, do you feel you're getting closer to the truth?' Sam asked. They were sharing a bottle of wine and Robyn could feel herself relaxing, her shoulders slumped.

'I do. It's as if I've been walking a journey and I can see the end in sight. I have no idea if tomorrow Annemieke will be able to tell us anything about Freida I haven't already discovered, but bringing the map here, it feels like it's coming home. If I'm going to discover its tale, then it'll be here.'

'Here's to finding the end of the story.' Sam raised his glass before draining it. He held up the empty bottle. 'Shall I get another?'

'Noo.' Robyn laughed. 'I don't want to have a headache tomorrow; it's far too important a day. And you shouldn't really, or you'll be in your room nursing a hangover and miss all the excitement.'

They were interrupted by Robyn's phone ringing. The number was familiar but she couldn't place it, and she answered it with a tentative 'hello?'

'Hello, Robyn, this is Margaret again. Margaret Cordwell. I said I'd call if my daughter had any more information about our family tree. She arrived home and I remembered last week to ask her. She said I've got it wrong – it wasn't a Henry who brought the map with him; his name was Henrik. Henrik Ortel. I'm not sure if that is of any help to you?'

Robyn punched the air silently. Sam's eyebrows raised as he mouthed, *'What?'*

'Thank you, Margaret, that is indeed extremely helpful.' Robyn ended the call as quickly as she could and explained what she'd just learned. 'If Annemieke Ortel is related to Henrik and we can trace him back to Johanna Ortelius, and from her to Freida, then that gives us the provenance I've been searching for. The final piece of the puzzle.'

Robyn laid the tourist maps and leaflets out across the table and began to plan the final step in her journey.

Chapter Forty-Seven

June 1581

Freida did not dare turn around to see what had happened
to Emanuel or indeed if he was still wading through the
mud behind her. All she could do was keep pushing forward
behind Willem, who was carrying the most precious of
bundles, and Christiaen who had not turned once to see if
she was still following. She could just about make out the
crimson of his cloak a smudge of red through the rain. Her
own cloak, so much longer than his, had been discarded
after five steps through the mud as it dragged her down,
the brown slurry clinging to the bottom of it.

Above them on the embankment she could hear shouts
and knew the guards had worked out where they were. A
flash rent through the mist and rain and she heard the
explosion of gunpowder as someone fired a gun again, closely
followed by several more reports, making her ears ring.
Now she couldn't hear a thing and prayed Willem wasn't
shouting any instructions to them, or she'd miss them.

Christiaen was still walking and she carried on following him, praying to her God that they might all be saved. She was no longer sure Emanuel could be.

As her hearing began to clear she caught more shouting from a distance away, then another volley of explosions lit the sky above them and small pieces of metal and nails sprayed across the water beside her. She wondered if the Spanish thought that they were out in a boat and hadn't realised they were cowering beneath the river bank itself, wading through London's filth as slowly they gained on the *Windfly*. Once there, they'd have no option but to try and battle through the guards to get on board, there only being a ladder and gangplank on the shore side. It felt like an impossible task and for the first time since she'd set off from Lime Street, she began to question her judgement that she could protect her family from danger. That this time it would all end differently, with no blood on her hands.

The firing continued as the freezing river water splashed up against her legs, pellets from the guns landing beside her. At one point she felt a sharp stinging pain momentarily on her arm. Had she been hit? She had no idea but she couldn't stop to check, and still she waded on. They were getting closer to the dock now, and almost safe. If they could just avoid the soldiers' fire as they climbed up from the riverbank and onto the quay then maybe there was a chance, but this was by far the most dangerous part – they'd be open targets once they were on dry land.

As they got to the bottom of the steps, she finally caught up with Christiaen and Willem. Her legs felt like lead, her thighs burning and her chest hurting with the effort of walking and the fear of losing those she loved. Her heart was pounding so hard in her chest she thought it would burst from her body. By some agreement that must have been arranged previously, Christiaen climbed up the steps first, attempting to take the initial fire away from Willem and Jacob and finally she realised what added danger she'd put the others in. But it was too late for remorse now. She needed to concentrate on helping in any way she could to get Jacob on the ship and away from Mendoza's men who, from the shouting in Spanish she could now hear in the commotion, were the ones up on the dockside. She could only imagine the ambassador's face when he realised that there would be no raid on Flushing and he'd been fooled.

Willem paused in front of her. She could see Jacob wriggling in the blanket and she caught occasional cries from him. At least it proved he was still alive and she could only hope his crying was just fear and not that he'd been caught by the flying shrapnel. It looked as if Willem was about to usher her past, but she pushed against him, shouting, 'You go!' and was relieved when he turned and started to climb up the ladder attached to the wall. Despite only having one arm free he hauled himself up easily, his head bowed over that of their son, and when he got to the top, she saw his boots disappear as he ran towards the gangplank. She knew his crew would be protecting them as best they could, and they would all be armed with cutlasses.

The time had come when she needed to haul herself up the ladder, even though she was certain she had no breath left in her body with which to do it. Her strength had gone and yet she knew she had to dredge some up from somewhere. She felt a hand at her back and, turning, she almost cried with relief to see the muddy, exhausted face of Emanuel looming out of the darkness beside her. He was still safe and seeing him gave her the power to carry on. She couldn't let her family down now. She turned and started to haul herself up the ladder, one rung at a time.

A fierce fight was underway between the night guards who'd appeared from out of the darkness and the Spanish soldiers and she wondered momentarily who she had to thank for the English coming to their aid. In one mad dash she clambered up the final three steps and, crouching down, she ran across the quayside, the lack of skirts making it far easier to run, despite how wobbly her legs felt. She spotted the gangplank where Willem's men were fighting hard. If she could just slip between them all, she could get on board. In front of her were three of the crew with huge knives, fighting with two guards carrying pikestaffs in a fierce battle. Beside them Willem still clutching Jacob.

Horrified, she spotted a soldier running across from another fight with a knife held high as he attempted to stab it towards Willem. Fury and fear flooded her in equal measures and, not giving it a second thought, she ran at the assailant, pulling her burins from inside her jacket. Holding two of them clutched in her fist, the blades sticking out from between her clenched fingers, she stabbed repeatedly at the guard until a spray of blood splattered across her and he fell to the floor.

A hand gripped her arm tightly and she turned, her other hand raised to stab again, but she recognised the scarlet cloak beside her and she allowed Christiaen to pull her, running, towards the ship. Ahead of them she spotted Willem jumping from the gangplank and onto the deck and she followed him as he passed Jacob into her blood-soaked hands. Never had she been so relieved to feel the weight of her son in her arms and she ran towards the steps that led to Willem's cabin.

Above her were shouts as the battle carried on and then the whole ship rocked with the sound of her small fore-cannon fire, hopefully giving them valuable time to get away. Beneath her feet was the vibration of the oarsmen starting their rhythmic pull of the oars and the ship slowly began to move in the water. She could still hear the fighting on the quayside but slowly it began to fade as they continued to move along the Thames.

She unwrapped Jacob from his tightly swaddled blankets and quickly checked him over but there was no blood on his clothing. His face was red and wet from crying but never had she been more pleased to hear his angry wailing. He was safe, she was safe, and so was Willem. This time her family had been saved. Her arm was smarting and looking at it quickly she could see her shirt was stuck to it with blood that ran down and over her hand. It would need seeing to but it could wait. Thank goodness Liskin had insisted she brought a selection of her herbal remedies.

Pulling the map and her tools from inside her jacket she was dismayed to see that the blood that had soaked through from her arm — and possibly some from the man she'd injured on the quayside — had seeped onto her map. But there was no time to worry about that now and after sitting Jacob on the bed beside her, her arm tightly around his body she pulled out the small chest she had packed with medication and rummaged in it, finding some ointment made of lady's mantle together with strips of linen to bind her arm up. She wasn't going to try removing her shift until she was somewhere with access to water. Settling back on the bed she pulled Jacob onto her lap where he burrowed into her. His crying finally stopped and his ragged breaths slowed down. Wrapping her arms around him she rocked him back and forth in time with the oarsmen.

It was another hour, the sounds of fighting now having faded in the distance and muffled by the rain, when she heard the snapping of canvas as the main sail was hoisted and the ship began to move at a faster speed, slicing through the water and heading towards the open sea. She knew they wouldn't be safe even out there but facing a Spanish galleon after what they'd just battled felt less of a worry. She wanted to go and make sure the other men were not injured but she knew better than to get in the way as they concentrated on making their escape. The wooden deck outside the cabin creaked and thumped with men running back and forth and the effort of the ship trying to race through the waves as they made their escape.

She was thankful Mendoza wouldn't be able to get word to his ships currently waiting at Flushing, and hopefully it would mean there were none guarding the port at Amsterdam so the *Windfly* could slip in unnoticed.

Eventually Jacob fell asleep and she laid him down on the bunk. She knew she should lie down too – her arm felt as if it were on fire – but she couldn't rest until she'd checked the others were not hurt. And she wasn't looking forward to facing Willem's fury that she'd put them all in more danger by not doing as she was instructed to. She felt sorry for Guy who'd have found her gone, and her horse too.

Stepping outside the cabin she breathed in the cold salty air, which caught and scratched at the back of her throat.

The crew were each busy at their allotted tasks and nobody noticed her standing there, her eyes on the most important man on deck. The most important man in her life. Now she understood that he'd done what he believed to be right, what his heart had told him was honourable and true, and she loved him even more for upholding his values and supporting their king. That he had followed his heart. The anger that had previously suffused her dissipated in the cold night air, whipped away by the wind. She watched as he looked up at the skies, pinpricked with a myriad of glittering stars, until he located what he was looking for. Then he held something against his face and in the moonlight that shone off it. She realised he was using his volvelle to determine the time and subsequently ascertain the tides for when they arrived in Amsterdam. Her gift was proving its worth just when they needed it most; it may well save all their lives.

She didn't want Willem to see her, knowing how angry he was with her, and she returned to the cabin to lie down next to Jacob. Exhausted she lay her head down on the bolster and feeling Jacob's soft breath against her face as he slept, she succumbed to the exhaustion that swamped her.

A rough shaking of her shoulder woke her after what felt like minutes although she could see through the tiny porthole that outside the sun was on the horizon, a round orange ball beckoning them towards their homeland. As welcoming as it looked, that sentiment wasn't reflected in Willem's face as it loomed over her. She felt her heart quail. The anger in his eyes made them flash and she steeled herself for the onslaught she was expecting.

'I do not think anyone has ever done something as stupid as you did last night,' he said. She was sure it was only the presence of their sleeping son that prevented him from shouting at her but his lowered voice was, if anything, worse. 'You put everyone's life in danger even more so than they already were. Why did you not just do as Guy bade you? What inspired you to come to the embassy? You could have lost your life in that fighting and you put us all in more danger.'

Still exhausted and overwrought by his harsh words, even though she knew she deserved them, she felt tears running down her face, burning her skin. She could taste the salt against her lips.

'I am sorry,' she whispered, 'but I could not allow you all to face that threat without me. It was my appearance at court that alerted Mendoza to our presence in London. It was my duty to be there by your side. I do not regret what I did.'

'Despite the wound you have sustained?' He indicated the bloodied linen strips around her arm.

'It is not deep I am sure,' she answered. 'Once we are at our destination, I shall find an apothecary who will have other herbs and I can make an ointment to help it heal. What about Emanuel and Christiaen and your crew? Does anyone else require any of my remedies? I still have some knit-bone and some feverfew in my chest here.'

'Emanuel was knocked by a pikestaff into the water but he has sustained no serious injuries. He will travel with us to Holland and then continue his journey onwards to Antwerp to stay with Abraham.' Beside her, disturbed by his father's voice, Jacob stirred, sitting up and rubbing his eyes. His soft hair was stood up along one side and his cheeks were flushed. Seeing his parents though his face broke into a huge smile as he threw himself across the bunk towards them. Willem picked their son up and hugged him tightly until Jacob began to squirm. He then passed him over to Freida who covered the little boy's head in kisses.

'Come up on deck and get some food,' Willem said, his voice a little warmer. 'Cook has some pottage ready. The wind is behind us and we shall be in Holland by tomorrow nightfall. Thanks to your gift of the volvelle we will be able to slip into port under the sight of the Spanish without them even realising we are there.'

At the mention of the instrument Freida suddenly remembered what she had brought with her from Lime Street and she pulled it out, handing it to Willem.

'What is this?' he asked, opening it out.

'When I made the map for Drake,' she explained, 'I also made one for you. It appears that it was damaged a little during our escape—' she indicated the bloodstain across the corner and the backing '—but I wanted you to have one too. See here, I have added your volvelle to this copy.'

'Thank you.' His face finally lightened and his familiar smile appeared. 'I shall treasure this forever. Even with a bloodstain that will forever remind me of the risk you took for the safety of your family.'

Freida managed a shaky smile as her eyes welled up. Now she had achieved what she needed, in her heart, to do.

Chapter Forty-Eight

September 2022

After walking through many streets and traversing several bridges over the canals they finally arrived at the street on the map Robyn had ringed.

'We're in the right place,' she said. 'I can feel it.' The air about her vibrated as if trembling in anticipation and the map in her backpack felt warm against her back.

It didn't take long to find the shop and, her heart thumping, Robyn walked in. Sam had insisted she went first; she was holding the final piece of the puzzle. Inside it smelled of the mustiness of old paper, ancient manuscripts. It reminded Robyn of her father and Hay-on-Wye and for a moment she felt a pang of homesickness, a prickle of tears behind her eyes and the kindness her father had afforded her, allowing her to chase across Europe to solve the mystery of this map.

The young woman behind the counter looked exactly as she did on her avatar and immediately Annemieke came around the counter to hug Robyn and shake Sam's hand. She called up the stairs behind her and they heard the sound of someone slowly making his way downstairs until he shuffled into the shop. There was a quick exchange in Dutch between the two of them and then he smiled and waved them both over to follow him upstairs.

Once they were sitting around a table in a bright and sunny open-plan kitchen, Robyn realised she needed to explain why she was there. Thankfully Annemieke's English was exemplary and she was able to translate for her father as Robyn told them about the map that had been found hidden beneath another. Of how it had arrived in the shop, her latest discovery of how it had been brought to England, and her research into Freida Ortelius and the map made to be a gift for Sir Francis Drake from Queen Elizabeth I.

'Yes.' Annemieke nodded. 'We know of this map. It has been lost for centuries. Are you saying that you have found it?'

'I think so,' Robyn said. 'I have it with me.' She picked up her backpack and started to undo it. Annemieke looked at her incredulously, before quickly explaining to her father what was going on.

Robyn laid her map out on the table, carefully arranging the specialist tissue paper beneath it. As she did so there was a sharp intake of breath from the old man opposite and another fast interaction of words.

'It's very unusual isn't it?' Robyn said. 'Not like anything I have seen before of that era. And here—' she pointed to the corner '—you can just about make out her signature. There's an instrument in the top corner here, but what is a little concerning is that there appears to be a bloodstain

352

across here. It continues onto the backing too.' As she stopped talking, she realised everyone else was silent and she looked across the table. 'Do you think this is the map made for Drake?'

'No, it isn't.' Annemieke spoke slowly and Robyn felt her heart sink. She'd been so convinced and yet after months of research suddenly it appeared she was right back at square one. 'It isn't Drake's but we do know whose it is, and for us it is far more important.' Now Robyn saw that Annemieke was smiling at her. Around her the air that had previously crackled in anticipation now settled with a sigh.

'You have a special piece of the story of this map, which has also been missing,' Annemieke said smiling at Robyn, 'so let me tell you what we know of Freida, a mapmaker's daughter.'

Slowly she told the story of their ancestor, a cartographer who enthralled the English queen with her skills. A young woman whose life had begun in tragedy with the slaughter of her parents at the hands of the invading Spanish soldiers and how she'd been brought up by a distant cousin, Abraham Ortelius.

'It must have been a hard life,' Robyn said, 'to have lost her parents so horribly like that. Losing someone who holds your heart in their hand is the hardest thing to come to terms with.' Beneath the table she felt Sam's fingers close around hers and squeeze them.

'Indeed,' Annemieke agreed, 'she must have been broken. I know I would have been. However much I complain about my father.' She smiled at her father before briefly translating what she'd just said. He gave a bark of laughter and flapped his hand at her before leaving the table to start making more coffee. 'But I believe you English have a saying: what doesn't kill you makes you stronger. And the story of Freida proved that. She didn't let a tragedy ruin the rest of her life. The family tale says that she was commissioned by Queen Elizabeth to create a map for your mariner Francis Drake but she decided to make another copy for her husband Willem. He, like Drake, was a sailor, a dangerous choice of career with the Spanish sitting off the coast of Holland. These days we guess that he was a privateer; some would say a pirate, although we know he also took parcels and packages to the botanists who lived on Lime Street and we also know the man who coordinated it all was another relation of Freida's. We can only assume that's how they met.'

'Lime Street.' Robyn repeated. 'On the map see here? Lime Street is named together with some of the houses. So why are there two maps?' she asked. 'I read in a letter from Elizabeth to Drake that she had a map as a gift for him. I've suspected all along although I wasn't certain that this was what we have here, but you say it isn't?'

'I believe not. Our family history always said that when Freida made an identical map for Willem, she added a navigation instrument on his. And that is why I am sure you have Willem's map and not Drake's.'

'How incredible,' Robyn said. 'I assumed we had Drake's because there is no record that Freida made a second one. I shouldn't have brought it with me really, but now I'm glad I did. It's home where it belongs. And although I've done some basic research it'll need proper experts to verify it's the map we believe it is. And this instrument, it's a volvelle; it's in the British Museum in London. It's engraved with an F and W just like on the one painted here.'

'Someone needs to do some tests to discover what this stain is—' Sam pointed to the corner of the map '—because if it is twentieth-century coffee that will devalue the map somewhat.'

'No, I think you will discover that is blood,' Annemieke replied. 'I haven't told you the rest of Freida's story.'

As she explained about the battle along the Thames and how Freida had maimed or possibly killed a Spanish guard, Robyn's eyes grew wide.

'So she used the tools of her trade to save her child's life?' she asked.

'Well, or her own life – we don't really know,' Annemieke replied, pouring more coffee into everyone's cup. 'But the story passed down through our family is that she was carrying the map and it got soaked in blood. We don't know if it was her assailant's or her own, but with modern techniques, they should be able to test some fibres of the linen and compare a sample of DNA from them with mine to discover if it was Freida's.'

Robyn looked across at Sam and smiled at him. The final piece of the story finally slotted into place. And the end of Freida's tale filled her with joy and inspiration. Even with the constraints of being a woman in the sixteenth century and with such a huge tragedy in her life, she still rose above it all and became renowned for her skills. And made a name for herself at the English court, the most esteemed of places, as a favourite of the queen. She'd managed to overcome her heartache for the tragedy that had befallen her and live her life to the full. It was a lesson that she, Robyn, had also finally learned.

Chapter Forty-Nine

June 1581

Just as Willem had promised, the *Windfly* silently slipped into port at Hoorn just north of Amsterdam on the high tide before moving around to the Markermeer Bay and dropping anchor. Freida looked across at the buildings, so different from London and yet so familiar from her childhood they made her heart hurt. Tall with deep pitched roofs and many square windows. She knew now she'd never return to London; that part of her life was over. Now they'd make their home in Holland where, Willem reassured her, the Prince of Orange was winning the battle to remove King Philip of Spain's armies from the Low Countries and soon they'd be living freely as Huguenots.

Below her, she heard the knock of the pilot boat. She clambered down the ladder to step into it, followed by Willem who carried Jacob, then came Emanuel and finally Christiaen. The ship's crew would hide the *Windfly* further inland before returning to their families.

Willem rowed them all ashore and Freida, on shaking legs as she adjusted to dry land, hugged Emanuel before he slipped away to make his way in the dark towards Antwerp.

'Thank you, cousin,' she whispered, 'thank you for everything. For making my life in London so happy, for the laughter we shared and for all the fascinating conversations about the objects that came through your hands on Lime Street. I will never forget you and I hope we will meet again.'

'I am not sure I deserve your thanks—' he pursed his lips, shaking his head '—for it was in my home that you met Doctor Dee. If that had not happened, I believe you could have lived your life out in peace, away from the English court. Where you were not visible to the Spanish ambassador.'

'Nay, the path of our life is determined for us on the day we are born,' she replied. 'It was always meant to happen this way. But you helped save me and for that I owe you my life. And my son's life.' They hugged goodbye and with a raise of his hand to Willem he was gone, swallowed up by the dark streets. Christiaen followed him a few minutes later, his presence in the city less dangerous, for nobody in London knew he'd been involved in Jacob's kidnap.

'Come.' Willem took her hand, lifting Jacob up onto his shoulder where the small boy laid his head down and closed his eyes. 'My family home is close by and we will be made welcome there.' Picking up a bundle of belongings she had brought from the ship, she followed him along the edge of the waterway that disappeared into the dark city, the familiar smell of home enveloping her.

★　★　★

As Willem had promised his family welcomed her with open arms and almost immediately a child's maid was appointed, the upper floors of their large house reopened and a nursery suite installed. Freida's natural instinct was to keep Jacob with her at all times night and day, but it only took two days for her to realise he'd suffered no lasting ill effects from his ordeal and he wanted to be playing with his young cousins who all lived in the family home. She could hear his laughter mixed with that of the others echoing through the house.

Her arm was re-dressed properly by a local physician and although she'd be left with a scar it was healing well. He complimented her on her use of the herbal remedies she'd brought with her.

After a month, Freida was beginning to feel restless. She wasn't used to sitting around doing nothing and so she was delighted when Willem reappeared after two days on the *Windfly* and announced that they'd be going on a journey the following day to visit Amsterdam. They would be away all day and she was to dress up warmly. Jacob would be safe at home while they were gone.

They left early the following morning, Willem having hired a coach to take them. Freida thought that riding a horse in her skirts, which she was once again wearing, would never have the same freedom as it had when she'd worn her breeches, so she was happy to travel in the coach although she felt every bump and hole in the road and her back began to ache the longer they travelled. She was relieved when they stopped in a wide street in the centre of the city and Willem jumped down from the coach, holding his hand out for Freida to follow.

'Where are we?' she asked. Willem pointed to a tall building ahead of them in the traditional Dutch style, its dark wooden frame and outer walls tall with a steep pitched roof and groups of identical glazed windows.

'I have leased this house for our new home,' he explained. 'I still have work to do to help the prince regain his throne and it will be easier here in the city. It is perfectly safe.' He held his hand up to stop the inevitable questions. 'And I do not wish to put upon my family forever. We need our own home as we did in London. But I have something else to show you.' He held out his arm for her and led her down a street to their right, until he paused at a small building squashed between two larger ones as if they were trying to squeeze it out completely, and he opened the door, ushering her in.

The room she stepped into was flooded with light from a window in the rear wall, which overlooked the waterway behind the building, but it was empty. She looked at Willem and raised her eyebrows.

'Why have you brought me here?'

'Because I think it is time you set up an atelier here in Holland and this is a suitable place to do so, do you not think?'

Freida's hands flew to her mouth. 'Willem, this would be perfect! I would love to continue my cartography; I am sure my cousin Abraham would support me in doing so. I must write to him and ask where I may source an easel and the plates I require.' She could tell by the smile on Willem's face that her face was glowing with pleasure. It was the beginning of their new life together.

Chapter Fifty

September 1582

Life in Amsterdam was everything that Freida had hoped it would be. The Prince of Orange had made a declaration of independence and at least for the time being there was peace in Holland; a new Huguenot Dutch Republic was emerging.

After she'd set up her atelier, she had a steady stream of customers wishing to commission maps, especially when it became known she had engraved a map for Queen Elizabeth of England. The Guild of St Luke's whose members included the very best of the artists and painters in Amsterdam invited her to join, the first woman to do so, and a huge honour for her.

It was in her workshop that Willem found her late one afternoon, the setting sun outside reflected off the rippling water as a cargo barge moved quietly past, creating sparkling patterns that danced across the ceiling. They reminded Freida of the brilliance and pirouetting light that had lit up the queen's privy chamber. Where the candlelight had reflected off a thousand jewels encrusted on the monarch's gowns encompassing her in a host of fireflies. It felt like a different life now. It had come to such a terrible climax and yet despite that, she couldn't regret it all. The conversations with the queen had inspired her at the moment she needed it most. If another woman could protect all her subjects, then she Freida could do it for her family. And she had proved she could.

'Come, wife,' Willem interrupted her musing, 'the hour is late and our son is waiting for supper. You need to eat too. You must keep your strength up.' Holding out his hand she carefully pushed herself up from the low stool on which she sat to work, her hand in the small of her back as she stretched. Her belly was extended with the new child she was carrying and she stepped into the cloak that her husband was holding out for her. A new child to be born into a life in the new Dutch Republic. Her life had come full circle and now finally she had moved forwards.

Chapter Fifty-One

September 2022

Within days Robyn and Sam had returned to England. They promised Annemieke they'd keep in touch and let her know when they'd found a laboratory that could carry out the DNA investigations. Despite all that Robyn felt about the map finally returning home to Holland, she had no option but to take it back to her father. He may not be its rightful owner, but he was its legal one. The map had burrowed under Robyn's skin and enveloped her in its past, showing her that it was a part of Freida's story, her own story, just as it was for her new friend's family.

They arrived in Dover on a sunny afternoon although a cool breeze was blowing in off the sea and Robyn was pleased to get in her car and drive home, her mind churning with everything that had happened over the past week. And the summer.

'A quick coffee before you leave?' Sam asked and she agreed, knowing it would probably be many months before they'd get together again as he prepared his yacht for its next race. Listening to him talking about what he needed to do she could see the excitement and joy in his eyes and remembered just how Nate's face had looked when he'd enthused about the races he was embarking on. She'd forgotten that in the sorrow and anger that had shadowed the past seven years. The happiness and fun had faded into the background like pale sun-bleached wallpaper, the pattern scattering in time.

'It's going to be a while before we can get together again,' he said, 'and as it's finally time for you to say goodbye to Nate, I thought this had better be the wake for Nate we'll never get to have. Just you and I, the people — apart from Wendy and Dan — who knew him best.'

His words made Robyn swallow hard, waiting for the inevitable tears, only to find that they didn't come. Had she finally run out? Declaring him dead was such a huge step, she hadn't thought about all the accompanying parts of dying. They had no body to bury, she'd never have a gravestone to visit and lay flowers on, or talk to him even if he couldn't hear her. Instead, she had to admit that he was buried at sea, which he'd doubtless have preferred anyway. Perhaps they could have some sort of gathering for him though, when all the paperwork was signed, the last dot of an I and the final cross of a T. A party to celebrate his amazing, wonderful life and how he'd died doing what he loved. A final farewell to a life well lived.

When she arrived back in Hay-on-Wye it was early evening and dusk was falling. She knew the shop would be closed and that her father was expecting her. She'd called to let him know they were back in England and she was driving home, but first she had somewhere to visit. Leaving her car in the public car park where it wouldn't be noticed, she walked along the familiar path to the river, and to their tree.

Night was beginning to fall, the twilight thickening as the day lost its grip on the sun as it lowered towards the hills in the distance. Robyn leaned against the tree and looked up at the sky. Her hand went into her hoodie pocket to the leaf she'd caught before she left for Holland. Now dried and brown, the pieces crumbled between her fingers and she let it drift to the ground.

She'd learned a lot while she'd been away. That she wasn't the only person who'd been through a terrible time, but she knew that already. She watched the news every night and all over the world people were living through sadness but they learned to accept it and move forward. She hadn't for so long, caught in a stasis of time, but now finally she understood she couldn't change what had happened. Nate wasn't coming home, and tomorrow she'd call James and tell him to press submit on the declaration of death form, to set her free. Allow her to fly again and to live her life wherever it may take her. To sail her own waters as Nate would want her to. Finally, she could say goodbye to him.

Getting to her feet she picked up a handful of the gold leaves and threw them into the air whirling around beneath them, the dying sunlight bouncing off their surface, their brilliance lighting her in a shimmering cascade. Tilting her head to one side she paused as she realised the ticking inside her head had stopped.

THE END

Acknowledgements

No one is more than surprised than me when I realise I have produced another book, but I certainly don't do it all on my own - I have help from a lot of lovely people and this is my chance to thank everyone.

First of all, a huge thank you to my editor Radhika Sonagra for all of your work on my behalf, you're brilliant. Also thanks to the whole team at Avon, Ellie and Becci in marketing, Helena Newton for your editing, and the cover design team who always do such an amazing job, thank you all.

And of course massive thanks to my agent Ella Kahn at Diamond Kahn and Woods, your help and advice is always spot on, it's great to know you're in my corner.

A special thank you must go to Penny Hampson, your knowledge about the Bodleian Library was invaluable, I must share an afternoon tea with you more often!

As ever thanks must go to my lovely author friends who are always so supportive. Jenni Keer, Heidi Swain, Rosie Hendry, Ian Wilfred, Claire Wade and Kate Hardy thank you all for the chats and waving of pom poms. And Ian your social media support is second to none, I can never thank you enough. Jenni, my virtual office buddy, I couldn't do this without you and your endless encouragement, beta-reading and virtual hobnobs, thank you a million times.

Writing a historical novel always requires a lot of research and when I first had the idea for *The Mapmaker's Daughter* I was delighted to realise I could legitimately undertake a visit to Amsterdam (so easy when you live in Norwich!) for research purposes, but unfortunately 2021 had other ideas. Nevertheless, there were some books which proved to be invaluable whilst I wrote *The Mapmaker's Daughter*. Ellen MacArthur's *Taking on the World* was so helpful, I've never been sailing and nor do I have any intention of doing so, but her description of participating in the Vendee Globe Race was extremely useful. My investigations of women in medieval cartography were much helped by *Map Worlds* by Will C Van Der Hoonaard, and the Lime Street community in the sixteenth century was brought to life by the wonderful Deborah Harkness's *The Jewel House* which is now well-thumbed and high on my list of favourite books.

Finally my thanks go to my amazing family, without their patience and encouragement this whole writing lark would be a lot harder – I love you guys! And of course to my husband Des at the helm of this ship, always laid-back, always level-headed and calm, my biggest thanks goes to you.

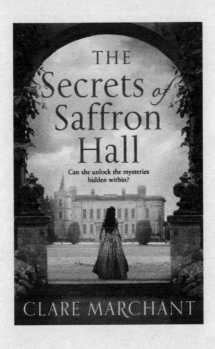

A perilous mission. An unforgivable betrayal. A secret lost in time...

Effortlessly merging past with present in an unforgettable tale of love, courage and betrayal – the perfect read for fans of Lucinda Riley and Kathryn Hughes.

Buy now!